NO
HERO

NO
HERO

JONATHAN WOOD

TITAN BOOKS

NO HERO
Print edition ISBN: 9781781168066
E-book edition ISBN: 9781781168134

Published by Titan Books
A division of Titan Publishing Group Ltd
144 Southwark Street, London SE1 0UP

First edition: March 2014

10 9 8 7 6 5 4 3

Did you enjoy this book? We love to hear from our readers.
Please email us at readerfeedback@titanemail.com or write to us at
Reader Feedback at the above address.

To receive advance information, news, competitions, and exclusive
offers online, please sign up for the Titan newsletter on our website
TITANBOOKS.COM

For Tami, Charlie, and Emma,
who asked me to tell them stories

1

It's the pretty blond that completes the scene. No question. Pressed up against the side of a building? Check. Life-and-death situation? Check. Significantly more sweat running down my back than really seems appropriate? Big check for that one. And yes, against all likelihood, there's a pretty blond by my side. Check.

Because now, after years of paperwork, after years of trawling through minutia, police work is finally fulfilling the promise *Tango and Cash* made to my impressionable teenage self.

It is time for action.

Except that, in the heat of the moment, my heart beating a sharp tattoo against my ribcage, I rather wish that Kurt Russell had taken the time to turn to the camera and explain the sheer bowel-loosening terror involved in doing this sort of thing. Because right now, even with a killer so close, even with a life on the line, paperwork has never seemed so appealing.

SIX MONTHS EARLIER

The office block is under construction—still in the skeletal stages—so it's the stairs for Sergeant Swann and me. She just transferred in from Peterborough, lured by the Dreaming Spires, or by dreams of reprimanding drunk students, or some such, but it's most definitely their loss. I'm huffing a bit by the time we reach the top, which is hardly likely to impress a pretty girl, but so far the most flirtatious thing I've managed to say to her is, "Good work, Swann," so it's not like I've got chances to damage.

Plus, seriously, she's not even thirty, so it's about an eight-year age difference or something. And I'm her boss, and that sort of thing is totally frowned upon. And she is far too pretty to be the sort of thing that happens to someone like me.

So, in conclusion, buying Starbucks and staring at corpses are likely to be the main activities we share together.

Anyway, today's corpse is lying in the middle of the concrete floor five stories up in the air. He's in more parts than normal. Everything's business as usual right up until his eyebrows, where someone's given him a rather extreme haircut. Diagonal slice down through his skull. The scalp lies a few yards away. There's quite a lot of blood.

First off I think about how I'm quite glad I missed my alarm and therefore my breakfast this morning. Then I think about how, as crime scenes go, this one is actually pretty cool. Then I go back to my first thought because that's a horrible thought to have when it's real life. Then I think about how I really need to watch fewer movies.

"Top o' the morning to you both." Doc O'Meaney is poking at the scrap of scalp with a ballpoint pen. He looks up and waves as we come up the stairs.

Bit of a strange fish, Doc O'Meaney. We both joined Oxford police force around the same time and back then he had a cockney accent and no "O" in front of his name. Then there was a rather fateful trip to Ireland and he came back... well I heard someone call him born-again Irish. Right now he's wearing a shamrock pin through his blue coveralls. Still, he's a nice enough chap and handy with a scalpel, so it's probably best not to mess with him too much.

"So." Swann looks at the body. "Heart attack, was it?"

I laugh. Possibly too loudly.

"Not so much the cause of death that's a stumper on this one," says the doc, "but more the cause of the cause of death, if you catch my drift."

"Come again?" I raise both my eyebrows. Never learned the trick of just lifting one.

"Well." Doc O'Meaney scratches the back of his head. "See it's just the one slice we've got. Comes right through the ear—" he traces a line "—and through the hindbrain. Hits all the important lizard brain bits that control your heart and your lungs. All that good keeping-you-alive stuff." He shrugs. "Insta-death. Just add machete."

"A machete?" Quite an exotic weapon of choice for a sleepy university town like Oxford.

"Might have been. Might have been." Doc O'Meaney chews his lip. "But, well, if it was… I just can't imagine how it was done, see? I mean, the skull is tough cookie. And this was just one blow to cut through it. I mean, that's a hell of a lot of force. Mucho newtons. More than a person could manage, I should think. And it's a downward slice, so that means they're taller than him, or above him." He indicates the empty expanse of floor. "Best I can come up with is something mechanical. A machete and an industrial strength spring, perhaps. But…" He indicates the empty space.

"Too empty," Swann says.

I nod. "No reason to come here. Off the beaten track. It was a Sunday, so no workmen."

"Someone looking for a quiet place?" says Swann.

"To…?" I don't have answers. I don't have any vital clues. I don't have a German with a suspicious accent and a bald cat standing in the corner of the room.

"Meet someone? Avoid someone?" Swann's guessing. It's all just guessing now. Even if it's the right guess we won't know for a long time. Interviews. Statements. Forensics. The dreary machinery of detection.

"Could have been a meeting," says Doc O'Meaney, nodding at Swann.

And it could be the right guess. Except... "Can't really see a chap standing there," I say, "while someone lines up the blow. Can you?"

NOW

Couldn't see it then. Couldn't see it for another six months. There were five more bodies to work with in that time, and I couldn't see it once. No signs of restraint. No signs of drugs in the system. For a while we toyed with the idea that maybe the victim had been led there and hypnotized. Except... well, it was a bloody stupid idea really.

Still, I can't help but wonder now if it was a failure of imagination on my part. Because now a life may be on the line and all I can do is imagine things: great tracts of machinery hastily assembled; a gleaming machete blade, tarnished by only a few traces of blood; a few hacked-at hairs; a coiled spring; a trip wire; me sneaking around this corner and the sharp tug of it on my ankle; a snag, a stumble, a swish... Swann screams. Or... well, maybe she just shrugs and thinks she always knew her bloody awful boss would come to a sticky end.

I'm frozen. I can't move for the imagined possibilities. I've become the inverse of my dreams—a man of inaction.

Insta-death. Jesus.

Behind me I hear Swann shifting her weight. "You planning on moving any time soon, Boss?" she whispers. "I sort of had plans that didn't involve standing around and freezing my tits off quite so much."

THREE HOURS AGO

"One more time," I say.

Swann sighs loudly.

"You don't have to stay," I say. Everyone else buggered off down the pub a few hours ago. It's Friday night. The weekend beckons. "No need for you to suffer just because I have police officer OCD."

I open a folder, start leafing through notes. Bank records. School reports. Employment certificates. Coroner's report. Minutia. Details. And the devil is hiding in them somewhere. Just need to find him and arrest him.

"Nah." Swann picks up the next folder in the pile. "One more time."

I smile. She's a good cop.

"Six victims," she says, shutting down my grin. "Six months. No pattern that we can see. Time between killings varies from ten days to five and a half weeks. Both male and female victims. Still no pattern. Ages spread between twenty-eight—"

My eyes flick up to the whiteboard, to the photo of that first man we found, back before his head became a two-piece jigsaw puzzle.

"—to sixty-three."

My eyes travel to another photo—a serious-looking woman, all perm and pearls.

"That leaves us with two links." There's a tiredness in her voice as she says it. Because both are bloody useless. "One—they're all newcomers to Oxford. Two—they're all independently wealthy. Minimum bank balance of…" She consults a Post-it note.

"Eight hundred and thirty-seven thousand pounds," I quote.

"Eight hundred and thirty-seven thousand pounds,"

she confirms. She looks at me. "Good chance you need to get out a little more, Boss."

I shrug. I'd defend myself except she's got a point. Details. Always with the details.

She smiles, but maybe that's just to soften the blow.

"So," I say, "rich bastard, newcomers."

"Money scam," she says. "Got to be money."

"Except there's no angle," I say. "No profit."

"A very bad financial scam?"

"Worst scammer ever." I smile.

Swann is serious though. "So he doesn't like rich people," she says. "Some chip on his shoulder."

"Whole bag of chips." Still no smile. "What else do we know about the killer?" I ask.

"Fuck all." Swann turns her back on me, fists curled. Sharp white knuckles on delicate hands.

I'm wandering off-topic…

So I stand there, watch her frustration, trying to think of something to say, to diffuse it all. Except she's totally justified. Hers is the reasonable reaction.

"Go home," I say after a while. She pushes her hands through her hair. "Sleep on it. Do the sensible thing."

"We should both go home," she says.

For a second I almost ask if she means together.

She doesn't mean together.

She…?

She picks the folder back up. "He always kills them on construction sites," she says.

My hopes fade. Well, my hopes take a kick in the nuts and fall over.

"Always at night. Always…" Her hand rises unconsciously to the back of her head. She makes a face.

"No physical evidence. Never the same site twice." I sit down. Put my head down. Think. I need to bloody think.

"Money and construction sites," Swann says. "Got to be the money."

And something clicks in my head. Something about absolutes that I've learned to distrust. "What if it's not?" I say.

"Come again?" says Swann.

"Well…" Gears are beginning to churn in my brain. "We've pretty much cavity-searched cash as a motive. Nothing doing. But what if it's the construction sites?"

"But that doesn't even make any sense, Boss."

Which is a fair point really. But… "What else have we got at this point?" I ask.

"Sod it," she says.

We hit the paperwork. And an hour later I've got it. Right there in my hands. The devil himself. Hiding right where I knew he'd be.

"Electricity," I say. "They were all having the electricity put in." And it feels like electricity, running right through me. An actual bloody break. And it may be a tedious job sometimes, but in moments like this it's worth it.

"Someone in city planning?" Swann asks.

"Let's stick with the sites for now," I say. "Time to make calls. Find out where the electric is being put in, and if there's nowhere, where the next place is."

Finding out at eight on a Friday night which construction site is having the electric put in is not the easiest thing in the world. Swann ends up on the phone with a lot of drunk foremen making a lot of wrong assumptions about why an unknown lady might be calling them. One of them kindly offers to put her electric in. Still, the words "Police" and "Department" stop him before he goes too far.

Finally, at ten-thirty, we have it. A growing business park to the east end of Cowley Road. Started putting the wires in on Wednesday.

We stare at each other.

"We should call someone," Swann says.

She's right. I know she's right. But suddenly this is it. This is the moment. I can almost hear the wheels of a car squealing. I can almost hear the synthesizer start to play. The guitar solo begin. This is a chance. To be a man of action. To do something I can be proud of.

"There's no time," I say. It feels like an out-of-body experience as I say the words. This is it. "Let's get the car."

NOW

I'm an idiot. I'm a little man kneeling out in the cold, gripping a baton. No hero.

Swann makes an irritated noise behind me. The pretty blond. And she may not be in a cocktail dress. She may not have a hairstyle two decades out of fashion. But it's as close as I'm ever going to get. This is as close as I'm ever going to get to heroism. And suddenly that is enough for me to put one foot forward.

I wince as I do it. I wait for the trip-wire's line of pressure, for the blade, for death.

"What are you waiting for?" Swann is losing patience with me.

Another step. Another. And still nothing. I'm still alive. A fact that brings a small amount of confidence with it. More steps. We're in.

I sweep my flashlight round in a broad arc. I hold it out wide. No need to advertise the location of my vital organs. The light picks out architecture that's become familiar—a concrete framework, interior walls sketched out in plumbing and nascent electrical work. Round and round I go. My baton is sweat-slick in my hand.

Nothing. No movement.

I flick my flashlight at the stairs. Swann's light follows

mine. Up we go. One of us on each side of the wall. At the top we go wide. Another sweep. Stepping lightly toward shadowed corners.

Still nothing.

Another flight of steps. Another empty floor. My heart is beating heavy and hard. My breath is shallow. I have to stop from jumping at the shadows I'm making. Swann is steely-eyed, her flashlight gripped like a pistol.

And then… I hold up a hand for Swann to be still. I want to be sure. I close my eyes, try to calm my breathing. And yes. There it is again. I hear it again. A sound from above. Like metal across concrete.

I look at Swann. And she's heard it too. We move together. Tight and fast. Fourth floor. And the noise is still above us. More definite now. More certain. We move to the steps. A definite clang. Metal on metal.

I pause. Swann, already a step above me, turns, looks at me.

"What?" she mouths.

I'm thinking. My imagination at work again. He's got someone up there. He's setting something up. Some part of his ritual. And when he's disturbed… He will not go gentle into that good night. He'll resist. And he's fast and he's strong. He has to be. Or he has a gun. Probably a gun. And Swann is the obvious target. Take out the girl, make the escape.

No. It shouldn't go down like that.

"I go first," I whisper. "You stay down here. If he gets past me, he thinks he's home free. But you're here. You get the drop on him if I can't."

She hesitates, her face slowly curling up. "Wait…" she says. "I don't think…"

"Don't make me pull rank, Sergeant." That sounded cooler in my head. In the real world it's just a bit harsh.

And I'm still not convinced I should really be in charge of anyone, but I think the irony of that is lost because I really am in charge of people, and Swann's face just goes sour.

"I think you just did," she says.

Another noise above us. And I don't want a fight here, now. I don't want her to be pissed at me. I don't want... I don't want to lose this collar.

So I head up. A man alone. With each step the thunder of my heart grows. With each step I slow, I crouch lower. By the time I get to the top of the stairs my eyes barely make it above the final riser.

The roof's not been done yet and it's colder up here, the wind blowing stronger. A few stars manage to shine through the glow of Oxford's streetlamps. I don't need the flashlight to see.

Outlined by moonlight, a figure crouches down by a pile of electrical cable. He's dressed smartly—dark suit, a navy-blue tie that flaps in the wind. There's an incongruous red toolbox on the ground next to him. His back is to me. I can't see what he's doing. But he can't see me either.

I tighten my grip on the baton. Tighten it further. It feels like either the steel or my knuckles are going to have to give out. My teeth are clamped down so hard I hear a filling creak. I can make out each bump and crevice in the concrete beneath my hand. I hear the rasp my fingertips make as I move them, getting ready to push myself up into a stand. I hear the movement of my ribs as I fill my lungs to shout.

Then—

—where the hell did she come from?

A woman—five foot six, maybe a little shorter, hair loose and flapping; she's wearing a large, red, flannel shirt, scuffed jeans. Her back is to me as well. She's moving silently. Walking toward the man in the suit. And she's got a sword.

A real bloody sword.

It's about three feet long, the blade shining white in reflected moonlight, curved slightly, balanced lightly in her hand. She lets the tip fall, brush the ground. It scrapes, fires off pale blue sparks.

The man at the wires hears it, stands up fast, turns around, sees her. He takes a few steps, out into the center of the room.

I want to shout, to yell, to move, to do some-bloody-thing. But I stay there crouched, silent, paralyzed. Just waiting for it. Just like the man in the suit waits. And if I could just curse under my breath, some whispered litany of obscenity, if I could just turn away, do anything, if I could just exhale, get rid of this pregnant breath caught bloated inside me... But I just crouch and I just watch.

She's about a yard from him. A blade's length away. He stands, both hands held out, but low, loose, already defeated. She still has the blade by her side. They are both as silent as I am.

Then the woman jumps. It's so fast I barely see it. But she's abruptly airborne, abruptly up and to the man's right, twisting in the air, her arm moving, and Jesus, Joseph, Mary, anybody, it's so fast I can barely make it out, there's barely even a blur. One moment her arm is still down, and then it's up. Straight and high. She seems suspended for a moment, everything hanging still. I know what's going to come next. I just know. But still when it does, oh God, oh Jesus.

She snaps the blade down. Again I miss the motion itself, only see the aftermath, the arm pointed down, the blade red and slick. Part of the man's skull is in the air, flipping over and over. The tips of his ears tumble down to the ground, like discarded earrings. But there is something else, something more.

White beads burst from the wound, like translucent pearls, like giant fish eggs, each one half an inch across or more. They shimmer and shine, lit by some inner luminescence. They spray out like the seeds blown from a dandelion. And in the center, thrashing in what is left of the man's head…

My gorge rises. I taste bile.

It is something like a maggot, something like a caterpillar, except it is the breadth and length of my forearm. It's the same translucent white as the giant pearls sifting down through the air around it. It seems to flicker just as they do. I can see through it, can see the awful sheer wound surrounding it, can see the blood spraying through the space it seems to occupy. It has a mouth like a beak, a dirty yellow color, and all around are tendrils, string-thick tentacles that thrash through the air as its segmented body bucks back and forth, back and forth in what is left of the man's skull.

Jesus.

I… Jesus… Maybe the victim isn't the only one losing his mind here.

Still, it's the sight of that thing, that inhuman, alien thing writhing as the body slumps to the floor, it's the way it and the pearls simply wink out of existence that finally loosens the breath caught in my chest. I exhale, a great screaming, braying exhalation of fear, and horror, and sheer bloody outrage that such a thing could exist let alone occur before my eyes.

I breathe in but it doesn't catch, and I whoop out a noisy spray of breath again. The woman looks up. I hear Swann below me. She's starting to move, but she might as well be on the other side of the world.

I try to stand up. I jerk spastically. I can't quite bring everything online, can't quite get my shit together. The woman with the sword crosses the roof. It seems to only take her an instant. Even her speed is terrifying.

I try to look at her face. Some part of me that is autopiloting the role of policeman in these final moments tries to jot down the details. Long bangs, so I can barely see her eyes. Long nose. Long cheeks. Sallow too. An underfed look. The red flannel shirt flaps loosely over a dark green tank top.

And the sword. The brilliant white sword.

And then the tip is gone from sight. All I see is my chest, and red, and the blade sticking from my chest, and red, and that is where the tip is, right in there, right inside of me, and red, and Jesus I never thought I could hurt like this, and red, and red, and black, and red, and black, and black, and black.

2

THEN AND WHEN AND IN-BETWEEN

An alleyway. Dirt-strewn. Trash-spattered. And I think I must have fallen down, must have landed badly, because everything hurts. My chest hurts. Jesus, it feels like I'm splitting in two, starting right there, right between my ribs. And how did I get here?

Behind me I hear a rustle of movement, like a thousand petticoats all moving out of sync, yet together. And then…

…black

NOW

The first thing I'm really aware of, that is really solid and true to me as I come out of the morphine dream, is the beeping. Even before the red vagueness of my closed eyelids. It's something like an alarm clock. I want it to stop, before it reels me fully out of sleep. I reach for the clock, to flip the damn thing off—

—and then the pain.

My eyes snap open with a gasp, my chest fills with air and the pain comes again, sharper. I go to gasp again but catch myself, the air coming in a thin sucking whistle instead.

"Ow," I say. "Oh balls, ow." Not quite up there with Shelley or Yeats, I'll admit, but honesty is a virtue, as my mum always taught me.

"Ah," says a woman's voice I don't recognize. "Finally."

The room comes into focus slowly. I want to blink it in faster but I'm afraid that'll bring the pain back somehow, so I let it come at its own pace.

At first all I see is the shadow of the voice's owner, then the outline of her, then the dark swathe of her hair contrasting with the whiteness of her skin, and then finally her features.

She is very close to having a pretty face. But there's a hardness to her that seems reluctant to lapse and let her cross the boundary into simple prettiness. She has a structured look, everything ordered. Her hair is carefully clipped into place. Her suit is straight edges and diagonal lines. Fashionable without being flashy, but without looking comfortable either. She seems a rather severe woman. The sort who'd play a nun in a movie and hit your knuckles with a ruler.

Reflexively I clench my fists to hide the fingers. Then I rather wish I hadn't because that hurts too.

"Detective Arthur Wallace?" she asks.

I go to answer but it turns out that my mouth is rather dryer than I thought and so my tongue does some ungainly flopping until the woman fetches me a glass of water.

"Yes," I finally manage, though I suspect she might have forgotten the original question by this point.

"You suffered a punctured lung," she states without preamble.

"Oh," I say, and then sit back as the memories pick themselves up off the floor of my mind and organize themselves like some kind of automated jigsaw. Vignettes assemble out of order, slowly taking their place in the whole. I remember the pain. I remember the blade. I remember being stabbed. The whole thing takes me a while, but I'm beginning to suspect I might be a little higher on the morphine than I originally thought.

Finally, I conclude with, "Bollocks."

The woman clears her throat. "Yes."

And then, another jigsaw piece floating up out of the miasma. "Swann," I say. "Sergeant Alison Swann. What happened to her?"

"No need to worry, Detective," says the woman. "Sergeant Swann went quite unharmed. Your attacker is reported to have jumped off the side of the building."

"Jumped off... We were... How many stories?"

"Five," says the woman, "according to Sergeant Swann." She shrugs. "She lost track of your attacker after that, more concerned with your well-being than making the arrest it seems."

The arrest... the victim... The victim. I see it again. I see what was in his head. The maggot, worm, thing... I see the impossibility of it all. The reality. I close my eyes.

"Oh shit..." I moan, passing up another opportunity for eloquence.

"Detective Wallace?" The woman sounds concerned, which is decent of her.

A decent woman. A nice businesslike woman, in a nice businesslike suit, in a nice businesslike hospital. And how exactly am I meant to tell her than I saw a monster in a man's head? An alien?

Stress. It was just stress.

"Nothing." I shake my head and wish I hadn't. The world feels loose, wobbly.

"Do you feel up to talking, Detective Wallace?"

I look at her. I imagine a worm, a maggot, an alien in her skull. Another bad idea while on morphine. I close my eyes.

"Not really," I say.

"Later then," she says.

I close my eyes, hear her footsteps. The door opens.

"Wait," I say. Because I'm reviewing the conversation and I realize she told me that the killer escaped. So I still have to get my man. My woman.

"How long until I'm up and about, Doctor?"

She cocks her head on one side. "I have no idea. I'm not your doctor, Detective." There's a very thin smile on her face. And then she's gone, and I think that's pretty weird right there. But then I sink into sleep and morphine demonstrates that when it comes to weird, it has my visitor rather outclassed.

THE NEXT DAY

The quality of visitor I receive definitely picks up the next day. Swann comes in just as my doctor is about to leave. She stops him in the doorway.

"How is he?" she asks, favoring the doctor, a tall Kenyan, with a dazzling smile. He returns it, possibly at even greater wattage.

"You're disregarding eyewitness testimony," I point out. Only slightly jealous of the smiling match playing out before me.

"Men's stab wounds are like the fish they claim to catch," she tells me. "They keep on getting bigger and bigger."

"He's much better," the doctor says. "Even took a short walk to the bathroom."

Which is true, but not really a heroic feat of endurance. But in the absence of genocidal terrorists threatening the hospital, chances to prove my fortitude have been a bit thin on the ground.

Once she's seated by the bed, Swann checks that the doctor is definitely gone. "When I was a kid all my doctors were giant gangly blokes with sunken cheeks and narrow teeth. You get all the luck." She pauses, tugs at a strand of hair. "Well, aside from the being stabbed thing."

"Silver lining to every cloud," I say.

"Plus," she says, "this cloud rains chocolates," and she holds out a small wrapped present. Which is incredibly nice of her, and genuinely sweet, and really is a silver lining, and I'm about to tell her she shouldn't have when she tells me she didn't.

"Boys and girls at the station had a whip round," she says.

"Very decent of you all," I say, though my enthusiasm is about as punctured as my lung. But that's an ungrateful thought, so I attempt a more genuine smile, and ask, "How's the case going?"

"Well," a small smile plays around the corners of her mouth, "we do have an eyewitness."

"Wait… we… you… you mean… we…" I spray words around the room, taking out innocent bystanders with my abrupt enthusiasm. "This is huge! This is enormous! This is like the Godzilla of breaks. It's the sort of break that destroys large chunks of Tokyo!" I stop, take stock, try and gain perspective. Punctured lung and all that. "Who is it?" I ask, unable to stop one toe from tapping.

"You, Boss."

My toe ceases its tapping. I take a mental step backwards. "I'm going to blame the painkillers for me being slow on this one," I say, "but can you run that by me one more time?"

"He stabbed you, Boss. Stuck a sword in you. He must have been close. You must have seen something."

A sword. I saw a sword. I saw it going into my body. Blood and black. Black vision. White blade.

I blink, rub my eyes. Memories—a nice place to visit but not necessarily somewhere you'd like to live.

"She," I say, attempting the whole stiff upper lip thing. "Not a he, a she."

"See!" Swann shifts from her hospital standard-issue chair to the corner of my bed. "We're making headway already."

"Yeah." I smile but I… No. I don't want to go back there, I find. The girl, the sword. The thing… My moment of madness. I'm not a reliable witness.

"I'm afraid I don't remember much else," I say.

"Come on," she says, "what do we always tell the witnesses?"

"A pack of lies," I say. Which is true.

"You remember more than you think," she says.

"Yeah," I say. But it's hard to express that that's what really scares me. I don't want to remember any more.

"You're going to bust this thing wide open," she says and she pats my hand.

It's an odd moment. Something between affection and condescension. I think I might be blushing. Then she's blushing. We stare at each other. I think maybe this is what it would be like if one of us suddenly grew an extra head and it started spouting profanities.

"Sorry," she says.

"Quite all right," I manage, and then we disengage the offending body parts and then suddenly her phone goes off and equally suddenly there's an emergency involving blood work and contamination, and missing paperwork, and all sorts, so she doesn't even get to hang up before she's waving goodbye, so I'm left alone with some chocolates and the desire to eat them until I feel nauseous.

Five minutes later I'm still thinking about the hand pat far more than is either healthy or reasonable. It's almost a relief when Ms. "You-suffered-a-punctured-lung" walks in again.

Turns out that's not her real name.

"Felicity Shaw," she says and sticks out a hand. Her suit is paler today but no less severe. "You look like you're feeling a little bit better, Detective."

"Thank you," I say. "Fresh air and exercise. Drugs and doctors. All that."

She doesn't smile. I think Swann would have smiled at that. Which I hope makes me funny and not Swann a woman with a terrible sense of humor. Could go either way on that one, though.

"I'd like to ask you some questions about what exactly happened the night you were injured," Shaw says, because Shaw is serious and businesslike.

Which is fine, of course, except I don't even want to talk about what happened to someone who thinks I'm funny, let alone to someone who thinks I'm juvenile.

"I don't suppose you have some ID?" I say, which is a dodge that's been thrown in my face enough times that I feel it's only fair I should get to use it.

That does elicit a smile from Shaw. Except I wasn't trying to be funny. Something is off here, and I don't know which one of us it is.

Shaw reaches into her pocket, pulls out a card. "Felicity Shaw, director of Military Intelligence, Section Thirty-seven."

"MI37?" I sound incredulous because I am. MI5, yes. MI6, I'm with you. And if logic persists in military intelligence, though I'm not sure it does, you could probably convince me over time about MI1, 2, 3, and 4. But MI37? Really?

"Yes, Detective," Shaw says. "MI37. We are a reality. We certainly don't advertise our existence the way MI5 and 6 do, but that just means the politics of intimidation are not useful in our arena. It doesn't mean we're not real. We are real, Detective Wallace, as real as the consequences you'll face if you discuss this conversation with anyone else."

I take the ID card from her. It has her face, though maybe five years younger, from before she tipped over into forty, and she has shorter hair and longer bangs. But it's her picture, and it's her name, and her title, and it does look terribly official, but I have to say I wouldn't know a military intelligence ID badge if one approached me at a party and offered to show me a good time.

"I'm sorry," I say. "I just don't know…"

Felicity Shaw nods, which is a better reception than I'd anticipated. "Your cynicism stands you well," she says. She looks away from me, out of the window. "Still, I'm surprised to find you with such a mindset after all you've seen."

It's the conversational equivalent of slapping me about the face. I sit up straight as a bolt, stare at her, while she continues to study the window. "What are you talking about?" I ask her. But I know exactly what she's talking about.

And she knows I do. "They're called the Progeny," she says. "The creature you saw in the victim's head. It's called a Progeny."

"Shit," I say, which is about as honest as I can get at that moment. "What do you want to know?"

"Actually, Detective, it's the other way around. I want to tell you about what I know."

She's crazy, of course. That's the obvious explanation, I realize. She's escaped from another wing of the hospital. Except her madness is the same color and shade as mine. It has the same details. It's as if she pulled the madness out of my head and into the world. But that's not what happened, I know. So that means she's not crazy, and I'm not, but that the world is.

"What is there to tell?" I ask.

Shaw's eyes leave the window, look around the rest of the room. "Not here," she says. "I'll fetch you a wheelchair."

3

I always assumed that if you have a clandestine organization then you'd have a clandestine headquarters. Stands to reason. And—I concede this point—Oxford is, admittedly, short on skull-shaped volcanoes. Shark-infested waters—ditto. But there is some pretty awesome architecture. Dreaming spires and all that. I always thought you could bury something beneath the limestone columns and copper dome of the Radcliffe Camera. Hide something in the depths of the Bodleian Library—down between the winding stacks, through miles of books, with just one ancient tome that acts as a lever to open some hidden passageway. So when Shaw tells me, "It's about two miles to the office," I can't help but be a little disappointed.

There is no romance in the term, "the office." Then again, Shaw seems more likely to fantasize over spreadsheets than biceps and bodice-ripping. I don't exactly see her as the type to adore purple prose or books with Fabio on the cover.

There again, neither am I.

She pilots the van through Oxford's tourist-loving heart, and heads toward the train station. She pulls up outside a shabby building thrown up in the sixties by an architect who clearly was less into dreaming spires and more into concrete squares. Shaw fetches the wheelchair from the boot of the car and I heft myself into it.

"We're in the basement," she tells me. Which briefly conjures images of secret passageways and hidden riches, but I'm not that hopeful anymore.

Shaw punches a six-digit code into a pad beside the door, her fingers a staccato blur. I can't follow the keys she hits. The door buzzes. A second door, another code. No beeps, just the rhythm of her nails on the keys. No clues for me. To take the elevator down requires a key.

"No thumbprint scanner?" I ask. Not my best joke, but I'm trying to make light. Then the elevator doors slide open and, of course, there one is. So I don't even manage that.

Considering how insecure I'm starting to feel, it's almost a relief when the elevator doors open onto an utterly mundane corridor, lined with mundane gray office doors. The first word that really springs to mind is industrious, except... the place feels too still for that. I expect to see men in gray suits and sensible ties clutching teetering stacks of folders, running from door to door in acute diagonals across the corridor, but instead when I glimpse through windows in doors I see empty rooms, chairs stacked in corners. The word is less industrious, and more abandoned.

"We're going to the reading room," Shaw says, taking a firm hold on my wheelchair and pushing me ahead before I have too much time to stare. "I'll talk while we walk, give you some background."

I hesitate, suddenly wondering if this is going to turn out to be a rather involved hidden camera stunt, but then take the plunge and ask anyway. "So," I say, "the Progeny."

"The Progeny," Shaw replies. The wheels of my chair make a light thrumming noise over the linoleum floor. "Are you familiar with the Fermi paradox, Detective?"

A distant bell rings but I can't place it, and shake my head.

"At its most basic," Shaw says, "the paradox points out that the absence of alien life in the universe is unusual. The universe is big. Big enough that life should have evolved elsewhere, but not so big that we shouldn't have found any examples. But we've found nothing. There's nothing there.

"This is a puzzle to scientists, to UFO speculators." Shaw speaks at a measured, even pace. Still, it sounds a little like a pitch. Maybe I was off with the hidden camera idea. Maybe Jehovah's Witnesses have just gotten all sorts of creative with their recruitment plans. Shaw continues, "Here at MI37 we have the answers. Both of them."

"Both?"

"Yes." Shaw keeps her measured tone. "Two interrelated answers. I am going to tell them to you. For the first one, I need you to think of a radio."

"I can do that." I go with my car radio.

"So," says Shaw, "a radio. FM and AM. Both radio waves, both ways of transmitting sound. But imagine the dial is stuck on AM. The FM stations are still there, but you can't get to them. In fact, if no one told you about FM you'd have no way of knowing they were there. For all intents and purposes, they wouldn't exist for you."

Just like my car radio then.

Still, flippancy aside I think I get the metaphor. "You're saying people are like that radio." I'm a little hesitant, but more because I'm worried about getting it right rather than getting it wrong.

"Exactly." Something in her tone makes me think she's smiling, is proud. Her footsteps sound a little brighter.

"So, the Progeny," I say. "They're FM?"

"Not exactly." We turn down more corridors, past more doors. This place is a warren. "You see, there are multiple realities, Detective Wallace. There are, to stretch the metaphor slightly, the equivalent of long-wave stations, medium-wave stations, satellite stations. And yet, eventually, the analogy breaks down. In the end we run out of radio stations. The universe, however, doesn't suffer from similar limitations. There are myriad realities, Detective. And many of them house intelligent life."

"How many?" Another question that I don't really want to know the answer to, but asking questions is a habit detectives pick up.

"I honestly don't know. Thousands. Hundreds of thousands. Millions perhaps. But for all that it matters, they don't matter to us. We're tuned to one reality and can't get to any others."

"So, you're telling me that's why we can't find any other life in the universe and why it can't find us?"

"I'm telling you that's one reason, yes."

We arrive at a second elevator. A retina scan this time. I'm beginning to think there's no way Shaw is a Jehovah's Witness. This is way too big budget for them. She's probably a Scientologist.

"If you don't mind me asking," I say, as Shaw pushes me into the elevator, "if it's impossible to detect these realities, how do we know about them?"

Shaw hesitates for a moment. As if I've caught her with a real stumper, as if she hadn't thought of that one. And maybe it is all just a big fat happy lie. And then she says, "We have a book."

"A book?"

"Yes, Detective, a book. A book the British government believes… that it believed…" She hesitates. I want to ask the questions about those holes in the conversation, but it seems that other information is more pressing. "It is a book of significant importance." Shaw has gathered herself, speaks confidently. "A book that contains information which, if disseminated, could unsettle the power balance of the entire world, which, in the hands of just one of the petty despots or egomaniacs in the world, could crack the very surface of our reality like the shell of an egg."

She pauses, lets the seriousness of her tone, her look sink in. "I'm sure you'll find it an interesting read."

It is by far the most threatening offer to read a book I've ever received. It's like an Ayatollah holding out a copy of Salman Rushdie's *The Satanic Verses* with a wink and a dangerous smile. And right then I bottle it. It's not worth it. I think I'd prefer to live with the idea I had a moment of madness, and that Felicity Shaw is just a good guesser.

"You know what," I say. "I'm not sure I really do remember anything from that night. It's all a blur. I was very stressed. Think I got some things muddled."

"It's not much further," says Shaw, pushing my wheelchair resolutely on. I don't think I can get out of here on foot.

We round a corner. The corridor is short and ends in another dull, gray door. Interest has been added by way of a muscular-looking man in fatigues holding the sort of oversized machine gun no one can ever hit Arnold Schwarzenegger with. I have no illusions that I could prove to be similarly elusive.

Coming along with Shaw is starting to seem like a very bad idea.

This time it's a nine-digit code, plus the thumb scan, and the retina scan, and some voice recognition just for kicks.

I swallow a lot, and rub sweat off my palms onto my pants.

The room Shaw wheels me into is bare except for a single low table. Four steel legs, a chipped particleboard surface. There's a book lying on the table. A four-inch-deep doorstop of a book. Heavy leather covers patinated with age. Moth-eaten pages hanging out at odd angles.

The sort of book John Carpenter would throw in to let you know Kurt Russell's day was about to go south.

But that's it. There's no chair. No windows. The door swings shut behind us. I swallow again. Hard.

"We're off the grid in here," Shaw says. "No wires in and out. Not even radio waves. We're in a completely sealed environment."

"And this is where I read the book?"

"Not exactly, no."

Oh shit. Oh balls.

Shaw walks away, leaves me sitting there. She reaches out to a small switchbox on the table, next to the book. For the first time I notice that the book is clamped to the table by a metal casing. Wires connect to it, trail down the back of the legs. Shaw flicks a switch. There is a hum like a generator.

"No one reads the book," Shaw says. "That's not quite how it works." Which seems an odd thing to say, because how else could a book work? "It was discovered by a British government expedition to the summit of Everest in 1933, twenty years prior to Edmund Hilary's ascent. You will find no record of that expedition anywhere. But that expedition—and this book that they found—led directly to the founding of MI37 in 1935, and to the magic arms race of the seventies and eighties. Not many people have experienced what you are about to, Detective Wallace."

What am I about to experience? What is wrong with the book? Why me? But I don't have time for any questions because then, without any more ado, she turns back the cover.

For a moment all I see is looping handwriting on a browning page. It's not a Roman script. Cyrillic? Pictograms? Something between the two. For a moment there is a smell like an ancient library.

Then the page ripples. There isn't a breeze, but still I see distinct movement.

"What—?" I ask.

The page flips. Then another. Another. One by one. Slowly at first. Then quicker. Until they are riffling past a blur.

"Holy—" I manage.

Then the book explodes.

It is noiseless, but I feel the shockwave blow back my hair. Pieces of paper fly past me in a flurry. And then they stop. Then they hang silently in the air. I sit and stare. It is as if I am in a snow globe, the water abruptly frozen, fixing everything, holding it fast

I gawk. I stare. I try to find a vocabulary for my wonder, my confusion, my fear. I reach out with one hand. I can see the hand shaking, like a schoolboy reaching for his first dance.

The paper moves, is suddenly galvanized. Like a thousand tangram pieces they whirl in a blizzard before us. They reassemble. Slowly they construct a vision before us.

It's me. It's me, standing there in the room. A perfect paper replica, my hand outstretched just so. I stare in awe. I smile. It is so... simple, perfect, beautiful... And the paper model smiles with me. I almost clap in delight.

Around the model, paper whirls, a fresh snowstorm. And the statue is shrinking, bleeding paper, receding. Surroundings build about it—the corridor outside, the elevator shaft, the whole building mapped out—but then they too are shrinking, being enveloped by the expanding horizons. Oxford is below me. Before me. The surrounding countryside. There is London, the slow twist of the Thames marked out in rippling sheets of white. Then I see England itself. Europe. Eurasia. The globe spins beneath my feet.

I have lost my sense of space. The walls are somewhere else, some place mundane and abandoned. The zoom out has picked up pace now. The solar system swirls before me. Shaw and myself—suspended in space, even as time accelerates, the planets blurring, stars. Everything receding, shrinking, and it must stop, the sense of vertigo is overwhelming, but it doesn't, it keeps going, and I keep falling away. I am too large, the universe too small, I am filling the whole of creation with my own existence, something must break.

And then it does. Something tears. Something rips. The white blizzard snaps and darts and something comes through, some barrier is breached, I am sure, a certainty beyond what I see. We are abruptly elsewhere.

But it doesn't stop. Shockwaves run through the paperscape before me, layer after layer of... something bursts. It feels like the whole of reality is splitting, dividing down and down into infinite slices, and I am stretched thinner and thinner between them.

And this is the truth of things. These—the rational part of me still left in the swirling madness realizes— are the dimensions Shaw was speaking of. Each of them a universe to itself. Infinite infinities. And with this realization comes a change. The space around me is no longer expanding, I no longer expand with it. The paper blurs, rustles, whispers over my skin. A change in focus. I am some place now, somewhere definite. Not here, but somewhere.

It is cold here. I feel it, a chill, my breath suspended as a thousand ice particles before me. I shudder and the paperscape shudders with me—a tremor through reality. Shaw is there. As frozen as the water in my breath.

Something is coming. I can feel it, a pressure in the air. I cannot see it yet. But something in the way the paper moves, the way it shifts and presses in. Something vast. The world is crushing down. And still I cannot see it. Until I realize that everything I see *is* it.

This thing, this presence—it fills the sky, fills the world. It is everything around me. Some vast scaled sheet of its being obliterates all horizons, all distances. And I am insignificant before it. I know that. A dust mote. Nothing more.

I am sobbing or screaming. Because I know. This is death. This thing in the sky, that is the sky. It is death pure and implacable. For it is hunger and I, even small insignificant I, am food, and I must be consumed. I must be. I must fill the vast void of its hunger. Everything must. Even the heat of this place has been consumed. It is death and it comes on.

I barely realize I am on my hands and knees. I barely realize the paper is retreating, blowing away, rearranging itself neatly, page after page lying down to rest between leather covers.

Shaw closes the book. Tears and snot dribble from my face. They puddle on the bare concrete floor beneath me.

"They are called the Feeders," Shaw says. "The Progeny are their children, and they are bringing them here."

4

Shaw helps me back into my wheelchair. I feel like a puppy someone just kicked. Shaky in a way I haven't been since I was four and couldn't find my mother in a department store.

"Others have done worse," she tells me. And there's a kindness in that, but it's going to take significantly more to reassure me everything's all right on the Western Front.

Because everything isn't all right. That's the whole point of this, I begin to realize. You don't have secret military intelligence departments to look after things that are just peachy on their own. They put things together because—

"The Feeders are coming." Shaw repeats the fact. "It's important you understand that."

Understand? I can barely comprehend. She's trying to expand my mind, but I think my mind's rubber might have perished. It won't stretch that far.

"The Feeders are the other reason for Fermi's paradox. Just as we know of the multiple realities, so have other races known. But those other races are gone. Are dead. They have been consumed. The Feeders have consumed everyone and everything capable of communicating with us. And they intend to do the same here."

"Why?" I ask. "Why here?"

Shaw shakes her head. "There is no why that we'd understand, Detective. They are aliens. Their thoughts, motives, are alien. We are simply a place where their spawn, the Progeny, landed. They send them out like spores. At least that's how we understand it. Blast them out into new realities without thought or reason. The Progeny that landed here found Earth fertile ground. Now they seek to draw their parents to them. To feed us all to them."

Oh God. Oh bollocks. That's enough. Staring into the future is like staring at that unrelenting paperscape sky.

"However," Shaw says, "that does not mean we intend to go down without a fight."

There's steel in her voice. Flint and iron. A little bit of bombast to be sure, but to be honest I could use a little jingoism right here, right now. Fighting back. Making a stand. That feels like the right response, like what should be done. I attempt to make my jaw as steely as possible, but I fear all I've done is give myself an underbite.

"The Progeny are here for a reason, Detective." Shaw talks with the same sense of efficiency, the same economy of words as she has since picking me up at the hospital. "The Feeders have not sent their children here simply as a homing beacon.

"The barriers between realities are not as easily broken as suggested by the book. One does not simply fumble through, like a child wandering into a magical wardrobe. It is a difficult process. We are on one side of a locked door, the Feeders upon the other. The Progeny are here to pick the lock. We, MI37, are here to stop them."

I nod. This is the hard sell, part of me knows that, but still… what am I supposed to do? Shrug and say it's not my problem?

"Stopping them sounds good," I say.

Suddenly Shaw smiles. Something warm and wide,

and unexpected. "Yes," she says, "Yes it does. Now, come with me, Detective. There are a few more things I want to show you."

She grips the back of my wheelchair and we head out of the small bare room with its opulent horrors. I'm happy to leave. To just be in a normal corridor, in a normal building, with a normal woman in a sensible suit.

Part of me still hopes I'm crazy, that this is some morphine hallucination. In fact, even a coma-dream might be preferable. But I'm not crazy, or dreaming. Deep down, I'm sure of it. I can see, as clearly as I see the linoleum floor tiles, the thrashing tentacles inside the man's head, the alien body twitching inside the human one. It was real. It's all real.

Shaw opens a door, and abruptly the smell of the sea hits me. There's a saltwater tang in the air. She wheels me through. A large space. The light is dimmer here, only a few lamps suspended above us. Instead the smell wells up out of a massive swimming pool set into the floor. There are shapes flitting back and forth, casting large deformed shadows over the ceiling.

"It's time to meet the Twins."

I twist, look at Shaw. "The Progeny. The Feeders. The Twins." I nod. "I am loving the nomenclature." Minutia. My comfort zone in times of stress. And this definitely counts.

Shaw straightens a little, a little smile on her mouth. "Thank you," she says. So I guess she's responsible.

As we get closer I can see the shadows in the pool more clearly. More than just two shapes. Not just the Twins. Unless Shaw means something more when she says "Twins" than I think she does. Can't discount that possibility at this point.

But then there are two heads poking from the side of the pool, long hair hanging, bedraggled over narrow shoulders.

"Ophelia and Ephemera," Shaw says. "But everyone calls Ephemera 'Ephie'."

"Ephemera?" I look back again, quickly, eyebrows raised. As a pair.

"That's what Kayla, what their... foster mother calls them." Shaw hesitates over the appellation. I'm about to ask why, but we're close enough for the girls to call to us.

"Hello, Miss Shaw." Two voices, young, make a reedy chorus.

"Hello, girls." There is a softness in Shaw's voice I haven't heard before.

The Twins are identical, black hair framing pinched faces with large eyes. Eyes like the lamps of a lighthouse— that's what I think at first. I can see why Shaw breaks out the warm and fuzzies for them. There is something oddly endearing about them. They are not wearing bathing costumes, but rather sun dresses with bright floral patterns in pink and yellow and white that bloom out around them, oscillating in the gently rippling water.

One of the shadow shapes twines between their slowly kicking legs. It's a...

"Jesus!"

"The squid are our friends, Detective Wallace," says the girl on the left, matter-of-fact and polite.

"The octopuses too," says her twin.

"The octopuses too," repeats the first, solemnly.

I stare, caught between being amazed and being aghast. The water is thick with them. With tentacles and gelatinous bodies. Here and there a sucker-strewn arm breaks the water, like a diminutive sea monster come to claim the pool's diminutive occupants. And where the hell... what the... how...? I turn to Shaw.

"She's not sure," says one of the Twins before either Shaw or I say a word.

41

"They were with us when we came here," says the other.

"There's more now. We feed them and they have babies."

My mind still reels. "How" doesn't seem as important as "why."

"She thinks it's something to do with the ink." Again the Twin answers the question before I ask it.

"What's the word you use, Miss Shaw?"

They are both looking up inquiringly at her. My jaw hangs. Not a good look on me but my mind just got blown for about the fifth time today and I'm starting to have trouble bouncing back. What a bloody week.

"Psychotropic," says Shaw. "The ink the creatures release is a powerful psychotropic drug."

"That's it," says the Twin on the right.

"Yes it is."

I open my mouth to say something, to try and put my confusion into words. "How do they…?" I manage.

Shaw shrugs. "It's something to do with the ink. I'm not completely sure."

"We told you that," says the one on the left.

"I'm Ephie," says the one on the right.

"I'm Ophelia," says the one on the left.

"Nice to meet you, Detective Wallace," says Ephie.

"Very nice," says Ophelia.

"Yes," I say, and stare about, still trying to get some life into my hanging jaw. I kneel down, hold out a hand. I'm not sure what else to do. "Nice to meet you."

The Twins stare at my outstretched hand.

"They don't really touch people," Shaw says.

"Because of the psychotropic ink," Ephie offers, helpfully. She pronounces the long word carefully, each syllable neat and distinct.

I stay kneeling, then slowly reel in my hand. "What are

you doing here?" I ask the girls finally. Because, I mean, I'm sure it's more complicated that it looks, Shaw doesn't seem the inhumanly cruel type... but it does looks like she has two ten-year-old girls locked away two floors beneath the ground in a swimming pool full of cephalopods and psychotropic ink.

"Kayla brought us here," says Ophelia.

I remember Shaw saying the name. "Your foster mother?"

"Our *mother*." Ephie corrects me.

"And she—" I start.

"Careful with your words here, Detective," Shaw says from behind me.

My brow creases. I hear the warning loud and clear, but I'm missing something. I don't think I'm being asked to table the conversation just for the girls' sake. I want to ask her more, but... another time and place. Probably be better anyway. Give me a chance to process things. As much as I'm able to.

"We help stop the Progeny now." Ophelia plugs the hole in the conversation. She has a helpful smile. Behind her an octopus rises to the surface. Two tentacles loop over her shoulders, grip her in some loose embrace. She turns, grinning; drops beneath the surface without causing even a ripple. I watch as she tackles the creature, revolving round its globular body, some strange iteration of roughhousing.

"We know about them," Ephie says. "About the Progeny." She speaks with sudden solemnity, in contrast to her sister.

"The girls know things we can't about the Progeny." Shaw's voice is businesslike now. The warmth drops away. "We have no way of detecting infected individuals. We can only hope to identify them by their actions, and the Progeny are very good at keeping those quiet. But the Twins here, they… they are able to access alternative channels of information. Ones that are not entirely clear to us at this moment."

"Something to do with the ink," I offer.

"Yes. Exactly. Their information has allowed us to track down several Progeny and eliminate them before they breed."

"They breed?" In some ways it just seems unfair that Shaw has added this image on top of everything else. I could have really done with getting through the day without the image of copulating mind maggots.

"I believe you saw their spawn," she says. And here we go: alien nookie 101. Buckle up for safety, kids.

"When the head of an infected victim is destroyed," Shaw continues, oblivious to my rising gorge, "the eggs are thrown out in a vast cloud. They look rather like giant fish eggs. They survive in our reality for," she squints, "around forty-five seconds. Maybe a little less. Our best theory is that our reality is corrosive to their outer layers. But during that time, any eggs that land in a nearby individual's hindbrain will nestle and hatch there. That individual will be infected."

"In a nearby individual's hindbrain?" Somehow that's both the least and the most disturbing image.

"OK, remember when I said we exist on one reality, and the Feeders on another?"

I nod.

"That's a simplification," Shaw says. "Reality as you and I perceive it is a composite. Hundreds of realities pressed into one. The Progeny exist in some of these but not all. Which ones exactly depends on their life cycle. It's more than you need to know now, but basically unless an egg or adult hits a suitable nesting site," she pauses, taps the base of her neck, "they're incorporeal. It allows them and their eggs to pass through some solid objects. For example, flesh and bone. Once they hit the nesting site, they're corporeal and we can chop them in two."

"Composite realities," I say, trying to grasp the whole. "Progeny exist on some. In hindbrain: can chop. Outside of hindbrain: can't chop." Reality feels loose. My mind has been expanded, and I'm rattling around inside it trying to find something I can actually grasp.

"Indeed." Shaw gives me a reassuring nod. I am not really reassured. Reality seems to be fracturing right in front of me.

I rub the back of my head. It, at least, feels reassuringly solid.

"OK," I say. Processing. Processing. I can almost see the progress bar in my head moving ever so slowly toward completion. I'm just praying the system doesn't crash.

"So," I turn and smile at the remaining Twin. My biggest grin. It helps hold my face together. "What's the latest word on what the Progeny are up to?"

"Ophelia's going to die," says Ephie.

Oh bloody hell.

She offers the words up matter-of-factly, as if this is a commonplace piece of information. I turn slowly to look at her sister, slip-sliding between tentacles out in the middle of the pool.

Bloody, bloody hell.

Mind worms I can take. Cosmic horrors I can take. The end of the world I am doing OK on. But this. A little girl. I can't… I mean… I don't… Shit. Just shit.

"Kayla can't save her," Ephie says, just as matter-of-factly.

I turn to Shaw. I feel completely helpless. Completely at sea. Drowning out in the Twins' pool. Drowning tangled in strange tentacular bodies I don't understand.

"What—" I manage. "What do you want me to do about it?"

And I know. I know what she wants me to do. But… shit.

There is a muffled thud to my right. Something heavy landing softly. I turn—

White. A line of reflected light. Brutal and simple. A blade pointed at my throat. Behind it a woman with a long sallow face. Long nose, long cheeks. Long bangs covering the eyes. A red flannel shirt over a dark green tank top.

Oh bugger me.

The swordswoman from the rooftop takes a step toward me, turning her blade so the edge now hangs before my bobbing Adam's apple.

"You feckin' save her is what you do." She speaks with a thick Scottish brogue. "You save her feckin' life."

My eyes are focused on the blade, my ears half deafened by the thunder of my heart, yet I am still dimly aware of Shaw moving to the swordswoman's side.

"Ah." She clears her throat, as if this is just an awkward moment at a dinner party. "Detective Wallace, this is Kayla."

Steel brushes my neck. Yesterday's stubble scrapes. "Yes," I hear myself saying, my voice thin. "We've already met."

5

Shaw lays her hand on Kayla's arm. Her sword arm. I fight the urge to genuflect as the blade bobs.

"Kayla," Shaw says. Her voice is soft as silk. "Maybe this isn't the time."

The sword doesn't move.

"It's OK." The voice comes from the middle of the pool. We all turn and look. It's Ophelia, surfacing from her game. "I like him," she says.

I glance back to Kayla. She's staring at me. A headlight glare, and I'm the bunny.

Then she takes a step back, and a moment after she retreats, so does the blade. With a practised movement she places it in a scabbard on her back. Probably what the flannel shirt hides.

Slowly I let out a long breath. "Jesus," I say. "I mean…" But I don't know what I mean. This woman stabbed me. Nearly killed me. She killed the Progeny. Which means… Shit, I've been hunting her for nearly six months. She's a serial killer. My serial killer. My whole life has centered around putting her behind bars for six months. Six months. One hundred and eighty-three days of my life. Rounding up. And now I'm on the same side?

Except… "She stabbed me." I say it out loud. I say it to Shaw, but I don't know if I expect her to answer. It's not really even a question. I just feel like someone, and really it could be anyone, should apologize. My lung was punctured.

I see it again. Her stepping out of the cloud of eggs, toward me. Coming toward me faster than I could track. Sword out. White blade. Black night. Red blood. Black vision.

Stepping out of the cloud of eggs. Something about that seems relevant. Something niggles…

And then—Shaw's words. *Any eggs that land in a nearby individual's hindbrain will nestle and hatch there.*

This woman, this murderer, she was in the cloud of eggs. She was hit, infected. She must have been.

"Progeny," I say quietly. "Oh fuck. She's Progeny."

I don't even see Kayla move. She is standing beside Shaw. Then I am suddenly falling, jarring against the ground, Kayla on me, holding me down. She is inches from my face, the blade pressed tight against my skin. I feel her breath as she speaks.

"You don't curse in front of my girls."

My head is pressed against the ground, cold concrete, light from the pool lamps playing around me. Ephie is holding on to the pool's edge, staring at me, wide-eyed. A squid nuzzles at her shoulder. Her sister swims to join her.

"That's a bad word," Ephie says.

"Very bad," Ophelia agrees.

And of course you don't swear in front of kids. Of course. I know that. I'm a policeman. I'm an upstanding member of society. But… But… I mean, aren't we missing the point?

"Progeny," I say again, barely a whisper as Kayla presses the blade harder against my neck.

"Apologize." Kayla's voice is as sharp as a second blade digging in between my ribs.

"S…" I manage. "S… I'm s…" I don't know if I can't

say it because I'm so scared or because I really don't mean it. "I'm sorry," I manage.

This time Kayla's sword precedes her own retreat. The blade is gone, but she remains, still staring, lip slightly curled. Then she steps back so I can actually get up.

"Please, Detective," Shaw says, voice still level, patient, as if dealing with irate toddlers. "Kayla is not infected. While you saw her within range for possible contamination, the Progeny have some issues with Kayla's... particular neurology. Neurology that makes her another vital agent in our attempts to stop the Progeny.

"You see, there is no cure to infection, Detective," Shaw says. "The Progeny do not give up a body without killing it. So to stop the Progeny you stop the infected. Kayla is uniquely capable in this. She has dispatched hundreds of the infected. You have been seeing the results of her work in Oxford. She is quite certainly on the side of humanity. On our side. And while you work for me, Detective Wallace, I will not have you question her loyalty."

But I miss the end of what she says, because hidden in there is, maybe of all the things I've heard so far today, the one that blindsides me the most.

"Work for you?"

"Have you not been listening, Detective? There is a war on. Our world, our reality is in danger. One of our key assets—humanity's key assets—in that fight, a young girl, is in danger. And you're thinking of walking away?"

"I..." I say. Because... well, I'm sort of in shock that I even have the option to choose. I've spent most of the time since I saw the Progeny either doped on morphine or being terrorized by the knowledge that we are most definitely not alone.

And it is terrifying. It is. Beyond measure. When I was in that room, with that book... It makes me shudder to think about it. And Kayla is terrifying. Utterly. And she kills. Has killed. And the way she moves... How can she really be human? How can she not be... something else? It's all too much and too big and too frightening.

But part of me is thinking that it's also kind of cool.

I really need to not watch quite so many movies.

"Look, Detective," Shaw says as I dither. "Arthur. You're not the first person to take an interest in Kayla's work. But you are the first to track her down. That makes you interesting. I've reviewed your police record, and it's exemplary. That makes you very interesting. And I've watched you today, as you absorbed what I've had to tell you. I want you on my team. I need you on my team. Kayla cannot defend Ophelia. I don't know why, but that doesn't make it less true."

Beside Shaw, Kayla shifts, a pent-up anger in her limbs, a desire to dismiss Shaw's statement but an inability to do so.

"But what Kayla can't do," Shaw continues, "I think you can. And I think, after all you've seen, you want to do it."

I look away for a moment, back at the door, away from the pool. It would be so much easier to walk away. In the long run. Bollocks, in the short run. Just so much easier.

I look back at the pool. At the two girls looking at me, both smiling softly. And what I have to do is obvious really. Terrifying and exciting and obvious.

"I'm in," I say.

Shaw smiles. Kayla looks away.

"Excellent," says Shaw. "Welcome to the team."

6

And that's it. I really am in. I'm a government agent. A member of a clandestine organization. No longer Detective Wallace, but Agent Wallace. Agent bloody Wallace. My mum would be so proud.

Well… if I could tell her she would be proud.

Well… actually, she'd probably be more impressed if I demonstrated competence at ironing. But…

Bollocks to it. This is exciting. Even if I do have to work with a terrifyingly psychotic woman who seems more likely to stab me than to actually support me in my attempt to… Jesus… to save her kids.

Jesus.

I'm actually pleased with how together I think I managed to seem at MI37's headquarters considering how freaked I was, and I was planning to freak out significantly more at home but Shaw has given me two little off-white pills saying they'd help with healing, and five minutes after I take them everything goes fuzzy and it's sort of fun to say, "Agent Wallace, Agent Wallace, Agent Wallace," over and over in my head, and then the curtains seem to come down rather hard and—

THIRTY-SIX HOURS LATER

A knock on the door wakes me. I manage to unglue my

face from the couch cushion I've been drooling on and stagger to my door to find the bloke in fatigues from outside the book room standing there. He's left his machine gun behind, though, and he's nice enough to let me shower and collect my somewhat scattered thoughts. I'm toweling off before I realize that I can breathe again, that I've only got a tiny scar on my chest instead of a great bloody sword-inflicted wound. I am healthy and whole.

Honestly, I think Shaw should give up the MI37 thing and take over National Health.

Anyway, then it's off through the tortuous streets of Oxford in a miniature Fiat, through three hundred different security locks, and I finally end up in empty corridors deep underground being marched to my first briefing. It's bloody brilliant.

"We don't feckin' need him."

Kayla's Scottish brogue is sharp enough to puncture my good mood. I hear her speaking around a corner, out of sight. I put my hand on my chaperone's shoulder. I don't particularly want to hear this, but I'd rather not confront Kayla before my first big meeting. Urine stains tend to make bad impressions.

"It's not your decision, Kayla." Shaw's tone is placatory but firm.

"They're my girls."

"We all want the best for them."

"And he's the best?"

Ouch. But the problem is that, somewhere in the back of my head, there is a gnawing fear that Shaw is clearly two sandwiches shy of a picnic if she thinks I can help her out in any way at all.

"He's the best I can do."

Well that's all my fears allayed... Oh wait.

"We don't need him," Kayla states.

"We need someone."

I'm half tempted to just turn and hoof it there. Except that's not what Kurt Russell would do, is it? And, anyway, that seems to have been enough to silence Kayla. There's the sound of a door opening and then closing. Then nothing. After a moment I touch the shoulder of the bloke in fatigues.

"Onwards then," I say.

He gives me an awkward half smile. A pity smile. But we go on. And then there's the door to conference room B, and my chaperone knocks, and I am delivered.

"Good luck, mate," he says. But I'm starting to worry if it might be too late for that.

Shaw opens the door.

"Agent Wallace," she says. She checks her watch. "You're a touch late."

Suddenly being Agent Wallace seems a lot like being myself at age twelve knocking on Mrs. Watton's classroom door for the first time. Still, Shaw stands aside, whereas Mrs. Watton gave me and the class a five-minute lecture on the evils of tardiness, complete with references to Satan, unwholesome thoughts, and potential blindness. Odd woman, actually, Mrs. Watton

Conference room B is as plain and functional as any room back at the police station. There's a couple of tables shoved together, a few office chairs scattered about, an over-sized whiteboard. I had sort of hoped for images of pentagrams and hieroglyphics, or runes and scientific equations, or possibly just the rough sketch of some hideous monster from the outer limits of space, but instead there's just the usual mess of half-erased lines that seem to appear whenever a whiteboard is exposed to the air for over six seconds.

I'd expected a veritable host of people to meet, and

palms to press. Even the smallest murder case warrants a team of at least a few police officers. The end of the world would seem to require fifty or more. But there are just three others sitting around the conference table.

Kayla is there, looking broody and murderous. I can't see her sword but her red flannel shirt is baggy enough to conceal multiple death-dealing instruments. I look for the seat furthest from her.

The best bet seems to be a chair next to a tall, skinny, collegiate-looking chap with a scruffy beard. He wears thick, black-rimmed glasses and a welcoming smile.

"Clyde," he tells me as I sit down, and pumps my hand vigorously. Nice chap, I suspect. "And this is Tabby." He indicates the girl sitting opposite him.

She's young, mousy, and I think Pakistani, though her skin is mostly hidden behind tattoos. Text scrawls its way up one arm and something like ivy pokes out from a thick sleeve that coats the other. Her nose is pierced once, her lip twice, I lose count checking out her ears. White streaks through her dark hair build to a checkerboard pattern around the base.

She places a foot, clad in a platform Doc Marten, on the table and informs me, "It's Tabitha."

Probably also lovely. Probably not nearly as terrifying as Kayla. Probably everything's going to be fine. Probably.

I wipe sweat from my palms and smile around the room. I try to make it seem like I'm jolly and at ease. Not sure how well that goes.

Shaw takes a seat opposite me and consults her watch again. "We're behind," she says. There's a quick glance at Kayla and me. The offenders, I guess. I try to look contrite, but I don't think Kayla bothers.

"I'd hoped we could do some formal introductions," Shaw continues, "but Clyde, you and Agent Wallace here have face-to-face with the Sheilas in just under sixty, and you know what the traffic is like." She doesn't bother looking at us for confirmation. Not exactly a democracy here. Still, bold leadership, and all that.

Probably fine.

"You'll be consulting them on a pronouncement Ophelia delivered at oh-seven-thirty-six this morning." She flicks through some notes lying on the table, pulls out one sheet of paper. "Beware the painted man's false promises until he shows his second face."

I grab my notepad from my jacket pocket and jot the words down. No one else bothers. The new-kid-at-school vibe intensifies.

Probably all Oxbridge geniuses with photographic memories or some such.

My palms are starting to sweat again so instead I look at the words I just wrote down. It looks like gibberish and I'm worried I'm no longer able to parse sentences properly. Excitement and nerves have the better of me and I'm making a hash of everything.

Probably going to doom the world to being consumed by giant soul-sucking aliens or some such.

Probably.

Shaw is still speaking. "Agent Wallace," she says, "as you have some experience directing a team, I'll let you take the lead on the Sheila conversation."

Wait. On my first day I'll be doing what?

But Shaw has already moved on. "Tabitha," she continues, "if you'd do us the kindness of researching painted men, especially prophetic ones. Maybe start with Native American mythology, see if there's anything there. Kayla, you're going to be sitting the early rounds out—"

Kayla grates her teeth like someone mashing the gears in a sports car.

"Is that a problem?"

Kayla says nothing. I have to learn how Shaw renders her so passive.

"All right, people." Shaw gives us all a tight little nod and a tight little smile. She looks at her watch again. She looks up and catches me looking at her. I think she reads the tremors of panic in my expression because for a moment her smile softens, broadens. Then the moment passes and she looks around the room. "Let's get moving," she says and seems to be out the door before I blink.

And with that we've started.

Bloody hell.

"This way," Clyde says with more gusto than I think I could manage even on a good day and suddenly we're whisking our way down a myriad of corridors, pushing through doors and security points. I tag along as best I can, feeling like flotsam caught in a wake.

Eventually we reach a moment of stasis, waiting for an elevator to take us up. "So," I manage to say into the toe-tapping silence, "who are the Sheilas then?"

Clyde turns, a look of sudden horror on his face. For a moment I wonder if he's foreign and I've somehow stumbled across a colloquialism that means I've slept with his mother.

"Oh God, I'm so sorry," he says, so contrite that I'm forced to wonder if the colloquialism is reversed, that I've accused him of sleeping with my mother.

"Why?" I ask, because what I'm thinking can't possibly be right.

"I can't believe I…" He shakes his head, touches his pants pockets then his breast pocket, as if checking he is completely together. "Director Shaw, you know. She's all business, and I get caught up in that, so then I'm all business, all go, go, go, and it completely flies out of my melon that you might not have a clue what we're doing. Totally discombobulating." He stares off into space for a moment, a quizzical expression on his face. "Is combobulate a word?"

This last question is a bit of a blow out of left field. It leaves me a little dazed and I eventually manage, "Is that important?"

"Probably not. No, no. Well…" Clyde stares into the middle distance. "You know. Never sure if these things might crop up in conversation at a later date. Might prove crucial one day. Never see it coming. Your whole life hanging on the knowledge of whether combobulate is a real word or not. Like *The Seventh Seal*, just with Scrabble or something. But not relevant now, no. Sorry about that." He shakes his head. "Gone and done it again."

I just stare. Despite having not actually talked about the Sheilas I've somehow become more confused about them. Clyde is shaking his head. "You ask me about the Sheilas and I go wandering up the garden path, on about classic Swedish cinema. Which, while noble and sparse enough to be noteworthy doesn't… doing it again. Not explaining. Sorry. Will focus." He taps his head. "The Sheilas. Three women. All called Sheila. Sheila, Sheila, and, well, Sheila."

Somehow I had imagined something a little more impressive, especially after all that. "Oh," I manage.

"Bit disappointing," says Clyde. "I can see that. Sorry."

"It's not your fault." Which in retrospect is a bit of an obvious thing to say. Clyde has me off my step still. Nice man, but… a lot of noise to the signal.

Eventually we make it to a garage where it turns out Clyde drives a Mini that neither of us really fit in. Still, it's a classic vehicle and seems to accommodate Clyde's personality if not his form. We fold into it as best we can and he dials us into classical music, which also seems fitting until "Ride of the Valkyries" begins to accompany our inching crawl down St. George's Street.

We ride along mutely for a while, Wagner smashing his way through crescendos and chords, while I try to think of something to say. Clyde seems equally dumbstruck and all we manage for a while is the occasional friendly grin, which somehow only makes things more awkward.

Finally I open my mouth with a last ditch, "The book's something, isn't it?"

He nods. "Rather messes with your head, doesn't it?"

We pause.

"That it does," I say into the conversational breach, which is a pretty pathetic save. I am vaguely aware I should be trying to live up to Shaw's dictum, that I should be leading our little duo. Except I don't know how to. I don't know which questions I need to ask in order to find out more.

"Did you get to the bit about the Dreamers?" Clyde interrupts my thoughts.

"The Dreamers?" I think. "I did the Feeders. Nothing about…" Then the implications of his statement dawn on me. "You mean there's more of it?" The idea of going back in that room makes me shudder.

"Oh yes. It's got about eighteen chapters." He fiddles with the stereo. "I've only read two. I think Shaw's made it through about three and seven as well. She's made of pretty stern stuff, though."

"And the Dreamers—they're related to the Sheilas?" I'm trying to tie this all together, get the big picture. Because once I get that, I can get back to minutia, to my comfort zone.

Clyde laughs. "Oh no. Sorry. Misleading. Just… no. The book." He changes the radio station. "Shaw told you about the whole composite reality thing, right? What we perceive being made up of multiple realities."

"Composite reality. None involving the Feeders. Some involving the Progeny." I recall the lesson.

"Yes, that's it." Clyde nods eagerly. "Well, the thing holding all the realities we perceive together is the Dreamers. They create the composite."

I know it's not Clyde's fault, and he really is a nice fellow, and he's trying to help, but it does feel like my head is being done in. I rub my temples.

"People?" I manage, trying to get the facts straight. "That's what holds reality together?"

"Probably not actual, real people. Reported to look like us, yes. Well not you and me, but, well, people. In the reports that there are. Not that many of them, you know. Sparse on the ground. Like four-leaf clovers. Well... never seen one of those. But haven't spent as much time looking for one as I have for accounts of the Dreamers, so maybe that's a persistency thing. Probably says something about luck, that. The more time you put in... But, anyway, they're a cagey lot, the Dreamers. Usually exist on some of the less probable realities apparently. Don't come our way. Sort of opposite of Jehovah's Witnesses. Except without the religion. Suppose that means they're not really opposites, actually. Maybe Satanists are the opposite of Jehovah's Witnesses. They tend to keep to themselves too. At least I assume they do."

"Did you say," I thumb through the mental mélange Clyde has summoned, "that the Dreamers exist on the less probable realities?"

"Did I?" Clyde hunches one shoulder; seems to cogitate on it. "Probably did, yes. You see, the problem with having more than one reality is that sometimes, well maybe often, I don't know, but sometimes they disagree. Opposite things happening in the same place. So the Dreamers pick which reality is more probable and we see that. That's how the composite can act like one reality, you see. Something happens on one reality, it happens on pretty much all the realities. Except in a few improbable background layers we don't see."

I take a moment. The Dreamers: holding reality together, hiding in the creases. It all sounds a little fragile.

Actually, sod fragile. Dreamers? Progeny? Feeders? It sounds bloody Lovecraftian. Any minute now my sanity is going to give way and I'm going to wake up in some New England mental asylum gibbering about unspeakable horrors and complaining about rats in the walls.

"What if they die?" I ask. "What if someone kills them?"

"Well, killing them isn't exactly the easiest thing for someone to do," says Clyde. He has a slightly professorial tone. He seems to relax in a way he hasn't done so before. The doling out of information seems to suit him. I wonder how much action there is in this job. Maybe not as much as Shaw made it sound. Maybe Kayla does all the action stuff.

Part of me is relieved at the thought. Part of me is rather sad.

"If anyone tries to get close to the Dreamers," Clyde is saying, "the realities they're on are just removed from the compound."

"Oh," I say. "OK." I wonder when I'll find out something that is more exciting than it is intimidating.

We drive on and it turns out the Sheilas live in Summertown, one of the less picturesque parts of Oxford. After the dreaming spires, it seems a rather drab setting for intergalactic revelations but beggars can't be choosers on this sort of stuff, I imagine. Still, it's a little tricky to sustain my sense of wonder as we mount the stairs to an apartment perched above a chain grocery store.

At the top of the stairs is a door painted a rather alarming shade of deep pink. Clyde knocks on it.

"It's open," calls a chorus of voices.

I let Clyde lead. I know Shaw said I'm meant to be in charge on this one, but letting the established contact take point here is a good dodge until I get my feet under me a bit more.

The door opens onto a tiny hallway—really just a four-by-four, square space separated from the rest of the apartment by a dividing wall. The pink theme continues beyond the hallway, with a Day-Glo pink print of the Mona Lisa on the living-room wall, and a shocking pink bookshelf squeezed underneath it. The TV is on and a man with hair so perfect it looks almost laminated is discussing crumb cake. On a pink couch perch the Sheilas.

There are, as Clyde mentioned, three of them. Except… well… I'm pretty sure there's a politically correct term for it but at this exact moment it escapes me. Probably because I'm too busy counting. And yes, yes there are definitely three heads. Identical heads, actually. Same one three times. Triplets. That term I have. And yes, there are six legs. And six arms. Six hands. Six feet. But, and this stays a sticking point no matter how many times I go back to it, there is just the one body.

Siamese triplets? Is that the term? It doesn't sound like it should be in this day and age.

They're all wearing the same T-shirt of a multi-headed Indian god, Brahma I think… Well, I mean, of course they're wearing the same T-shirt, they have one torso… but it's really the same T-shirt three times, sewn together somehow. The same deity staring out at me again, again, again. Three pairs of jeans handled in the same manner— one seat with six legs. From their faces—smooth-skinned and fresh—I'd put them in their twenties. They all have the same asymmetrical haircut, bangs slanting down across their foreheads. The one on the left is placing a bookmark in a copy of *Macbeth*. The middle one slurps ramen noodles from a plastic pot. The rightmost Sheila is the one watching TV. She uses the remote to mute it, but doesn't turn it off.

"Hello, girls," says Clyde.

"Hello, pet," says the leftmost Sheila, the one farthest from us.

"Morning, love," says the closest one.

"All right," says the one in the middle.

And thereby we arrive at the appropriate point for me to say that it's very nice to meet them all and that I have a couple of questions if they don't mind too much, and generally do all the things that ten plus years on the force has prepared me to do. What I actually do, of course, is my goldfish impression. Open mouth. Close mouth. Open again. No sound.

"This is Arthur," says Clyde. Then, after I open my mouth a few more times, "He's new."

"Barely shows," one of them says.

"Wallace," I manage. "Arthur Wallace."

"All right, Arthur," says one, then another, then another.

The middle Sheila extends a hand. I shake it. It grounds me. This is a real person. This is a real thing happening. I am being a real arse.

"I'm so sorry," I say. "It's been a rough couple of days." I shrug apologetically. "Not my best excuse, I realize. But, well, my mum taught me honesty is the best—"

"Shaw make you read the book?" asks the rightmost Sheila, cutting off my babbling. It's a mercy killing.

"Yeah." I nod. "Still a bit shaken up over the whole aliens going to devour me sort of thing."

"Clyde pissed himself after he read that," says the middle one.

"Sheila..." Clyde's protest either lacks conviction or backbone. Or both.

"You bloody did."

"True. Yes. But it wasn't really the validity of the fact that I was objecting to."

He's comfortable here, I realize. He's not exactly confident but he is comfortable. Maybe there's a way for us to work that. If I can fake confidence we might not totally half-arse this.

I pull out my notepad from my pocket, check the line Shaw gave us. I go over it a couple of times. I want to get this right. It's been a long time since I was the new guy. I need to use my police officer props until I hit my stride.

"Director Shaw gave us a line," I say. "Something Ophelia said."

"Business already?" says a Sheila.

"Enough of this social foreplay already?"

"Get stuck in, is it?"

They wink as one. I attempt a grin but I'm still on my back foot and my blush reflex decides to kick at the least opportune moment, so I just stare down at my notepad and read the nonsense statement a few extra times until my brain kicks in again.

One of the Sheilas laughs. "He's cute, this one," she says.

"You can bring him again," says another.

More notepad reading. And they're nice girls, they really are, and I think I'd probably love to come round here and share a pint and have a laugh, but today is totally not the day for it.

"Beware the painted man's false promises until he shows his second face," I manage to elbow into a moment when they all seem to be taking a breath at the same time.

"Come again?" says a Sheila.

"Beware the painted man's false promises until he shows his second face," I repeat.

"Well, that's marvelous to know, pet," says one Sheila, pushing her bangs back out of her eyes. "Never know when that'll come in handy."

"What if he's just been gone at with a crayon? Does that still count?"

The middle Sheila brays at this. The noodles hanging from her lips fly wildly and I am uncomfortably reminded of the Progeny in the dead man's brains.

"Come on, girls," Clyde says softly. "It's his first day."

And I could almost hug Clyde, except now I feel even more awkward. Some leader I am.

"Look." I push my hair back and use the hand to force my head back so I actually make eye contact. "I'm really sorry. I just… I'm kind of feeling the pressure on this one. What, you know, with things not looking so awesome for Ophelia. Not really used to being the frontline on that sort of thing. I'm just trying to get off on the right foot is all."

There is silence for a moment.

Finally the Sheila in the middle swallows her noodles and speaks. "Bloody buzz kill, you are," she says.

"Sorry."

"Nah," says the one nearest me. "It's fair play to you. Down to business."

"Well, painted man," says the one furthest away, "could be literal. Someone in a painting."

"They're not usually literal," says another.

"Poetic licence is what they have," says the third.

"Could be tats. Painted skin."

"That could be it."

"I like that," says the Sheila with the TV remote.

They all look at me, as if seeking some sort of approval.

I don't have a bloody clue. I sort of imagined something involving the word "scrying" and possibly rabbit guts, or at least a tarot card or two. I mean, I don't want to doubt Shaw or Clyde, but just making random guesses seems a little… prosaic.

I glance at Clyde, and apparently I'm not doing such a fabulous job of keeping that thought off my face because he chips in with, "The Sheilas have an excellent record for accurate interpretation. Far above chance. In excess of ninety percent, actually."

"You're going to bring up the chicken thing, aren't you?" says the rightmost Sheila.

"I wasn't," Clyde protests.

"Welsh loonies," says the middle Sheila.

"I mean," says the leftmost Sheila, "if you come to us with the phrase 'bird of terror,' then, I'm sorry, but we're just not going to go to chicken."

"Welsh loonies," says the middle one again.

"Seriously," continues the leftmost Sheila, "how are we meant to know about some cabal of chicken-phobic apocalypse cultists operating out of Cardiff? We're conjoined, not bloody psychic."

"Welsh loonies."

Conjoined. Not Siamese. That's the PC term. Conjoined triplets.

Which is a thought as off-topic as we are. Again, lovely girls, but it's a bit like trying to herd conjoined cats.

"So, painted man is probably a tattooed chap," I say, trying to bring things back on course.

"Most def," says the middle Sheila.

"Maybe it means you, Clyde," says the leftmost one.

The middle Sheila brays again while I raise an eyebrow. Tabitha, the Pakistani goth back at the briefing—she I can picture with tattoos. Probably because she has them. But Clyde? Really?

"Technically speaking," Clyde says, pulling his head down between his shoulders like a retreating tortoise, "they're not exactly tattoos."

"What's your girlfriend think of them, Clyde?" asks one of the Sheilas. "How'd you explain that one?"

I don't know if I'm more surprised that Clyde has tattoos or that he has a girlfriend.

"You seen his tattoos?" asks the leftmost Sheila.

"The painted man has false promises?" I ask, completely ignoring her questions, which is basically an arsehole move that I hate pulling, but, well, Ophelia, universe-destroying aliens, etc.

"All business with you, isn't it?" The rightmost Sheila doesn't sound offended exactly, but she's disappointed. I don't have to be a detective to work that out.

"False promises," repeats the middle Sheila.

"Pretty bloody obvious," says the leftmost one.

"A tattooed bloke is going to lie to you," says the middle Sheila.

Again my mind flicks back to the goth, Tabitha. But she is, most definitely, not a bloke.

"Until he shows his second face," adds the leftmost Sheila.

"Which is?" I ask.

"Erm..."

The three Sheilas look at each other.

"A mask?" says one.

"He takes off the tattoos?" says another.

Everyone else in the room creases their brow.

"Guess not then." She shrugs, and the motion ripples down the conjoined torso.

"Not sure," says the leftmost Sheila.

There's a moment's pause while I wait to see if there will be more, but the Sheilas seem to be done. I glance over at Clyde, trying to gauge what exactly we've gained here, how exactly we wrap this up, if we should push for more. He sees my glance.

"That sounds like that's all then," he says, clapping his hands. "You've all been marvelous, of course. As ever." He leans forward, starts shaking hands. "Definitely going to be on the look out for tattooed men with an above average number of faces."

The Sheilas all smile. Broad smiles. They like Clyde. This is his world. As for me… I'm still perched out on the periphery. Just like I am with this farewell. Nodding and hand waving around Clyde's goodbyes. An observer looking in. And I worry again about Shaw's decision-making abilities.

We're at the door when the leftmost Sheila says, "Of course, if it's tattoos you're after, you know who you should be talking to." She gives Clyde a significant look. I follow it up with a questioning one for good measure.

Clyde slaps his head. "Oh bollocks."

The Sheilas all nod together.

"What?" I say.

"You're too easy on him," says the rightmost Sheila.

"Who?" I say.

"Should've flushed the bloody key," says the middle one.

"Who?" I ask again.

"Bollocks," Clyde says again.

7

"Maximilian Lewis," Clyde says as a momentary lull in the Oxford traffic allows him to stomp on the accelerator for about half a nanosecond before a cyclist makes a kamikaze run at us.

"Who?" I say, my head bouncing against the Mini's headrest.

"Owns a tattoo parlor on Cowley," Clyde says.

Cowley Road—the start of Oxford's student slums. Cheap housing, cheap restaurants, cheap bars. And a cheap tattoo parlor strategically placed to catch them as they stumble back to the aforementioned cheap housing from the aforementioned cheap bars.

"A chap called Maximilian owns a tattoo parlor?" For some reason I sort of assumed all the owners were called Terry or Steve. Silly idea really.

"I think he goes by Max," Clyde says. Which makes more sense, I suppose. Good to know some things still do.

"And he... is involved with the Progeny?"

"No." Clyde shakes his head. "Well... no. Probably not. Not knowingly. Don't think so. Unless he's infected. But he wasn't infected last time..." He shakes his head. "Can't think why they'd do it. He's just a nuisance really. Likely still is. We've had to take him off the streets more than once. He's more than willing to give tattoos with metallic ink, you see?"

"Not really."

"Oh." Clyde chews his lip. "Probably should have seen that coming," he says. "It all goes back to electricity, you see."

"I'm lost." I think it's going to be best if I'm honest every time that happens, even if it means asking a lot of annoying questions.

"Well, electricity is the universal lubricant between realities," Clyde says, as if telling me that the sky is blue.

"Erm?"

Clyde tries again. "Any sort of cross-reality breach requires electricity."

"Can we try words of one syllable?" I ask. "And maybe diagrams?"

"OK." He nods. "Fair point. Well made. First principles then. There's more than one reality."

"Well established," I say.

"The Feeders are not in our reality, but they want to be, right?"

"So I'm told."

"So, QED and all that, it must be possible for things to travel between realities."

I think about it while Clyde swings us around the fifteenth traffic circle we've hit in quarter of a mile. "I suppose," I say.

"So how do you do it?" he asks.

I look at him, and apparently it's a serious question. "Haven't the slightest of clues, I'm afraid."

"Electricity," he says. "Universal lubricant. I've mentioned that. Remember it."

"Oh," I say, because he's right, but when he said it last time there wasn't really meaning attached to it, so I'm not sure if he's really right, but I'm also not sure if I'm pedantic enough to point it out.

Clyde nods, briefly manages to make it all the way to fifteen miles per hour but then has to go over a speed bump. "So, you can use electricity to get things between realities. Bigger the thing, the more power you need. Small things are the easiest." He looks away. "Well, the essence of things are the easiest. Say, for example, there's fire in another reality and you want to bring it here. You could use a decent chunk of electricity to bring over the flame, or you could use a little bit to bring over the essence of the fire—in this case its heat. Bring enough heat over and you'll probably start a fire anyway.

"Now to get something as enormous as a Feeder through," he continues, "would take an absurd amount of power. And then that power would need to be focused. It's not really feasible. Which is why," he takes his eyes off the road to give me a significant look, "the Progeny, who probably came here pretty easily, being small and mostly incorporeal, are now having such a hard time doing it."

"You focus the power?" Up until now I've been buying this, possibly more eagerly than I should be. Any cynicism I possessed has rather had its legs cut out from under it these past few days, but the idea of focusing magical power is beginning to seem a little too New Age mysticism to be real to me.

"Yes!" Clyde nods enthusiastically. "Hence the tattoos. QED again."

"Wait, what? Q E what?"

"Bugger," Clyde says. "Sorry. I'm not very good at this. OK. So, the power is electricity. So it flows down the path of greatest conductivity. Now, the body's a natural conductor so you don't have to do what I did, but…"

"What you did?" I ask. For a moment I have an image of Clyde in the middle of some group of death cultists in various states of undress. Possibly accompanied by sacrificial guinea pigs and the like. It doesn't seem to really match him though. "And this is to do with the tattoos?" I ask.

"Yes!" Clyde's head bobs up and down in a few swift nods. "See, different parts of the body are more powerful for doing magic than others. Your chakras, as it happens. So to get the most juice out of, well, the juice, you want it to be concentrated at those points. The tattoos provide the path of least resistance to the chakras. Except, well... like I said, they're not exactly tattoos. Here, look."

His hands come off the wheel, but at this speed it doesn't really matter. It's not like we could really do anything any harm. He pushes up a sleeve. There is a fine black line running down the center of his forearm. Occasionally black threads break off from the main line and form small spirals.

"Holy McPants," I say, "how did you explain those to your girlfriend?"

"What?" Clyde says. "Devon? Oh I'm not really sure. I think she thinks it's a security system for work."

"What?"

"I'm not sure how it happened." He shakes his head. "Devon has a creative mind."

"But how would a tattoo be a security device?"

"Well." Clyde hmmms. "It's not actually ink, you see. It's copper wire beneath the skin," he says, finally grabbing the steering wheel in order to dodge a student on a bicycle. "Following the main ley lines of my body. The spirals mark various chakras. And that's what focuses the power. That and words. Words are important."

"Words? What words?"

"Well, you know." Clyde oscillates between enthusiasm and sheepishness again. "Once you've got the juice to breach realities, then you need to make sure you're breaching the right ones, that the energy does what you want. You have to shape it. Human will and all that. So there are words to help you do that. All sorts of nonsense. Help you think in the right ways, so you don't end up blowing off your nether regions instead of turning someone into a toad or some such."

"Wait a minute," I say, the penny dropping, "are you talking about spells?"

Clyde shrugs several times in rapid suggestions. "Erm... well... in lay terms, I suppose, yes."

Spells. Magic spells. OK, that's cool.

TWENTY MINUTES AND ONE MILE LATER

With a certain deftness I hadn't credited him with, Clyde pilots the Mini into a parking space about the same size as a grapefruit. Quite a feat to behold, actually. Kayla stands by the curb watching events with disdain. As we unfold ourselves from the confines of the car she thrusts out a hand. I flinch but all she does is open her fist to reveal two tan-colored earplugs sitting in her palm. I stare at them, nonplussed. Clyde takes one and hands the other to me.

"Tabitha," he says, in a moment of surprising conciseness.

He pushes the bud into his ear and I follow suit.

"Warning next time," says a tinny little voice in my ear. "Little bit. Before a bloody field operation. Be nice." It's good to know Tabitha is still in intimate contact with her inner misanthrope.

"Hello! Tabitha!" Clyde sounds far happier than I imagine is usual when there's someone telling you how much you screwed over their day. "On location. Cowley Road. The sights, the smells, down among the people. Terribly exciting to be out of the office for so long."

"Shut up, Clyde," says Tabitha. For some reason he

beams. Something's going on there but I'm not sure exactly what.

"Erm... I..." I say, thus cementing my role as a keen and decisive leader.

"All right," Tabitha says. "Arthur. New boy. I'm in your ear. You tell me problems. I do research. I fix your shit. So you be my eyes. Don't want to listen to Clyde mumbling over batteries."

"Batteries?" I look over at Clyde who pulls two flat silver-cadmium batteries from his pocket and tucks them into his cheeks, gerbil-like.

"Erm?" I say again, just in case anyone missed the benefit of my incisive intellect the last time around.

"Electricity," Tabitha says into my ear. "He explained, right?"

"Oh," I say. "Right."

"Q, E, bloody D then," she says. Which is actually quite funny, but she delivers the line so aggressively I realize the humor too late to laugh.

Kayla just glowers at me. I don't look her way for long and I certainly don't meet her gaze.

Instead I look over to the tattoo parlor three stores away. "So this bloke, Max," I say to Clyde, "he puts copper wire in folk too?"

"Not exactly." Tabitha speaks directly into my ear before Clyde can even open his mouth. He doesn't look at all put out by this, maybe seems even to expect it. "Uses metallic inks. Not as effective. Effective enough, but not as hardcore as Clyde."

Clyde. Hardcore? The only thing I can really imagine Clyde getting hardcore about is D.H. Lawrence. Probably another imagination failure on my part. And I don't want to comment until I work out the nature of their relationship. So instead I say, "Metallic inks. Right."

"Yes," Clyde says. "It's students mostly. That's the problem with the Bodleian being a copyright library. Just about absolutely everything is in there. Makes it hard to sort the grimoires out."

"Every six months." Tabitha harrumphs. "Bloody cleanup duty." She harrumphs again. "Bloody students."

"And this guy tattoos on the… focusing lines?" That's probably not the term. I need a cheat sheet.

"Just follow our feckin' lead, all right?"

It's the first thing Kayla's said. She walks away from us; pushes open the tattoo parlor's door.

She still seems pissed. I probably shouldn't have called her Progeny. Except I can't shake the feeling that there is something profoundly off about her. And I can't help but think of Shaw telling me that there's no easy way to tell if someone's infected. So Shaw might not truly know.

I'm not really sure what I can do with my suspicions. Use them to get stabbed again?

I look to Clyde, searching for a lead to follow, when I should be offering up one myself. He hoists his shoulders sheepishly and shambles off after Kayla.

I swallow my pride and follow along. Definitely need to work on my leadership skills with these guys.

The inside of the tattoo parlor is close and dark. The walls are crowded with pieces of paper tacked there, each bearing some twisting design inscribed in black ink. Skulls leer, women pout, vines creep.

The artist, a man who knows his audience at the very least, is bent over a chair. In it is a young lad, nineteen, twenty perhaps, shirtless. The artist holds a buzzing needle over his sternum, finishing a vast spiral that stretches from one nipple to the other.

The kid being tattooed defies the Oxonian stereotype of gawky and bespectacled youth. Instead he is lean and muscled in a way that has always eluded me. His skin is ruddy, and too tan to give the impression he has spent years riffling through the depths of the Bodleian Library.

He notices us first. His eyes narrow. I guess we probably don't look like customers. The tattooist follows his gaze.

"Oh bollocks," the tattooist says.

"Hello, Max," Clyde says conversationally.

"Third strike, you feck," Kayla says, not so conversationally.

Clyde puts a finger to his ear. "Large funicular circle. Whole abdomen. Minor thorax involvement. Unilinear."

The tattoo, I realize. He's describing the tattoo.

"Cross-referencing now," Tabitha's voice comes back.

"I was just copying a pattern from a book," says Max. He indicates the offending item. It's on his tray next to his inks. I've heard drunken men pinned by their car airbags lie more convincingly about how the wall came out of nowhere.

That said, the book looks too new to be a tome of ancient magicks. It's a neatly bound hardcover, with a faux-leather spine. Still has the sheen on it. Something's not right.

"It's just something I sketched out myself," the student says.

Beware the painted man's false promises. Don't believe his lies. Q, E, bloody D, he did not sketch that himself.

"If you could just put the needle down, Max," Clyde says, ignoring the student. "Be a decent chap."

"Before I make you, Max." Kayla's Scots accent somehow makes the words even more threatening.

"This is not even close to being f—" he says, and it's about that point that I realize that if the student is the painted man, which seems fair enough given that Max himself doesn't have a single tattoo on him, then really we shouldn't be worrying about him. And it's also the point when the kid we're ignoring legs it.

He moves like lightning. I turn trying to grab him, but his elbow whips out and slams into my gut. I collapse on it like a deflated balloon, air whining out of me.

Clyde manages to half-turn his head by the time Kayla is fully turned around, but even she is too slow. The kid grabs the notebook as he legs it, uses the momentum of his motion to catch Kayla on the back of the head. She steps to steady herself and he's already passed her. Then the bell on the door rings and the student's outside.

"Feck!" Kayla bellows in the small space.

I try sucking in an experimental lungful of air. It doesn't go as well as I'd hoped.

"What's going on?" Tabitha says into my ear. I don't bother trying to reply.

"You," Kayla points to Max.

"Y-y-y-yes?" Any cocky swagger he has put on, any defensive bluster melts in the face of her anger, steams up and evaporates. All that is left is fear.

Kayla steps forward, punches him. His head snaps back and his legs go out from under him. Kayla looks around at Clyde and I. "Why are you still feckin' standing here?"

I feel that I actually have a decent excuse for this one, but I still can't get enough breath in to explain that, and anyway, Kayla's already out the door, and then Clyde is too, his tweed jacket flapping behind him, and I'm not sure that Max, in his unconscious state, would really appreciate the observation. So I make my wheezing way to my feet, and stagger after them. The spot where I was stabbed burns.

"What do you mean he's running?" comes Tabitha's voice in answer to some observation I don't hear.

I can see Clyde a dozen yards away, hand still to his

earplug. Kayla is more like a hundred. She's moving at a terrifying pace. People on the streets leap left and right. She's heading to a parked car. Some clapped-out old thing, rust showing through the paint. The hood has been popped.

"OK, databases gave me a hit," Tabitha barks into my ear as I stagger forward. "Tattoo design. Mazalian spiral. South American origin. Originated circa fourteen hundred BC."

Kayla jumps. It's twenty yards or more to the car. She arcs through the air. There's a grace to her. Her arm reaches back almost lazily. Except it's as if everything has been put on fast forward, everything moved up so fast my eye can barely follow it.

"Mostly used for rejuvenation spells. Crop stuff." Tabitha drones on.

I catch up to Clyde, wheezing, bent over. He's standing still now. No need to catch up. Game over.

"Also altered consciousness. Sex rites. Fertility."

The sword sweeps through the steel of the car's hood. It rips and splays, falls away. The bare-chested student is standing there. He staggers backwards. He's holding the car battery.

"And transmogrification. Of all things."

"Oh bugger," Clyde groans. Then he breaks into a run.

"Trans what?" I say. "Why are we running?"

"Battery!" Clyde is yelling. "He's got a car battery!"

"Move it!" Tabitha's yell is an electronic screech in my ear.

Transmogrifi-what?

I can see Kayla raising her arms. The sword doesn't come up, though. She's not going to strike. It's a defensive gesture. She's protecting her face.

There's a magnesium-white flare, bright and brilliant,

like the birth of a star in the street before me. My vision goes white, then red, then black. I stumble back, grabbing at my eyes. And Jesus does that hurt.

Slowly the street comes back to me, slowly it resolves. Black, to red, to blinding white. Then blurs of shape. Focus evolving out of chaos. Into chaos. People about me are down on their hands and knees, pawing about blindly. Screaming. Cursing. I rub my eyes. The car. The detached hood. A shadow shape still standing on the car's roof. Kayla. I see Kayla. And the student, where's...?

Holy shit.

There's something where the student was. Something massive. Something growing. It's human in shape, I'll give it that. Squat powerful legs, broad as my chest, thickening at the thigh, ropes of muscle bursting through the jeans he was wearing. Above the waist—an inverted pyramid of flesh, each abdominal muscle a chopping board of flesh, the pectorals as wide as the hood of the car Kayla just cut away, but thicker, vault door thick. And the arms... They grow longer, knuckles strike the ground. Forearms thicker than the thighs. Biceps thicker still. Shoulder muscles like a cow's carcass dragged over the joint. He's colossal, ten feet tall and still going. Twelve foot now.

And perched on the massive crossbar that is his shoulders is a curiously small head. Not the student's head anymore. A second face.

His hair grows as I watch, is longer, blonder now. The cheekbones lift, the chin thins, the eyes grow larger. It's a girl's face, a child's face, pretty, actually, despite the monstrosity beneath. And then it twists, contorts, one side of the skull crumples, caves in, its tongue lolls out and it sneers. It roars. It bellows, from its crushed head, and the street vibrates with the sound.

If ever there was a moment to bail, then this is it.

Running and screaming are pretty much the only rational things left to do.

So I start running. Except... well, if I ever meet Kurt Russell I think I'm going to have to give him a piece of my mind, because I'm running toward the bloody thing.

8

I'm halfway to the car when the monstrosity swats Kayla like a Scottish fly.

She watches it happen. She stands there. Does nothing. Her sword dangles by her side. She stares up at the misshapen head while the fist goes back. While it comes back down.

At first I think something must be happening so fast I don't even see it. I almost expect to see her dancing up the thing's arm, standing astride its shoulders. But she's flying through the air like a broken mannequin. And it doesn't seem like part of the plan when she lands and lies there unmoving.

Our biggest gun was just taken out in under six seconds.

My pace slows. And... isn't she...? Isn't the plan that...? Aren't I backup? Kayla does the whole inhuman speed and agility and stabbing things with a sword bit. And I...? I've never even punched a wall.

Why did she take that hit? Why would she do that?

The thing that was the student closes a massive fist on the roof of an old Ford Escort. Metal crumples. He hefts it, one-handed. Weighs it. Muscles ripple—inhuman anatomy flexing. In his spare hand, he still holds the car battery, two fingers pressed to the contacts. I wonder about that. Not for very long. Too busy wondering about the best way to dodge a flying car.

I dive left. There's a sound like the sky cracking. Chunks of glass and metal fly. My ears pop painfully. I eat pavement, scraping to a stop, skinning my chin. I roll, breathe, come up and the street keeps rolling. The student… Where's the student? And then there's another car. It's in the air, already coming at me. And it's unfair to blame Kayla for the whole thing, but I do anyway.

Why did she take that hit?

I brace for a vehicular enema.

The car lurches sideways in midair. Something invisible slams into its side and knocks it spinning away. It crashes into the middle of Cowley Road. Rolls like a barrel. Bounces over the roof of another car. Collision glass shatters in an explosion of white shards.

Clyde stands there, hand outstretched. There's a tear in the elbow of his jacket. He brings his second hand to bear on the student, the monster. A slow deliberate movement. He bunches his shoulders. Pulls back, curls into himself. The student takes a step toward him. The ground shakes. Clyde explodes outward, flings his arms out. A great shove into midair.

The student slams to a halt. His feet grind backwards. He stumbles, goes down on one knee. Clyde takes a step forward.

Holy crap. *Clyde* is the backup.

The student grunts, something animal, something guttural. He bellows. Everything vibrates. Clyde's feet shake; he's putting everything into the invisible shove. The student smiles. The student leers. The student stands. Clyde staggers back.

I lurch to my feet. I stare.

They come at it again. Clyde slams something massive and invisible into the massive and very definitely visible student. I see the student's muscles quake. But he doesn't go down. He just pushes back. They stand there. Stalemate.

I think about the two flimsy batteries in Clyde's mouth. I think about the car battery the student is clutching. Clyde's power level isn't even close.

But… maybe, yes, maybe there's the start of an idea there.

"What's going on?" Tabitha's voice is sudden and sharp in my ear. I shake my head. I need to concentrate.

The student needs power. That's why his fingers are still pressed to those contacts. Electricity is power. Electricity powers the break in reality that's causing this spell. Electricity needs a circuit. Break the connection, break the spell. We don't have the monster to deal with, we have the man.

All I have to do is think of a way to get the big bastard to loosen his grip.

And the thing about movie cops is that they have guns. Magnum 45s and Uzis. They have biceps the size of my head. I don't even have my steel baton so I can give him a rap on the knuckles.

The student lets out another bellow from his misshapen child's mouth. He takes a step forward. Clyde's sneakers skid back down the road, soles screeching. He grunts. The student takes another step.

All I'm left with is running for cover. Head down. Feet slapping against the asphalt. I half expect a Peugeot up the arse.

"Keep using Elkman's Push." Tabitha comes online again answering some unheard statement from Clyde. "Emphasis on the second syllable. Searching for something bigger. More oomph."

I slam into the limited shelter of a doorway. Tabitha is whispering a stream of curses into my ear. Whatever she's trying to look up, she's not finding it.

From my momentary cover I look again at the student's car battery. I look at the fist gripping it. It's as big as my chest, fingers near the width of my forearm. I can't get it to let go. There's no way to prize those fingers apart.

Still, there's more than one way to skin a cat. Even a twelve-foot-tall slavering monster cat. I hope.

"Tabitha," I say. "I need something sharp. Something with a rubber grip." Something that won't fry me like an egg when I jam it into that battery. "A fire axe would be nice."

"Have fun with that. Kind of busy."

I scan the street, the rubble. Nothing. I look over at Clyde. Doesn't seem to have a fire axe on him.

"Come on," I say to Tabitha. "Please."

"Where are you?"

"Cowley."

"I fucking know Cowley. Where on Cowley?"

Adrenaline is screwing with my ability to keep up with conversation. I look left, then right. There's not much to go on. "Opposite an Indian restaurant," I say.

Nothing. No reply. Clyde is in full retreat now. The student is grinning, mashing his way down the street.

"Turn around," Tabitha says.

"What?" I was rather hoping to keep my eyes on the terrifying, death-dealing monster stalking down the street.

"Turn around," Tabitha repeats. "Pretty simple."

I hesitate, and then I turn.

I'm looking into a hardware store. I'm standing in the doorway of a hardware store.

Talk about staring you in the bloody face.

I kick in the glass of the door. Which jars my leg in an uncomfortable way but still looks sort of awesome. Then I go and spoil the effect by trying to avoid slicing myself open on the remaining jags of glass as I edge through.

The lights of the place have gone out. I can see people cowering in the aisles, heads down. Someone standing behind the counter furiously rubbing his eyes. Axes. Axes. Which aisle for axes?

I can feel time running out. I can feel Clyde's batteries running out. I hear a yell from the street and see him flying backwards, sailing through the air. Time's up.

No axe.

Then I realize I'm staring at crowbars. Crowbars with easy-to-grip rubber handles.

I grab one, turn, feet skidding. Adrenaline flushes my system and this suddenly feels like it might even be a good idea. I start running. My feet pounding down. I smash through the remaining shards of the door. I hit the street sprinting. My legs burn. A good burn. The burn of fire. Of power. The world is slipping past me in slow motion. It's like a dream. The student is hefting another car. But I'm going wide, and he doesn't see me. He looses the car at Clyde. I don't have time to look. I'm coming up parallel with it. I've got the crowbar lifted like a javelin. The student looks left for another projectile. I'm coming up on its right.

I jump. Right foot on the hood of a car. The twang of steel beneath the impact of my foot. The thing starts to turn. My left foot hits the roof of the car. Smack. And then I'm in the air, crowbar lifted above my head. A steel snake about to strike.

The student swats me. Dismissed by the back of his hand.

I am vaguely aware of pain. I am vaguely aware of my vision jagging abruptly sideways before it blurs. I am even vaguely aware of the pavement as it robs me of my senses.

9

THEN AND WHEN AND IN-BETWEEN

An alleyway. Dirt-strewn. Trash-spattered. And I think I must have fallen down, must have landed badly, because everything hurts. My chest hurts. Jesus, it feels like I'm splitting in two, starting right there, right between my ribs. And how did I get here?

Behind me I hear a rustle of movement, like a thousand petticoats all moving out of sync, yet together. And then, as I let out a grunt of pain and surprise, a woman's voice says, "Hush."

I get my right arm working. Lever myself onto my back, and lie facing up. The sky is a dead, dull gray. It was blue back in Oxford.

Back in Oxford?

Yes. I don't know how I know it, but somewhere deep in my bones I can say for sure that, Toto, this is not Kansas anymore.

A woman stands at the end of the alleyway, framed by steel fire escape stairs that stretch up to the swatch of cloud-choked sky above us. She's beautiful. An incredible softness of features. Large, pale, gray eyes framed by thick black lashes. Hair held up by an architecture of jeweled pins, a few loose curls spilling free to hang around her ears.

She wears something like a princess's dress, though that phrase makes it sound gaudy, and she is to gaudy as matter is to antimatter. She's wearing the dress that every other princess's dress echoes—layered cream fabric, lace, and silk. She's as out of place as Halloween in the middle of July, yet somehow she seems to make the rest of the world seem out of place. There is something utterly genuine about her in a way I cannot quite describe.

To be honest, I'm rather impressed with my own subconscious. Who knew I could summon these sorts of images? I'm going to have to get knocked out by giant monstrosities more often.

She puts a finger to her lips and again says, "Hush."

I open my mouth to explain that I hadn't said anything and she gives me a benevolent yet reprimanding look. I feel like a naughty child.

The princess, the vision, takes two steps toward where I lie, crouches down with the rustle of fabric and crinkle of crinoline. She leans forward like a conspirator.

"She is not what you think she is." Her voice is soft and melodious.

I let that percolate a moment.

"Who?" I say.

The woman pulls back sharply.

"Hush!" The word is a demand now. Then she softens. She steps forward again, comes to crouch beside my head. It feels as if light radiates from her dress.

"You do not want to wake me up," she says. She lies a cool finger on top of my forehead and—

COWLEY ROAD

—Kayla is lying next to me. She is wide-eyed, breathing shallowly, close to hyperventilating. Not unconscious but caught in the grip of something.

More unfair thoughts rise up. She bailed on us. When she took the punch. Why did she—

"She is not what you think she is."

No. Obviously not. That's just subconscious burbling, just me letting my thoughts run away with me.

The ground shakes. Footsteps—slow and ponderous and inevitable. I look up. The student is advancing on Clyde. I try to get up. I don't. My arms barely even twitch. My chest aches. Each breath burns. I taste blood and gravel. A stone is embedded in my lip.

Clyde pops AAAs like Alka-Seltzer. His cheeks bulge with them. Hardly a threatening image. Still, he musters some power. He flings his hands out, as if throwing air, and with each movement the student visibly reacts to some impact. But it's not enough. The student keeps walking.

"Tabitha!" Clyde shouts. There's an edge of desperation in his voice.

"Not getting anything." Tabitha's voice is thin and reedy, a sense of hysteria slipping through the rising static. "Databases are blank."

The student pauses, looks from Clyde to me, a bored expression on his face. Clyde sees the hesitation and throws both his hands forward, like some mad shot-putter hefting a leaden beach ball.

The student's head snaps back. Something gives with a sharp crack. The remaining cheekbone. The student twitches its head back, stares at Clyde. The other side of its face sags. The leer is mockery now. Lips droop, cracked yellow teeth exposed. The student grunts. He moves toward Clyde. Fast now. The air of boredom is gone.

"Tabitha!" Clyde is almost shrieking.

"Just buy time! Anything! Trip it. Bind it. Blind it. Just slow it fucking down!"

Clyde spits out a mouthful of batteries and shoves in a

nine-volt. He closes his eyes. His mouth moves but I can't hear the words.

Blackness. A cloud of darkness. It's as if night has descended on one tiny corner of the world. The student's head disappears inside an inky cloud.

One massive foot snags on a partially collapsed streetlamp. The student stumbles. One knee crushes a car; a hand only just stops it from face planting.

The student howls. A sound so loud my vision blurs. I'm about up to my knees but that takes me down to all fours again. The student flails. Objects fly through the air. A postbox. A street sign. Then the clawed hand hits a telegraph pole and it stops. The hand grips. The hand pulls.

Wood gives way with a crack. Splinters explode outwards. Wires twang and snap. The monster wields the pole like a staff, sweeping it round and round in great circles. A car is totaled. A shop window vanishes as the thing blunders forward.

The collateral damage is insane. On and on goes the dervish of destruction. The student clears a path for himself in great arcs. He doesn't stumble. There's nothing for him to stumble over.

I'm close enough to Clyde now to hear him as he feeds information to Tabitha.

"Well, it's blind."

"Nice." Tabitha sounds satisfied.

"Not totally convinced that's working out as well as we planned." The student stops, focuses on the voice. "Oh pants," Clyde adds.

"Any chance the student just heard you?" Tabitha says. "Worked out where you are?"

"Maybe."

"Then shut your hole, you idiot."

But her advice comes too late. The student is moving with purpose again.

I'm so focused on the destruction that at first I don't notice Kayla moving beside me. I miss her breath slowing, coming more regularly. I miss her getting to her knees, to her feet. But then she moves. A blur of limbs, a glint of shimmering steel. And I see her then.

She hits one car roof, then another. There is no stealth to her approach. There is grace, certainly—something of her ungainly figure becomes fluid in the attack—but in her own way she is as blunt as the creature she's attacking.

She's fifteen yards away when the student hears her. He careens around as her feet smash down on the hood of a car. He flings the telegraph pole in a wild arc, smashing at everything he can.

He misses. Of course he misses.

Kayla is just ten yards away. She leaps.

The student swings again. And somehow, through some fluke, some piece of chance, the blow is wickedly accurate. Babe Ruth swinging for the bleachers.

But the balls thrown at the Babe never had swords.

Kayla catches the pole with her free hand. She twists in midair. The dive becomes a pirouette. Her blade arm juts out at a sharp right angle to her body. The sword tip buries itself in the monstrosity's arm, even as Kayla spins. She unpeels flesh, as if skinning an apple. A great peeling swath of skin. Muscles suddenly exposed. Gouts of red. Kayla completes her spiraling circuit of the pole. Her body whips out in a sharp diagonal. Her blade leaves a doodle in gore across the blinded student's chest. And then, finally, its trip completed, Kayla's sword smashes into the car battery still nestled in the monster's hand.

I feel the explosion first, a soft wind over my face, a light lifting of dust that gusts in my face. Then the shockwave hits me. Air kicks me in the face. It lifts me up off the ground and dumps me a yard down Cowley Road. My head cracks. Limbs smack. More gravel grates against my face.

And then the sound. Not the great bloody kaboom of Hollywood, but just a short bark and then silence, slowly, slowly replaced by a high-pitched whine. The death shriek of nerve fibers in my ear. A tone I'll never hear again.

Eventually I pry myself off the floor. My knees shake hard. Clyde sits on the crumpled wreck of one of the monster's projectiles. He shakes beads of collision glass from his jacket with a trembling hand. And Kayla—

Kayla stands in a mess of blood and bone, the epicenter of some explosion. Gore spatters her—chunks of flesh plastered to her shirt, her jeans, her face, her hair.

Jesus. I mean... Jesus. I've seen dead bodies before, but this is something different. This is like a warzone. The body... The pieces of the body... of the inhuman body.

Slowly my mind starts to parse what just happened, what I just saw. And it was real. Not some Hollywood effect, not some post-production computer wizardry. Flesh warped here. Reality broke here. And this is the world in which I live. This is my home. Fucking Oxford. Dreamy, sleepy, little Oxford. The best minds of the next generation pickling themselves in alcohol. It's stupid and small and calm and quiet. And I'm standing on Cowley Road with a woman who breaks the sound barrier. A woman with a sword.

It's unreal. It's too much. I don't understand. I don't understand anything.

One answer. I'll take any answer. Just one answer to one question.

And Kayla standing there.

"Why?" I ask her. "Why did you stop? I don't understand.

You stopped and then you—" I point to the corpse.

Kayla turns her back on me. Starts to walk away. "No," I say. "Please. I just want to... I need to understand. I mean, you let him hit you. And he was huge. I mean, that's got to hurt. That hurts you, right?" I'm following her as she keeps on walking.

"Shut up, Arthur." Tabitha's voice is clear in my ear. I ignore her. I really need an answer right now.

"You're... You're like me, right?" I persist. "A person, right? No..." I shake my head. "That sounds wrong. I didn't mean... Shaw said. You're not Progeny. I know that. But the things you do. They're... You're..."

She is not what you think she is.

"Shut up, Arthur." Tabitha is insistent.

"Why?" I ask Kayla's back. "Why would you stop? Let him do..." I sweep my arm around; try to encompass the entirety of the destruction. It feels futile. Still Kayla ignores me. I catch the arm of her shirt.

"Please—"

Suddenly Kayla is inches from my face. I can feel her breath on me when she speaks.

"Shut. The. Feck. Up."

She walks away and I stand there. I sit down. On the tarmac. Alone. Confused.

After a while Clyde come up. He limps slightly.

"Bloody idiot," Tabitha says into my ear. Clyde hears it too because his voice twists into a grin.

"She's talking about the student," he says.

She's not, but I let it slide. There's a chance I was being a little needy, but, well, I've been through a lot recently.

I close my eyes. Try to focus. "The student?" I ask.

"Didn't even know to let go." Clyde says.

"Let go of w—" I start to say and then balk at uttering the interrogative. I give a quivering look at Kayla's retreating form. But just one answer. Surely that's all I need.

"He interrupted the power source," Clyde says. "Electricity is the universal lubricant between realities. No electricity, no lubrication. Inter-reality friction. Rapidly generates a vastly exothermic reaction." He looks at me, at my expression. He tries again. "If you don't stop casting a spell before the electricity runs out, everything goes boom."

"Ah," I say. But it's another explanation that doesn't help me understand anything.

I look at the devastation, at the wrecked cars, at the smashed blacktop, the shattered shop fronts, the downed telephone wires. Around us, people start to pick themselves up off the ground, start to look at each other, to sob hysterically. People start to look at us.

Something dawns on me. Witnesses. Oh shit.

"We screwed up," I say.

"Oh, did you guys screw up." I decide to pretend that wasn't just glee I heard in Tabitha's voice.

"Big time." Clyde chews his lip.

"Shaw's going to tear us new ones," I say. She doesn't seem like the sort of woman who'd take this well.

"Could be worse," Tabitha says. And this time I can't ignore the audible smile. "You could be the cleanup crew."

10

"A complete and utter shambles. A disaster. It stretches the limits of comprehension that such a thorough display of incompetence could have been managed without willful bloody intent. Such a f—" Shaw trips over the curse word, swallows it back down. "Such a damned disaster."

She is white-lipped, wide-eyed. Every muscle in her face seems tensed. Two red spots stand out on her cheeks like a clown's make-up.

To my right, Clyde and Tabitha shuffle their feet. To my left, Kayla stares intently at one corner of the room, as rigid as the moment the monster hit her.

Shaw's stare is a frosty searchlight. Someone needs to fess up. Someone needs to take charge.

Oh bugger.

So, I clear my throat and everyone looks at me. Everyone except Kayla. My mouth is very dry. "I think," I say, resisting the urge to look at my hands while I talk, "that the problem is—" and here goes nothing "—teamwork."

Tabitha's eyes narrow. Kayla's head twitches momentarily toward me. Apparently not a popular play on my part.

"Look," I say. "I mean, mea culpa. You asked me to take point on this one—" I nod at Shaw "—and evidently I blew it. Teamwork is my responsibility, I get that. But,"

I permit myself a brief shoe shuffle, "well, I hate to play the new guy card, but, well, I'm the new guy. And it's not a very good excuse, and I apologize deeply, I should have been more familiar with things, and I wasn't." Which may be pushing the humble pie thing a little far, but I want to buy as much goodwill upfront as possible.

"And," I say, "I think individually everyone did their jobs great." I can't help but flick my eyes to Kayla, but it's not time for that yet. "Clyde really came through with... what he does. Tabitha was on the research. Kayla put the student down." I don't say the word: eventually. "It's just, when we had the hiccup. When Kayla... Well, I'm sure there's an explanation—"

She is not what you think she is.

I need to shut that little voice down. Get my fears back in my subconscious where they belong. Still, I'd love to hear the explanation.

"But it was... When Kayla... stopped, well, then it became pretty apparent that we weren't entirely comfortable playing together. Everyone seems to have a very specific role. If someone has to back someone up then we fall apart a bit. With one leg of the chair knocked out, to use a metaphor, the other three couldn't really take the weight."

I try to gauge Shaw's reaction to my little monologue. Her face is a mask. Her eyes are jumping from face to face.

"That's your assessment, Agent?" The title doesn't sound quite so awesome all of a sudden.

"I mean..." I say, "only one day on the job, but..." Her face is still a mask, but I think this isn't leading to a good place.

"And what do the rest of you think?" Shaw snaps her head around the room.

There is a very pregnant pause. I think I even hear its water break.

"Honestly?" I'd expect the comment to come from my left, but instead it's Tabitha who speaks. I look at her. She seems unhappy. More so than usual.

Shaw nods at Tabitha.

"Bullshit," says Tabitha. "This is. Turned into a bloody monster. Bit of an advantage on us. But we stopped him. Could have torn up Oxford. Rampage. But we were there. We did good." She looks at me. "'Cept what the fuck did you do?"

Ouch. And it hurts most because she's right. Lay there. Mostly. In a lot of pain. I did jump off the hood of a car wielding a crowbar which might have looked momentarily cool, but it was about as effective as throwing wet pasta at the bastard.

"*We* did good," Tabitha repeats. And then she turns and pushes out the door. All done.

Not a resounding endorsement of my point of view, I admit.

Shaw chews her bottom lip.

Silently, Kayla follows Tabitha. Shaw closes her eyes.

I look at Clyde, wait for him to follow suit. But he just shrugs. I can't tell if it's an apology, condemnation, commiseration.

"Right then." Shaw sighs. "Spectacular." She's not really talking to us. "We'll wrap this up later then." She picks up a pile of folders, exits stage left.

"Oh balls," I say and sit down in one of the chairs around the conference table. What a colossal cock-up. I put my head down on the table with a dull thunk. It's cool against my forehead.

"I wouldn't take it so personally," says Clyde. "Tabitha, obviously, well, she disagreed with you. Probably can see that. Binoculars not required for that one. Not like bird watching. Which I never enjoyed. But..." There's a pause.

My head's still down, but I can imagine him shrugging furiously. "I'm trying to say… She's loyal is Tabby. Doesn't like a word said against her team, her people. That's all. It's nothing personal. Well, except that part where she asked what you did, which might have been taking things too far, really. Just like you said, really. First day and all. And your first day is a Tuesday. Terrible days, Tuesdays. Bane of the week if you ask me."

I manage to prise my head up off the table. "Thanks, Clyde," I say. And I mean it. Support from one out of three. That's not… well, actually that is quite bad. Piss poor in fact. I put my head back down.

"Chin up, old man," says Clyde. There is quite a long pause during which I don't comply. "Well then," Clyde says eventually, "best be off then. People to do, things to… no wait, other way around. Anyway, I'll…" And then the door swings shut and cuts him off.

THREE HOURS, A BEER, AND AN ICE PACK LATER

I almost don't answer the door. I'm still deep in my funk. I screwed up. Not the team, but very specifically me. And not just because I didn't lead on Cowley Road, but because I didn't lead in that conference room. Kayla leads. Without even saying a word. Which makes sense of course. Sociopathic killer though she might be, she can actually do something. She can actually fight the Progeny. She can make a difference. I can get knocked out and summon pretty hallucinations. Which is of limited use when you're trying to save the world.

Except that punch… It occurs to me that, in fact, my only reason for believing Kayla's not infested with duplicitous mind worms is that Shaw says she isn't. And what reason do I have to trust Shaw? What if Shaw is infected too? Both of them, sabotaging the efforts of

MI37 from within. Which, yes, I am willing to admit, is a little paranoid. But there are mind worms, damn it. A little paranoia might not be amiss.

And all this is weighing on me a little bit, and I'm not really in the mood when the doorbell chimes. But then it occurs to me that it will probably be a Jehovah's Witness or something and seeing someone even more pathetic than me might cheer me up a bit.

"Sorry, not today," I say, opening up the door. But actually it's Swann standing there which catches me off guard, so I say, "Actually, yes, today." Which is both not funny and reminiscent of a bad pick-up line. But it's still Swann, which is a little cheering.

"Boss," she says, "with all respect, you're one stupid bastard."

Not how this scenario had played out in my head, I have to admit.

"What is it, Swann?" I sound tired and impatient, which I suppose I am, but I wish I didn't sound it.

"Oh, come on, Boss." Swann rolls her eyes. "Don't act like you don't deserve that. You burst a lung because someone actually stabbed you with an actual sword, like a real actual sword, and then you check yourself out of hospital without telling anyone, go completely missing, and worry everyone half to death—you're a stupid bastard. It's obvious."

Not the finest example of her detective skills, but I've got to say she makes a convincing argument.

"Good to see you too," I say. She smiles at that.

"You look a bit rough, Boss," she says. "If you don't mind me saying."

And while I'd rather she point out that I look rugged and handsome, I say, "No, I don't mind." I smile. She doesn't.

"Look, Boss," she says, "when an injured copper goes

missing then your co-workers may get a tad worried about the whole thing. Wonder what you've been up to."

If I was cooler, I would say something disingenuous about not knowing she cared, but as it is I just sort of shuffle my feet the way I did when Shaw had me on the spot. "Well, you know," I say, "the whole stupid bastard thing got in the way."

"Seriously, Boss." Swann looks momentarily anxious, a brief moment of vulnerability I haven't seen before. "What happened to you? The superintendent is going around bitching about some government letter saying you've been co-opted, which no one seems to be able to prove is a fake, but it stinks so bad of bullshit he's leaving his office windows open. And now here I am and you look like a car hit you. What's going on?"

"Well…" I say. And how do I answer that? How do I lie to her face after she's come here to check up on me? Above and beyond the call of duty on her part that is. But I can't tell the truth. I like the way she doesn't think I'm insane, or a pathological liar. "Good news is," I say, "that actually the car missed me."

"What?"

"Look, do you want to come in?" I ask. The question feels loaded in a way it shouldn't. I'm just asking a co-worker in. Just trying to make a long story short. That's all.

"Sure," she says.

So she comes in and takes a beer, and examines my CDs, and asks me who Miles Davis is, which breaks my heart a little, and finally finds a seat, and makes herself comfortable.

"So." She takes a swig. "This is the bit where you tell me everything and put my mind at ease, right?"

"Not exactly," I say. Not at all. "It's complicated," I say. She stands there, one eyebrow up. Wish I could do that.

"Look…" I say.

Still the lone eyebrow mocks me. And I have no point to make. I have nothing for her to look at. I sit down on the couch, which makes a sad little groan that sounds like disappointment.

"I want to be honest with you," I say. "You deserve that." And it is and she does. "But the honest thing is I don't know what I can tell you. What I'm allowed to tell you. You understand?"

The eyebrow climbs back down. The other one goes up instead. "Well," she says, "I mean, yes, I understand the sentence. All the right words in all the right places. But, you know, I come here because half the bloody force is worried about you, and now you're not going to tell me shit? And, look, I realize that, well… you know… you're the boss. But, I mean… I was bloody there. When you were stabbed. I was there. When we almost had her. I was there. I'm involved."

God, I wish I could tell her. Just to ground myself. Tell someone I trust what the hell is going on. Someone who isn't part of the madness that my life has become. But how can I tell her that there are alien mind worms, and other aliens the size of Texas coming to eat us? How can I tell her I know a chap who can access other realities by sticking batteries in his mouth?

The silence stretches between us. I see that sad look again.

I can't. I can't tell her.

"Fine then," she says abruptly. She stands. "If that's how you bloody want it."

"Swann," I say. Then, "Alison." I don't think I've ever used her first name before. She turns, some mix of hope and sadness and anger there.

"I want to tell you," I say. "I honestly do. But…" I trail off.

"But, what?" It looks like anger is winning out, eclipsing other emotions.

"But it would be really selfish."

She stands there for a moment, unreadable. And it sucks because she's as good a person as she is a cop, and it sucks when you realize someone's a friend just when you lose them.

Swann stoops, picks up the half-empty bottle of beer she left on the countertop and takes a swig.

"Fine," she says. And she sounds like she means it. Like things really are fine.

"I'm sorry," I say.

"Don't push it," she says. "I'm not going to feel sorry for you." She takes another sip. "Stupid bastard."

It's OK after that. Maybe "fine" would be pushing it, but there's an understanding. We make small talk. We smile at the right moments. She doesn't stay for a second beer, though. Of course she doesn't. But it would have been nice if she did.

"Guess you won't be in the office tomorrow either, will you?" she says as she stands in the doorway.

"Don't think so," I say.

"You going to take care of yourself?" She pushes hair back from her eyes.

"Yes," I say, and I even smile reassuringly as I lie to her.

11

THE NEXT DAY

Clyde is like a child in a candy store. He runs his fingers over the spines of books, tracing our route through the Bodleian Library's stacks.

"It's a genuine copyright library," he says. "A copy of nearly every book in the world." He turns round in a circle, a smile on his face. "You can almost feel it."

I know everything he's telling me—which is a nice change—but I don't mind him repeating the information. Pretty much anything delivered with this much enthusiasm would be a nice pick-me-up.

The place itself feels dark, musty, and rarely visited. The librarians at the front desk seemed to know Clyde—they only gave his credentials a cursory inspection before letting us back here. I saw one student staring at us with obvious envy as we walked through the "Staff Only" doors. This is hallowed ground for the serious bibliophile.

"Just a little further," says Clyde as we make another tight turn between the encroaching bookshelves. "He's normally somewhere back here."

Clyde has been unusually coy about who we're seeing this morning. Seems to be the morning for surprises.

AN HOUR EARLIER

"Agent Wallace is right," Shaw says.

The complete absence of precedence for this statement causes my mouth to hinge open. I glance left and right around the room to see if other people have heard this. They all look as astonished as I do. Which, while it confirms that I'm not suffering from auditory hallucinations, is not quite as reassuring as I'd hoped.

"We need to work on our teamwork," she continues. "We need to work on people being able to fill dual roles. We need to work on team redundancy. We also—" and this with a quick, not-quite-nervous glance "—need to work on being less reliant on Kayla.

"We are going to try to decrease Kayla's involvement in subsequent operations until such a time as the team can operate more successfully independently. Once that is achieved she will once more be integrated into full team membership."

Kayla doesn't say anything but I can almost feel the temperature dropping from that end of the table. Tabitha isn't looking at anyone either. Clyde, though, smiles and gives me a surreptitious thumbs up.

Personally, I'm a little blown away. I had even considered having a quiet word with Shaw about whether she's really sure I'm the man for the job. I mean, yes, I care about the end of the world, but Tabitha's accusation kept on playing on the mental soundtrack all night. Because what did I really contribute? Even if it hadn't been my first day, what could I have contributed?

And now, out of nowhere, Shaw has my back. Apparently I have contributed something. Though it does seem to be something that pisses half the team off something awful.

Maybe fifty percent isn't bad...

"So," Shaw says, "with that understanding, let us

proceed." She pulls out a folder, extracts some notes. "Now," she continues, "we know from the Twins and the Sheilas not to trust the words of a tattooed man until he shows his second face. From yesterday's debriefing I understand we had a tattooed man who changed his face. So, what did he say?"

"Did he say something?" Clyde asks. "I don't remember him saying anything."

"Yeah." Tabitha nods, unexpectedly breaking her moody silence. It strikes me that I really have no idea if the mood was genuine or just posturing. Maybe Clyde's right about her not hating me. "Said he'd sketched the picture. Drawn the tattoo himself."

"Which was a lie," Shaw says.

"Pretty bloody obvious," Tabitha said. "Bollocks clue." She looks over to Kayla. "No disrespect to the Twins."

Kayla doesn't reply.

"So where did he get it from?" I ask.

Tabitha finally looks at me. "What?"

"Well," I say, feeling like I just flunked occult research 101, "if he didn't draw the tattoo himself, he must have copied it from somewhere, right? I just was wondering where?"

"Well, I mean, I'd guess, probably a book from the Bodleian," Clyde says. "I mean... You see... Usually..."

"Tabitha," Shaw says, riding over Clyde's sputtering, "access our student's library records."

Tabitha pulls out her laptop and within two minutes has managed to violate everything I was ever taught about computer security. If I get back to the police force, I'll have to talk to the chief about questioning the usefulness of corporate-sponsored training seminars.

"History stuff mostly. Primary sources. Usual crap. Plus," she pauses, runs a finger over the screen, "*Thaumaturgic Practices in Milton Keynes.*" She raises her eyebrows. "Shit you not. Wish I did, but I don't."

Clyde must see my befuddlement because I don't think anyone else learns much when he says, "Thaumaturgy—big fancy word for magic."

I flash him a smile. My first of the day. And I think maybe I'll give the whole thing one more day.

"Clyde, Agent Wallace," Shaw says, "I want you two to head to the Bodleian. Find out what you can."

I don't think Clyde could have looked happier if he'd plugged his nipples into the mains.

NOW

Clyde peers down one aisle, then another, another. We're not getting anywhere particularly fast, but I appreciate the change of pace.

Still, something is bothering me, and in the Bodleian's musty recesses it seems safe enough to voice the concern. "Clyde?" I say.

"Yes?"

"There are aliens out to destroy the world, right? The whole universe, et cetera."

"Unfortunately I'm going to have to go with the affirmative on that one, old chap."

"And we're funded by the British government, who I imagine do not want their nation, nor any other nations, to be consumed by hideous aliens from outside reality, right?"

"Again, a thumbs up for accuracy."

I nod. Something doesn't add up. "Well, then," I say, "where is everybody then?"

Clyde stops peering down rows of books and peers at me. "Ah," he says.

"I mean," I say, "if the world was on the verge of destruction, I'd imagine we'd be throwing a few more people at the problem."

"Yes, about that." Clyde shrugs a couple of times, I think to calm himself. "Bit of an old lacunae in the orientation there, that. Intentional on Shaw's part I'd guess. Not malicious of course. Far from it. Lovely lady underneath, I suspect. Just doesn't like talking about the matter. Which is totally understandable of course. Prickly subject and all." He trails off.

"What is?" I prompt.

"Oh yes, sorry. Going on about lacunae and then leave a great gaping hole in the story myself." Another shrug. "They're shutting us down."

"Wait." This requires a moment. "Who? Why?"

"The government. See... well, when MI37 was set up—"

"Back in the thirties," I say, remembering Shaw's story about the Everest expedition.

"Yes." Clyde nods. "Well everyone was mad for the magical and spiritual and occult back then. Very keen. And what with Hitler and the whole occult thing in World War Two, we had about a hundred or so agents in the forties. And then there was the magical arms race in the seventies and eighties. But that all ended horribly and really no one felt like they'd really got anything out of it. At least nothing like nukes, which is really what they were after. Everybody obsessed with destroying the world several times over. Crazy days, or so I'm told. Not quite my era.

"Anyway, after the eighties the whole magical, alien, MI37 thing ended up rather out of favor. And folk go on about the Progeny and the Feeders, except the Progeny have been here for decades and don't ever seem to interfere with the sort of stuff governments care about—national security, international finances, that sort of thing. And I think they've been pretty much written off as a credible threat. So instead of a hundred agents, right now, with you, we've got four."

I stare at him. I try to comprehend. There are aliens trying to destroy the world, and no one cares? Because it doesn't affect the GDP?

"What the hell?" I splutter.

Clyde retreats into his shoulders. "Turns out we're both a bit late on the scene, old chap," he says. "The old guard's gone. All the people who've seen what we've seen. They're retired. Reassigned. No one in government comes to read the book. They don't see the Progeny. They don't really know. So we just rattle around in the old space. Alone and forlorn. Except, well, not forlorn, because, well, despite it all, I quite like my job."

"We have to get them to come down and see," I say. This is a travesty of justice. "We have to force them."

"Shaw tries," he says. "She's always trying."

I shake my head. I feel like reality just slapped me a bit. Four of us against the end of the world.

"But we keep on fighting, don't we?" says Clyde. He gives me a little smile. "What else can you do?"

I shake my head. I don't know. Because there isn't anything else to do. You just fight. Good old-fashioned Kurt Russell man alone stuff. But that doesn't seem such a good thing when it's me playing the role of action hero.

"Come on." Clyde gives me a pat on the back. "Let's go find what we're looking for."

I trail after him as he resumes looking down corridors of books. I'm genuinely gobsmacked. I can't believe they're killing the MI37 budget. I am so totally voting for the other guys next time the elections come up.

"No," Clyde is muttering. "No." Then, "Quicker way to do this." He pulls out a flat silver battery and pops it into his mouth.

"*Arcum locium met morum um satum Winston.*"

"Winston?" I ask. Because it genuinely did sound like he said that, but that sounds about as magical as my arse.

Clyde is a little too preoccupied to answer though. His head tilts back. His eyes roll back, something like static playing across the lower row of eyelashes.

I take a step backwards. Whatever just happened it doesn't look like it went right. I wish I had my baton with me. Instead, I heave something substantial-looking off one of the bookshelves, and wield it above my head.

Clyde opens his mouth. A shuddering groan creaks out. Then, the groan mutates, becomes words.

"Of all the spells I ever cast," Clyde croaks, "this one stings the worst."

He's up on his tiptoes now, and suddenly his body jerks forward, like someone is reeling him in, a rope tied around his midriff. I stuff the book back on the shelf and follow. He jostles and bumps down a long corridor until we're deep in shadows and the faint smell of mildew permeates the air.

Clyde points a hand down one row of the stacks.

"This one," he croaks. The sound makes me cringe. It's like someone's down in his throat, working on it with sandpaper.

I follow his hand and peer into the narrow corridor of books. It's been blocked off halfway down by a wooden bookcase. The bookcase's shelves are as stuffed as anything else here, but still it seems out of place, somehow. And there's furniture here too, I realize now, but each piece made from piles of hardbacks, paperbacks, loose-leaf documents. A bedsheet has been spread over a pile of them at the base of the bookshelf. A stack of atlases makes something like a bedside table. There's an anglepoise lamp wedged there and a glass of water. And a plastic container of rice and gyro meat.

"Someone lives here?" I can't keep the astonishment out of my voice.

Clyde coughs and spits out the batteries. He doubles over wheezing for a moment, then straightens.

"Yeah," he croaks, then coughs again. He pulls out a large white handkerchief and spits into it. "Sorry," he says. "Yes, someone does. He moves about quite a bit, hence the handwavery to find him, though." He looks away from me. "You can come on out now Winston, he won't bite."

There's a rustling sound from a shelf to my right and I snap around. Some of the books shift, start to tumble off the shelf. Someone is hiding behind the stacked books I realize, someone crouched tight in-between the shelves.

But the person doesn't appear and the books keep falling, and then I realize that the person isn't going to appear. Because the books start to pile into legs, into a torso and arms, and then I realize that the books themselves are Winston.

A man made out of books. Of course. Should have seen it coming really. I wonder, yet again, if I've gone mad.

The book-man, Winston, stands about five feet tall, his feet made of heavy reference tomes, his legs an accordion stack of paperbacks, on top of which balances a jumble of pamphlets and pages. Covers wheeze open and shut as Winston shifts his weight, as his chest rises and falls. His eyes are finger puppets mounted into circular holes in infants' board books, his mouth is a dictionary laid on its side that snaps up and down when he speaks.

"All right, Clyde, mate," Winston says.

I look from the dictionary mouth to the gyro.

"What?" Winston asks me, taking a step forward. "I don't bloody spill shit, all right. I'm incog-fucking-nito, mate. I move like a shadow, all right? They don't know I'm here. You didn't know. Did you?" One of the finger-puppet eyes—a small yellow-faced bee—waggles knowingly.

"It's all right, Winston," Clyde says with a soothing tone. "He's with MI37." He looks at me. "He's new."

"Fresh as a fucking fish, is he?" Winston asks.

"I'm Arthur," I say after a pause, during which I try and get my sense of wonder to be quiet so I can make polite conversation.

"Nice one. Nice one." Winston takes a step forward and slaps me congenially on the shoulder with one hand—a copy of *Pride and Prejudice* that snaps open and shut like a lobster claw. The moment exists in some limbo place between awesome and hideously creepy.

"All right then, gents," Winston says, stepping back, "what can I do you for, then?"

"A book," I say.

"A book he says," Winston barks, his rough voice sharp and loud in the quiet space. "Of course a fucking book. I'm made of fucking books. I'm in a fucking library. You're hardly going to be here to ask me about the pleasant summer weather, is you? What book, mate? A name, an index reference, a Dewey fucking decimal number, if you please."

"*Thaumaturgic Practices in Milton Keynes,*" Clyde says quickly.

"Hmmm." Winston cocks his blocky head onto one side and makes a great show of cogitating. "This way gents, if you please."

He lopes off past us and we both have to hurry to follow him.

"Don't mind him," Clyde says conspiratorially as we pursue. "He's just a bit put-out because he knows he must have messed up. He knows we only do this when he missed a book."

"Missed a book?" I'm not sure the answer to the

question will help me, none have so far, but if yesterday taught me anything it's that I need to try and get answers when I can.

"Well," Clyde says, "I made him to catch any suspicious texts coming into the library. Obviously he didn't catch this one."

"You made him?" My ability to be surprised is being steadily eroded, but Clyde still manages it.

"Well," Clyde says, and shrugs, because it's been about five minutes since he last did it, "technically I brought an animating force over from another reality, invested it into a pile of books and set it certain tasks that were within the parameters of an ancient agreement I found in a couple of Sumerian texts, but 'made him' is easier to say."

I stopped listening after the bit where I went cross-eyed so I just nod. "But you made him…" I search for the words. "The way he is?"

"A little too much Dickens and Irvine Welsh in the stack of books I used."

Which makes about as much sense as anything else I've heard so far. Still, I wonder what would happen to Winston if MI37 was finally closed up. Would he stay here, munching on gyros and reading books? Would he just fall apart? Would anybody except Clyde care?

Winston stops at a small stack of file cards. He fiddles with the drawer for a minute cursing quietly under his breath, and I clearly catch the phrase, "opposable bloody thumbs," but eventually he gets it open. He… well, he doesn't thumb through the cards, exactly… but he's able to get through them pretty quickly anyway and pulls out a card.

"Here we are," he says. "Bob is very much your uncle. Paternity suit denied." He extends the file card. "*Thaumaturgic Practices in Milton Keynes*, if you please."

Clyde plucks it from between clenched pages. He skims it quickly. "So?" he says finally.

"So what?" It's hard to read expressions on Winston's makeshift face but I can still see that he's suddenly as shifty as a used-car salesman.

"How did you miss it?" Clyde is not exactly confrontational, but there is a tone of paternal disapproval.

"Look," says Winston, "I mean, come on. Seriously?" Clyde just looks at him. "It's a fucking copyright library, mate. You have any bloody idea how many fucking books there are here? How many come in every day? I can't keep up with that. You having a laugh? I very much doubt it, but I've got to live with practicalities here, mate. I'm in the fucking trenches I am. I've got to prioritize." He manages to emphasize each syllable in the last word.

"Ancient texts, mate," he continues. "Primary sources. The real fucking deal. That's what I look for. That's what I get you. I mean, what's that?" He snatches back the card. "Published 2009? I can't be dealing with that. You want someone checking the modern stuff you give me subordinates, mate, you give me a workforce. Then I'll get you your work done."

"Winston," Clyde says. "It's called *Thaumaturgic Practices in Milton Keynes*, that couldn't be more suspect if they'd tried. Milton Keynes was only built in the sixties." He shrugs. "It's hardly going to be a hotbed of thaumaturgy. And—" he grabs back the card "—print run of two. There's only one other copy."

"Hold up on that," I say. A little shiver of adrenaline runs through me. Because I think I finally have something to contribute.

"What's that, mate?" Winston turns. So does Clyde.

"Two copies?" I ask.

Clyde looks back down at the card. "Yes."

"One for the British Library and one for here."

"Yes."

"Why bother?" I ask. "Why bother copyrighting it? Why not just print it for yourself and never bother copyrighting the thing? Not even... Unless you want to guarantee that it's here, want to guarantee that some idiot student comes across it and tries out the stuff written in it."

There's silence as I think.

"Got me stumped, mate," Winston says.

"It's a plant," I say. "It's a plant with a booby-trapped spell in it. Someone stuck a bomb in this library and waited for a student to set it off. And they know who the disposal squad sent in will be. You guys. MI37. Us." I say the last word with a sense of slight shock. Because it still doesn't feel like "us."

"Whoever wrote and printed this book," I say, "was gunning for MI37."

"Bit fucking unpleasant of them," Winston chimes in.

Clyde looks down at the card. "Olsted," he reads. "Benjamin Olsted."

I smile. "Looks like we got ourselves our next Progeny," I say.

12

"Benjamin Olsted," Tabitha says. She points abstractedly at a PowerPoint presentation, as if daring us to give a shit about it. She does, however, seem to have taken a lot of time and care with it. There are clear, concise bullet points, and animated graphics, and the whole thing is rather professionally done. It seems only fair to give it as much undivided attention as I can. But Tabitha is wearing a huge black dress today—like the negative exposure of one of those meringue wedding dresses from the eighties—and it rustles every time she turns to click a slide. The sound triggers memories I'd almost forgotten.

She is not what you think she is.

Who isn't? Tabitha? Kayla?

Except, of course, that phrase is just paranoia and blows to the head.

I try and focus. I need to know about Olsted. So we don't screw up.

Tabitha's slide shows a small man in his late sixties. His skin is worn and folded like ancient leather. He does not look happy to have his photo taken. Probably because of the whole shoe-leather-face thing.

"Owns Olsted PrintTech," Tabitha continues. "Manufactures laser printers. Not the sort to do limited runs of thaumaturgy texts." She looks significantly at

Clyde, the recipient of most of her gazes today. Kayla's not here per Shaw's new ruling. And I'm still in the doghouse because of that.

"Personal life—" Tabitha clicks and a series of black-and-white photos spiral onto the screen.

"Nice." Clyde nods his appreciation.

"Whatever," Tabitha says, and then turns with a particularly extravagant swish of pleasure. "Anyway. Widower. One daughter. Creutzfeldt–Jakob disease." She finally looks at me. "Mad cow."

"Cheers." I knew that, but I'm going for brownie points. Not earning them though, apparently.

Her gaze flits back to Clyde. "Anyway, Olsted. Very wealthy. Disproportionately wealthy." Dollar signs explode over the screen. "Everything looks above board, but way above average with investments. Almost prescient." She raises an eyebrow. A significant eyebrow. Because apparently everyone can do that except me.

"Plus, passionate for ancient anthropology. Studied it at university. Lots of visits to old tombs. And—" another significant eyebrow waggle "—investment success skyrockets within six months of visiting a Peruvian temple. Bad trip reportedly. Tunnel collapse. Dead guides. Only he survives. Fewer trips after that. All to Peru though."

"Grimoire?" Clyde asks.

"Grimoire," Tabitha answers.

"Grim-what?" I add—a faulty echo.

"Spell book," they say in unison. Clyde grins broadly at Tabitha. She almost lets a smile flicker at the edges of her lips.

"Most of what we know about thaumaturgy," Clyde explains, "all of the spells we know, basically, come from old texts. See, a spell is electricity violating the boundaries between two realities. Our reality and another one. You focus the electricity, either with thought patterns caused by the words of the spell, or you can make a machine do it. They focus the electricity with mathematics and totems instead. Fascinating stuff actually. Lot of texts written on it in the eighteenth century. Mad for it they were. But machines are a bit limited though. You can only program one spell into a machine. People can cast all sorts, different spells. Because we can say all sorts of things. Machines, a little lackadaisical in the vocab. Specific…" He catches my blank expression.

"Anyway, not totally relevant. But basically the electricity reaches out of our reality into another one and pulls something through. The problem isn't reaching out of our reality; it's knowing where exactly you're reaching into and what you're going to pull out. So it's nice to know someone else has tried it before. See, a spell's like a map. It lets you know where your spell is going and what it's going to bring back with it. If you just randomly open holes in reality you have no idea what might come through. Nasty stuff, often."

"Chernobyl," Tabitha says.

"Exactly." Clyde is animated now. "See, Chernobyl wasn't really a nuclear meltdown. That was the Russians trying to pioneer their own spell. Tried to punch a particularly tricky and experimental hole and it did not go quite as well as they had hoped."

"Wait a second," I say. I blink several times. The gears are turning. I feel like I can almost get a handle on this one. "You're saying the Chernobyl accident was caused by a communist Harry Potter?"

"Little more complicated." Tabitha gives a disingenuous shrug and seems about to leave it at that, but then can't help herself. "Experienced bastards, actually. Too ballsy for their own good, though. Ended the magic arms race.

Pretty much. No one wanted to mess then. Beginning of the end. For us. This place."

Clyde nods. "After that nobody wanted to play magic anymore. Everyone pretty much just gathered up their marbles and went home. Which, you know, understandable. Bit knee-jerk perhaps. I mean, depends on your point of view. Made things harder for us, though."

"Freak out," Tabitha says. "Massive. Collective trouser-shitting."

"So a lot fewer funds. And a lot fewer people hunting down the remaining grimoires," Clyde says.

"Speaking of which…" I start.

"Yes," Clyde says. "Well, basically, a grimoire is like an atlas. Or a travelogue. Big list of where someone's spells went, what they brought back. So you can reproduce the effect if you want."

"And Olsted probably owns one," Tabitha says.

"And now," I say, finally connecting dots, "he's using it to target MI37."

"Working hypothesis." Tabitha nods, still not quite looking at me. "So: either in league with the Progeny or is one of the Progeny. Neither scenario is very good."

"Why, in God's name, would anyone help the Progeny?" The idea is beyond me.

"Daughter," Tabitha says.

"That makes sense, doesn't it?" Clyde says. "What Tabby says." He shrugs.

Tabby? This time there's no reaction from Tabitha to the nickname. There is something… But didn't Clyde mention a girlfriend? Something else I can't wrap my head around.

"What exactly did Tabby say?" I ask, trying to catch up.

Tabitha gives me the finger, so I'm still shy my Brownie points for the day.

"The Progeny do brain stuff," Clyde continues. "Olsted's little girl has got a brain problem. The whole mad cow thing. And I think… we think… Tabby thinks and I agree that there's got to be, you know, some sort of overlap, some sort of knowledge. I don't know. Even if there's not, maybe one of them is riding around in a brain surgeon or something."

I nod slowly. "OK," I say. "Makes sense." Probably. And Tabitha looks at me without abject disdain for a fraction of a millisecond, so maybe it really does.

"So," I ask, "what's next?"

There is a long pause.

"Get the grimoire." Tabitha shrugs.

"Do we know where he's keeping it?" I ask.

"Internet a bit light on that." Tabitha doesn't smile.

"I sort of… I don't know—" Clyde shrugs "—just rather assumed the what-do-we-do-next bit was your sort of territory. Didn't want to tread on toes."

And there you go. Kayla's gone and I already have a niche. I smile. "So we need to find out where he has it. Well, have I got a great idea for fans of coffee and body odor."

Clyde cocks his head. Tabitha rolls her eyes in as disinterested a way as I think is humanly possible.

"Who's up for a stakeout?" I say.

EIGHT EXCESSIVELY LONG HOURS LATER

Stakeouts. The paragon of policing tasks. Tedium at his most absolute. We've spent the entire working day parked outside Olsted's apartment, crammed into Tabitha's beaten-up Honda, and so far our most significant learning is that it only takes four cups of coffee before Clyde's hands start to shake.

Tabitha could be happier about the situation. Actually,

she could be happier about most situations, but this particular one seems to have irked her more than usual. The phrase "I'm a fucking researcher" has become her mantra. I hear its echoes even though it's been about ten minutes since she last said it.

There again I think I made a pretty good argument about needing as many eyes as possible. Which she ignored. And then Clyde made a terrible one on the same point, and she agreed to come along.

There is seriously something going on there.

She sits in the driver's seat, he in the back, but I keep catching nervous-looking glances between them. Clyde seems to unconsciously touch his ear every time he speaks to her.

Working that mystery out seems like the least of my problems, though.

The doorman at Olsted's building has a serious aversion to remaining behind his desk. He patrols the glass-fronted lobby, striding between leather couch, stone fireplace, and mahogany end tables. He doesn't stay still. His eyes don't stay still.

"He's patrolling," I say eventually. "Walking the perimeter. Guarding the place." I shake my head. "That's not what doormen do."

"Wasn't a doorman all his life." Tabitha is sitting next to me. Despite her insistence that she shouldn't be doing fieldwork, she's good at this.

"Definitely," says Clyde from the back seat. "I mean… probably. I guess. If you guys say so."

That is actually one of the more exciting moments. And the sad bit is that part of me likes it. I feel comfortable in the car. Despite the pleather seats.

But the patrolling doorman makes me think that maybe we know where the grimoire is.

Then, just before midnight, a limo pulls up. Olsted gets out. Clyde jots down the plate number. And watching Olsted walk away from us, toward the building, I realize that our big takeaway from the evening is going to amount to knowing which door he prefers—left or right. A piece of minutia. Something that might be useful if we were going to carry out this operation in a month or two, but I don't know if reality has that long. If Ophelia has that long. What we're doing is sensible, but there's no time for it.

This, I suddenly realize, is the moment for something reckless. This is the moment when Kurt Russell throws over his desk and screams that he can't sit by and watch things happen anymore. It's the time to storm out and right serious wrongs. Except it's me sitting there. No hero.

Olsted uses the left-hand door. He likes the left door.

And a little bit of me snaps at that. I can't leave just knowing that. I just can't.

I open the car door. "Follow the limo," I say.

"What the hell do you—" is all Tabitha manages to say, before I shut the two of them in the car.

I jam my hands into my pockets, put a little stumble in my walk. I'm twenty yards behind Olsted. Tabitha's clapped-out Honda chugs past me. I'm pretty sure she's giving me the finger. Adrenaline is buzzing in my system. I'm terrified, and overjoyed, and on the verge of voiding my bowels. I am excited. After twelve hours of mind-numbing, jittery boredom, I am excited.

In the lobby, the doorman welcomes Olsted, but he's already looking at me. The pair move toward the back of the room, toward the elevators. I push through the same door. Olsted's palm print is still on the brass plate.

"'Scuse me," I say, talking too loud.

"If you could wait a minute, sir." The doorman has put himself between Olsted and me.

"Wouldn't know if there's a curry place round here, would you?" I advance. My heart is hammering in my chest.

The doorman stops, turns fully. And I realize then what an enormous slab of a man he is. Bodybuilder and champion breakfast eater, I'll be sure. Olsted's at the elevator bank, third on the left. It has its own separate panel.

"No, sir," says the doorman loudly, forcefully.

"No, there isn't one, or no, you don't know?" My voice is shaking a little at the end. I wonder if he knows how scared I am.

The doorman lets his arms drop. They're big arms. And that's it for me.

"I'm going. I'm going." I back away, palms up, keeping my eyes on the doorman. He ignores me with studied patience—threat assessed and dismissed. He slides a card into a slot next to Olsted's elevator. The elevator doors open. And then I revolve back out through the door and into the night.

I find Tabitha's Honda idling in the entrance to a loading bay between a purveyor of fine Oriental rugs and, of all things, a curry house.

"What the fuck?" Red spots shine in Tabitha's dark cheeks as I climb back in. "Heads up please. Next time. Except, no next time, please. Discussions help. Stop you from being fucking stupid. From letting Progeny-aiding magicians seeing your face. Stop them from remembering you." She waves her hand around the car. "Fucking team here, jackass. Resources. People to trust and who need to know they can trust you."

Up until then I'd been rather pleased with myself, but then I realize I did something a little bit stupid. And it's not exactly like I'm high up on Tabitha's list of lovely-people-who-deserve-a-cuddle. I need to curry trust. I mean, I'm sure she distrusts me as much as I distrust Kayla. Shit, there are alien mind worms about. Everyone's going to be a little short on trust.

I look to Clyde for support. He doesn't accuse me, but he's not defending me either.

"Sorry," I say. "Impulsive. Stupid. I shouldn't have…" This is not the sort of speech that great leaders make. Can't imagine Mel Gibson in a kilt saying, "Well, chaps, I was sort of hoping… if you don't mind much… Well, to put it one way, would you mind fighting for our freedom?"

So I try again, and say a little more assertively, "I wanted to see what sort of security he has. Ex-military, I'd guess. And I think he was carrying a gun, because there was no way he was that happy to see me." A small smile from Clyde. "Uses some sort of card to call the penthouse-exclusive elevator. Which we'd have to take from him. I guess there's more like him up at the top of the elevator as well."

Tabitha looks at me. She's still pissed but she's curious now.

"Can we take the card off him?" Clyde asks. "I don't think we can take the card off him." He pauses. "I can't take the card off him."

"I don't think any of us can."

"How do we get in without Kayla?" Tabitha asks.

Or do we back away from stupid fucking ideas and get her back on active duty, is the question I think Tabitha is really asking.

For a moment I don't say anything. I've got nothing. But then I realize I'm thinking like a policeman. And I'm not a policeman. A policeman wouldn't barge into a suspect's lobby and scope the place out. I'm Agent Wallace. I am ballsy and impulsive, and screw the minutia. Go big or go home.

I smile. "We con our way in."

13

I'm sure it's difficult to organize a conference, more so than you'd initially suspect, but it hardly seems like it'd be brain surgery. Yet, the Fourteenth Annual Conference of the British Neurosurgery Society seems to have a strong resemblance to Bedlam. Clyde and I are jostled by crowds as we hunt for Olsted. It's like playing *Where's Waldo*, except Waldo is a besuited older gentleman in a mass of besuited older gentlemen.

"There," I say, finally, after two hours. I point from the back of the lecture hall we've just sidled into. "Second row, three in." He's sitting there. Leather-face himself. And after all the hunting through random conference rooms and seminars, he's not actually that hard to find at all. Because none of the other scientists are flanked by bodyguards the size of water buffalo.

"I think we should just turn around," Clyde says. "Probably. Don't you think? No. You probably don't think. That. Certainly do think. *Cogito ergo sum* and all that. But yes, turning around, silly idea. Shouldn't do that. Should we? Could we?" He shakes his head. "No."

I'm a little worried that Clyde is so nervous. This is meant to be his show. These are his people. His skills are at the core of this plan. But there's no need to put him on further edge by pointing any of that out, so I just ask,

"You think you can fudge on this topic?"

This Fourteenth Annual Conference is meant be to where the latest and greatest breakthroughs in neuroscience are presented. And occurring in this very room is one of the key talks about treating encephalopathies, which, Clyde informed me out in the corridor, is why Olsted is taking time out of his busy destroying-the-world schedule to listen in.

Clyde pulls a face. Slowly, his hands shaking slightly, he takes one of the little earbuds from his pocket and plugs it in. Up close it makes him look very CIA.

Well... as CIA-like as it's possible for Clyde to look. Actually not that CIA at all.

"You getting any of this, Tabitha?" he whispers. He squints at whatever reply he receives. Quickly I plug in my own earbud.

"—the subject?" I hear.

"Basically recombinant DNA in CJD," he whispers. "Protein biomarkers. Couple of other things. Preliminary stuff."

"Lit search. Incoming." Tabitha's voice is tiny in my ear. There is an ease and efficiency in their voices and manner that was missing during the stakeout. They seem more comfortable with each other when there's electronic interference they can hide behind.

Clyde looks at me. "I think we can fudge this," he says. "Maybe. Not really sure. Hope we can. Sort of need to of course. So, yes, I'm sure it'll all be fine. Fudge-tastic. I love fudge. Caramel too." He looks away. "Not truffles for some reason. Not sure why."

I give a nod toward the stage. "Probably help if we..." I start.

"Oh, gosh, yes. Paying attention now." An affable smile from him. Something similar for me, nerves at the edge of it. But I am gung-ho now. Fearless and impulsive. I need to remember that.

"Not planning any coups are we, Arthur?" Tabitha's voice sounds in my ear again.

"Not yet."

She harrumphs but I don't say anything else and she lets me be. Then it's just toe-tapping time. I sit there, one hand covering my ear, hoping no one sees the earbud. It's hard to blend in when you look like you're some dubious government agent. Which actually, thinking about it, I am. Still, not looking to advertise the fact.

Finally the talk winds down, the room clears, the guys on stage start to wrap up. I look to Clyde. This is the bit where I just smile and look pretty. Well… where I smile, anyway.

The two guys look up as we approach. They're about my age, well entrenched in their thirties, I'd guess. One is tall and rangy, the other just, well just sort of average-looking really. Sort of person I'd have hated to have as a suspect. Which, I suppose, is good for us.

"Can we help you?" the taller one asks.

Clyde stares at them for a moment that becomes increasingly awkward as it becomes less and less of a moment.

"We had a couple of questions," I start.

There's a pause. The two men look expectant.

"Jesus," Tabitha says into the silence. Clyde twitches slightly at the abruptness of her voice. "You two never had a conversation? Make nice. Compliment them."

"Great presentation!" Clyde lurches as if someone suddenly switched him on. "I mean, yes, I… Great. Really… great." He pulls his head back between his shoulders.

"Thanks!" Nondescript guy looks genuinely pleased. "Obviously it's all early stages right now, and there are some horrible holes in the literature, but—"

"Now move on to the research," Tabitha guides him.

"Start with the riboflavins or—"

"Riboflavins!" Clyde barks. He looks around as if horrified by what he's said. It's as if he's been suddenly struck by a bout of scientific Tourette's. "Transcriptase factors!" he blurts.

"Sod it," Tabitha says. "I'm having no part in this. Bloody idiots."

Clyde stares desperately at me.

Impulsive. Fearless.

"Yes," I say. I say it quite loudly. Possibly too loudly. I try to think of something else to say but my impulsiveness seems to have left me. Probably did it fearlessly. The two scientists are looking at us and at each other trying to work out if we were both just bludgeoned on the back of the head by some invisible assailant. Which will probably happen to me before the week's out, seeing how it's going.

Clyde is still quiet. I scrabble for words.

"Idiots," I hear Tabitha mutter again.

"Transcriptase factors," I say. "Riboflavins." I'm playing for time. "Two paths of research that we have combined in examining genetic cures for…" I pause, I'm running out of steam, "…modern ailments."

"Yes." Clyde echoes my own monosyllable and we stand mutely again. I wince. But then, out of nowhere, a stream of words blurts out of Clyde's mouth.

"You see, we're currently engaged in some pretty unique research, which gels quite excitingly with your own. We're working up in a lab in Swindon, you see, and we've been doing some very interesting work on pigs, using gene therapy that crosses the blood–brain barrier."

And suddenly, to my utter disbelief, Clyde is actually on a roll. The words are coming faster and faster, the buzz words thicker and thicker. And suddenly I think despite the disastrous start, we really could pull this off.

"This is horse crap," one of the men says abruptly.

Clyde freezes. "What?" he croaks.

"What?" I echo.

"This is quack bullshit," says the tall guy. "Look, you may be able to take advantage of frightened patients who don't know any better but we do know—"

Clyde steps away. He's done. Folds as his bluff is called. And we're done. Except we can't be done. We have to know more than which door Olsted prefers. Which is a lousy metaphor.

Impulsive. Fearless.

"Look," I say, cutting off the guy, "all we should need for this process to work," I have no idea if what I'm saying gels with what Clyde was saying, but it barely even matters, "is a sample—" I take a quick step forward and put my hands on their heads, like I'm carrying out a benediction or something "—of DNA." I tug.

Both guys yell.

"I'm calling security," says one.

"Do you even have membership rights?" asks the other.

Clyde has my arm, is pulling me away.

"Stop!" shouts the taller one, but he doesn't make a move.

I stare at the two tiny strands of hair in my hand. I feel like a hero. It's like I just wrested a pair of handguns away from a terrorist. For some reason I can't quite fathom, I cannot quite resist calling out, "Philistines!" as we leave the room.

"Yeah," comes back Tabitha's voice. "Those guys are the morons. Totally."

TEN MINUTES LATER

"You're sure this is going to work?" This still feels impulsive, but some of my fearlessness has definitely abandoned me since Clyde pulled out the car battery.

"Relatively," Clyde says. It's the fifth time he's told me that. It's the fifth time he's failed to reassure me.

At least Clyde told me we needed to remove the earbuds. It's nice to do this without Tabitha telling me what a paranoid idiot I am.

We've managed to find a storage closet, and next to the battery lie the other contents of Clyde's rucksack: copper wire, acupuncture needles, clamps of various sizes. It looks less like the paraphernalia of the supernatural and more like hardcore S&M gear.

"How does it work again?" I sound the way I did when I first got an electric razor and was perhaps overly concerned about removing my entire face with it.

"The spell calls upon a mutagenic force from another reality. Then, because I don't know the exact words to make us look exactly like the guys we want to look like, we're cheating a bit and just throwing a bit of the impersonatee into the circuit. Should channel the spell nicely."

"Should. OK," I say. Words are spoken. Knowledge imparted. I'm still far too afraid.

"Clip the needles to the wire," Clyde says. His attitude is different here, I think. There's authority in his voice. And, I realize, it is not out with the boffins that Clyde feels comfortable, but in here, violating the boundaries of what is real. He is, as Tabitha put it, hardcore when it comes to this stuff.

"So, what next?" I ask when I'm done.

"I'm going to take my clothes off," Clyde says.

Not exactly what I was hoping for.

I avert my eyes while he strips to a pair of tighty-whities. He hands me a couple of the needles that he's rigged up to the copper wires and taps four spirals of wire embedded under the skin of his chest. "You need to put the needles in these four chakras here." He taps between his eyes. "And then one in my third eye."

"Seriously?" I ask.

"Yes, please. The wires—" he gestures to his tattoos "—help get the power to the chakras, but using the exact spot to infuse power is even better."

And so I stab the poor guy. The fifth and final needle spears low in his forehead, like some sort of crazy unicorn horn. He flexes his eyebrows and it bobbles madly. I look at the car battery, at the wires beneath his skin—the path of least resistance. Not how I usually spend my weekends...

Clyde picks up a piece of aluminum foil and wraps one of the stolen hairs around it, fixing it in place with some clips. He nods. "OK, we're good. Just hit the juice when I say, 'ashrat.' OK?"

He gives a perfect private-schoolboy grin, wonky teeth and all. His face is bright and clean. Almost as if he is not mostly naked in a hotel cleaning closet with giant needles sticking into him.

"Sure," I say, "whatever you say."

Clyde hands me two large clamps, electrical tape wrapped thickly around their handles; one red, one black; positive, negative. "On ashrat." He closes his eyes. He slows his breathing. His chest rises and falls. In and out. In and out. "*Sellum,*" he says. "*Moshtaf al partum.*"

Static electricity sweeps like a wave up my arms and legs. Each hair standing on end, one by one.

"*Kel saloth cthartin. Anung ash partek. Felim um ashrat—*"

I almost miss it, caught up in the madness of the moment. But then I realize and slap the two clamps down onto the battery. And, even as I do it, part of me, yet again, wants to be put on lithium and told the bad dreams will go away.

Clyde convulses. His mouth mashes down on his

tongue, mangling a word. The wires under his skin are glowing, red at first, then brighter, whiter, to blue. It's like they're going to burn right through him. There's the smell of ozone, of crisping flesh. Above us the bulb flickers, a strobe flash, and then it dies. The only light is the magnesium flare of the wires, making Clyde a stick man, a scribble pattern of light lifting up, up, off the floor of the room, off into the air, his mass a bubbling silhouette, blacker than the black of the room, shifting, stirring, in flux, his arms and legs spasming, coming in and out, in and out, clenching down into a fetal position then out as a star, some bizarre exercise program, and then there is a snapping sound, like a hundred bones breaking at once, and a cry, and I think I'm finally just going to go ahead and vomit, and the light bulb flares to life once more, and I'm standing in a room with a tall rangy scientist I called a Philistine just a moment before.

"Clyde?" I cannot keep the edge of tension out of my voice.

The scientist's double shudders, grabs the edge of the table. He exhales. "All right," he says, "that went better than I had hoped."

"Better?" I cannot quite keep the incredulity out of my voice.

"Yeah." Clyde nods. "The wires stop it from stinging too bad."

"Really?"

"Oh." Clyde looks apologetic.

"What?" I say.

"Well…" Clyde shuffles on the spot. "Now it's your turn."

14

When I was a kid I used to dream about magic. It took both my parents to physically peel me off a copy of *The Hobbit*. And I don't mean the stage tricks of David Copperfield. Not the levitating cards of David Blaine, but real magic. Actually violating the laws of physics. Twisting reality to your will, transmuting matter. Magic! Summoning something from nothing. Calling on the powers of the heavens. There was romance to it, poetry.

But, childhood discarded, now I know.

Magic sucks.

I'm in bloody agony. These are not my limbs. This is not my shape. It's as if my body has been crammed into a shell it doesn't fit. I'm pressed up against the limits of new skin while my body screams to be free.

Clyde tells me it'll get better soon.

I would love to say that I accept this news with affable good humor, but in the heat of the moment I tell him to shove his magic bloody wand where the sun doesn't shine. Not one of my finer moments, truth be told.

Clyde, thankfully, is the bigger man. Literally now, it transpires. He smiles, tells me not to let go of the D battery he's given me and then leads me by the elbow out of the broom closet and back into the conference. And he's right; it does get a bit better.

I apologize, and, knowing the lay of the land this time, finding Olsted goes quicker. Spotting his two buffalo-size security guards is easy enough anyway. I mentally dub them Tweedledum and Tweedledee.

Olsted's leathery face becomes momentarily more scrotum-like as we approach, though after a moment I realize he's actually attempting to smile.

"Mr. Olsted," I say, taking the lead as we approach. I attempt my own smile but I'm not totally used to these new muscles so I'm not sure I'm any more successful than he was.

"Mr. Olsted is busy," says Tweedledum, which is an obvious lie, but I'm guessing from the size of his fists that he's the sort of man who doesn't have to worry about such trivial things as factual accuracy.

"It's about your daughter, Mr. Olsted," I say with the same teeth-grinding smile.

Tweedledee balls his fists.

Olsted lays a hand on the big man's shoulder. "Heel, Christopher."

Tweedledee satisfies himself with an aggressive leer.

"I enjoyed your presentation, gentlemen," Olsted says. "But, as ever, things seem very distant."

"That's what we want to talk to you about."

Olsted works his jaw. Something flickers behind his eyes. Not quite hope. Something too tired for that. And is this really the bad guy? Someone just looking to save his daughter?

"I am too old for promises of better tomorrows, gentlemen. And my money is invested in other lines of research."

"A Phase One trial," Clyde snaps. The words lurch out of him. He repeats it, more quietly, "A Phase One trial."

"You're years away—" Olsted starts.

"Publically," I say. "Yes."

That hangs in the air a while.

"You have thirty seconds," Olsted says, "before Christopher and Samuel here take you outside and break your fingers."

We lose three seconds in staring. Clyde at Olsted. Me at Clyde. Go, I will him. Talk. Please. Talk. Two more seconds go by without a word.

And then Clyde talks.

It's almost bloody poetry. If poetry was carried out mostly in acronyms.

It's not perfect because he stares over Olsted's shoulder the whole time, because he speaks in a monotone, and because he spends another five seconds trying to grab at the word "precursor." But then thirty seconds are up and he's still talking. He's still going at a minute.

Olsted holds up a hand and stops Clyde. A card appears in it. As if by magic. Comfortable David Blaine magic. I pluck the card from between his fingers.

"Next Tuesday," he says. "Eight p.m. My home. You can meet Ilsa then."

"Yes. Yes." I am almost babbling. I want to high five Clyde. Probably would be bad form. "We'll see you there," I manage.

Olsted and his goons depart and we stand there staring after them. A result. For a moment I'd feared Clyde didn't have it in him, that I didn't have it in me. But we did it. I turn and look at Clyde. There is panic on his face.

"What did I just say to him?" he says. "I have no idea what I just said to him."

"You know what?" I smile. "It doesn't even matter."

NEXT MONDAY, TWENTY-FOUR HOURS TO GO

"So, wait a minute, Boss," says Swann. She sips her beer

but doesn't take her eyes off me. "You, a government employee, are telling me, a police officer, about your plans to break and enter?"

There is a chance I have said too much.

At least I left out the bit about the aliens, and the magic, and prophetic twins living in a pool full of squid. In fact, I think the sheer amount of "saying-too-much" I am now capable of may be throwing off my sense of what it *is* OK to talk about.

"There again," says Swann, "probably a good thing you told me. You're going to need a friend on the force to bail you out when they call the cops on you."

"What?" It is my general understanding that men as bad as Olsted do not call the cops when someone's trying to expose their nefarious plans. Pools full of piranhas: yes. Police officers: no.

"I mean, seriously, Boss," Swann pats my hand. "Do you really think you're going to get through the front door? I mean, you've already screwed up by telling me about it here and now. And this is hardly a high-pressure situation."

I bridle a little at this. "Look, Swann," I say. She smiles. Apparently I don't bridle as intimidatingly as I might wish. "For starters this is not a government employee telling a police officer, this is some bloke telling his friend about a difficult work situation."

"Course it is."

"And secondly," I say, "yes, it was part of my plan to get past the front door." I sag a little. Chew my lip. "You really don't think that'll happen?"

"Boss," says Swann. She has a maternal expression, which I don't think is entirely appropriate to our relationship. "You're a good copper. You're a great boss. You can solve a murder like nobody's business. I'll give you all that. But is this cloak-and-dagger stuff really your thing? Really?"

Balls.

"I'd rather hoped this would be the conversation where you told me how easy this sort of thing would be and how nothing could go wrong."

She pats my hand again. I do have to concede that the hand patting almost makes up for the brutal beating my confidence is taking.

"Look at it this way, Boss," she says. "I'm sure the guy in charge will be a competent military intelligence ninja bastard, and probably won't let you screw up too bad." She gives me an encouraging smile.

Oh double balls.

TUESDAY

I pick Clyde up from a surprisingly modern flat overlooking the canal. I've barely knocked when the door flies open with an exuberance that borders on the explosive. I take an instinctual step backwards but the only thing behind the door is a woman who looks about as deadly as a teddy bear.

"Hello!" she booms as the door flies wide. "Arthur! You must be Arthur! This is fantastic!"

She resembles a peppier, younger version of Santa Claus's wife. All ruddy cheeks and boundless curls of brown hair. For a moment her sheer enthusiasm keeps me on my back heels, so I stand there silently collecting myself as she beams a hundred-watt smile at me, before managing, "I'm here to pick up Clyde."

"I know!" she shrieks. "Clyde! It's Arthur!" she bellows without looking over her shoulder. Then out of nowhere she grabs me and hugs me. I'm enveloped in a cloud of perfume and soft flesh. Not entirely unpleasant but I do briefly worry about asphyxiation. Still, she releases me before I start to spasm. Complete escape is still beyond me though. A meaty hand on each arm, she continues to hold me close and booms, sotto voce, "Clyde never goes out for drinks with work friends." She dazzles me with another one of her magnificent smiles.

I think I rather like... oh bugger, what's her name? I should know it. Clyde has mentioned it before. I know he has. It's just the whole Clyde–Tabitha thing has seemed so palpable that the girlfriend thing didn't seem like it could be real. But now there is nigh overwhelming physical evidence.

I'm surprised Clyde would want to go from her to Tabitha. There seems to be simply so much of her... And what Tabitha has... Well, Tabitha's very nice in her own way. But her way seems more of a hard spiky way compared to this.

Clyde's head suddenly appears over the woman's shoulder. "Hello Arthur," he says to me. "Devon, this is Arthur."

Devon. Her name is Devon.

"We just met." I smile as winningly as possible.

"He's lovely," Devon bellows. Then she grabs Clyde in what is either a hug or a very complicated wrestling hold. "Not as lovely as you, of course. My glorious geek." A very large kiss is planted on his cheek. She looks utterly enrapt.

"Met at Cambridge, you know," she tells me, failing to release Clyde, who can apparently hold his breath longer than I can. "Lab partners. I set him on fire with a Bunsen burner. So romantic."

"That sounds..." I realize I have no idea what that sounds like.

Finally Clyde manages to disengage from the embrace and make his way from doorway to hallway. "Best be off," he says, leaning forward to give Devon a peck on the cheek. "Love you."

Devon grabs him in another spine-crushing hug then lets go.

"Get wasted for me," she booms as he backs away, then looks at me and mouths, "No," several times.

"Lovely to meet you," I say. Which it is. But that's about it for things I can think to say until Clyde and I are at the car.

Our eyes meet as we open the doors. Clyde seems to think some sort of explanation is in order. "We met at Cambridge," he says, still holding the door handle. He hoists his free shoulder awkwardly high. "She burned me with a Bunsen burner." He chews his bottom lip. "Surprisingly romantic, really." But he's not holding my eye when he says that. Instead he hums quietly and monotonously to himself and then gets into the passenger seat.

FIVE MINUTES BEFORE EIGHT

I've been trying to ignore what Swann said for nearly twenty-four hours now, and I'm getting worse at it as time goes by. As we watch the door to Olsted's apartment block there's a lot of rubbing-sweaty-palms-on-thighs and avoiding-Clyde's-eye going on.

It's not helping, either, that Clyde has dissolved over the course of our car journey and now seems to be in a worse state than the one I'm in. Or that I've got several large needles stuck into me. Or that Clyde keeps losing his concentration partway through the spell and saying the wrong things, so rather than channeling otherworldly forces he's just electrocuting me.

"It's OK," I say. "Everything's going to be fine." I'm not a hundred percent sure, but I think that's about the billionth time I've said that. It's about as convincing as it was when I started.

"Just think," I supplement, "if we screw up you can

throw blasts of invisible power at people using a couple of AA batteries. That's pretty damn cool."

"It's just kinetic energy," Clyde says, not looking at me. "Not my spell. Transcribed by a chap called Elkman back in eighteen forty-five. Elkman's Push. Just pulls kinetic energy from some reality where things are moving very fast a lot. Easier than bringing the thing through. That's all. Just physics."

"It's still pretty cool though."

He finally looks at me. "If I cast any spells tonight that means we've already screwed up, doesn't it?"

That one stumps me because he's technically correct. Tabitha is listening in through the tiny earbuds; I don't think we're overwhelming her with confidence.

"Just stick to the plan." Her voice snaps in my ear. "Do what you're meant to do. Be fine. Clyde, you'll be fine."

Clyde is hyperventilating. I'm not far behind him.

Bold. Impulsive.

But it's easier to be bold and impulsive when you're up against scientists. Armed security guards require a whole new league of boldness, and I haven't given up my amateur status yet.

Still, we stiff upper lip it. Open the car doors, elevate our chins and march off to our dooms. The doorman checks our names and then ushers us across the lobby floor. Still, he gives us an odd look as he calls the elevator. Can't really blame him. My kneecaps are doing the tango up and down my legs. It's not a good look on me.

"Steady breathing." Tabitha barks commands at us. "Conference went well. This will go well. Stick to the script. No deviations. No improv. Do your jobs."

It's somewhere between cheerleader and boot camp drill sergeant. I know she's doing her best, but I rather wish she wasn't. My nerves are fraying by the second. I pull out the earbud and stuff it into my pocket.

The elevator doors ping open. Clyde collapses against the back wall. I tug him gently by the arm.

"Come on, mate," I say, but that doesn't work so I bodily haul him out. Which probably looks a little odd to Tweedledum and Tweedledee, who are staring at us from down the hallway. I smile and wave. Probably not the most reassuring thing I could do.

I'm sure the guy in charge will be a competent military intelligence ninja bastard...

Oh balls.

The amount of corridor between us and the Dee–Dum duo seems infinite. I try to keep in mind the map of the building Tabitha found us. It's not some non-Euclidean nightmare of impossible angles, just a simple corridor running the periphery of the building. Keeps the penthouse isolated—no outside walls, and no windows. In fact, I think Olsted might be even more paranoid than I am right now.

There again, I'm willing to give him a run for his money. Everything Clyde and I do seems suspicious—when we walk out of unison, when we walk in step. It looks too practised. Too studied. And as soon as I start over-thinking the way I walk I'm on the verge of screwing even that up. And tripping over my own feet doesn't seem like the best way to convince a man you're a potential Nobel candidate.

Tweedledee's eyes are tiny black beads as we reach the door, his brow knotted. Still he opens the door, and there is Olsted, tiny and wrinkled inside his pristine suit.

"Gentlemen," he says and seems about to go on but then stops.

"Hello, Mr. Olsted." I put as much sunshine in my voice as I can muster. It's hardly Royal Shakespeare

Company, but I'm surprised at how chipper I can sound when I'm in this sort of state. "Thank you so much for inviting us to come by... and talk..." I grind to a halt. Olsted isn't looking at me. No one is looking at me. They're all staring at Clyde. He's turning a strange shade of green.

"Guh," he says. "Ack. Cah." He coughs. I think he's trying to shrug but his shoulders just waggle randomly up and down.

Tweedledum balls his fists. Tweedledee starts reaching for a bulge in his trousers. I still don't think anyone's happy to see us. Which means...

A gun. He's most definitely going for a gun.

Oh balls. Oh bloody fucking hell. Swann was bloody right. We're not even going to make it through the front door.

And I was right too. They are most definitely not going to call the cops.

I'm sure the guy in charge will be a competent military intelligence ninja bastard...

Except it's me. And I am not bold. I am not impulsive. I'm just a little bastard out of water. And I don't know what to do. I do not. I do not have these kinds of impulses.

What would Kurt Russell do?

I don't know exactly where the thought comes from. It's certainly not the most rational thing to pass through my head, but it's like a brief window, like the eye of the storm opening around me before I am brutally cast out. It's the moment before I think, *I'm nothing like Kurt Russell*. A window of madness. A window to be a man of action.

So, in defiance of rationality, in defiance of the plan, and most definitely in defiance of what Tabitha would have me do, I turn and punch Clyde square in the face.

15

Clyde slams back against the wall, head bouncing off the doorframe. I step into him, following up with a sucker punch to the gut and Clyde doubles over, grabbing his stomach. I try to whisper to him to just go with it, as he goes past me, but there's no real time.

"What the hell?" Olsted barks.

Tweedledee has the gun up now. It flicks back and forth between Clyde and me.

"Easy now," I say. My heart is pounding like a jackhammer. My hands do not so much tremble as bounce as I reach into my inside pocket slowly, very slowly. The gun is trained right on me now. Sweat is coursing down my brow. I pull out the ID Shaw gave me. "Arthur Wallace," I say. "I'm with MI37."

"Who the fuck?" says Tweedledum.

"That's not fucking you," says Tweedledee turning over the ID, demonstrating that he is the more eloquent of Olsted's security men.

I let go of the battery in my pocket.

The release is immediate. A nausea-inducing shudder of flesh. And then the pain falls away, like a discarded blanket. My hands. My arms, my body, my legs.

"Oh," says Tweedledee.

"MI37 deals with thaumaturgical threats to the

United Kingdom's sovereign borders," I say, doing the best I can to keep my voice calm, even. "Obviously you don't hear about us in the press that much." I have no idea if I pronounced "thaumaturgical" correctly. I don't even know if you can use the word that way. I just need to keep talking.

"This man is not who he appears to be," I carry on talking into unbelieving faces. "He is Clyde Marcus Bradley, originally of Lithuania—" because that's the first country I think of "—and the member of a dangerous cabal." It all sounds paper-thin to me. I get the feeling it's all paper-thin to them as well, but the gun is down as Tweedledee checks my ID.

Clyde makes another guttural noise and I punch him again. I try to pull it, but I'm not really sure how to go about that. Clyde goes down on one knee. If we get out of this alive I really am going to need to buy him several beers.

"I don't know," says Tweedledee. "Sounds like bullshit to—"

"It's your grimoire." I talk straight to Olsted. It's him I have to sell it to. He's the boss. The bad guy. Dee and Dum are the ugly movie henchmen. And henchmen do what the bad guy says. And when I say grimoire, Olsted's eyes go wide. "This man—" I point to Clyde "—is after your grimoire."

Olsted opens his mouth several times. He looks to Tweedledee and Tweedledum, uncertain, unsure. And I realize that out of nowhere this plan is working. I somehow have him on the back of his heels. I just need to push him one more time to get him reeling.

"The British government believes that the security of your grimoire is an issue of national importance," I say.

"It does?" Olsted looks utterly bewildered. And considering the bastard is using it to betray humanity to bloody aliens, I don't blame him.

"The British government has great faith in you, Mr. Olsted," I lie.

"Th— Thank you," says Olsted.

We stand there in silence. Well, silence if you ignore Clyde's moans of pain. Which I'm definitely trying to do. I keep my eyes on Olsted.

"Do you…" He looks down at Clyde. "Should you…"

"The grimoire," I say to Olsted. "I need to see the grimoire." I try to say it like he's an idiot. Like I'm not on the verge of soiling myself. Because this is it. Make or break. This is where I either get to walk away or get to go to sleep under six inches of England's good fresh soil.

"What?" Olsted is still confused. I reach for some deeper layer of bullshit. Kurt Russell, I tell myself. Do what Kurt Russell would do. In a world gone mad, that this plan should work almost makes sense.

"Mr. Bradley, here," I indicate Clyde, "represents but one strand of his cabal's web of deceit. MI37 has intercepted him, has intercepted his part of the plan, but I have no idea if you have been targeted by other parts of his organization, or by his competitors. As I said, the British government views the security of your grimoire as being of vital importance. I need to ensure that it is indeed safe. If you would please show it to me."

Olsted stares at me. The gears are still skittering in his head, I can tell, but they're turning. Something is going on back there.

"Christopher," he says to Tweedledee, "Samuel—" Tweedledum "—take this" he kicks Clyde "—*thing* into Ilsa's room. Bind him." He looks to me for confirmation. Which is good. Which is very good. Not for Clyde, of course, but… I nod.

"Stay with him," Olsted continues. "Make sure Ilsa

doesn't…" he trails off. The goons nod. Something is not being said. Something I don't understand. But I don't need to, because the next thing Olsted says is, "Come with me, Mr. Wallace."

Dum and Dee drag Clyde off in one direction, Olsted leads me in another. The main body of the apartment is open-plan and modern. A kitchen opens onto a dining room, which merges with a living room. I can almost imagine Swedish people emerging from hidden cabinets.

Olsted swipes an AA battery off a counter top and mutters something I can't quite hear. On the wall in front of us, between two Van Gogh prints, a door appears. There is no shimmer, no moment of in-between. It's more like an awkward cut in a film, an abrupt jump. It's not there. It is. Olsted opens it without ceremony.

I almost hesitate going through. I feel there should have been more… theater to the big reveal. This feels underwhelming, as if I've missed something.

The room Olsted has revealed is equally unassuming. It looks more like a junk room—a square metal cube lit by halogen strip lamps. Boxes of junk lie around the floor— rusted metal sheets, bent tailpipes, chunks of rebar, all in beaten-up wooden crates. And cats too, of course. Because why just use your top-secret magical safe for storing scrap metal when you can throw in a tabby, a tortoiseshell, and a scratching post, as well?

The more of this magic stuff I see, the more I'm certain it drives you crazy.

Olsted moves across the room quickly, ignoring its contents. There is a second doorway. A purple velvet curtain blocks it but he pushes it aside and I get a glimpse of what lies beyond. And that is a little more like it.

The room is circular, the ceiling high. There is a pentagram in gold upon the floor. In the center of the room and the pentagram is a lectern of polished wood. The natural rhythms of the wood have been carved into the pattern of twisting limbs—half human, half other—that reach up its elegant splayed shelf. On it lies the cracked leather tome.

It is so Hammer horror, I expect Christopher Lee to rise out of a tomb at the back of the place. I love it.

Olsted lays a hand on the book. "Safe," he says.

But that is the last thing he says, because then I hit him on the back of the neck with a length of pipe purloined from his junk room. The metal vibrates and the shock goes up my arms to my shoulders. I almost drop the pipe with a grunt. But Olsted doesn't make a sound as he falls like a narcoleptic.

I nearly shout in victory, but I'm still undercover, even if I'm undercover as myself, so I satisfy the urge with a fist pump. Next, I get to the business of actually thieving the grimoire, which is heavier than it looks, but otherwise unsecured. Its only guardian is on the floor sleeping like a babe.

Now just to rescue Clyde from two heavily armed men. But I can do this. I can bloody do this.

I turn and pull back the velvet curtain to reveal the junk room. A massive spark fills the room with blue light. I reel backwards, arm up. But even as I move a massive wind seems to rise from nowhere, buffeting at me like a giant snatching hand. Junk whirls past me and I duck back from the flying debris.

Suddenly the center of the room is a cyclone, whipping the metal trash around faster and faster into a jagged, deadly mess. Even above the rising howl of the room I can hear metal screeching as chunks of ironwork smash into each other, warping and tearing.

I've triggered one of the magical machines Clyde told

me about. I've triggered a trap.

I'm cornered. Oh shit and balls. I can't go in there. I'll be smashed to bloody pieces. Jesus—the cats. They must be pulp by now. What sick bastard keeps cats in a booby-trapped room? I should have hit him harder.

But what the hell do I do? On the one hand, I do not want to end up like the cats. On the other, I'm coming up a little short on alternative exits.

I look down at Olsted's comatose form. There has to be some switch, some trigger, I missed. Some infrared device in his ring, or glasses, or something. Bastard. Some wicked, frustrated part of me wants to chuck him in the junk room with his dead cats.

Still, it's not all bad. If I can't get out, then Tweedledee and Dum can't get to me. I just need to think of a plan while the spell lasts.

Except suddenly the tornado finds a whole new gear and suddenly I am losing my footing, being sucked toward the grinding mass of junk.

I brace myself against the doorway. Then I clutch at it. It's as if gravity has shifted, has become a point at the center of the room. I think about black holes, about event horizons, about being liquidized by a tiny point of gravity.

My feet are off the ground. I grab the door tighter. My fingernails dig into the wood. The curtain tears off the rail above my head. And oh shit, and oh balls, and oh—

And then the wind drops. I drop, smack down on my knees. And that is going to leave a mark. And the wind has dropped and I still need to formulate my plan of escape.

Olsted. I have Olsted. A hostage. Yes. That'll work. I risk a quick glance to survey the landscape before me.

And I stop. And I stand very still. And now I understand why Olsted kept cats in the room.

Not for fun. Not for recreational animal abuse. To

provide a focus for his spell, his trap. To give things shape.

There are two… beasts in the center of the room. There's something feline about them. Something feline and something metal. They're made out of junk, the junk that filled this room. Scrap-metal tigers standing on their hind legs. Steel sabertooths, walking as men. They shift their massive weight and their joints screech. Rust teeth, knife-blade claws, rebar thighs as thick as my waist. They have tails made of steel bars, twisting and lashing. They leer at me.

What would Kurt Russell do?

I have no idea. I really have no idea.

16

Just for kicks, I throw the pipe I used to club Olsted at one of them. It bounces off one massive, steel-clad shoulder. It lands, ignored.

"Shit." The expletive spills out of me.

One of the beasts opens its mouth. It seems to go on forever. A throat of wire and rust. Sledgehammer molars. Steak-knife canines. A sound emerges, something between a roar and a burst of static.

"Balls!"

I run. There's nothing else to do. It doesn't matter that the pipe didn't work. It's either die standing or die running. And running feels like doing something. And I can't run away, so I run at them instead.

They lurch toward me. Their limbs jerk. As if they're only just getting used to their bodies. As if the confusion of birth is still on them. It almost feels like a chance.

One beast jams out its arm, as if to clothesline me, jagged claws poised to take my head off at the neck. I let my feet fall from under me, throwing my legs forward, praying for some momentum, ducking and sliding, a mad limbo to freedom.

Except the one on my right seems to have remembered how to move. Its foreleg is a blur, and I barely realize what's happening until I'm lying in a heap on the floor, gasping, my right flank blazing in pain. The thing punches like a jackhammer. I'm not bleeding, but at least one rib must have broken.

I just about make it to my feet, just about make it one step, two, and then they're both crouching to jump. The room wavers before me. Three more steps, almost a run.

Even though I know it's coming, the leap still comes as a surprise. The speed of it, the ferocity.

I freeze.

That saves me—that abrupt failure of my limbs to do as I tell them to do. Some survival instinct bred into the old lizard brain that ignores the idiocy of my higher functions. The beasts fly past me, through the space I was about to occupy. The sound as they crash into each other is like an auto wreck. They tumble, their limbs madly locked, spitting and screeching, a sound like feedback on speakers.

And suddenly the path between me and the door is open. My limbs come unglued, or just know that now is the time to start cooperating. I'm out into the open-plan living space. White couch. White chairs. Fireplace. Kitchen.

Where the bloody hell is the door?

But Clyde. I need to get Clyde. I got him into this. This is all my fault. This is my own idiot fault. Because it's easy to be a hero when you're trying to con a couple of scientists out of a hair follicle or two. But when there are genuinely bad people, and genuinely bad things. Shit. People are only heroes in movies. Where it's fake. Where it's special effects. Where the blood is glycerine and food dye. Shit.

I stagger across the living room. Everything's open-plan. No Clyde. A door. I need to find a door. Any door. Give me a goddamn fucking door. I'm panicking. My eyes are flickering. They can't rest anywhere. I paw my way along the wall. My hand closes on something. A door handle.

This is a door handle. Focus. I can hear metal crashing from beyond the gaping doorway to the grimoire room.

I pull the door. Nothing. I push. And then I fall. I sprawl through it. Forehead meets floor. I scramble forward in a haze of pain. Kick the door shut. They didn't see me. Pray they didn't see me.

Static scrawls of sound echo from beyond the wall. Still prone, I flip onto my back, stare at the door. Nothing. Metallic footsteps. But the door isn't torn open. I turn around. I need a way out. I need Clyde and a way out.

And I have Clyde. There is Clyde. Right there. Staring right at me. Lucky door.

Except Clyde is gagged and bound, arms and legs wrapped up in silver duct tape, like some half-finished Egyptian mummy. Except there are two dead bodies lying across the floor. Tweedledum and Tweedledee. Identical holes punched in their foreheads. Identical brains spilling across the floor. Except there's a girl. A girl with a gun. A gun pressed to her temple.

Outside, something lets out an electronic scream.

No. Not a lucky door.

17

"You must be Arthur," says the girl.

"I…"

Clyde's eyes are almost out of his head. He's making muffled shrieking sounds from behind the duct tape. I look down at the dead bodies. At the girl. At the gun. Why is the gun to her head? Why would she—

"I should probably thank you," she says.

"Ilsa?" I say. "Ilsa Olsted?" Isn't Ilsa meant to be bedridden? Doesn't she have Creutzfeldt–Jakob disease? Isn't that what the research notes said?

"I've been trying to infect Olsted forever," she says. She sounds almost bored. "And now you go and bring me a magician of my own, so I don't even need the old bastard. You're so kind."

Infect? Infect Olsted? And the penny drops.

"Progeny," I say. "You're Progeny." Ilsa Olsted. Infected. Of course. Of course that makes sense. That's why the old man is cooperating. He's over a barrel. And so they get him to plant the book. He does whatever they ask.

"Not Progeny for much longer," Ilsa says with a soft smile, almost a dreamy smile. "You, though…"

The words hang. I remember the cloud of eggs exploding out of the skull of the man in Cowley. I remember Shaw's words. *Any that land in a nearby individual's hindbrain will nestle and hatch there."* I look at the gun again. The gun pressed to Ilsa's temple. Oh shit.

Ilsa thumbs back the hammer on the gun.

I'm still lying on my back, looking up at her. I whip my legs around; spin my whole body like a breakdancer. Or an epileptic, depending on your standards.

Grace, thank God, is not required to tangle Ilsa's feet. Mine connect with hers and she heads south. Legs out. Arms up. Gun up. She fires. Plaster falls. The shot's echo rebounds. The gun spills loose.

I jump for it. I don't know what I'll do with it. But it's a gun. Surely you always go for the gun.

Ilsa howls. Her hand grabs my ankle. I come up short. I kick back down. Something gives beneath my foot. A crunch. Part horrified. Part glorying. I broke a girl's nose. But I'm free.

Something crashes behind me. I spin. Five claws have smashed through the plasterboard of the wall. They scrape sideways, tearing great gashes through the wall. They tear through the door. It falls in two. Gunshots are, apparently, not the best way to keep a low profile.

The beasts scream in unison. I finally make it to the gun. I spin. Point. Shoot. By some miracle I hit them. Probably because they're so bloody big.

The bullets ricochet off them. They don't slow down.

"Shit!"

Ilsa Olsted stands, beaming. A look of rapture on her face.

"That's it," she calls to them. "That's it. Come to me. Take me apart. Scatter my children."

"Shit!"

I'm back up against the wall, crouching. Clyde is at my feet. He's screaming behind the duct tape. I pull it from his mouth.

"The gun!" he shouts. "Give me the gun!"

"But it's—"

"Give it to me!" He looks mad with panic. And I don't know what to do. I don't know what to do. I press the gun into a hand taped close to his side.

One of the beasts punches through what's left of the door. The next one just punches a path through the wall.

Gripping the gun awkwardly Clyde fires a shot down the length of his pants. He's aiming at nothing. Just the wall. An electrical plate shatters.

An electrical plate.

One of the beasts lifts a paw and prepares to decapitate Ilsa.

Clyde grunts and rolls forward. He grabs a wire that spills out of the shattered plate on the wall.

"*Kton achton mal racthon al mannon...*"

The scrap-metal tiger with its claw raised freezes. Its limbs grind and scream.

"*...feton mal rannon tel shathal ac rannon...*"

The beast comes apart. Its paw shudders as if struck, and then quite simply, quite gently each constituent part separates itself from all the others, and in a slow-motion explosion, shrapnel drifting lazily through the air, it collapses to the floor.

From the center of the mess, a tabby cat scampers away.

The second beast backs away, mewling, something like shock on its face.

Ilsa turns to stare at us.

Clyde mutters another word. The duct tape around his arms and legs burns away, disintegrates into ash in a moment. Clyde tosses me the gun. "Your turn," he says.

Wait. What? My what?

I look at the gun in my hands.

Ilsa is screaming. She is bending down. Grabbing

something. A knife. A jagged shard of metal. Some part of the dead tiger. Some weapon. She's snatching, and screaming, and she's going to—

My first shot punches Ilsa back a step. I didn't even know I'd fired. The gun goes off again. My hands jump. Ilsa reels into the doorway. Two bright roses of blood bloom on her chest. She stumbles over scrap metal, wavers, clutches at the frame. Not dead. She's still holding the metal. Still... I have to shoot her again. Oh shit. Oh fuck. I have to...

I close my eyes. I fire. Open my eyes.

The bullet takes the top of Ilsa's head off, opens her like a can. Blood sprays straight up, like a fountain.

"No!" A scream. A sound dragged out of a man. I look up and see—beyond the corpse, beyond the mewling scrap-metal tiger, in the doorway to the grimoire room—Olsted, bruised and bloody and horror-struck as he watches his daughter die.

In the wound in Ilsa's head I can see the Progeny thrashing. Tendrils whip the air, sprouting from around the beak-like mouth. A white, segmented body. A maggot's body with a thousand short legs spasming in the air.

I wait for the eggs. The white spray of alien young. I wait for confirmation that the thing is dead. I wait to see if Clyde and I are out of range.

But it doesn't come.

The Progeny kicks free of Ilsa's body, kicks free of the corpse. It is moving. Still whole. My shot didn't have the angle of Kayla's sword blade. It didn't hit hindbrain, where the thing nests, squirms, and roots. It didn't get it when it was corporeal, when it was nesting. I killed the host but not the Progeny. I set it free.

18

I open fire again but my bullets fly through the Progeny's transparent body. It's like shooting at air.

Olsted howls again. His eyes scan the devastation of his home. He looks at me, at the gun I hold. There's murder there. Of course there's murder there. He just witnessed murder. I just murdered his daughter. Oh shit. I just murdered... Oh shit.

Before Olsted can react, before he can spit me on some pole of magical spite, the Progeny moves. It lances through the air toward the old man. The speed is incongruous from its fat body. The tendrils spear forward. It heads straight for Olsted's skull.

The old man flings up an arm and there is a crack like a lightning strike. Every hair on my body stands on end. I can feel warm air blowing over me, as if an oven door has been opened.

The Progeny stops. It hangs in midair, mouth tendrils and tail thrashing. Olsted stands, his hand outstretched, as if holding it in place.

No, that's wrong. Actually holding it in place.

Beside me, the remaining beast snarls. It turns. It leers at the small white creature. It flexes scissor-blade claws. Then it moves.

The Progeny does too. Suddenly jagging left. The beast

and Progeny careen toward each other.

"No!" Clyde screams, but I can't see what he's frightened of. All our enemies are fighting each other.

And then the Progeny glides through the outstretched claw of the beast and slams straight into its chest.

The beast stops moving. Shudders.

The cat. The cat is still in there. In the heart of it. The cat has a brain. Has a hindbrain. Has a place for the Progeny to nest.

"Run!" screams Clyde.

Which seems like such a remarkably good idea, I'm already doing it.

The massive metallic cat hurls itself at Olsted as I hurl myself at the door. The grimoire is lying on the floor, discarded in the chaos. I reach down, grab it, as the infected beast slams into some invisible wall between it and Olsted. Its claws scrape down the air as if against a chalkboard. Olsted flings out another hand. Something explodes. The beast wheels away, claws dicing the air.

I'm down, running crouched over. Like a roadie at a rock concert. The grimoire is clutched to my chest. A steel foot mashes down on the floor beside me. I fling myself back. I spin. I run.

I am upside down, or sideways, or falling. Coffee tables are exploding into splinters. Somehow I'm in the kitchen now, behind a counter, now a line of cabinets. There is a snarling gnashing from the middle of the room. I pop up, fire randomly, hit nothing. I see Clyde running for the doorway. I run after him.

Out in the hallway. Look left. Look right. A sound like a train disaster behind us. Left. Right. The elevators. We run. Feet pounding over the carpet.

And the elevator doors are opening as Clyde and I sprint toward them. They slide apart. The doorman is standing there. Concerned. Confusion on his face. He sees us. Reaches for a gun.

My fist flies out before his catches the handle. Adrenaline has taken over. I'm holding the pistol. Cold-cock him right on the side of the head. My hand sings with pain. He staggers back, into a wall. I grab him by the collar. Knee to groin. Hurl his doubled-up body out into the hallway. The elevator doors slide shut.

My breath comes in ragged bursts. Clyde is on his knees whimpering.

Kurt Russell is a terrible, terrible role model.

The sounds of chaos fade above us.

Going down.

19

"A complete and utter shambles."

It's not depressing to hear the words because we failed but because we failed again.

"A disaster."

Shaw is shaking her head. Tabitha, Clyde, and I are lined up in front of her. Another bollocking. Only Kayla is missing this time. Can't blame her.

"Now," Shaw paces back and forth, "the idea was that, by taking Kayla off the team you three would learn to work better together, correct?"

The silence is long and awkward. Finally we all seem to realize she actually wants an answer.

"Yes," Clyde mumbles. Tabitha and I mm-hm our responses.

"How would you say that went?"

She's not as pissed as I expected, just tired-looking. Disappointed.

"Not as well as hoped," I finally say into the gaping silence.

Shaw nods solemnly. "Yes," she says. "Punching Clyde in the face was probably a good sign you'd derailed."

Part of me wants to argue about how unfair that is. Part of me wants to say that the plan had already gone awry at that point. That no, it wasn't probably the best decision, but I was dealing with an evolving situation. Except, I was meant to be in charge. I'm where the buck stops.

"We got the book," I say. It sounded like a repudiation in my head, it sounded like a whine out in the wild.

"Yes." Shaw nods. "The minimum bar for success, but you did do that." Again she sounds tired. She shakes her head. "I don't know," she says. "I don't know." She looks up at us. Smiles. Grimaces. Shakes her head. "Just find out what it tells us," she says. "Make this worthwhile."

Tabitha and Clyde scurry away, Clyde snatching the grimoire off the table. Shaw and I are alone in the room. She looks at her watch.

"Not as well as hoped?" She shakes her head again. She looks at her watch. "We'll talk about this later," she says. "I have to be somewhere." And then she leaves and I'm alone.

I stand for thirty more seconds, stare into space, then find a chair and sag. Head to table. This again. Here again. Messing everything up again. Wasn't I a competent policeman a few days ago? Wasn't I good at my job?

Yes. Yes I was. That perks me up a bit. I was good at something once.

I am not good at this. This is stumbling from disaster to disaster. And I know the life of a little girl is on the line, I know that. But I think the really responsible thing to do is to put those lives in the hands of someone who can actually do something to save them.

I don't need to wait to have a talk with Shaw. I need to just quit.

There's something liberating in the thought. Which in turn makes me feel guilty. But knowing someone else will be dealing with this makes me happy. Some competent military intelligence ninja bastard, to quote Swann. It'll be nice to go back to working with her.

It takes me a while to get to Shaw's office because, I

realize only after embarking on my journey to it, I don't actually know where it is. Yet another indication that quitting is the right idea. And I open doors onto a lot of empty and dusty rooms, and even find out where the library is, before I finally find a door labeled "Section Director."

It's open slightly, and I hear voices, but I'm so excited by the idea of getting out of here that I don't want to delay. Anyway, resigning shouldn't take long, and the quicker the better. Then, my palm about an inch from the wood, I hear my name.

"—really even need this Wallace guy? The local police force is screaming that someone in the government stole their man without even asking."

It is not Shaw's voice. It is a whiny, nasal voice. Too close to nails scratching a chalkboard to be comfortable to listen to.

"Is this a joke, Robert?" The tiredness in Shaw's voice has been ratcheted up a notch even from the conference room.

"No, it's not a joke, Felicity," says the whiner, Robert. "You know full well your department is out of favor. The government has ambitious plans and it is looking to cut. And after the stunt on Cowley Road you are looking like a good place to find a little spare change. So, is Wallace necessary?"

"There are creatures, Robert—" Shaw sounds like she's burning through her last gallon of gas "—looking to destroy the entirety of creation. To stop this, I have three agents I can send out into the field. Two are glorified researchers, a chemist from Cambridge with a surprising aptitude for thaumaturgy and a serious case of nerves." I don't feel good matching Clyde to that description but it seems to fit. "The other is just as smart but more eloquent with her middle finger than with anything else." Tabitha. "And the third, while she fell into our hands with superhuman abilities, has several serious psychoses you tell me I can't afford to have treated." Kayla's easy to spot. But this diatribe doesn't make me feel good about what I'm going to hear about myself. "And now, I finally manage to get half a grip on someone who actually seems competent, someone who knows how to run an investigation, someone who may be able to save the life of a girl who you know has saved many lives herself, someone who I can actually trust to herd the cats I have running around out there, someone who was quick-witted enough to actually get a new grimoire into the agency out from under the nose of an actual Progeny, and you want to take him off my hands? So I repeat, are you having a joke at my expense, Robert?"

I just stand there. Because... No, I still need a minute.

I did good? After all that...

Holy shit. I did good. I got the grimoire. When Shaw's telling it, I'm the hero of the piece.

And maybe I owe Kurt Russell an apology.

My hand still hangs in front of the door. In the office, silence hangs.

Then, Robert's nasal whine cuts through whatever moment it is we're having.

"So, if Wallace is in, who can we cut?"

Shaw sighs deep and loud and long. I slowly back away from the door.

TEN MINUTES LATER

I sit in an empty conference room and try and work out what I'm doing. My watch says ten in the a.m. Clyde and Tabitha are researching ancient tomes, and I don't know what I can do to help. Shaw is... I don't know what Shaw is doing.

I need to get my head straight. I'm either in this game or I'm not. And it sounds like... God, it sounds like I'm in.

No easy way out. No making this someone else's problem. No working with Swann. I've got a little girl to save.

And if I'm going to save her, I really need to be in this game. I need to know what I'm doing. I need to understand this world I'm in. I need to stop just reacting. I need to commit. Learn this world. Learn its minutia.

Except it's a whole new world to learn. Where do you learn about a new world?

Basics. I need to start with the basics. I need to start with the girl I'm meant to save.

A BRIEF ELEVATOR RIDE LATER

The saltwater smell of their pool hits me as soon as I step off the elevator. In the glare of the pool lights, the shadows of cephalopods play on the room's ceiling.

"Hello, Detective Wallace," calls a voice.

"Agent Wallace," corrects the other. The acoustics of the room make the words bounce hollowly around.

"I know." There is laughter and splashing.

"Hello, girls." I kneel by the edge of the pool. They swim over. Quick efficient strokes. Beaming faces surface.

"Hello," says one, Ephie maybe. "Agent Wallace," she adds. Both girls dissolve into giggles, submerging beneath a web of wriggling tentacles. Still not used to that.

They surface with little gasps of breath. "To what do we owe the pleasure?" asks the one who may be Ophelia. She performs a small, aquatic curtsey.

And what is there to say? What do I ask them? How can I ask the best way to stop one of them from dying?

"Erm…" I say. I stare at them. "I suppose," I say, "I was wondering… Is there an easy way to tell you apart?"

"Of course," says the maybe-Ephie.

"Our names!" says the other.

More laughing. More splashing. I laugh too. It's nice

to know there are still laughs on this job.

"Seriously," I say when they finally settle down. "Is there?"

"Yes," says one.

"Freckles," says the other.

"Two," says the first pointing to two brown specks on the right corner of her jawline.

"Three," says the other, pointing to the same spot. And sure enough there is a rough triangle of three freckles there.

"Ophelia," says the first.

"Ephemera," says the second.

Which of course means I had them backwards. But that's why I'm doing this. Learning. Understanding the basics. Easier to save them when I know who they are.

"It's OK," says Ophelia, abruptly serious. "We think you're doing a good job."

I look at them both. The giggles are gone. Two serious little girls. Old beyond their time. But there is a stillness to them, a confidence.

"So does Shaw," says Ephie. "Don't worry so much."

I look at them. And it's right there—they do trust me. Which is an insane responsibility. It's a responsibility like a weight on me. But at the same time… someone here has confidence in me. They may only be ten, but, still, they trust me.

"Twelve," says Ephie.

"What?"

"We're twelve," she says.

I smile. I shake my head. It doesn't stop. But here and now, for the first time, I really think I can handle it.

"How come," I ask, "you two aren't the prune-iest two people in the world? Seriously, you should both look like Mother Teresa by now the length of time you've been in there." And then there's laughter again, and splashing, and I don't know if they really feel better about things or not, but I actually do.

I check my watch again as I head up in the elevator. Still not lunchtime. And I feel like doing something. I feel like my feet are on the ground again. Like I can achieve something.

What would Kurt Russell do?

A stupid thing to think, but it brings a grin to my face.

I think I'll swing by Olsted's place. Just in the car. Scope things out. There's not much of a chance of learning much, but I don't see how it can hurt anything.

THIRTY MINUTES AND TWO MILES LATER

I see the smoke from a mile away, a dusty dispersing cloud. My stomach starts sinking about half a mile away. A quarter of a mile and I almost turn the car around just so I don't see what happened, but I keep going in the blind hope that maybe, just maybe, there's a pizza place right next to Olsted's building and they just happen to have left the oven on too long.

As it turns out, confidence and coincidences are not going hand in hand today.

I pull up where the police tape marks off the end of Olsted's street and stare up at the smoking ruin that is the top floor of the building.

It wasn't us. It almost seems unfair. This really wasn't our fault. When we left the place was whole. This was that damned Progeny. And Olsted. Damn him too.

We got the book. But I'm beginning to worry we missed the ball.

20

It feels important I find out what happened here, but I want to avoid awkward questions with old co-workers. They'll have too many questions I can't answer. I'm about to turn the car around and try and catch Shaw before she checks the local news, when I spot a familiar blond head amongst the crowd. I pull out my cellphone. Press the number three.

I'm sure Swann would be fine with the fact I put her on speed dial. She patted my hand. A whole number of times. And it's not about that anyway. I just don't have many people I call regularly. My parents in Australia—as infrequently as possible—and the front desk back at the force. That's about it. That's why she got number three. No other reason.

I can see her pick up. "One street west, two minutes," I say. She looks up, looks around and I duck back into the car. But, she watches me pull away. Because she's a good policewoman.

ONE STREET WEST AND TWO MINUTES LATER

"Don't tell me you're responsible for this." Swann's expression is half smiling until she sees my expression.

"Oh shit, Boss."

Apparently I still have to work on playing things cool.

"No." I hold my hands up. "Really. I promise. This wasn't my fault."

"So it was an accident? Tell it to the judge, Boss." She's joking but the smile is getting smaller.

"Last time I was here, this place was completely intact."

"When were you last here?" There's an edge to her voice. She's not quite interrogating me, but it's close. This isn't going quite how I wanted.

"Last night." I sound sheepish. I'm not making things better.

"Talk to me, Boss," she says.

We exchange a look. I chew my lip, she chews hers. Then she laughs. "Come on, Arthur, Boss, please. Give me a break. I just... I don't know what happened here. I know you can't talk much about what you're doing now, but can you give me something? You have an idea about how this happened?"

I picture the scene when we left. The whole magician fighting an alien-possessed giant metal cat-monster thing. How do I explain that? Do they make straitjackets in my size?

"What do our guys... your guys think caused it?" I say, dodging the question.

"There was some sort of detonation," she says, looking back over her shoulder toward the slowly drifting smoke haze. "Looks directed. Almost no damage going downwards. All out and up. Took off the roof of the place and flattened a chunk of the walls. No flame that we can tell of from the blast. Just the shockwave itself. Which makes no sense. But then, with the walls down you've got all sort of pipes exposed. Water, electricity, gas—bad combination. But the initial blast has us stumped." She raises an eyebrow expectantly.

"What about the guy who lived there?"

"Come on!" Swann throws her hands up. "Give me something, Boss, Arthur. Come on, we're friends. Answer a question."

"I want to tell you. I want to. I do." I'm almost pleading. "I'm trying to find something." I take a step toward her. I almost take her hand. "You are my friend. I don't want to…" I almost say I don't want to screw her, but my brain balks at that wording, too close to too many other things I don't know how to say. "I don't want to mess you around. I want to help. Help me help you." It sounds like a line, like some bullshit a TV spy would tell someone before he shot them in the back. And I hate it. Because I can't think of anything I could possibly tell her.

Swann sighs, chews her tongue. "We can't find the guy, Olsted. We found what we think is his daughter. Dead. Nasty gunshot wound to the top of the head. No one else." She pauses. "Lot of scrap metal too." She scrunches her face, confused.

God. The girl. The girl I shot. I shot a girl. A Progeny. But… still. No, I can't think like that. The Progeny killed a girl. I killed a Progeny.

"You're looking awful guilty all of a sudden, Boss." Swann isn't smiling.

Oh piss. God, I just want to tell her. I just want her to know. And then she can judge me crazy. And then she can think I'm spinning her some bullshit. And then she can write me off as an asshole. And then she can never speak to me again.

Actually, no, I don't want to tell her.

Hello, rock. Hello, hard place.

The thing is there's no solution to this case for her. There is no way to explain it calmly and rationally. A wizard and an alien-possessed magic cat had a fight. That's what happened. I don't even know if the Oxford police force has jurisdiction over alien-possessed magic cats.

I hum. I hah. I keep looking at Swann. I keep on not telling her anything.

"Jesus Christ, Boss. Grow a pair!"

The words explode out of Swann with a violence I never expected from her. She looks at my shocked expression.

"What?" she says. "I mean, seriously? You don't see where I'm coming from. Jesus, Boss. Ever since you took this job... It's like they gave you a badge and took your balls. You used to... You were a good cop, Arthur. You were large and in fucking charge. You were the boss. And look at you now. I mean, just tell me to fuck off or tell me what you know. Have an opinion for longer than six seconds. Be the fucking boss." She presses her hands to her temples. "Jesus, I used to think you..." She shook her head. "And look at you now."

And there's something there. Something beneath the surface of our friendship.

"What?" I say. "You used to think what about me?" And don't let me have blown something I didn't even know was there.

Swann is staring at her feet. I want to reach out to her but—

"Tell me to fuck off or tell me what you know." She repeats it.

I can't do either of those things. I have to do one of those things.

I wish I knew magic. I wish I were Clyde with hidden answers stitched into my skin. Or Kayla—something more or less than human. Because the answers aren't something I can tell. They're something I need to show. And I have no way to show her.

"F—" I say, but that's as far as I can get. How can I tell her to go away?

"Olsted—" I start. "He—" She won't believe me.

Nothing. I say nothing.

Swann looks up. "Fuck off, Boss," she says. She turns away.

"Wait, Swann. Sergeant. Alison." Every name I have for her. And she responds to none of them. "Please, I—"

"Talk to me when you have an answer. Because this is bloody pathetic."

"Alison. Alison, please." But my voice just echoes around her, doesn't touch her. I watch her go, listen to the click of her heels on the road as she walks away.

She gets to the corner and I pray she just turns around, just gives a hint of a second chance.

She pauses. I pause breathing.

And then something comes running from the cross street. Someone. He's dressed in white, long blond hair billowing out behind him. Almost impossibly thin arms and legs—slender and elegant. There is an amazing grace to his movements. He's almost beautiful at this distance. Going a hell of a clip, too. Fast as a bloody bicyclist. Faster.

The runner collides with Swann. His arm does. It snags her, and she flies through the air. That impossibly thin arm caught around her waist. I hear her yell of surprise, of anger, then it cuts off as her head snaps abruptly sideways.

The runner doesn't miss a beat, a step. He just keeps going. Tugs Swann out of sight.

I stand for a moment trying to work out if I saw what I just saw, if what just happened was real. And then I wonder what the hell I'm doing standing around when reality has been so thoroughly bloody breached for so bloody long. Someone's just abducted Alison in front of my eyes and I'm bloody standing here.

I move. Get in my car. Turn the keys. Floor the gas. And I pursue.

21

The runner is already two full streets away when I round the corner. He's going a ridiculous speed. Impossible. Inhuman.

Progeny. It has to be. Or something they made. Or Olsted made. Something with a spell. Magic and aliens. Just my bloody luck.

I accelerate hard, hit a speed bump, hear the bottom of my car scrape against it then I rebound up and smack my head against the roof. Disorientated, it takes me another moment to find the runner.

Goddamn Oxford traffic.

There are cars just swirling round in aimless traffic circles. There are traffic lights every six feet. Stop signs. Random protrusions of concrete blocking the road.

The runner is going to beat me. He's pulling away, Swann flapping like a rag doll in his arms.

"Shit!" The word bounces emptily around inside my car.

The runner turns a corner and without really thinking I punch the accelerator, slam over the median of the traffic circle with a scream of horns and brakes, and pull into oncoming traffic. I slalom between cyclists and cars. People yell, gesticulate, curse, but I leave it all behind. I reach the corner and crank on the wheel. My suspension groans, tires squeal, and various electronics ping angrily at me as I violate the manufacturer's parameters in a variety of new and exciting ways. The runner is still two blocks away, and a bus is turning into the space between me and him.

I am pleased to say that I do, at least, think twice before mounting the sidewalk. I still do it. I crash through a trashcan in a burst of litter. My car lurches violently. I flirt with the curb like a ham-fisted schoolboy on a first date. Women and children run. So do men, for that matter. But I gain on the bastard.

It's down to a block between us and I have to plunge back into traffic. The car twists and I skew wide up on the other pavement. People are running. Somewhere I can hear sirens. Friends of mine—probably the ones from Olsted's place. I stamp my foot on the accelerator, pop the clutch, listen to the wheels spin, and swing back into pursuit.

My heart thunders, my palms sweat, the wheel is slipping in my grip. Part of my head is yammering at the impossibility of the runner's speed but the rest of me is screaming at that part to shut up and let me focus on driving.

We head back up Cowley. Long and straight, finally free of traffic, of traffic calming measures. Finally I can make a decent run at the bastard. I floor it. My needle heads toward sixty, seventy, eighty. Still the bastard is in front of me. His feet are a blur. Swann's head snaps up and down. She must be unconscious.

This is a dream. A nightmare. Nothing seems real. I swerve across lanes. One hand is on the horn as long as I can keep it.

Then the runner jags left into a construction site. I'm going to miss the turn. I'm going to overshoot them.

I yank on the handbrake.

Kurt Russell movies really are bollocks.

The car screams. The tires scream, then think, "sod it," and just give up. The car flips, first up on its side, careening

madly sideways on two wheels and then goes into a full
barrel roll. I'm thrown sideways. The airbag explodes
from the wheel and slams into one of my cheeks, twisting
my neck violently. The world is a blur, a vortex, snapping
me round, round. The sky dances about me, caught in a
breakneck tango with the earth. Metallic thunder booms.

Then silence. A gentle creaking. The car rocks back
and forth on its roof. I am dangling upside down, my
seatbelt doing a decent job of crushing the life from me.

After a minute I manage to get the shaking in my arm
to calm down enough so that I can unbuckle myself. I drop
awkwardly, smack painfully into the crumpled fabric of
the roof. The car window is smashed and I crawl out onto
the rough asphalt. Pebbles push into my skin. I can smell
my own sweat. It's in my eyes, thickening my eyebrows.
My breathing is ragged.

I use the car to pull myself up. I'm looking at the
construction site. I know this place. I've been here. I've
been stabbed here.

I know where Alison is.

The sirens grow closer as I start to run.

22

They're waiting for me on the top floor. The police tape blocking off the stairway has been ripped in two. I look for blood on the steps and there is none. Doesn't calm me down. I'm about two heartbeats away from cardiac meltdown.

I'm expecting just the two of them. The runner and Swann. Looks like I hit the jackpot, though.

The runner is there. A tall man, slender to the point of starvation, his whole body strangely elongated, almost stretched. Piano-player's fingers, hangdog eyes perched either side of a roman nose. His blond hair stretches to his shoulder blades. Long bangs sweep over porcelain-pale skin. Bastard hasn't even broken a sweat.

Beside him, another man stands, holding Alison's unconscious body—

"Olsted," I say.

"Not exactly." He smiles back. He is not like he was last night, when I was in the apartment with him. He stands taller, more confident. He's not tired. He smiles a lot more.

Progeny. When Alison said they found a lot of scrap metal in the apartment the night before I assumed Olsted had won. But the Progeny didn't need that body to win. It won Olsted's body.

The two Progeny aren't alone. Around them—I count

quickly—five, six, seven creatures that were once human. Now they're something like the student we fought. Twisted by magic into something vast and monstrous— faces pulsing with overgrown veins leer out from between colossal shoulders; arms as thick as tree trunks; fists big enough to make my balls retract into my body.

One has devolved further than the others. His eyes are insectile, fractured. One arm dissolves at the elbow into tentacle-like reams of flesh. His legs end in elephantine paws, feet fully gone. He leers at me, a lolling tongue six feet long or more spilling from a mouth like a gash in his skin.

"You really are a lifesaver," says Olsted, the thing that was once Olsted. "I mean, I should have realized myself that capping the little girl was the best way to crack the old man's nut—" he taps his own head "—but there you were to point the way." He shakes his head. "I was just about ready to give up the ghost and just infect your friend, but it's not like we don't already have eyes in MI37."

He's not looking at me as he says the last. Drops it in like bait and just lets me react. And I have no idea if he's lying or not, but it's way too far off-topic for me to care right now.

"Give me Alison," I say.

The Olsted-thing looks to the runner, who shrugs mutely.

"You're not even a little bit curious?" he says. "Is it the lovely goth girl just dying to sink her claws into young Clyde? Is it Shaw? The ice queen? Is that why she's such a fucking horrible leader? Is it Kayla? Ah, Kayla. Not quite human is she? What she does? And how does she do that? How does my friend here run the way he does? Something else at the wheel, perhaps. Someone not concerned with the limits of your pathetic species' bodies?"

"Give me Alison!" I scream. Every nerve in me is scraped raw. I cannot have this friendly fireside chat. I do not care about the end of the world. Just the end of my world. The end of my friend. Everyone in MI37 could be Progeny for all I care right now.

Olsted sighs. "All business, is it? Well, I must disabuse you of a misunderstanding." He stops there, seems to lose interest, looks over at the runner and rolls his eyes.

"I'll kill you," I say. Quietly. Because I mean it. I actually mean it. In cold blood. Whenever. Wherever. "If you don't give her to me, I'll kill you." No matter what is between us. No matter how many monsters.

"There you go again," says Olsted. "I mean, what on Earth makes you think I'm going to give her back?"

"What," I hiss through teeth clenched so tight I can hear them grating in the gums, "do you want?"

"Ah!" Olsted claps his hands. "We reach the very nubbin of the misunderstanding, the very beating heart of it." He smiles broadly, no humor in it, just a baring of teeth.

"I'm warning you, you bastard."

"Of what exactly?" Olsted spreads his hands. "How do you think you can harm me? What weapon do you have? What forces to support you?"

"I'll think of something."

Behind him the once-men shift their weight, alien muscles bulging in exaggerated poses. Reality punches in at the edges of my fear, my fury. What can I really expect to achieve?

"What," I say again, "do you want?"

"Ah yes." Olsted claps once more. "The misunderstanding. You seem to believe Alison here is a bargaining chip. That she has value. She is not. She does not. She is a demonstration."

Something is off here. Even through the adrenaline-fueled hatred I can feel it. Something greasy in my stomach. Something slipping away from me.

"A demonstration of what?" I ask.

And just like that he snaps her neck.

23

It is like falling through ice into a river. A moment of blinding, almost unbelievable pain—something systemic, a pain that seems intense enough to cause pain itself. And then numb. Nothing. Sensation robbed from me. Yet inside me, some buried pressure building, the need for air, for what has been taken, slowly increasing until it occupies all space.

Olsted drops Alison's broken body. It falls heavily to earth. All its grace is gone. Just meat and bones smacking onto concrete.

"A demonstration—" Olsted is speaking and his words come to me from a great distance filtering through my numbed neurons "—of how little we are scared of you, of how futile your achievements are. We are not afraid of you, Agent Wallace. We are not afraid of MI37. But you, all of you, should be very afraid of us.

"We walk among you, Agent Wallace," Olsted says, "very close, very quiet, and you never know when you're going to piss us off."

"You won't walk so feckin' far without your feckin' legs."

I didn't hear Kayla come up the stairs behind me. I can't think where she has come from. I don't truly care. It just means that this is her problem now. The violence is all her problem. I can just stare at Swann's fallen, broken body, at the terrible awkward angle of her neck, and just collapse in on myself, on what I have lost.

I have lost a friend. I have lost the chance to ever tell her the truth of things.

Kayla moves like liquid fire. She burns across the distance between me and the Progeny. Her blade is out, is up. But the monstrous things are moving in, closing the distance, slow and clumsy as they are compared to Kayla, but massive and close. They form a wall of flesh around Olsted sealing him off.

She is dwarfed before them, waist-height on some. She does not pause, does not hesitate. The pattern of her limbs goes on. She dances up one's outstretched fist, the blade trailing behind her, scoring a spitting wound of pus and blood as the skin and muscle peel from the bone. She jumps sideways, using the sword to lever off another, plunging it in and out of his chest as her feet beat a path across its abdomen, its pectorals. Then she is up and on its shoulder as it falls forward, and she balls up, rolls down its toppling corpse, blade out to one side, churning through the flesh of yet another creature, and she has breached their defense and stands before Olsted.

Except Olsted is gone. The runner has him, cradled as a babe in those thin arms, and together they are hurtling down some pylon wire, a tightrope act in fast forward. And then, one of the four remaining creatures plunges a fist the size of a TV at Kayla and she has to pirouette sideways to avoid the blow, then brings her blade crashing down, smashing through sinew and bone to sever the fist so it rolls away like some incongruous boulder invading this construction yard.

The monster geysers blood, dropping to its knees, howling. Kayla turns back to the wire. Olsted and the runner are on the ground now, a hundred yards or more away. The remaining three monsters smash at Kayla. She dances up their swinging limbs, stands astride the swaying head of one, almost casually reaches out and slits the throats of the other two, then brings the sword down, point first. The skull shatters. The sword sinks to its hilt. The thing falls to its knees. As it does Kayla pulls out the sword, wipes the blade clean on the taut purple skin of the creature's skull. Two quick swipes and then she steps free as it finally crashes to earth.

She looks to the pylon wire, to the earth beyond. There is no sign of Olsted, of the runner. They are gone. We are alone.

I have made it to Alison's body. Crawled on my hands and knees. I have her head in my lap. I am a mess of snot and tears. I can never tell her now. Never tell her anything. All the things to come that I'll never tell her about.

I think Kayla is going to say something. She works her jaw, her tongue coming out, licking her lips once, twice. She looks away from me.

She seems barely human to me there. Gore splattered across her face, soaking her sleeves to the elbows, staining her jeans. There is a piece of shattered bone sticking from one shoe. I wonder if perhaps she will kill me too, if perhaps she cannot stop herself.

"Feck," she says, and then she jumps from the side of the building, and only Alison and I remain.

24

Shaw finds us before the police do. They are milling around the crashed car and the construction site. Uniformed officers are phoning up construction companies worried about entering partially-constructed buildings. They are an ocean of buzzing activity, of static and nonsense, of insignificance.

Up here, on my island, I cling to Alison.

"It's OK, Arthur," Shaw's voice comes from behind me, from the stairs, "you can let her go now."

But I can't.

There are footsteps. She comes closer. "Kayla told me where to find you."

"Kayla." I echo her. It is the first word I have said since Alison... since she...

"She told me what happened."

"Why?" I say.

Shaw pauses. "Wallace..." Again she pauses. "Arthur, let Sergeant Swann—"

"Why didn't she save Alison?" The question comes to me and suddenly seems all-consuming. It seems necessary, as if perhaps in the answer there is meaning to this, as if the signal amongst all this noise lies hidden within Kayla's motives. "Why did she come too late?" I shake my head trying to clear it, but the words won't stop now, they have control because I have none. "She must have known we were here. She found us here. She knew. But she came too late. She chose to come too late."

"She was following you," Shaw says. "I asked her to. After what happened with Olsted I wanted eyes on you, to ensure your safety. I wanted—"

"She followed me. She knew where I was." I am chasing logic. I am in a maze of meaning, circling round and round, trying to find a center that can hold. "She came too late."

"You were doing ninety down Cowley," Shaw says. "Even Kayla has her limits."

"She came too late!" I bellow the words, rip them from my lungs. "She knew. She didn't save Alison. She chose." I shake my head.

"She's not human." I say it. Try out the feel of it. "She's not human," I say it again, grimmer, with more satisfaction, because, yes, that I can hold onto. "Olsted told me," I say, "eyes on us. Spies walk among us. She's not human. She's with them. One of them. She chose to let Alison die. She chose. She knew. She did."

"Agent Wallace!" Shaw's voice is a whip crack. "Put Sergeant Swann down now!"

I stand. I let Alison's head drop. It cracks down on the floor, and with that sound another little piece of me is chipped away. "You're protecting her," I say. "You always protect her." I advance on Shaw. My fists are balled tight. My knuckles are in my palms. "You're with her. You're with them. You're one of them. You. You're... You..."

I can't get the words to work anymore. There is a lump in my throat hard as an iron bar. I cannot swallow. I clack and spit as grief and fury mingle, choked back, ready to burst. And behind the tears there is murder in my eyes. Fury I cannot chase down. I don't want to chase down. An alien anger possessing me: that this fucking woman came into my fucking life, started tearing it fucking down, and she is with them, the Progeny she took Alison, she took, took…

I am going to fucking take the life from her.

I take a step toward her.

"Agent Wallace!"

I pull back my fist.

Her hand lashes out faster than I can track. There is a deep, hollow feeling in my neck. Everything blurs and slips sideways. Everything is dark before I even hit the ground.

25

THEN AND WHEN AND IN-BETWEEN

I'm starting to get the feeling there may be more to this place than just my subconscious fantasies.

Same alley.

Same dead sky.

Same woman dressed in white.

Why do I keep coming back here? What has this got to do with anything?

I stand up. The beautiful woman puts her finger to her lips—a mime's exaggerated mummery. But I don't have the patience for this. I can feel the throb of reality at the back of my head. The dull ache of loss.

"Yes," I say, waving my hand at her. "Hush. I know."

A look of outrage crosses the woman's face, spoiling her prettiness. She looks mean and petty. She suddenly looks mundane, like everyone else. And part of me is glad of that, and part of me is sad, but I can't decide which is the larger part.

She leans in, urgent now, beckoning me closer with one finger. "She is not what you think she is," she says. Then again, "She is not what you think she is."

"Who?" I scream it at her. Because I am tired. Because this doesn't help me. Because I'm at a loss and I have lost. Too much today. Too much. "Just tell me a goddamn name," I ask. I beg. "Tell me!"

The woman's face curdles, twists upon itself. Fury and horror. And then the world frays like a piece of old celluloid. Holes in reality. Voids swallow me, the woman, everything. And I am empty and alone, and then I am not even that.

A COUCH. SOMEWHERE

The first thing that comes back is the pain. The physical pain. A little slap of it to wake me, to ground me back in reality—whatever that is these days. And then a dull ache, radiating out from my neck, pulsing to match the pain in my heart.

Alison.

Fuck.

I try to sit up and try to get my bearings. I don't do very well on either task. The room is small, cramped, bookshelves on three walls, all overflowing, the couch and a doorway jammed against the fourth. The exposed wall is a deep red and mostly covered by a Klimt print I don't recognize. Something from an exhibit at the Tate apparently. Someone is in the next room. I can hear a kettle whistling.

I make it upright, put my head in my hands.

Fuck.

I shouldn't have gone off like that at Shaw. I shouldn't. Especially considering… What exactly did she do to my neck? My whole arm still feels numb. The headache throbs up from the base of my neck, wrapping around my skull, stretching down my shoulder.

Is it Shaw? Is she not what I think she is?

What do I think she is? Friend? Enemy? Kung fu master?

And what is happening to me when I fall unconscious? Where am I going? Does this always happen to people? I've never been knocked out before. Typical really. You wait for one knockout forever and then three come all at once.

But that alleyway doesn't just live in my subconscious. I know that. It's not like I've been doing this job that long, but it's too long for me to keep making that mistake. There's something else going on. Something else to talk about with the team.

God, I don't want to talk to anyone.

Which is, of course, when Clyde comes in with the cups of tea.

"All right, old chap?" he says.

I put my head back in my hands.

"Understandable," he says then stands there awkwardly. He shrugs a few times. After about thirty seconds he holds out a mug. "Fancy a cuppa?"

On the whole, I realize, I rather would. As we sip he sits down beside me. We sit in silence for a while.

"This your place then?" I say after a while. Of course it is, but I need to say something, to get out of the confines of my own aching head.

"Yes. Well, mine and Devon's. Me and Devon and the cats."

"Cats?"

"We have seven cats."

"Wow."

"I like cats." Clyde sips his tea.

"Be tricky if you didn't." It's not a funny joke, just an automatic one. A social reflex.

"True." Clyde nods. We both stare at our cups of tea.

"I'm sorry," I say, finally.

"Whatever for?"

"For punching you. Back at Olsted's. I shouldn't... I mean... I didn't know what else to do. And I suppose... I don't know, maybe I had to do it. Maybe I didn't." I'm waffling, saying nothing. Alison's words echo too fresh in my ear. *Grow a pair.* "I'm sorry," I say, more definitively, though still repetitive. "It had to be done—"

I think it had to be done.

"—but I'm sorry it happened."

"It's all right," Clyde says. "Good plan in the end. Sort of worked out. All except, well, you know, the Progeny in Olsted." He pauses, looks stricken. "Which, I mean, obviously you realize, given…" He pauses again. "I mean. Well, I don't want… Just that… Oh God. Foot. Mouth. Shutting up. Going to be completely silent. No more talking." We sit there quietly, Clyde occasionally muttering the word, "Idiot."

I sit and stare at my feet. Images, moments, keep floating up. Bits of scum coming to the surface. Bodies floating. The image of the runner grabbing Swann. The sweat pouring off me as I took the car onto the sidewalk.

"How do they…" I start. "He wasn't… human. The one who grabbed her. I mean, I know they're not human. But they're in human bodies. How could he run so fast? How couldn't I… How couldn't I catch him?"

"Well." Clyde shuffles his feet and contemplates his tea. "Sort of interesting in a, you know, totally academic way. Horrific in other ways, of course. But you know there's this idea that we don't use all of our brains? Total myth in a very specific sort of way. All sorts of bits of it are useful. But we do all use our brains in, ostensibly, the same ways. This bit connects here. That bit over here. Nowhere else. But the theory is—I can't state any of this for certain you realize—but the theory is that the Progeny rewire stuff. Bugger with the connections. Do things we can't do. Establish neurological parallel processing. They can get more out of the brain than we can. Inhuman thing to do of course. Alien thing. Can make their hosts a little odd. Buggers to deal with. But then, you know… well, yes. I mean you… Shutting up again."

There's more silence. More tea drinking.

After a while I ask, "If I told you that she's not what you think, what would you say?"

"Erm," Clyde makes a final bid for composure, gets close and settles for that, "probably, you know, ask you who you're talking about."

"Yeah," I say. "Same here."

Clyde gives me an odd look.

"Don't worry about it." I can't deal with whatever that means right now. Maybe I should ask the Twins about it. Or the Sheilas. Or Shaw. Unless it's about the Twins. Or the Sheilas. Or Shaw.

Crap.

More silence. More tea.

"So," I say after a while, "how did I get here?"

"Oh," Clyde says, "of course, stupid of me. Should have explained. Shaw said to bring you here. Thought it might be less stressful for you to be out of the office. Didn't want you to be alone."

"Babysitting," I say.

"No, no, no. Nothing like that." He pauses, examines the dregs of his tea. "Well, yes." He shrugs, apologetic. "You know, friendly face and all that."

I smile. Well, I twitch my lips. Smiles still feel a bit beyond me. A friendly face. Except who exactly has a friendly face these days? *We walk among you*, claims Olsted. Claims the Progeny that possesses Olsted. And if he's telling the truth I wouldn't know.

Paranoid thoughts. Maudlin thoughts. The inside of my head is an ugly swill. I put on the smile again.

"Good to know I haven't disappointed everyone down at the agency."

"What are you talking about?" Clyde says.

"Well." I tick off on my fingers. "Kayla thinks I'm a screw-up and she should have stabbed me harder. I just tried to physically attack Shaw. And I'm pretty sure Tabitha wants to use my testicles for golf practice."

"Oh no," Clyde says. "Tabby rather likes you."

Both my eyebrows shoot up.

"You know Tabby," he says. "That's just her way. Hard and crunchy on the outside, soft and gooey on the inside. Like nougat."

"Like what?"

"Bad metaphor." Clyde shakes his head and looks embarrassed.

There is a noise from another room. A key in a lock. A thump of a body against a door. A bustle of clothes. I jump up, knock over my tea. My heart is thudding, my fists balled.

"It's Devon," Clyde says behind me, talking quickly. "Just Devon. Calm down. Nothing to worry about. All fine."

I sit. "Sorry," I say. "Sorry about the tea." A brown stain is spreading across the carpet.

Then Devon comes in, all half-shed coats, and eco-friendly bags.

"Honey, I'm home!" she bellows in a singsong voice, then sees me. "Oh, hello. Visitors is it? Fantastic. Want a cuppa? Oh you've got one. I'll just clean that up." And then she's barreling past me, past Clyde, with a massive peck on the cheek and a cry, "My glorious geek!" and then she's into the kitchen.

Clyde's composure seems to have abruptly left him. His eyes are wide.

"What?"

"Just play along."

"With what?"

And then Devon is back, paper towels clutched in one meaty fist.

"There we go," she says as she completely fails to remove the stain I have created on their carpet. "Good as new." She stands, claps a hand to her forehead. "Good lord," she exclaims, "where have my manners gone? Must have left them out in the hallway. Too much to carry you know. Forget my head one day, won't I? That's what I tell Clyde." She turns, pecks him on the cheek again. "But, God, listen to me. Blather, blather, blather." She grabs my hand and pumps it. The crushing grip manages to make it through the blanket of numbness that envelops me.

"Terribly good to see you again," she says, pumping my arm up and down. She looks over to Clyde, still working my arm, "More drinks?" She examines her watch, finally releasing me. "Little early, isn't it? Sun above the yardarm and all that naval nonsense? Is that naval? Not really sure what a yardarm is, actually. Is it a flagpole? Always rather thought it was. No good rational reason for that, I suppose. Little early though." She clucks theatrically.

Clyde looks like he's about to bolt from the room. "Erm... there was this, er, this meeting—"

"I don't know how you do it," Devon says. "I'd rather top myself than go into accountancy. Terrible at math. All those numbers and symbols. Terrifically bloody boring stuff. To me. Not to you I imagine. Not to Clyde. Loves them he does. Utterly incomprehensible. Like German. I was taught it as a child but it still sounds like monkeys gibbering to me. Can't make head nor tail of it. Me. Not Clyde. Well... Wait, do you speak German, Clyde? Should I know that?"

"No, love," Clyde says distracted. "See we stopped back here for a cup of—"

"No I shouldn't know it, or no you don't know it?"

Clyde blinks rapidly several times. "I don't know German, love."

"I don't think anyone does." Devon nods emphatically. "Not even the Germans. I think they make it up as they go along. Start speaking some other bloody language as soon as our backs are turned. Giant practical joke. I've heard Germans can be surprisingly funny people. You wouldn't think it, but apparently so."

Devon, I notice, has massive square teeth. She gnashes out her words.

"We should probably be getting back to the office," Clyde manages weakly.

"Of course," Devon says. "Beck and call of the books, 'ey? Make sure all the rows and columns add up and all that. Do you wear glasses for it? Don't know why I've never asked you that, Clyde honey. I always imagine you all perched over ledgers with those jeweler's eyeglasses screwed in, peering at stuff. Probably not like that at all. All computers, I suppose. Do it all for you. Probably just sit around and drink tea all day. No, I suppose not. Be nice though, wouldn't it? I could use one of those." She abruptly stares off into space, and I have to imagine that maybe this is where she sucks in the next colossal lungful of air before bursting into the next breathless speech.

Clyde pecks her on the cheek. "See you later, love."

"Yes, yes. Marvelous. Come again, Arthur. That'd be lovely."

"OK," I manage.

Clyde leads me out to the car. We drive in silence. I can't really concentrate on conversation right now. Part of me just wants to get out of the car. Never wants to be in a car again. All I can think about is how slow everything is, how terribly late I feel, about how much faster we need to move to make it... to make it...

I put my face in my hands.

We walk among you.

She is not what you think she is.

Mysteries. Wheels within wheels. I am confused, beaten, and grieving. I want to lie down. Just go to sleep. Give up.

But then... Then this will just happen again. To me. To others. More lives lost. Every life lost. Ophelia first. A sweet little girl.

And who can stop it from happening?

I know some people think it's me. I don't think they're right. After everything, I think they're probably quite mistaken in fact. But does that really mean I shouldn't try? I pull my head out of my hands. Look at the world slowly trundling by. Shouldn't I be looking for a way to go faster? Shouldn't I be looking for a way to stop those Progeny bastards?

Just because I'll probably fail doesn't mean I shouldn't try. And any victory, no matter how small, any chance to see those bastards lose their smug fucking smiles, shouldn't I take that?

What would Kurt Russell do?

A stupid bloody thought. Some idiot mantra based in bad movie choices and a too-quiet life. A philosophy stupid enough to have Hollywood's false promises at its heart. But it takes my anger and it gives it an edge. It takes my fury and it uses it to bury my guilt, my sorrow. It gives me a cruel, cold smile.

I'm going to fight those Progeny bastards, I realize then. There in the car. I'm going to do what Kurt Russell would do. I'm going to fight to win.

"I hate lying to her." Clyde interrupts my thoughts. It takes me a moment to realize he's talking about Devon. "I hate it," he says, "and I do it all the time."

I think about that for a bit. I think about Clyde and Devon at home in their comfortable apartment, the comfortable bustle of the other, the warmth of that place. And then I think about the way I've seen Clyde look at Tabitha.

"It's not like that when you're with someone you work with," I say.

He doesn't answer that, and I don't push it.

HALF AN HOUR LATER

On the way back to my place we get a call to go straight to the conference room. I don't want to go but I grab onto my newfound resolve and give a nod to Clyde's questioning look. Probably the best way to stop Shaw from tenderizing me with karate chops anyway.

The meeting is Tabitha's show again. No laptop this time. Instead she stands at the head of the table trying to navigate a path between her desire to seem like she doesn't give a damn and her palpable excitement.

Shaw looks up as I come in. She gives me a surprisingly soft look. Very decent of her, considering last time I saw her I was trying to murder her.

Kayla's there, too. I take a seat as far away from her as possible—opposite Shaw. I can't look at Kayla without thinking about the rooftop. Without thinking—

We walk among you.

She is not what you think she is.

I glance at her, at Shaw, at Tabitha. And can I really trust the woman in the alleyway? What if what's in my head is Progeny smoke and mirrors? What if they want me paranoid? Should I trust subconscious visitors, or the people in this room, or no one at all?

Tabitha swishes about, all nervous energy. And is that out of character for her? Is that a Progeny screwing up on its acting?

Jesus.

I put my head in my hands again.

"Got some news might cheer you up," Tabitha says.

I look up. And she really is talking to me. I raise my eyebrows. Both of them.

"The Progeny," she says. "We got them by the short and curlies."

26

"We've translated Olsted's book," Tabitha says. "Clyde and me." She favors him with a nod. Then she looks away, a slightly confused expression on her face. I glance at Clyde. And it is a confusing look he's giving her. Not quite happy. Not quite sad. Longing? Suddenly, I wish I'd kept my mouth shut in the car.

"Anyway," Tabitha continues, "translated. The book. Not all of it. Enough. A couple of spells. A whole lot of history. The usual. But not that usual." A grin almost cracks the surface of her face but she manages to suppress it.

"See, Olsted had a book that talks about The Book." The capitalization is audible in her voice. "The Book that begat other books. Big poppa grimoire. The Source."

Clyde taps the table he's so excited. The longing look is replaced with wide-eyed wonderment. Personally, I'm going to keep on working on morose until something actually makes sense.

"The Source is one of the original grimoires," Tabitha says, eyes flicking between Shaw and me. "Most others are derivatives. Copies of fragments. Corruptions. The Source is a big prize. Read lots about it before, but not details. Olsted had details. Now we have them."

Even Shaw is leaning forward in her seat now, so I

figure it's time to start paying attention properly. I fish for a notebook. Tabitha seems to suddenly realize she's the center of attention and starts talking more quickly, trying to wrap things up.

"According to Olsted's book, the Source gets into some fundamentals. Realities intersect like this. Or that. Or this and that. Gives us the rules. Lets us know how to shut other realities out. Lock the door to our reality. Permanently."

Suddenly the grin that's been threatening her face does break through. It's a wicked-looking thing. Probably bludgeoned its way onto her face with an axe.

"No way for the Feeders to get in," she says.

Clyde actually squeaks.

"Oh, and, yeah," Tabitha's grin grows, almost looks like it won't stop, "we've got a map."

Clyde stands up, arms upraised, fists balled. Then he realizes what he just did and sits down very fast. "Sorry," he says. "Little carried away. Academic at work and all that. Always enjoy a breakthrough. Silly of me. Probably shouldn't have—"

"Be quiet, Clyde," Shaw says.

"Good idea," he says.

"This map," Shaw says, speaking to Tabitha now, "we can crack it when Olsted couldn't?"

"Well," Tabitha says, "respect to Olsted, but he's not a government department with an extensive library built on seventy-five years of raiding tombs, museums, and libraries, is he?"

"So," Shaw says, "there's a chance this Source is still where the map is pointing to?"

"Decent one." Tabitha nods.

"Where?" the word bursts out of Clyde. "Where? Where? Where?"

"Where do you think?"

Is Tabitha actually playing it coy? She and Clyde are as bad as each other.

"I knew it!" Clyde bounces in his chair.

"Would one of you care to actually enlighten the rest of us?" Shaw says. Apparently I'm not the only one who thinks something is up between these two. I really should have kept my mouth shut in the car.

"Peru," Tabitha says. "Where Olsted kept going back. But I can get more specific. Did some cross-referencing. Other stuff we had. We need to bloody digitize, by the way. Do some scanning." She pauses, looks at Shaw suspiciously. "Not volunteering."

"Of course not," Shaw says. "You're going to be busy in Peru."

27

There's about fifteen minutes of profanity after Shaw says that. But Tabitha folds in the end. She's going. And once that's settled, it seems like everything's settled. We'll be flying out in the morning. Shaw gives us a time and the location of a military airbase. We stand up and start filing out.

Shaw catches my arm as I get to the door.

"A moment," she says. "Please."

"Sure," I say. And we do need to talk. I don't want to but I think I need to start doing more things I don't want to do. This isn't an action movie; it's a job. Aping Kurt Russell is only going to get me so far.

"About Tabitha," she says, which I wasn't expecting. "She's a good researcher. We recruited her from Oxford after we promoted Clyde. She'd had our eye for a while. Her work is very impressive. And I want you to have the right information when you're out in the field."

Something in her stance, her tone—this isn't what she really wants to talk to me about. It's certainly not what we need to talk about, but I think she knows that too. I think we're both trying to negotiate how to tackle the tricky subjects. Maybe we're more alike than I thought we were.

Shaw opens her mouth but is interrupted by a violent string of vulgarities coming from the corridor outside.

They largely center on the fact that Tabitha is, "a bloody fucking researcher."

"Occasionally she could work on being a better person," Shaw says. "But she is an excellent researcher."

"I'll remember that." It sounds awkward. It is awkward. We're standing in a conference room, but there's a rooftop and my terribly confused attack between us.

"Look," I say. "Sorry about, what I said, what I did, up on…" I look at my feet.

"You're sorry about me hitting that nerve cluster in your neck? I don't think you need to apologize for that." I look up. It's not quite a smile on Shaw's face, but it's something not too far removed.

"I'm sorry you needed to hit it." I twist my neck, stretching the crick that still lingers there. "Sorry you hit it too, actually." And that does get a smile. Wasn't expecting that. Then it fades.

"I'm sorry about your friend," she says.

"Me too." I look away. But I don't want to over-dramatize this. I want to get back to work. I want to do my job. And I want it to hurt the Progeny very badly.

"Kayla's back on the team," I say. Focused. Shop talk.

"You understand why?" she asks me.

"If anything goes the way it normally seems to," I say, "I'll probably be glad to have her along."

Shaw nods. "She's dedicated," she says. "She's an essential weapon against the Progeny. She can be difficult but you should never discount her."

"I won't." I can't promise to trust her either, but Shaw's right—if I'm wrong I'll really regret not having her along. And if I'm right…

If I'm right, then it won't matter whether she's close or far away. We'll all be screwed.

My thoughts are spiraling down again. Down into an

Alison-shaped pit. And I don't want to go there. The best way to deal with everything is to stay out of there. Stay focused.

"We're going to do this one better," I say. "We're going to get the book. We're going to win this."

"I…" Shaw looks suddenly awkward. It doesn't really suit her. She shrugs it off with an expression as if she's swallowing something bitter. "I'm glad you're on board, Agent… Arthur."

"Agent Arthur?"

"I meant Arthur." She closes her eyes, pinches the bridge of her nose. "There's been too much of keeping everyone at arm's length. Enough with titles and formality."

Enough with formality? Maybe she really is Progeny.

Oh balls. That wasn't funny.

"Thank you," I say. "I appreciate the support on this trip."

"You're going to get the book." She smiles again, and it feels genuine. That does suit her.

"Smooth sailing," I say. "We'll be back here with the book before you know it." And for a moment I even believe it.

FIFTEEN HOURS AND OVER SIX THOUSAND MILES LATER

I really should go hunting for long-lost grimoires more often. Yes, the flights are long, and military planes seem to have been involved in some warped design competition to produce a seat with no comfortable parts, but when you get where you're going…

Yes. Most definitely, yes.

I can feel Oxford, the detritus of the past week sloughing away. There are no clouds, no rain; there is no craggy, ancient limestone. And there is a charm to that, to Oxford, of course, but this… Peru…

Massive open skies, patchwork fields and then jagged

peaks jutting up—green and gray—like the world has teeth. There's a sense of space, of breathing room. Here I can see Clyde, Kayla, Tabitha, the pilot, and the van driver—his smile a broken mosaic of mismatched teeth—but that's it. All of it. I feel lighter. Freer.

Clyde keeps turning with the camera. I assume it's a panorama shot he's going for until I realize he's tracking Tabitha around the plane. Her dark legs, dense with angels, demons, and seventies' metal icons etched in white ink, and some very short shorts seem to have him hypnotized. I think of Devon again, her bustle and hurry and warmth. But I don't think Clyde is.

Totally shouldn't have said anything in the car.

The van can get us within two miles of the temple the grimoire, The Source, is supposedly at. After that, apparently, it's pretty much vertical, but a little exercise can't hurt. At least, not as much as the Progeny or one of their creatures.

Clyde and Tabitha sit in the front, as they apparently know where we're going, or have mapped it out on Google, or something. Tabitha's laptop is open anyhow and they're both hunched over it.

I'm in the back of the van with Kayla. We sit in silence. I try to think of something warm and witty and general ice-breakery to say, but instead all I think—

She is not what you think she is.

I have to say, that would be my first move if I were a hideous mind parasite. Get in the head of the person trying to wipe me out.

But she did save me. Only a couple of yards from where she almost killed me. Without her I'd have been torn apart.

"Thank you," I say finally. It sounds as awkward as I feel. Kayla turns and looks at me, a look of confusion and irritation. "For on the rooftop," I say. "For coming."

Kayla keeps staring at me. "Feck off," she says finally.

Not a butterfly kiss on the cheek but she didn't stab me, so that definitely could have gone worse.

I'm still working on a follow-up when the van pulls to a stop. The road has devolved into mud and now just stops entirely. Most of what is beyond us is above us. Rough rock and scree.

"It's up there." Tabitha points. "Buried." She yanks a smartphone from her pocket and reads, "Under sky, under earth, under stone, underneath notice, hidden from the eye of the jealous Lord, it slumbers. Enter its chambers as the snake is cursed. At the base of the forbidden tree." She looks up.

Kayla, ignoring the rest of us, is already several hundred feet up the mountainside.

"What does that mean?" I ask.

"Religious references," Tabitha says. "Snake. Forbidden tree. Adam and Eve. Apple. Apple tree. Something we have to crawl into on our bellies."

"Wait," I say, because I feel like I just spotted a flaw in this plan too late, "when was this grimoire of Olsted's written?"

"About four to five hundred years ago," Clyde chips in. "I mean, give or take. Basing that on some of the grammar usage, way the book was bound, et cetera, et cetera. Nothing definitive. Ballparking you really. Didn't carbon-date it or anything. Too much paperwork, you know. No, probably don't. Why would you? Silly thing to say really. Don't know…" He notices Tabitha and I staring at him. "Apologies. Sorry. Shutting up now. Being quiet—"

"But," I say, "wouldn't the tree have died about… forever ago?"

"Well, a five-thousand-year-old pine tree was chopped down in the United States in the sixties," Clyde says. "I mean, that's an extreme example. Not many that old.

Well maybe, could be, just people get bored counting the rings. But probably not. That's probably silly. And five hundred years is an old tree. Of course. Not insignificant. But it's possible."

"Course," says Tabitha, "could just give up. Go home. Let Ophelia live up to her name. Let the Feeders come through." She raises an eyebrow at me. Just one.

"No," I say, "I wasn't—" But I was. "Fair point," I say. "Best foot forward, everybody."

Tabitha rolls her eyes while I roll up my sleeves and prepare for the mother of all scavenger hunts.

Suddenly, Kayla lands in the center of our little circle. She drops to one knee. Dust and sticks billow up around us in the small shockwave of her landing. I look up trying to work out how far she just jumped down. But I have to keep on looking up and up and up and on second thoughts, maybe I don't want to know. I'm going to be up there soon.

"Found it," she says.

Tabitha gives me the finger again and heads off up the steep incline. After a moment, I follow.

28

NEXT MORNING

The sunrise is glorious. Almost hymnal. We're camped up on the mountain outside the tunnel entrance. It took Kayla five minutes to climb up to it. Took the rest of us closer to five hours, lugging our backpacks of equipment. The last hour wasn't the most fun. And considering the mountain had already handed our asses to us we thought we'd wait to give ancient Peruvian magic a break until morning. But this morning, this mountain daybreak... yesterday's exhaustion was worth it. Most definitely worth it.

The apple tree is still growing here. It's gnarled, mostly dead, and it wouldn't be too hard to confuse its two growing apples with walnuts, but it is still here. It's almost more impressive for being in such a state. If it was a disco song I think it'd be Gloria Gaynor's "I Will Survive." But it's not. It's an apple tree.

I sit with my back to it and use the satellite phone I lugged up the slopes to call Shaw back in England. Let her know what's happening.

"Good morning." Shaw's voice is brisk and surprisingly clear after I fumble my way through a couple of security passwords I was given. "How's the search for the temple going?"

"Sitting right outside it," I say.

"Excellent news." Shaw sounds genuinely pleased.

"We'll be heading in shortly," I say.

"You've got a plan, in case you run into trouble?"

"Does letting Kayla go first count?"

There is a sound from the other end of the line and for a moment I can't think what it might have been.

"Director Shaw," I say, "did I just make you laugh?"

"Just because we're not being so formal, Arthur, doesn't mean we're being flippant."

Except… is she being flippant?

"Yes ma'am," I say. Just in case she's not.

"Do you have a plan?" Formal. Whatever that moment was we're back to business.

"The book's pretty light on specifics," I say. "So we're flying a bit blind. We'll just take things slowly, not rush in. I'm more than happy to pull out and reassess if things feel off."

"The Peruvian weather agrees with you, does it?"

I actually smile at that. The first time since… since Alison was killed. And here I am, in a foreign country, halfway up a mountain, staring at light spilling into a valley beyond, and I'm smiling.

"Yes," I say, "I think it does."

"I'd like to see that," says Shaw. Which seems an odd thing to say and for a moment I'm not quite sure how to respond. Shaw seems to fumble about as much as I do.

"Well…" She coughs. "Yes. Well, I'd appreciate updates on your progress. And a full debrief when you get back here. There's a lot we might be able to learn here. And not just about the Progeny. There's a lot of gaps in our knowledge this book, The Source, might be able to fill."

"That sounds doable," I say, still wondering about the weather comment. But then I turn, look back at the camp, and catch sight of the hole leading to the cave. The cloud to all this silver lining. "You're assuming, of course, that when I get back I'll still have a vital function or two left."

"You might be surprised by my faith." It actually sounds like I might.

Clyde's disheveled head appears through a tent flap. He nods sleepily at me.

"I should go," I say. "I'll report back once we're out of the temple, let you know how it all went, how many limbs we lost, that sort of thing."

"Excellent." There's no humor in Shaw's reply but there might still be a touch of warmth. It's nice to hear. Odd. But nice. "I look forward to it," she adds and then clicks off before I can say anything else.

AN HOUR LATER

The glory of the sunrise fades the deeper into the earth I go. Cold rock and dirt envelop me. I find myself wishing there had been a Starbucks near the apple tree. They do seem to be pretty much everywhere else.

Kayla leads the way, as that only seems sensible, then me, grubbing along on my belly just like the snake, post-Biblical curse. Then it's Tabitha because, and I may have used Hollywood logic here a bit, in most movies that seems to be the safest place to be. Surprised no one called me on that… Then there's Clyde to occupy the being-picked-off position. But I think he might have volunteered for it because it means he can stare at Tabitha's legs some more.

I'm beginning to suspect Tabitha's noticed the increased level of attention, though I'm not sure she's interpreting it correctly. I overheard her asking Kayla if there was a stain on her shorts.

We've gone about a hundred yards and I'm starting to think that while he knew all about ancient apple trees, Olsted's author might have known less about hidden

Peruvian temples, when finally the space opens up ahead. The light on my headlamp spills out, first over Kayla's ankles, and then, as she steps out the way and I fully emerge, over craggy moss-dotted rock. Tabitha and Clyde emerge as I swing my headlamp around, illuminating the massive cave.

Four beams of light reach out from our helmets, like the fingers of some giant hand. They trace the limits of the walls. And some of the dawn's beauty is recaptured as we stand there in the darkness.

The cave's ceiling seems incredibly distant—a great cathedral-like arc. Roots have pushed through the rough rock, some dangling like patches of fur, others that are great thick twisting things, broad as I am, which, admittedly, is not particularly broad or anything to be remarked at in a person, but which in a root may, I think, be noted as being of significance.

We circle the space slowly. And then, one by one, the fingers of light come to rest on the same point: carved into one massive slab of rock—an archway. And it's not just something somebody hacked away, even though that would hardly be an achievement to be sniffed at, but someone really went above and beyond here. Twisting, carved figures, baroque details, pictogram script. It's beautiful.

Tabitha is the first to speak.

"Bugger me," she says.

And somehow the arch has enough poetry in it to make up for Tabitha's lack.

While it's tempting to just stand and stare, the headtorches are on battery power and we're trying to conserve that for Clyde. So I give Kayla the nod, and she's not one to stand around gawping, so off we go again. I ask Clyde to walk in front of Tabitha this time. I hope it's not obvious, but I have the feeling we're going to need him undistracted later on.

The corridors of the place are choked with roots. As we pick our way between them we catch occasional glimpses of intricate wall carvings—people lost to time frozen in poses, raising livestock, tilling fields, worshiping absent gods.

Here and there in the carvings I see a giant figure dominating all the others. The muscles are curiously exaggerated and I think of the magically twisted creatures that the Progeny seem to employ as shock troops. There is something different here, though. The figures are more graceful. Still, it's doubtful any of the art is truly representational. These giant figures, for all their decoration, have utterly blank faces, not a single feature described—seems unlikely we'll have to worry about them.

After ten minutes or so of twisting between the roots I see light up ahead. The space opens up into a square carved as decoratively as everything else we've seen. The roof has two long cracks that shed trickles of rainwater onto thick patches of moss. Massive roots hang down like so many stalactites.

At the center of the room are four statues, far more detailed than anything we've seen before. Four representations of the faceless figures. They're no longer giants. Just average-looking men. At least, in the way Arnold Schwarzenegger is an average-looking man. They all sit, muscle-bound and silent, back to back in a tight square, one facing each corner of the room.

"I've seen them," Clyde says, "on the walls."

"Probably religious," Tabitha says, squatting, opening the laptop. "Or royal. More important than most. Why they're carved so big."

Kayla circles the room, giving the statues a wide berth. I'm inclined to agree with her trepidation, but on the other hand there's a slim chance I may have seen one too many action movies. Clyde, however, does not seem to feel any caution. He peers at one's face.

"They're masks," he says. "They're wearing masks. That's why the faces look so blank."

"Masks?" Tabitha asks, looking up from the glare of her computer screen.

"Yes," Clyde says, nodding. "I can see straps round the back. Two of them: one above the ear, one below. About an inch thick. Bald heads beneath. Workmanship on these is pretty much amazing. I don't think stonework like this should have even been possible."

"Masks. Two straps." Tabitha taps more. "Fuck. Please tell me they're not wooden. I cannot be dealing with the Monks of Queatel today. Not tomorrow either."

The elevator operator in my stomach presses the down button. Here we go. Kayla keeps circling the statues.

"Don't know," Clyde says, "looks like stone." He reaches out a hand.

"No!" I bark, but it's too late. His knuckle taps the mask. A hollow, distinctly wooden sound.

The statue moves instantly. I barely even see it stand up, but suddenly it's vertical, a hand gripping Clyde's extended arm. His face distorts in pain. Then a fist or a foot, or something else too fast to see, buries itself in Clyde's midriff and he flies ten feet across the floor.

The other four statues are on their feet. Quick as blinking. Not statues at all. Or if they are, they move like men. Four colossal monks, wearing masks, sitting utterly still, covered in dust and grime, waiting. And waiting. And now they move. I see their muscles move. Flesh and bone, just like me. But they move so bloody fast. Move a way I never could. They move like Kayla.

She comes at them with terrifying speed. Inhuman speed. *She is not what you think she is.*

Her sword comes up. Comes down.

And one of the bastards catches it.

He claps his hands together and holds the blade there suspended three inches from his face.

Kayla grimaces, pushes. I see the muscles in the monk's arms knot. And I've seen this movie. This is the bit where he snaps the blade, attacks her with the tip.

Kayla goes with the motion. Her face relaxes. She jumps, moves with the monk's straining muscles, and spins in the air. He carries her up over his head. She twists. Her knees clamp tight. Locks them around the back of his head. And she brings him down. Lands kneeling, crushing his head between thigh and calf.

But another masked figure is there. He slams a fist at Kayla. She blocks, pushing it aside, as the monk she's sitting on bucks and thrashes beneath her. Then the third figure comes in, then the fourth. Blows rain down. Kayla's hands and blade are a blur. And then there is a cracking sound and Kayla flies out of the group. The four figures rise, limbs flexing, as Kayla is tossed aside like so much firewood.

29

Clyde comes around at about the same time Kayla lands next to him. Her head cracks against the stone floor. Blood flows. Not good. Not even vaguely good. Way beyond bad, even.

The four masked figures start spreading out, a loose semicircle fanned out before us.

Clyde rolls over, vomits onto Tabitha's knees. She's kneeling next to him. I'm not sure how she got there. It doesn't seem very Tabitha-like. Especially not when she wipes the corner of his mouth with one frilly sleeve.

"Get up," she says to him. "You stupid bugger."

Kayla beats him to it. An abrupt kippup and she's on her feet, heading off toward the clenching fist of figures. At first I think my vision is still off. Everything is a blur. But then I realize that it's not me, but the speed the five of them are fighting at. I can't track a single limb. They're all moving at fantastic speeds and I can only catch glimpses of movement. A raised sword. A fist drawn back. A deflected kick wheeling away.

There is something breathtaking about the whole thing, something almost as wonderful as it is horrible. Something like ballet. But, when I glimpse it, I can see a look of absolute fury on Kayla's face, something desperate and something terrified.

I think of the Twins. I think of Ephie saying quite calmly that Kayla can't save Ophelia. That must be what Kayla is thinking now. She's being held in place. Total stalemate.

"We have to do something," I say. Helplessly. Because I can't think of any way to help.

"Be my guest." Tabby stands, supporting Clyde. And despite the flippancy, I can see anxiety and frustration written all over her face. Because I'm right.

"Rocks," I say. "We need to throw rocks."

"What?" Tabby shakes her head. "What if you hit Kayla?"

"There are more monks," I say, even as I realize I'm not really thinking straight. "We're more likely to hit one of them."

"But what if you hit Kayla?" Tabby's question has grown teeth while I answered.

"I hate to be constantly siding with Tabby against you, Arthur," Clyde starts.

"I know," I say. "I know. But something. There has to be something…"

We stand helplessly, like absurd spectators as the four masked men pound on Kayla's ever-twisting defense.

Can we just slip by them? While she holds them at bay? Leave her keeping this problem trapped in stasis?

Except… well, sod it, she may have come too late on the rooftop for Alison, but she did come. She tried. So unless I know for sure she's Progeny, no, I can't leave her behind. There's got to be something we can do.

"Tabitha," I say, "we need to know about these things. Anything. Everything. Whatever we can." I grab her by the shoulder. "Right now. Please."

She blinks, nods, disengages from Clyde who is clinging to her like a drowning man. She grabs her laptop.

Behind me I can hear Kayla grunting with exertion, her

breath coming in whoops and gasps.

"OK," says Tabitha. "Monks of Queatel. Masks... Recorded memory. Very advanced. Close to magic. Maybe magic. I'm not sure."

Behind us steel smacks flesh and flesh smacks steel back.

"Come on," I say.

"Circuits beneath the wood. Old monks' brains written in zeroes and ones. Put on the mask, put on the monk. Personality override. So you train one bugger instead of generations."

A shower of sparks lights up the room as Kayla's sword rebounds at speed, carving a jagged channel through the stone.

"So..." The gears of my brain churn more than my adrenaline wants them to. "Take off the masks. Turn off the monk."

"Kick the bloke's arse," Tabitha supplies.

All five figures are off the ground. Limbs pinwheel in midair. Limbs snap out at awkward angles. Knuckles pound skin and wood.

"How do we take the masks off?" I say. Next logical step.

"Erm..." Tabitha says. I echo the sentiment.

Kayla lands first, whips out her sword. Monks land on the flat of the blade, balance there. Impossibly. Kayla dodges kicks to the head.

"I have an idea," Clyde says. He speaks quietly at first, hesitant.

"Yes?" Tabitha and I both wheel on him. He half recoils. I nearly grab him by the lapels. This is not the time for tentative modesty.

Kayla ducks as four blows reign down in a single instant. The monks' fists slam together. I feel the shock wave where we stand.

"Well… it's probably not a good idea…"

"Tell us!" My voice almost cracks as I yell.

"Sorry," Clyde says, then sees the expressions Tabitha and I are wearing and finally spits it out. "Well, the masks… magical, electric. There is a chance that I could, so to speak, in a sort of manner—"

Kayla reels back as a kick catches her in the stomach. Another grazes her lips. Enough to draw blood. She catches the third blow but the monk twists away. She barely ducks the fourth.

"Say it!" Tabitha does grab Clyde by his collar.

"I think I could hack one."

Tabitha and I exchange a genuine look of astonishment.

Kayla lands a blow. A monk staggers into another. She lands a kick. Then a monk has her leg and the dance begins again.

"Say again?" I say to Clyde.

"Well," he says, "with Tabby's laptop, the wireless stuff, I could perhaps… it's a form of, erm, well in layman's terms it's sort of astral projection, spirit leaving the body sort of stuff. Never really tried it before. Read about it. Get my, you know, mind, soul, spirit thing out of the old flesh and bones—" he taps his chest "—and into the mask. Then I just overwrite what's written there with my own personality, which, I have to concede is a little short on the ninja monk training. Probably obvious really. Good on French composers of the twenties to be certain, but again, a little lacking in ninjujitsu and so forth. So then, while that masked chappy has his posterior handed to him by Kayla, hopefully breaking the deadlock, I hoof it back to the old body thing and hope I haven't made a really bad mistake."

"Mistake?" I say. "What sort of mistake."

Kayla goes down for a moment. Four savage punches

later she's on her feet but one side of her head is caked in blood.

"Oh." Clyde shrugs. "You know, usual. Completely failing to overwrite the mask, and having the monk dump his personality into my body as well. Which is pretty much sayonara for me and throws another monk into the mix. Standard we-all-die-horribly-sort of stuff."

Kayla is against a wall. She looks tired. The monks don't.

"Anybody able to come up with a better plan in the next ten seconds?" I count to five and then just abandon that one. "You want to go for this, Clyde?"

"Not particularly."

Kayla dances against the wall, blows chasing her.

Of course he doesn't. Who would. "Can I—" I start.

"I'll do it," Clyde says. "Has to be me. Specialization and copper wiring and all that. Tabby," he turns to her, "I don't suppose you could pass me the laptop, and then catch me when I fall over?"

"I'll catch the laptop," she says.

With it in hand, Clyde pulls out two thin strips of copper from a pocket. He jams one in on either side of the battery. He sits cross-legged with it on his lap. "Once I start," he says, "I can't let go. Otherwise the circuit breaks, inter-reality friction, and kablammo for everyone."

I remember the explosion that took apart the student in Cowley Road. "Duly noted," I say.

Clyde starts muttering, one incomprehensible word, then another. Then he grabs the strips and immediately keels over.

The four monks press Kayla harder. I can see her sword blows now. Slower. They're wearing her down. Each time she slices with the blade a forearm, or a palm, or a calf, or heel strikes the flat of the blade knocking it off course.

They constantly circle, two monks working high, raining down blows, while two strike low. She's pinned in and she knows it. She tries to spin free but is forced to break into a series of parries and thrusts that the masked monks twist around.

Clyde's body convulses, once, twice. I see Tabitha biting her lip.

Kayla jumps, a fist lands on the side of her head and she crashes down. She spins like a dancer. One monk jumps the kick, another, another.

The fourth monk falls.

He stands there staring dazedly at Kayla and then her legs smash into his. A jagged extra angle appears in his legs as the bone shatters. And then he falls, like someone pulled the plug from him. He crashes to the ground and her sword finds his throat as the mask rolls free.

The other three monks pause. And that's all Kayla seems to need.

Suddenly her sword blade is through the mask of one, protruding from the back of his skull. The front of the wound spits sparks, the back blood.

The other two monks start moving, but Kayla is levering off the sword even as the speared man falls, arching up into the air. She catches her initial attacker with the same trick she first used, catching the mask behind her knees, crushing down. There is a splintering sound, a burst of electricity, and then the third monk goes limp.

The fourth and final monk leaps at Kayla as she lands on her knees. She whips her legs out from under her so fast I can hear the wind cracking behind them. Her feet go into the man's chest, keep going. She lifts him over her head, rolling onto her back, pivoting on her shoulders as she grasps his hands, swinging him down to earth in a vast curve. And still she holds him as his face plows into the rock. She holds on, rising up, flying over him. She lands between his flailing legs. Steps onto his back. Puts a foot onto his spine. She pulls his arms hard. The joints pop loudly and the shoulders dislocate.

The monk lies insensible at Kayla's feet, legs kicking. She flips him over, raises a foot, buries it in his face. The mask caves inward and he goes limp. Blood pools around his head.

"There," she says, "that's you in your feckin' place."

30

Still Clyde just lies there. A low babble emerges from him, like the muttering of a mad man. Tabitha and I kneel, looking at his twitching lips, the hands clenched spastically around the copper strips attached to the laptop. The muscles of his arms are convulsing slightly. Drool is beginning to trickle down his cheek.

It doesn't look particularly good.

"Come on," Tabitha says. She puts a hand in his hair. A tender gesture. Not Tabitha's style at all. "Come on, Clyde," she says again.

"What the feck's up with him?" Kayla hasn't approached, still stands over the collapsed body of the last monk.

Tabitha stands. "Don't fucking start. I don't give a shit what you can fucking do. I'll fucking neuter you. You fucking understand? Not the time for your fucking shit right now."

"Any time." Kayla barely breathes the words, but Tabitha catches them all the same. She lunges.

I grab Tabitha's arm, haul her back. She fights against me. "Not now," I hiss. "Any time but now. Clyde needs help now." Tabitha strains once more then gives up, goes to stalk away then kneels next to Clyde again.

"You," I say to Kayla, then lose my nerve. "Just…

Jesus." I shake my head. "He saved your arse from getting kicked. All of our arses."

"Not what I was feckin' asking." Kayla shrugs, stays where she is, stares at me, as if daring me to disagree. I'm not about to. Kayla genuinely pissed off seems even more homicidal than she does in her usual bad mood.

I turn my back on her, kneel down next to Tabitha and Clyde. He has the laptop on his chest, like a knight laid to rest still gripping his sword.

Tabitha looks at me. Underneath the make-up she looks small and scared. "I don't know what to do," she says.

I don't either. "Maybe the sound of your voice," I say. It's the best thing I can think of. Because if Clyde would come back for anything, I think, it would be Tabitha. "Maybe that could ground him."

"Yes," says a weak voice, "I think that would be lovely."

We both stare down at Clyde. He has one eye half cracked. With a grunt he lets go of the copper strips. "Ow," he says.

Tabitha lets out a very un-Tabitha-like squeal and bounces on her knees. She dips her head down for an instant as if about to plant a kiss on his forehead, or cheek, or... well, that's when she seems to remember herself. She pulls up sharply, sneers at Clyde. "Gormless prat," she says.

Clyde cracks a tired smile. "I missed you too," he says.

She smiles at that. I think of Devon, look at the two of them, and think maybe it wouldn't be such a downgrade after all if Clyde decided to make the trade.

"If he's all feckin' right," Kayla says, "can we get moving, grab this book and get the feck out of here?"

"What?" I ask. I'm so elated I even find that I momentarily have the balls to ask, "This place giving you the creeps?"

"Feck off."

217

Together Tabitha and I get Clyde to his feet. Tabitha reclaims her laptop.

"That seemed to work," I say to him.

"More or less."

"More or less?" That doesn't sound as reassuring as maybe I'd like from a man who just violated the rules of pretty much all the sciences I can think of.

"Well," Clyde shrugs, "I do seem inexplicably to know fifteen ways to kill you with my little finger now."

"Bloody hell," I say, as I try to grapple with the concept of someone with Kayla's skills and Clyde's disposition.

Clyde cracks a grin. "Having you on, I'm afraid. Absolutely fine, actually. Bugger of a headache, but that seems to be it on the side effects front. Plus…" He bends and lifts up the mask that rolled free from the first man to fall. It is the only one left still in one piece. "Now we have an extra copy of me."

"Oh fan-fucking-tastic," says Tabitha, but she's still smiling.

Using the straps of the thing, Clyde slips the mask up his arm until it's on his shoulder. "Armor," he says. "Never know when I'm going to get smacked on the shoulder. Could happen at any instant." He's grinning like a fool.

"So, you're telling us," I say, "that your copy is even thicker-headed than you."

Clyde thinks about that one. "Hmm," he says. "Yes. Bugger."

"I'm not waiting another feckin' moment." Kayla stalks off toward a tunnel.

Clyde looks at her, shrugs at us, and then scampers after her. Tabitha and I follow in their wake.

Whoever carved this place seemed to think the monks would be enough to deter most people, and we don't have far to go before we hit the main chamber of the temple. If anything, it's even more cavernous than the one the monks were in. The sense of grandeur is different, though. The architects dialed down the pomp, and turned the sinister up to eleven. The light that filters down from the fissures in the ceiling is thin, weak, as if reluctant to enter. I kind of regret teasing Kayla about the place giving her the creeps.

But the book is there. It stands on a plinth that rises from a circular platform in the center of the room. No moss grows there; no water has collected. Even the light seems thinner there. It is as if there is a slight pressure emanating from the center of the room, from the book itself, a subtle throbbing in the air. Clyde rubs his temples.

"Goes right down my wires, that does," he says and shudders.

"That's our book, for definite?" I ask.

"No," Tabitha says. "Planted a book so powerful it disturbs the bloody ether as a distraction. Dumbarse."

Nothing has changed in Tabitha's disposition, but I think I'm beginning to understand how she works a little bit more. That insult almost sounded like a form of endearment.

The four of us approach the plinth. I feel the resistance in the air and have to push harder with my feet to step up onto the circular platform—a small stage in the round.

For a moment it seems as if the walls around us fluctuate. There is a rustling from a dangling clump of ivy, a cracking sound from the thick roots. Then nothing. Just silence. Just stillness.

"Well," I say, "at least that wasn't creepy."

"Just take it," Tabitha says.

I reach out a hand. The book has a cover so black it could be a tear in reality. The spine is exposed. Age-stained pages sprout rotted twists of thread. The thing is over four inches thick. My hand pauses, shaking. The book is pushing back, pushing against me.

"How sure are we that this isn't a horrible trap?" I ask.

"About as sure as we were that those four guys were statues," Tabitha supplies.

"Excellent." I nod.

"Oh, I'll take the feckin' thing." Kayla reaches for it.

"Wait," I say. I catch her eye. And it's... well... *She is not what I think.* Or... Just... What if she's not? What if she's not? I can't take that risk. I can't let her touch this book.

"No," I say, with a certain amount of force.

She rolls her eyes and goes to take the book. I reach out and snatch the book, grabbing it off the plinth, from under her fingers.

She looks at me. She could have beaten me if she wanted. It's in her expression. She's indulging me.

"Children," Tabitha starts.

And then something starts to hum. A building whine that sounds like—

"Tell me that doesn't sound like a generator," Tabitha says. "Tell me."

But it does.

Sparks suddenly arc across the floor, blue light sputtering from puddle to puddle. They crackle and spit. And then the walls start to rumble. A deep, thundering bass that starts in my gut long before it makes it to my ears. The noise builds though, layers upon layers of sound—stone grinding on stone, water splashing, roots rustling and cracking. The noise builds and then it's not just the noise that is making me shake, but the very floor of the place quivers like a live thing. Clyde drops to one knee.

I look down at the book. And I really did like it when magic was something cool, when it was something Egg Shen chucked at Lo Pan in *Big Trouble in Little China*, and not something that tried to pound on me like a meat tenderizer.

The shaking intensifies. I have to grab hold of the plinth with one hand, the other clutching the book to my chest. Clyde and Tabitha are on all fours. Only Kayla stands free, seems to ride the shivering floor like a surfer navigating rough seas.

And then silence. Absolute stillness. Nothing. We all stand perfectly still.

"Maybe it's broken." Clyde speaks into the settling dust. "An old mechanism. The whole place is old. Maybe it just stopped."

"Do you really believe that?" I ask. And I rather hope he does.

"Not at all." Clyde looks miserable.

And it's at that point the stone plinth whips around like a spring sapling and hits me.

I stagger back. The plinth rears up like a snake. Then the broad flat top plunges into my midriff lifting me off the ground and slamming me off the platform and onto the ground.

The floor beneath me bucks like a bronco. I roll, head over heel, over arse and elbow. My head smacks into the floor. Then the floor smacks me back. A flagstone rises from the floor, catches me on the edge of my jaw. I sprawl back, fight for my feet, but there is no solid ground to gain purchase on.

I hear a crashing sound. Regular. Pounding. In a moment of nearly-grasped verticality I see the archway we came through contracting, slamming down the ground, a great blunt guillotine. The floor bucks again, sends me sailing toward it.

I scramble on the rough rock, find purchase in the space between floor slabs, jam my fingertips into the gap.

The floor heaves under me. I hang on. Then the floor slabs slam together crushing my fingers.

I howl in pain, release my grasp. Then the floor bucks and I sail through the air once more. The gnashing doorway looms.

31

I snag my foot on a vine, spin away from the door. I'm still falling. Falling sideways. And then I stop.

I don't know if I hit the wall or it hits me. It closes like a catcher's mitt around me. Then I'm thrown. Then I'm flying down the length of the wall, a great propelling hand of stone, shoving me in a stumbling sweep. The doorway. It's pushing me toward the doorway.

I do rather wish that fighting psychotic animated temples wasn't in my job description. Or, at least that I was prepared to deal with it.

I can see Tabitha, Clyde, and Kayla all bunched in the center of the room, trying to keep out of range of the sparring plinth. Pillars detach from the walls, sweep in long arcs, try to crunch their bones. Jags of floor try to spear them.

But they survive, they succeed, they fight back. Kayla and Clyde can do this stuff. They can achieve things against these odds. They have talents here.

I heave myself away from the wall. For a moment I stand still. A tiny oasis of calm in the madness. I can see Kayla actually blocking blows from the wall with her sword. And they drive her back, they physically move her, but she's OK. She's on her feet. She's mastering this situation, whatever it is.

Clyde has his hands up, has batteries hanging out of his mouth. Stone is hitting something invisible around him, some force field, some magic bollocks. Tabitha is huddled at his feet, clutching her laptop, as if somehow that will help, will let her survive, but it's Clyde that is keeping her safe, doing the white knight shit. He can do it.

Me? All I can do is stand here until my feet get taken out by a stone a rock wall spits at me.

Another blow to the head. The world spins. I can't tell if it's really spinning or if it's just my consciousness skipping a few beats. And there's the wall again. I taste it. Feel it. I hear the archway slamming down. I fight for finger holds, for any hold. Heave myself off the wall again. Jump something. Trip on something else. Crawl away.

And then feet are running past me. Clyde holding Tabitha's hand. Ta-ta, see you later. Nice knowing you. The pair of them fleeing the scene. And then I'm up, off the turbulent floor. Not sure how, until I realize it's Kayla grabbing me, pulling me.

"Feck this for a laugh," she says.

"The doorway—" I say, but then the doorway explodes. Stone dust fills the air. Kayla bats chunks away with her blade. Clyde is running forward, one arm outstretched, spitting batteries. More rock shatters itself on the invisible battering ram he holds out in front of us. I stagger along in their wake. And not for a moment does Clyde let go of Tabitha's arm. And if he was looking to impress a girl, that is some pretty bloody impressive white knight behavior right there.

The masked monks' room passes in a flash, then we're all through the next archway. Into the next corridor. Running hard. Pushing past roots. Everything still. All quiet.

Then the light disappears. Behind us, the archway closes up. Shuts tight as a sphincter. We flick our headlamps on.

We don't need to know what's happening. We hear the rumbling, the rock roar. The tight knot of rock is coming closer, the corridor clamping down to nothing, closing up, coming to crush us.

Kayla bodily shoves Clyde out of the way. Her blade is already a blur. Roots fly everywhere, and she carves a path forward. My head is still spinning. Tabitha loses grip on her laptop. Clyde pulls her on even as she grabs for it, even as the collapsing rock crushes it to a few plastic splinters. All the data, all the intel, all gone.

Then I'm gone too. Running. One foot in front of the other. Desperately trying to keep up with Kayla. Roots she missed explode behind me as the corridor shrinks and shrinks.

Then our headlamps light up a wall. A dead end. There is no welcoming archway, no light at the end of the tunnel. The other end of the corridor has closed up too. We're trapped in a shrinking pocket of stone. As if two hands are squeezing the ends of the corridor. Coming to squeeze us. Trapped. Dead.

Clyde lets go of Tabitha's hand. He pushes out with both his arms, braces his legs. He bellows something. Sprays batteries as he does it. The smell of ozone is crisp in the air. Static crackles in my hair. The air shudders, becomes dense. Like the book on the plinth. Everything is still. Then everything quakes. It's like looking through a heat haze.

Clyde's nose is bleeding. His ears are bleeding.

Then a detonation. An explosion. The rocks before us explode back, crash away. And there, right there—I can see our way out.

Now that is bloody impressive white knight behavior, right there.

But then rocks are falling. Earth is falling. Everything

is falling. The whole place starting to give away, to cave in around us.

Our charge out is blind and panicked. I trip but don't stop. I scrabble on all fours, on just my legs, just my hands. Anything that will propel me. We're in the final chamber, then in the final tunnel out to fresh air, grubbing forward, onward, out, and up. Not thinking of anything but escape.

Then open air. Then sunlight. Then I breathe. A great gasp of air. I can feel everything shaking. My face, my arms, my hands. Exertion and adrenaline. I can feel a hundred cuts on me. My face, my arms, my hands. I can barely see in the sudden light. I can barely stand.

Around me, shadows flicker. Only slowly do they take shape. Surroundings and… People? Things that are moving for sure. They must be people. But which people? Who else is halfway up this mountain?

I try to make the newcomers out. I blink and my vision tears. I wipe with dusty, bleeding hands. I try to make sense of things. Then Clyde yells.

Things come into focus with an immediacy that startles me. I take a step back. Then what I see registers, and I take another two.

Olsted is there. The runner is there. And not just them. More Progeny. Our driver. Our pilot. And, Jesus, were they Progeny all along? On the flight over here? But why didn't they just kill us then? Ditch the plane?

But there's a dead body on the ground too. Someone I don't recognize. And I realize that, no, the pilot and driver weren't Progeny. They've been infected. Here. A Progeny came with Olsted and shot himself in the head. Simply sacrificed itself to propagate the species. Like an insect or something.

And, of course, there are their shock troopers as well. Their mutated monsters. Things like the student. Except these weren't people once. They were animals. A couple look like cows, horns drooping around Minotaur faces. One was maybe a monkey, thick fur covering its limbs, a lashing tail, oddly human eyes. A spotted cat creature. Muscles move, almost ripping their flesh. They are awkward, hulking, trapped in their new frames, baying and howling. They are in pain. I can see it.

The runner is holding Tabitha. His fingers like steel wire on her throat, holding her up one-handed. And I wait for the crack of bone, for the spine to go. I can't quite look at Tabitha's face.

Something flashes in the runner's hand. Something white and gray. His hand lances toward Tabitha's side. A knife. He has a knife.

Tabitha arches. Clyde bellows. The runner's hand flicks back and forth, twice, three times, stabbing Tabitha in the side. Then red blooms against the blacks and grays of Tabitha's outfit. A brief splash of color in this bleached world. And then he lets Tabitha fall.

32

The runner stands over Tabitha's crumpled body. There is no expression on his face. No leer of victory. No sorrow. Utterly impassive.

"Give us the—" Olsted starts.

Clyde lets out a roar next to me. He's a mess. Dirt and blood-smeared, half doubled-over, hand blocking the sun. But he sees, and he bellows. Something in the guttural nonsense language he uses to sling his spells. His hand comes out, and Olsted never finishes the sentence. He flies through the air. Slams into the monkey thing.

Clyde yells again. Another invisible shove sends the runner tumbling head over heel. Then the monsters close in about Clyde. About me. About all of us.

Kayla goes to work. Her sword flies. Blood splatters. I'm backed against the wall. Something with fists the size of my head, with fingernails the size of my palms, with great big bloody horns the length of my forearms protruding from its kneecaps, closes on me. And then it's going down with a guttural scream, with something silver jutting from its throat. I'm soaked in blood. To the skin. It drenches my clothes and hair in one long hot arterial spray. I am screaming something incoherent even to myself as the thing lands next to me, the earth shuddering at the impact. Blood drips from my fingers. I stagger away.

Then something is around my neck, squeezing. An arm. I cough and more blood sprays from my lips. The arm squeezes tighter. I remember basic self-defense. Back from being on the force. Back from when my days were sane. I stamp my foot down, swing my head back. The toes crunch. The nose breaks. The arm releases. I push away, spin round. Our driver is there. No. Not our driver. Something wearing the skin of our driver. Our driver is dead. This thing will be too, very bloody soon.

I've never really been in a fistfight. Except Clyde back at Olsted's perhaps. Not that I'm sure I'd count that. Still, the punch lands square. Slams into the jawbone, snapping the head sideways. My fist throbs, so I punt the bastard between the legs. Not very sporting of me, but neither is infecting the brains of someone else, if you ask me. And anyway, I promised Alison, promised myself, I'm fighting to win this one.

The thing goes down. Good to see that still hurts as much if you're an alien. I put the boot in. Once. Twice. Thr—

It catches my foot. Twists. I go down. Not as graceful as Kayla by far. Then it's on me. Tooth and nail. Fingers burying themselves in the soft skin of my cheek. Clawing at me. One in my mouth and I bite down hard. Blood in my mouth. More blood. The Progeny is trying to grapple me, but the blood of the monster makes me slippery and I wriggle from its grasp. One hand grabs my foot. I stamp down into its face. Again. Again. It releases me. I struggle to stand.

Then it tackles me low, and I'm down again. My head smacks dirt, and the world loses focus. I turn, groggy. Something hits my chest and the wind bursts out of me. I lie wheezing, coughing, trying to make sense of things, like why there is grass pressed on my cheek instead of beneath my feet.

I work out which way is up and look there. The driver is standing above me. He's holding a very large rock over his head. I have enough sense to know where he's aiming. I try to roll but can't get my limbs to work. The Progeny kneels, one leg on either side of me, the massive rock still suspended above his head.

Kayla comes from nowhere. Some sort of kick and the Progeny is flying—literally flying—through the air. Six, seven yards. He'd go further if it weren't for the vertical slab of rock.

The Progeny's head caves. Caught between the rock he held and the rock he hits. Cracks like a coconut in a vice.

Eggs fly out. Tiny beads of infection, of infestation. They cover the area. I scramble backwards as they shower down to earth. Kayla is away.

"Look out!" someone is yelling. "Look out!" I look in the direction of the voice. Clyde has Tabitha in his arms, is shoving her away from the cloud. He leaps after her.

Then a massive fist obscures my view. I duck under the swing, roll beneath colossal hoofed legs. Kayla is on the thing's back, hacking at its spinal column. I can see bare vertebrae as the thing falls. I look for Olsted, for the runner. I don't see them. I pray Kayla has ended them. The pilot is still there. He and Clyde are going at it tooth and nail.

Then Clyde says something and the man flies away. Slams to the earth. Clyde is chasing after him, bellowing words in a language time was meant to forget. The pilot's body is tossed like a rag doll. Back toward Kayla. She swings her sword. The man's head comes undone.

More eggs. In the sky like a cloud. Clyde running toward them. He collapses. Lets his feet buckle under him. Rolls under the cloud. Kicks out his legs and jumps away.

"Shit!" he's cursing. "Shit!"

I look around. Dead bodies everywhere. Chunks of

flesh and shards of bone. No sign of Olsted or the runner. Cowardice proving the better part of valor and all that.

"Clyde!" I call. He is still cursing. He looks at me, hollow-eyed. "Are you all right? Did they get you?" Not the swords. The eggs. I don't think they got him. He was free and clear. "Are you all right?" I say again, insistent.

He looks at me as if I'm insane. "Tabby," he says. "They stabbed Tabby."

And if Tabby's still his main concern, I'm pretty sure he's fine.

We move toward where Tabitha has fallen. Kayla is already there, which surprises me. She's as drenched in blood as I am.

"Shouldn't touch her," she says to me. "Clean up." And she's right. The last thing Tabby needs is some hideous bloody disease I'm a vector for.

She doesn't talk to Clyde. He's not as bad as us. Only spattered, not soaked. And he wouldn't listen to us anyway. He's pulling off his shirt, balling it up, pressing it to the wound. He cradles Tabitha's head in his lap.

She's just about conscious, muttering something. She and Clyde talk back and forth with words I can't catch.

"I'll clean up," I say. "Get the first-aid kit." No one listens to me.

33

HALF AN HOUR LATER

Clyde is still raging. He paces back and forth, around and around Tabitha. She's stabilized almost more than he has.

I pick up the satellite phone, dial Shaw. Explain as best as I can. Another disaster. I wait for the reprimands to start.

"A mole," she says, instead. Her voice is flat, carefully controlled. "They knew where you were. We've got a mole."

Again I hear Olsted's voice. The Progeny's voice. *"We walk among you."* He wasn't lying. And he was here to prove a point.

She isn't what you think she is.

Two times Kayla has failed to kill Olsted now. Two times the runner has escaped.

Or Tabitha. It could be Tabitha. Sure, she's wounded. But it's not fatal. The runner could have killed her easily, but he chose not to. Could it all be subterfuge?

And Shaw. Shaw sitting out of danger. Shaw, perfectly placed to tell them where we were. It doesn't feel like Shaw. But... but...

But I can't collect evidence without caving in someone's skull. At the very least I can't conduct it without a forensic team. Without time. And MI37 doesn't have either of those things.

Clyde is still yelling in the background. Something in

him has snapped. He's spitting and frothing, alternately indignant and murderous. Curse words I didn't know he knew keep issuing from his mouth.

"What do we do?" I ask. Because I don't know. I'm all out of ideas. I'm all out. Just done for a while.

"Sit tight," Shaw says, "I'll send another plane."

"About the mole?" I say. "What do we do about the mole?"

A pause.

"You have the grimoire, don't you?" she says.

"Still do," I say. I'm sitting on it. Keeping it safe. "Clyde wants to use it," I say. "Now. Wants to evict them all from reality."

"Can it do what Olsted's book promised it could?"

And it's tempting, very tempting. Read the grimoire, cast the spell, screw the Progeny. Man, I want those bastards screwed. Very, very badly. And it's probably worse for Shaw, Clyde, Tabitha, Kayla, for all of them except the mole... Jesus... But they've been doing this for so long. They must have seen more loss than me. But with everything so close, I don't want to screw this up because we rushed things.

Because we involved someone we shouldn't have trusted...

"We need more time," I say.

"You've got some time," Shaw says. "A plane won't be there until tomorrow morning now. That's the best I can do. Have Clyde read the book."

"He'll cast the first thing he finds if he thinks it'll help."

"So be the boss. Be in control. Do what I recruited you to do. Take charge." There's a beat. "You can do it." Another pause, and I get the feeling neither of us are entirely comfortable with her assuming the role of pep rally leader. "Look," she says, "this was a win for us. We got the book. For the second time we got the book. Two straight-up confrontations with the Progeny and we won."

Three. Three confrontations. And one we lost. Swann lost. I lost Swann. But I don't say that, because this isn't the time for that. Still, a voice still mutters in the back of my head, *She's not what you think she is.*

But when I hang up, I give Clyde the book.

"About goddamn time," he says. It still sounds wrong coming from his mouth. Like he's breaking character.

Propped up against a rock nearby, Tabitha, dosed on morphine, smiles.

EIGHT MORE HOURS LATER

Night has fallen when Clyde has his eureka moment. He slams the book shut with a look of grim satisfaction. "Got the bastards," he says.

Tabitha, unconscious now, but still stable as best I can tell, stirs, but doesn't wake up. Kayla, sitting away from the campfire she set up, walks over.

"What's it say?" I ask.

"It says we get rid of them." Clyde has a tight little smile. "Ta-ta, you little bastards. Don't let the door hit you in the arse."

It seems unlikely that's the exact wording. "What are the specifics, though?" I ask. "This is too big to do blind. We have to be in charge of this. We have to do it right."

"Look." Clyde is impatient. "I can't tell you the exact wording. Tabitha is the language expert, but if you hadn't noticed, she's kind of in a bad way right now."

He is oddly focused in his passion. And I think about the cloud of eggs again, but it wouldn't make sense for a Progeny to take Clyde over and then act out of character so violently. The change in him feels more genuine for being so pronounced.

234

"I'd noticed, Clyde." I keep my voice soft, even. Clyde still feels like the one person I can trust. He can't lose the plot on me.

"Look," he says, pushing his hands through his hair, "I don't, I admit, understand every last word, but I get the basic gist of the thing. And no, I don't understand every last nuance either, but I get the big picture. I really do, Arthur. I understand this as much as I need to cast the spell, as much as I need to know casting it is a good idea."

"So give me the big picture." I still keep my voice low, even. "I want to make this deal. I want the Progeny to hurt. I want Alison avenged. But I want it done right. I have to know we're doing what we think we're doing."

"It summons a force, all right?" Clyde says. "I don't know the name of it. I can't make out the word. Some colloquial phrase or something. But the force, it's a… a sort of cipher. A cipher to reality. It gives you access to all the layers that make up our composite reality." A thought strikes him. "You remember the Dreamers?"

I've heard the word but it's lost under so many layers of crazy that I'm forced to just shrug.

"You remember—this reality is made up of more than one reality. It's a composite reality. And the people who decide which realities make up the composite are the Dreamers. They decide what's in and what's out."

"Yeah." I nod. Not because it makes sense but because it is at the very least familiar.

"This force, this power the spell summons, it gives you the powers of a Dreamer. It's as if the caster is a Dreamer."

Clyde—this version of Clyde—with the powers of a Dreamer. An angry, vengeful, lovelorn man with the power to rewrite reality. I… No. Tabitha has to be all right before I let Clyde cast that spell.

"We should wait," I say. "Sleep on it. Get someone else

here on this, make sure we've got everything right."

"Come on!" Clyde's shout is out of place in the peace of this place. "We can do this now. We can end this now. We can get the Progeny out of here. We can stop them from hurting anyone else. Not Tabby again. We can stop them from doing what they did to Alison to anyone else. Come on, Arthur, please. See this from where I'm standing. I don't want to see Tabby go the way Alison did. I don't want to see anyone go that way." He shakes his head. "Not Tabby."

Oh Alison. Alison. God, I want to let him do it too. It's a head–heart thing. And I know, I know, I should go with my head. We should wait. We should know.

But—

But—

And on the other hand—

Jesus Christ, Boss. Grow a pair. Swann's voice echoing from beyond the grave. Pick something. Shaw telling me to be the boss.

I look at Clyde. He's looking at me, imploring. And don't I have to trust Clyde? Just to stay totally out of the paranoid zone. Don't I have to trust someone?

"Oh shit and balls," I say. "It's not like things have gone any better when we planned them out ahead of time."

He almost hugs me. He almost hugs Tabitha. For a second I think he even contemplates hugging Kayla. I try to get a read on her, on how she sees this. And if she is Progeny, and if she thinks this plan will work then we are surely dead men. And if she is Progeny and she is letting us do this, then we've got this wrong, and well… we're dead men again. In fact, blanket statement—if Kayla is Progeny we're all pretty much completely screwed. Me, Clyde, the rest of humanity.

I still can't think of what to do about that. I need

some way to lock her up the way that Progeny did back in Oxford. I need to talk to Shaw about that.

A day, that's what I need. A day. Just one. To get my head straight.

Clyde is raiding his backpack, pulling out a dynamo or something. And this could buy us time. This could make all this go away. Surely we have to try it.

I put my head in my hands. I don't know. I don't know what the right thing is anymore. I've lost my way.

Have an opinion for longer than six seconds.

It's what Swann told me to do, so I do it.

"We shouldn't be interrupted," Clyde says, handing Kayla the dynamo, "so I think it's OK to use this. Just, whatever you do, don't stop cranking the handle until I tell you to."

Kayla takes it without giving any hint of acknowledgment.

"What about me?" I ask.

"Surplus to requirements, really," says Clyde, but he's not looking. He's too busy stabbing his various chakras with his various needles. "Just sit back, and watch the fireworks."

Fireworks. I can't help but feel we could use a night without fireworks. I wish Swann had given me some words of wisdom for if I picked something, and I picked wrong.

34

"Fer terrum. Ex locum. Venum um terrum cum veritem. Lom vienne. Mok retrem."

Clyde has his head bowed and he's floating a good foot off the ground. The wires leading from the dynamo are neon blue lines stretching through the darkness of the night. Kayla cranks the dynamo steadily, mechanically. I pace around and around the pair, occasionally pausing by Tabitha as she slumbers on. Clyde has been chanting for almost over an hour, incanting the same words over and over and over.

Nothing much has happened except for the floating. There have been no fireworks. Part of me is relieved. Part of me is bitterly disappointed.

But then, as I keep walking, I wonder if perhaps something is happening after all. Slowly but very surely. There is a familiar sense of pressure, of the air thickening. The aura that surrounded the book upon its plinth. It's not a pleasant feeling. The air is almost greasy about me. A nauseating pressure in my gut, as if someone cinched my belt too tight after a heavy meal.

And then something else too. At first I think it's dawn coming, but then I look at my watch and realize it's not even midnight. Not even the witching hour yet. Instead, the glow of the wires seems to be spreading. Or... it's hard to put my finger on it. It's as if part of the night is getting paler. As if someone is pressing an enormous finger against the sky, stretching it out. And still Clyde drones on. And still the pressure grows. And still the sky grows paler—a patch almost as wide as the clearing we're in, but not quite, so that I can see a ring of real night at the edge of the place.

The sky is definitely glowing now. It's not daylight, though. It's more like a fluorescent spotlight shining through blurred black glass. Clyde's speech is growing guttural, the consonants harder, the vowels swallowed, until it sounds like he's barely human.

And then reality tears.

It's not dramatic. It's not fireworks. But finally the great invisible finger pushes through. A hole opens in the sky. I can see the ragged edges of our reality hanging around it, tiny white tatters curled up against the blackness of our reality's night.

The space beyond… I expected stars I suppose. Not that this is the sort of thing you expect. But, well… I'd expected stars.

Instead the space beyond glows darkly—a blackness that illuminates, that somehow shines.

Clyde falls to earth, panting hard. Slowly Kayla lets the dynamo die. The lines of neon leading to Clyde's body fade and go out.

We stand there in the half-gloom all looking up.

"What now?" I ask.

"Now it comes," Clyde says.

Suddenly I realize I'm wrong. I have to be wrong. Clyde is the traitor, is the one I should never have trusted. And by allowing this moment, I have screwed over the world. "It" is the Feeder, vast and implacable. I've screwed us all.

And then "it" turns out to be a ladder.

We stare, almost overwhelmed by the sheer amount

of underwhelming the ladder radiates. It's wooden, old. Something my grandfather would have owned. It pops out of the darkness, the base of it landing at Clyde's feet with a loud thud.

I start to laugh. I can't help it. It's all too absurd. It's all too pitiably disastrous. This can't help us. There's no way this can help us. Clyde looks at the ladder as if it just broke his heart.

And then a leg.

Out of the bright blackness, a leg. A foot upon the highest rung of the ladder. And then a second leg. Which I suppose is natural, except there's nothing natural at all about two legs appearing out of nowhere, high above you in the Peruvian sky. Still, two legs are a reassuringly mundane number of limbs.

A body follows. A man dressed in coat and tails, a top hat balanced upon his head. He climbs down hand over hand. Then another figure follows him. A woman making her awkward way down, feet sprouting from the crinoline of a large ball gown. Then another. Then another. Ten, fifteen, twenty... more and more climbing down the ladder, out of one reality and into ours. All of them dressed as if they've escaped from a Victorian-themed costumed ball for the fabulously wealthy. And all of them, I see, have their eyes shut.

As they get closer, massing out from the ladder, it feels like there's something else wrong, or odd, or different. And then I notice their breathing. A shuddering susurration in the air. All of them breathing slowly, regularly, together. Their heads bob loosely on their shoulders.

"They're asleep," I say, suddenly realizing as the first one touches the ground. "All of them. They're asleep."

Clyde lets out a low whistle, almost a moan. "The spell," he says. "It doesn't... It doesn't summon a force like the Dreamers. It summons the Dreamers themselves. It brings them here."

They are collecting in a circle now at the base of the ladder. Clyde steps toward them but they take a collective step back. He stops.

"These are the people responsible for the world we see?" It suddenly feels a little bit like meeting God. If God were, you know, a whole bunch of people in very fancy dress.

And then she comes. The woman from the alleyway in my head. The woman who tells me that, *"She is not what you think she is."* The princess is a Dreamer.

That has to mean something. I think. I mean, it has to. Except I don't know what.

We stand and gawp at them, unsure of ourselves, unsure of what happens next.

They stand quite still, clustered. Like a herd. I take a step toward them. Again they back away. Their eyes are closed but I get the feeling they're looking at us somehow. Something beyond mere sight. And not just looking at *us*, but looking very specifically at Clyde. Their summoner.

Then one of them breaks from the pack. A short little man in a top hat. Not quite a run but a brisk walk, arms swinging stiffly at his side. Others take his lead, start to walk away at speed. Not following the first one, but all heading off in their own directions, dispersing out into the night. It's like a slow-motion rout. Panic under a veneer of respectability.

I exchange a look with Clyde. He shrugs, helpless.

"Hey!" I call, not really sure of what I'm doing. "Hey wait! We need you! We need your help!"

They ignore me. None of them are heading toward us. I step toward them, but they pick up the pace, arms pumping. They're leaving the edge of the clearing now, disappearing off into trees and scrub. Kayla stands there, watching them, letting them go.

The princess, the woman I know... Do I know her? In her white dress, with her beautiful icy face. She's still there, walking perhaps just a little slower. And maybe she will talk to me. Maybe she'll let this be the point where things start making sense.

I dart toward her. "Wait!" I say. "We need your help. Please—" I close the distance even as she accelerates. I reach out, grab her by the shoulder.

Suddenly I don't have an arm. One moment it's there, and next my shoulder ends abruptly, smoothly, a few inches down my bicep. I stare. Then something flickers and my arm is back, but it is bending like rubber, curling back on itself, the fingers arching back toward my elbow. I can feel the bones shattering and I scream. And then I have no arm but a slimy flopping tentacle—purple and white, slithering down my side leaving a cold wet trail. I collapse to my knees still yelling. Reality blinks again and I have a ragged bleeding stump. I have an arm of squirming worms. I have a metal arm, heavier than I can lift. I have an arm that ends in a baby's screaming head. We scream together, my mind overflowing with images. A plastic mannequin's arm. A wing. An extra leg.

I hit the earth, and I'm actually glad when my mind simply flees the scene, when I finally retreat into madness for a short but pleasurable while.

35

"They're gone."

I'm propped up against a tree near the still-sleeping Tabitha. My arm is just an arm. It's soaking wet, but it's an ordinary arm. Actually, all of me is soaking wet.

Clyde is kneeling down next to me. Probably the one who threw the water on me to wake me up. Kayla stands behind him, looking at me with mild disgust.

It strikes me that mild might be an improvement.

Then Clyde's words finally sink in.

"Gone," I repeat. "The Progeny?" Ever the optimist.

Clyde shakes his head and hope stops springing. "The Dreamers," he says, "they've gone, left."

"Is that good or bad?" I know which way it feels but...

Clyde shrugs. He looks gaunt. Defeated. "I honestly don't know."

Kayla looks away.

And we don't know. We can't know. That's the truth. And even if we knew the implications, there's no way to stop the Dreamers from walking off. They can turn your arm into a... a... I don't know. Anything. Everything.

Part of my brain is still screaming. Part of it is trying to rationalize the experience, pulling on half-remembered conversations with Clyde about more and less probable realities. And the thought that in less probable realities my arm is a leg, is a stump, is a… No. This doesn't feel like rationalizing something.

But it's easier to think of that rather than of what to do next.

What would Kurt… No. I'm not stooping to that level of idiocy. I have no idea what to do next.

"Nothing to be done," I say, finding a brave face to put on. "Just wait. Wait for the plane. Wait for morning."

Clyde sits and stares off into the dark remnants of the night and soon enough I drift off to sleep.

THE NEXT MORNING

Sunlight brings a new van, a new driver, and a paramedic. He produces a jar of ointment and smears the contents over the gash in Tabitha's side, getting ready to stitch her up. The ointment looks vile, and I swear I can see chunks of straw or something similar in it, but I remember the pill Shaw gave me, and the punctured lung, and that did a decent enough job of patching me together. Good to know somebody knows what they're doing.

Then we get back in the van and we drive back through the beautiful countryside, back to where our plane waits—a great military hulk squatting sullenly in a field of grass. We board it, rattle about in it, and we head for home.

We don't talk much. There's not much to say. Clyde sits with Tabitha's head in his lap. I sit opposite him, while the paramedic stands in the doorway between the main body of the plane and the cockpit chatting quietly with the pilot. Kayla sits as far from us as possible.

Somewhere over Mexico I get sick of the maudlin stew that is my thoughts. I'm chasing my own tail. So I give Clyde the best smile I can manage. Pretend everything's normal.

"You started out as a researcher, right?" I say to Clyde, recalling something Shaw said.

"Yes." Clyde nods. "I got into odd formulations back when I was working on my doctorate at Cambridge. Odd texts. Really interesting, actually. To do with the intersecting oscillations of…" He looks at me, sees my expression. "Shaw approached me," he says. "Seemed like a no-brainer to come on board. Good use of book skills."

He shakes his head. Grimaces. "Of course then I had to get interested in some of the books I was reading. Had to mess around with these old spells I was finding. Had to find out I could get them to work. And then Shaw found out." A rueful smile. "Everyone found out. Blew up a good portion of a lab on my lunch break. 'Chernobyl junior' Tabitha called it." His smile breaks.

"It's not like book learning out here." He's not looking at me anymore. He's looking at Tabitha. "It's always easy if it's in a book. You just read it, learn it, say it again. Ta-dah. Insta-knowledge. Just add student. It's the stuff they don't write down. Or the stuff they write down but they get it wrong, or just not… I don't know. Sometimes life's not the way people write about it. Sometimes it's different."

I'm not sure what to say. I'm not sure if he's even talking to me.

In his lap, Tabitha stares. Her eyes flicker.

"Thought you were brainy," she croaks. "Figure stuff like that out."

A smile spreads so broadly across Clyde's face for a moment I'm worried that the top half of his head is going to fall off. He pushes the hair back from her forehead.

In the doorway at the front of the plane, the paramedic stirs, takes a few steps toward his patient. Tabitha twists, grimaces as she does so, and gives the paramedic the finger. He backs away. She goes back to staring up at Clyde. He stares right back.

I knew that white knight stuff was impressive.

Kayla stands up, moves away to the back of the plane. I get the hint and head up toward the cockpit.

But part of me can't help but think I really should have just kept my bloody mouth shut in that car.

36

TWENTY JET-LAGGED HOURS LATER

"Someone's infected," I say. "I know it."

It's the first time I've actually made it into Shaw's office. The room is as functional as the rest of the MI37 complex, and being underground there are no windows, but she's got a row of daylight bulbs against one wall hanging over a miniature forest of potted plants. She even has an orchid in there. It gives the place an unexpectedly soft appearance.

The rest of the office is more as expected—an angular desk, a few perfunctory-looking office chairs, stainless steel bookshelves with a mixture of modern reference books, bulging ring binders, and ancient-looking documents.

Shaw drums her fingers on the desk and looks over my shoulder.

"The Olsted-Progeny basically admitted it to me. And the way the Peru trip was leaked. And it just makes—"

"I'm not disagreeing with you, Arthur," she says, holding up a hand, and stopping my exhausted babble. "I'm thinking."

I nod and then rest my head in my hands. It's been a long flight, and a long journey to Oxford. And I could, of course, be making a big mistake. Shaw could be the infected one. But the chances of that are only one in four.

And if she is the Progeny then I'm not really revealing anything she doesn't already know I know.

"It's not the only way," Shaw says at last. "We are largely off the grid, but there are ways to hack our system. Tabitha's computer, for example. You saw in Peru how Clyde was able to manipulate the wireless broadcast in magical ways. There may be methods of hacking into it remotely that we just don't know about." She shakes her head. "Metaphysical firewalls, that's the last thing I need to worry about.

"Then," she continues, "there's the fact that someone uninfected could be working for the Progeny. The way Olsted was before... well, before our involvement."

I thump my head against the table. Sometimes it feels like the biggest achievements so far have been blowing up Cowley Road and letting the Progeny infect a powerful magician.

"It happens." Shaw shrugs. I'm not sure she's telling the truth, but it's nice of her to say it. I lift my head up, smile.

"The Progeny could have a hold on the mole," she goes on. "The mole may not even know they're working for the Progeny. Money can be a significant blinder. And it's not just the five of us down here that have access to the files. We're not the most popular agency these days—" Her expression sours slightly.

"I know," I say. "Clyde told me."

Shaw nods. "We have to work with what we have, but that's not my point, Arthur. My point is that there are others outside our little network who may be the ones talking. We're not airtight."

"True." I nod. But I'm not convinced. It doesn't fit. Not with the picture painted.

"Look, I'm not trying to discount the theory," Shaw

says. "I just don't want us to ignore other potential avenues of investigation." Which is the right call, of course. "But you could well be right, Arthur." She twists a stray hair that hangs behind her ear. "So let's assume you are. What do you suggest we do?"

"Well," I start, but I'm still having trouble getting past that point.

"I mean," Shaw says, "I could take everyone off the team. Including you. Because I can't trust you. Including me. I trust me, but it would be suspicious if I stayed. No one else would trust me. But then who do we bring in? Who do we know for sure that we can trust?"

I'm guessing that's rhetorical.

"This is a job, Arthur, and I hoped you'd have realized this on your own by now, to be honest, where you can't trust anyone, and so you have to trust everyone."

My eyebrows go up.

She rolls her eyes. I remember the woman who greeted me at my first meeting with the news I was late. There's an incongruity. And is that… could that mean she… And then I realize she's right. That way lies madness. There's a leap of faith that has to be made.

"So," she says, "we carry on. We trust the whole team until we *know* we can't trust someone. Not just feelings, not suspicions, but genuine evidence. And I don't want you to waste time trying to find something to pin on Kayla." There is a trace of the schoolmarm to her tone. I used to use something similar when dealing with wayward members of my own team back on the force. "If we can trust anyone, we can trust her."

I pause on that. Chew it over.

"Now, on to what we can work with," Shaw says. "The Dreamers. Their presence here. That's an angle. We should be working it."

"About them," I say, still chewing on the Kayla issue, "about evidence."

"What do you mean?" Shaw asks.

So, hesitantly, because I'm still worried I'm a little mad, I tell Shaw about the Dreamer in my dreams, about her warning. About her words.

"She's not what you think she is."

Shaw looks down. "You think she's talking about Kayla."

"I…" I start, and I know how Shaw feels, about how she thinks this looks. "It's not that she stabbed me," I say. "I mean, that obviously didn't start us off on the best foot, but this isn't that. This is how she moves. This is how she acts. She's not human. What she does isn't human."

Shaw taps her pen on the desk. "You don't think she's human, and then when a Dreamer, for reasons I cannot begin to fathom, tells you that some mysterious 'she' is not what you think, you think that's confirmation? Surely the Dreamer is disagreeing with you. If you think Kayla is Progeny and the Dreamer really is talking about her, then doesn't that mean Kayla's not Progeny? That you should be trusting her?"

I shrug, helpless. What she says is true. It's logical. But there's my gut too. And I was never a policeman who put much in his gut, well, aside from burgers and fries, but this time I have a feeling, and it's hard to let it go.

But it's not like Shaw is going to shift either, and she is my boss, and she knows Kayla better than I do, so I don't push it any more.

"Still," Shaw says into the silence, "the Dreamers' involvement doesn't sit right. Their manifestation here— it doesn't seem like something that helps us."

"Can you tell me more about them?" I ask. Again, the more I know. But then a fear hits me. "Can you tell me about them without using the book?" I think I need at least one good night's sleep before I do the book again.

Another smile from Shaw. She's actually quite pretty when she smiles. The thought takes me rather by surprise.

"There's not much to tell," she says. "Because we don't know much. They control our reality, basically. Whether they created the composite or came afterwards and just handle maintenance, I don't know. But they're a fact of life. And because of their powers they're basically invulnerable to attack. If they don't like what you're doing they'll just screw with the particular reality you inhabit to stop you from screwing with them. What happened with your arm sounds like a fair example of what they can do. Fairly minor example, actually."

A baby's head for a hand—minor. Jesus.

"How did they even…" I shake my head. "There was no electricity. I thought everything required electricity."

Shaw shakes her head. She looks sympathetic. "They're not human, Arthur. Our rules don't apply to them. But it could have been worse. You still exist in this world. They could have blinked you out. They could have made the change permanent."

I blanch. But maybe that's good news. "That means they're pretty much impervious to the Progeny, right?"

"They're essentially minor gods," Shaw says. "The Progeny may be powerful and inhuman, but they're not powerful the way the Dreamers are. The Feeders are, but not the Progeny."

"And the Feeders…" I say.

"They'd destroy the realities the Dreamers exist on. So I can't imagine the Dreamers letting them in."

"Fair enough," I say, nodding. "So, the Dreamers' presence here maybe doesn't hurt us. Maybe it does help us somehow." I pause. "I just can't see how."

"Neither can I." Shaw cracks her knuckles. "But one of them making contact with you, trying to give you information. That can't be a bad thing."

I think about it. "They're trying to help?"

"I would guess so." Shaw shrugs. "They may not be very good at it, but they're a powerful ally to have."

And that actually makes me feel good. The Dreamers are on our side. My side. I smile. "Thanks," I say to Shaw. For a moment I almost ask her if she wants to grab a pint with me before I crash out.

A knock at the door cuts that idea short.

"Yes," Shaw says, but the door's already opening. Someone has a sense of propriety. So it's no one from the team.

The man is a narrow, gray-looking fellow. I think he was probably once my height but either scoliosis or terrible posture advice means that he's staring directly at our feet. His face has an emaciated look with thin lines crossing the skin. Gray hair is swept back away from a prominent forehead. He points at me with one spidery finger, which at first glance gives the impression of having more than the requisite number of joints, and it is a while before I can convince myself that it's quite normal.

"Is now a bad time?" he asks Shaw, then plunges on without waiting for a reply. "Well, this will only take a minute," he says. I recognize the high-pitched needling voice at once. Robert, the whiner. The one with the purse strings who wanted to cut me from the team.

"This Peru trip is bullshit, Felicity," he says to Shaw. "Bottom line. I'm not approving it. You're going to have to find alternate means of funding. And I don't think your salary quite covers it." He gives a nasty acrid laugh, as if this is meant to be a joke.

And someone does laugh. A woman still on the other

side of the door. I can't see her, but it's a lush sound, utterly in contrast to Robert's.

Neither Shaw nor I join in, though. "It's happened, Robert," Shaw says with a sigh. "I wasn't submitting for approval. I was submitting for reimbursement."

Robert turns a dangerous shade of purple. The word, "What?" manages to hiss out from between his quivering lips. And who is this man? What sort of game does he think we're playing? What sort of stakes does he think there are? I'm tempted to give him several large pieces of my mind.

"I submitted the forms Robert, expedited. I ticked all the boxes. But I didn't have weeks to wait for an approval. I needed a rapid retrieval."

"Look, Felicity," Robert says Shaw's name as if it were a curse. "I thought I had made the financial situation plain to you." He clips each of his words, keeping them separate from the others, giving him an odd stilted tone. "The budget is not there. You can hardly afford maintenance of another old book, let alone the price of going after it."

"Well, Robert," Shaw's tone is barely any more civil, "then we shall have to investigate new methods of finding the money."

"Maybe we'll have to cut some of the higher-paid staff."

It's a vicious little thing to say from a vicious little man. And before I know it my mouth is open and I have my own vicious things to say.

"How much do you get paid?" I ask.

His head snaps around. "What?"

I pause a moment. Because this is not the sort of thing I do. Or not the sort of thing I did. But it's the sort of thing Kurt Russell would do, goddamn it. And I have faced down bigger monsters than this guy in the past few days. And I think I can take him.

"Well," I shrug, "if we're cutting people, shouldn't we evaluate each individual's salary? Try and work out what it is they bring to the team?" While he splutters, I let a frown crease my forehead. "What is it exactly that you're bringing to the team?"

It is only there for an instant, but I swear I see Shaw smile.

"Can you not even control your staff, Felicity?" Robert hisses.

Shaw feigns confusion. "You seem to assume I disagree with Agent Wallace."

I almost reach over and high five Shaw.

He swings his gaze on me, eyes black and flaring. "Director Shaw cannot offer you protection for long. Too many black marks and you will not enjoy the benefits of this organization. There are things out there that I would not like to meet without backup."

"Oh shut up, Robert," Shaw says, and I could almost hug her for it. Instead I swallow the ball of laughter and clamp it down in my stomach.

Robert turns, stalks out of the room. As he does so, I, for a moment, glimpse the woman who was standing there, who laughed at the little man's little joke. I manage to get a glimpse of blond hair, red dress, and curves that would make the tires of a race-car squeal. And then she is gone.

And she laughed at his joke? There is no justice in the world. And I used to be a policeman. I should know.

I pull myself back together and turn back to Shaw, who's looking at her watch. "OK," she says, "now I could definitely use a drink." She pushes against her forehead with her hands. "Too long a week by half." She sighs, looks up. "Thank you. Robert is... manageable, but it's always nice to have…" she pauses, lets the smile creep out for a moment again, "…backup."

"I want you to know you can trust me."

She lets out something that's almost a laugh. Then she's serious again. "Look, Arthur," she says, "I don't know how much help I've been. The Dreamers concern me, but I can't tell you much more than you can figure out on your own. But you were a detective. Do some detecting. Try talking to the Twins. When we're confused they're often our best resource."

"Sounds like a plan for the morning."

"Indeed." She opens a closet, pulls out a coat. I hold the door. She pauses there.

"Would you—" she looks awkward— "want to join me for the drink?"

My eyebrows bounce up and I immediately pull the irresponsible little buggers right down. "Sure," I say, hoping she didn't notice.

We step out into the corridor and see Clyde coming toward us. He's still wearing the mask from Peru around his shoulder.

"Oh," he says, "not too late am I? Just wanted to talk about the book we found, about the Dreamers and such."

I look at Shaw, who looks tired.

"No," she says, "not too late." She turns back to her office.

"How about we do it down the pub," I say. "Easier to talk with a pint in our hands."

Clyde looks at me as if I've committed blasphemy. Shaw pulls the same eyebrow bounce I just did. And apparently this is an office culture faux pas I'm still too new to really grasp.

Then Shaw shrugs. "Yes," she says. "Yes, that would be easier."

I don't think Clyde would look more shocked if a Feeder punched through reality right here and now and started dancing the two-step.

37

We head over to the Turf, which is a charmer of a pub, tucked away near a few of the colleges. It's a bit of a trek from the office, but utterly worth it as I sag into an oak chair, and Clyde, who is decent enough to buy the first round, sets an amber pint down in front of me.

"So, this book," Shaw says to Clyde, "tell us about it."

"It's reality magic," Clyde says, "all of it." His fingers bounce on the table. He's excited. Has been ever since the flight landed.

So has Tabitha.

"I think this could be as big as the book about the Feeders. Just, well… less traumatic to read."

More pint sipping quickly ensues all around the table as we all briefly relive the horrors of that experience.

"I mean," Clyde continues, "I'm only just scratching the surface, Tabby's doing the real work…"

And there's that boyish grin again. It's a little bit infectious. I wonder if Shaw knows, if I should tell her. Or maybe I should let it alone. Reality will impinge on the relationship soon enough. Devon will impinge on it. My smile slips. I wouldn't want to be in Clyde's shoes for that one.

"I mean… using this—" Clyde is struggling to find words to describe the enormity of his vision "—we could probably plot out other realities. I mean, the whole thing is basically a guidebook for creating your own spells. And I know, I know, I know…" He holds up a palm to Shaw. "The whole Chernobyl thing. But they didn't have this book. We could do the experiments in Wales. Who'd miss Wales?"

I snort into my pint. Shaw clucks slightly.

"I'm sorry." Clyde rubs his hands. "But this is so exciting. Like getting the girl of your… well, you know, just, very exciting. And even if we can't… even if it doesn't do all it seems to be promising to do, I still think this is a genuine break. This gives us some real insight into what the Progeny might actually be doing, how they think they can bring the Feeders through."

Something clicks in my brain. Perhaps it's the beer finally unknotting some of the kinks I've had in my thoughts since starting this job. Maybe I'm just not thinking straight and I needed to go at a lateral angle, but events start collating in my head.

Something to do with unwelcome guests.

And throwing Robert out of Shaw's office.

Something about the Dreamers coming, entering our reality.

"Can we throw them out?" I say.

Shaw and Clyde both look at me.

"I mean…" I say, hesitate, almost lose the thought, then, "the Progeny. Out of people's heads. I mean that's the problem, right? And we've tried to get the Progeny out of our entire reality, and instead we pulled Dreamers in. But maybe we don't have to be that dramatic. Instead of getting them out of reality, we just get them out of people's heads. Because… well, if the Progeny don't have a nest what can they do? They can't breed. They can't operate. Is there something in the book that can help with that?"

They both stare at me. I feel like I just spoke in tongues

at them. Then Shaw's head swivels and suddenly it's me
and her staring at Clyde.

"Err…" he says, looks down at his pint, goes for the sip
to put some alcohol between him and the collective stare.
"Maybe?" He sips again. Then more enthusiastically.
"Maybe. Yeah maybe. I mean, I'd have to read more. A lot
more." He looks excited at that prospect. "But perhaps
there's something in there."

"Read," Shaw says. "Find out." She pats me on the
arm. "Good thought, Arthur."

We both look at the hand. Almost sheepishly, she pulls
it away. We both look up at Clyde, who takes a very, very
long sip.

38

THE NEXT DAY

There is, I admit, a decent chance my vision of magical research was overly influenced by Harry Potter. I was pretty sure test tubes would be involved. Jars of unnameable fluids. Bits of mythological creatures. Probably a cauldron. And, I was rather hoping, the occasional explosion.

In reality there is a table and a large pile of very old books with colored plates. Though, in defense of young Master Potter, there are two people making eyes at each other over the book pile when they think no one else is looking.

As much as I like Tabitha and Clyde, it's a relief when I remember Shaw's advice, and excuse myself to go and see if the Twins can shed any light on matters.

The elevator doors slide open. The familiar sea-salt smell. Familiar shapes in the water and shadows on the walls. One of the girls is leaning on the side of the pool, wet hair draped over the tiles around it. The other slips through the water around her, bobbing up and down, barely disturbing the water as tentacles wave around her— the Loch Ness monster in miniature.

What happened to them? What was done that made them into these aquatic, prophetic creatures? And what's going to happen to them? Am I really going to be able to stop anything?

More than ever I am reminded about what colossal bastards the Progeny really are.

"Hello, Agent Wallace," says one of the girls. I am too far away to count freckles and know which one.

"Can we call you Arthur?" says the other, surfacing and swimming to the edge.

"Agent Wallace is more polite," says the first.

"Arthur is what Shaw calls him," says the second.

"Director Shaw," corrects her sister.

Swann would have liked the girls. The thought strikes me suddenly, unexpectedly.

Ouch.

"You can call me Arthur," I say, smiling through the mental confusion.

"We're sorry about Alison," Ophelia says. I'm close enough now to see it's her. The first speaker.

"Time makes it better," says Ephie.

Ophelia nods. "We've seen it before."

Ouch again.

"Sorry," says Ephie. Ophelia just shrugs with the certainty of youth—this was something I apparently needed to hear. She's probably right.

"It'll hurt for a while," Ephie says. "But then less."

"Yes," I say. And then, "I'm not going to let them get you." I'm surprised by how fiercely I feel it.

"We know you'll try your best," says Ophelia.

I don't really know what to say to that. Not a ringing endorsement. But not a condemnation. Still, I mean what I say. I will do everything I can to stop the Progeny. Anything.

"You wanted to ask us something," Ophelia says. She's more serious than her sister. The difference is more pronounced between them than the last time I was here. Though there's a decent chance I'd get grumpy if I were living with a death sentence over my head.

Man, it's hard to have a happy thought in this place.

"Yes," I say. "I wanted to ask you about—"

I cut myself off. Something has caught my eye. Something red in the water. Black dots floating in the center of a red haze. Something shifting beneath the surface of the pool.

Blood. It looks like blood in the water. Clots at its heart slowly dissolving away.

Blood. Why would there be blood in the water?

Unthinking I reach out to touch it. The girls stare at me, uncomprehending. Then, with my fingers a fraction of an inch above the water, they seem to understand fully what I am about to do.

"No!" Ephemera shrieks.

Ophelia releases a high-pitched scream.

And I turn, but I don't stop, because I don't understand, and I don't remember Shaw's warning, and my fingers touch the water.

The pool turns black. A great flood of ink. Every animal in it releasing in one massive expulsion. My finger drips ink. And then I remember Shaw's words. I remember her using the word "*psychotropic*" as a strange tingling sensation creeps up my arm. And the tingling is burning, is crushing, each sensation coming faster up my arm, battering against my skull, thundering over my chest, making my legs kick and spasm. I flinch backwards, wrenching my stained fingers away far, far too late, because already I am—

THEN AND WHEN AND IN-BETWEEN

Ouch.

I'm not totally sure why I always end up in this alley face down… I need to work out a better way of getting here. Talk to a travel agent or something.

I push myself up and over, the smell of wet concrete

still in my nose. And I realize—this is a new alleyway. I can hear the sound of traffic at its end, oddly muted, but undeniably present. The sky has clouds. The trash smells a little worse.

But the princess is there still. Still in the same dress. I watch her hands. I don't want my arm to go all silly putty on me again.

"You're—" I start. Her brow creases, her finger goes to her lips.

"You're one of the Dreamers," I whisper, my voice barely audible over the sound of my own breathing.

She nods as I push myself up to stand.

"You're here," I whispered. "On Earth."

"We always were," she says. "Only a part few see." There is something lyrical and sing-song to her voice.

"But now we can all see you," I whisper.

She turns from me, takes a step away, then she looks over her shoulder. A white finger beckons me on.

Our destination isn't far. Just a fire escape door without a handle on our side halfway down the alley. It opens without her even touching it. A minor trick for her, I suppose.

The corridor beyond the door is dark and musty. There is a paint-spattered ladder leaning against one wall. On it is balanced a branching candlestick. Five candles drip wax down its bronze surface. The princess picks the candlestick up and, in its pool of light, makes her way down the corridor. Old newspapers and candy wrappers rustle as her dress sweeps over them.

She opens another nondescript door and we step into a dusty, shabby room.

Except the door opens onto more than that one room. There's another one as well. I blink at the hallucination, but it won't clear. There are two rooms here, layered one over the other. Like a picture developed from a double negative. In one version of reality this room is just a large storage room for something like a theater. Large flats lean against one wall. There are power tools and paint cans in odd piles. A rack of dresses. A make-up table with a broken mirror.

Then over or beneath or beyond this there is a second room. It has higher ceilings, and walls with plaster wainscoting that curls in great golden twists over blood-red paint, with massive oil canvases hanging heavily, glimmering slightly in the glow of massive chandeliers pregnant with glass and light.

The Dreamers swirl about in both rooms, avoiding piles of old magazines and picking at hors d'oeuvres scattered on gleaming mahogany cocktail tables.

Not all of the room's occupants are as ethereal as my guide. Not all are beautiful even. One has heavy jowls that wobble as he sprays crumbs over a crumpled silver waistcoat. Another woman has a face that appears to have been badly burned, white ragged flesh sagging around her eyes and mouth, lending a permanently melancholy expression. A third seems to have virtually no muscle or fat to his face, the skin stretched tight over the skull, eyes large and red-rimmed, teeth pressing clearly against the paper-thin lips. His massive eyes follow me as I step across the room and I can feel mine watering at the sight. I start sympathy blinking.

I stop in the middle of the room looking around, turning slowly on the spot, trying to take it all in—the squalor and the glamour. My princess moves away from me back into the crowd that mills around me. Only the skull-faced man keeps staring, working his jaw, the skin stretching out, cheeks almost purple with each of his movements.

"Why are you here?" I say. My voice is less than a whisper.

Instantly, movement in the room stops. The Dreamers

stand icily still. The princess raises a finger to her lips.

"Why are you all here? Why am I here?" I'm so quiet even I can't hear the words. The Dreamers all stare at me.

"Tell me something," I breathe. "Give me some clue. A break. Something. Someone."

They turn to each other. I hear the quietest of susurrations, a hint of a breeze almost as they talk.

"Come on," I plead. "Please. Come on."

The skull-faced one stalks forward suddenly. All eyes follow him as he crosses to stand in front of me. He stops a pace away. Sweeps an arm at one wall. Like the ringmaster at a nightmare circus. Gives me the shivers.

The wall shimmers, like a sheet of silk suddenly exposed then pulled away. I stare into a room beyond, dusty and dirty. Cobwebs seem to fill the space, to blur its edges, packed almost as tight as cotton balls. At the center, hemmed in on all sides, sit two girls. It takes me a moment to recognize them. I am not used to seeing them with their hair bushy and pinned in place, with their dresses plump and carefully arranged.

The Twins sit in the filthy room, slowly laying down tarot cards.

"Keep them safe," the skull-faced Dreamer speaks. "Keep them safe."

"But that's..." I press my hands to my temple. Because I'm back at the beginning. I'm here over and over and over... And I think the Dreamers are trying to be helpful. But, God, they're bad at it.

"That's exactly what I'm trying to do. What I've been trying to do." I try to keep my voice low, patient, but I must have gone up a decibel or two because everyone is back to frowning at me.

"Sorry," I breathe. "I'm sorry, but I'm going to need a little more help than that."

"Important," says skull-face, again indicating the girls. "Save them."

"I know," I say. "I really, genuinely know. But if you just give me a few pointers—"

Again the glowers. A few fingers to lips.

"Keep them safe." Again.

"I know!" I can't help it. I'm a patient soul, but this is just... I shout at them. I'm not stupid enough to grab the guy by the lapels and shake him, but I do shout in his face.

And the world rips and tears, holes burn through reality and through me and then—

AN INDETERMINATE TIME LATER

—I am lying on my back by the side of the pool, the back of my head throbbing where I was thrown backwards.

I groan as I open my eyes. The groan gurgles and dies. I look up into the silver tip of Kayla's sword.

39

"What the feck are you doing here?"

"You," I say. Because suddenly it's starting to make sense.

"I asked you a feckin' question!" Her eyes are furious dots in a contorted face. Somewhere in the background I can hear a girl crying. The sword floats an inch above my nose.

But all I can think about is the skull-faced man, about his command. Now. I think he meant now. Here. Now. In this moment.

"Of course you can't save her," I say slowly, ignoring her talking, ignoring the blade. I'm too busy figuring things out. "You kill her."

"What?" Kayla actually flinches at the words. "I... what? What the feck are you talking about?" There is a look of utter panic on her face. And this must be it. I have her. I've got her. I go to push myself up but the sword comes back. It is quivering now, though.

"You're one of them. You betray us, and you kill her. Her but not Ephemera. You can't kill Ephie. Something stops you and you're trying to figure out what." That must be it.

But that's not it. No. Because the sword stiffens, straightens. "I am going to cut out your feckin' gizzard, you little lying sack of shit," she says, and her voice is abruptly calm. "You don't ever talk about me and my girls. You don't have the feckin' right."

Her sword arm comes back. I am acutely aware that the girls are watching this. They shouldn't see this. What a stupid thought to end your life on.

There is a cough behind us.

"Sorry," says Clyde.

Kayla glares around behind her. Her sword doesn't move.

"Terrible timing," Clyde says. "Or, you know, alternatively, quite good. Depends on your point of view, I imagine."

"S... S..." I pull in a breath to get myself under control. "Something like that."

"What do you want?" Kayla hisses. The girls, I see, have let go of the edge of the pool, are floating lazily away. The excitement is apparently over. Which is good news.

"Well," Clyde swallows audibly. "It's just... Shaw sent me down here. She was asking... wants the whole team to assemble. All constituent parts attached. Well... she didn't specify that. Sort of assuming." He laughs high and nervous, not taking the Twins' lead.

"Why?" Kayla asks.

"Well, you know," Clyde blusters, "she seems like she's quite fond of us as we are. You know, whole, and hale, and hearty, and—"

"Why does she want us to meet?"

"Oh!" Clyde swallows again. "My prototype. The one to throw the Progeny out of people's heads. Think we've got something workable up and running. Want to... try it out and stuff."

"That was fast," I say, doing my best to keep my voice casual, trying to ignore the sword still hovering above my head.

"It was Tabby mostly," Clyde says. Even though the bulk of Kayla's admittedly petite frame blocks my vision of him, I can still hear the smile in his voice. Maybe Kayla and I are the yang to their ying. The better they get along the closer Kayla comes to using me as an anatomy lesson for the Twins.

"So," I say, playing it far cooler than I am, "better be getting along then."

"Yes," Clyde says. "Probably should. You know how Shaw's a stickler for timing."

Still Kayla doesn't move. Not for a moment. Then with a grimace of something very close to hatred she stands. It takes me a moment to follow suit. My hands are shaking badly. My breath is shaky. But I manage it, because in the back of my head a small victorious voice is shouting at Kayla—now you get yours. Now you get yours.

40

No one will meet my eye.

They won't meet each other's either. We stand in a circle and it strikes me that we look like the shiftiest prayer group to ever meet. The thought almost makes me laugh, which would be terrible timing.

We're gathered around a small black disk that looks like it's mostly held together with duct tape. A flat red button protrudes from the center like some day-glow mushroom.

"It causes interdimensional friction," Clyde tells us. "Anything that exists on more than one reality, a Progeny for example, should be pretty much fried. While one-reality folks like you and me should get a free ride."

"You *have* tested this, right?" I'm not overly keen on the word "should."

"Didn't kill any guinea pigs," Tabby says.

"Or rats. Or my cats," Clyde adds. "Good thing about the cats really. Penicillin kills cats actually. Or possibly guinea pigs. One of the two. Anyway, would have been a disaster if that, whichever one it actually was... is... had been the first test subject. Would never have made it to human tests. Robbed humanity of a great asset."

"Your point, Clyde?" Shaw asks.

"Oh. Yes," Clyde flusters. "A point. Well, just, I

suppose, you can't always be a hundred percent certain from animal tests. That's all."

He shrugs.

"Not completely reassuring, Clyde," Shaw says.

His head retreats between his shoulders.

But that's not it. That's not why we can't look at each other. Otherwise, when Tabby says, "We've checked it best we can. No theoretical way for it to harm people. That we can find," then Clyde would smile, or look at her. But he doesn't. None of us smile.

Because we're all wondering which one of us it is. It doesn't matter how many alternatives Shaw throws out, we're all quietly certain that the traitor is in this room. But if we talk we might give our suspicions away, and nobody wants to be wrong.

I don't think any of us wants to be right, either.

Which, in the end, is why we have to do this, no matter how unsafe it may be. We have to get some trust back. We're never going to be a team until we do this.

"OK then," I say, "let's do this."

Clyde hesitates.

"Do it," Shaw says.

He hesitates.

"Now," Kayla says.

"Just do it, Clyde," says Tabitha.

Clyde's hand comes down.

41

I'm on the floor. I don't know how I got on the floor. I feel broken.

Slowly I find my hands, my feet. They seem further away than usual. Getting on all fours is hard. Getting on my feet is harder. My head throbs. My stomach rolls. The world lurches left then right. I don't think all the signals are getting through. It feels like working a marionette. Apparently I am no good at working marionettes.

Next time someone tells me there's no theoretical way something can hurt me, I'm going to pop a couple of ibuprofen just in case.

Everyone else is lying where they stood. Tabitha sprawled out like some recently crashed bird—dress and hair spread out like broken wings. Kayla is sprawled backward, fringe thrown out of her eyes for once, revealing surprisingly long, soft lashes. Shaw is curled up on herself, as if knocked back into infancy. And Clyde…

Wait…

Clyde…

Where the hell is Clyde?

A wave of bile rolls through my stomach. A sickness greater than the one the little black disk brought on. And oh shit. Oh no.

I scan the room a final time. Clyde has to be here. He must be here.

But he's not.

The Twins.

I look at Kayla. Right now she couldn't stop a kid from crossing the street, let alone a Progeny-infected magician. And I don't have the time to wake her up.

I have to get to the Twins.

I stagger forward. My vision blurs. For a moment all I can see is blood. Blood in the water.

Another step. Another. I half brace myself against the wall, half crash into it. It takes me five tries to get the door handle to work. And maybe this is all Clyde did. Maybe he just came around and went to throw up in the bathroom, went to offer a sacrifice to the porcelain gods. It could happen. It could be.

And he had the presence of mind to shut the door behind him?

Another wave of vertigo and nausea. I hear a groan as I stumble out into the corridor, but if I turn around now, I'll never be able to keep going. It's a hundred miles to the elevator. I trip, bite the floor. I rather wish someone would show up with a shoulder to lean on and a glass of cold water.

I make it on my hands and knees. Feels like I'm swimming—desperately trying to come up for air. I'm not even sure if I've pressed the elevator button until the doors open and I fall in.

I throw up before the doors open again. I feel better for it. Just about make it to my feet. Stagger across the open expanse toward the pool. My vision is blurring, but I can already see the answer to my question. One girl. Just one girl, hanging on to the edge of the pool as if her world is crumbling, sobbing out her heart.

The sound of footsteps behind me. I half turn, half fall. Kayla weaving her way toward me. Sword drawn.

"No," she slurs. "No you feckin' don't. Not my girls. No."

In the background I can still hear Ephie sobbing over and over, "It was him. It was him. He took Ophelia. It was him."

Too tired to explain. Too sick. Too heartsick. Headsick. I lie back. Back here again. Back on my back again. Kayla advances.

And then, either Ephie realizes the effects of her words, or by chance she hits the part of the cycle that redeems me. But I don't feel any better at all, don't feel any hope, any relief as she says, "It was Clyde. Clyde took Ophelia. It was him. It was Clyde."

42

Kayla's gone when Shaw and Tabitha make it down. She was screaming. Howling. She saw the blood in the water. And I was trying to explain it was there before. But then Ephie said it was Ophelia's, and Kayla seemed to almost be pulsating with fear and rage. I thought she was going to pop something. Like some terrible eighties horror movie. Smash cut to an exploding head and a collapsing mannequin. She left then, her sword scoring an inch-deep groove in the concrete floor.

I wouldn't want to be Clyde right now.

Oh God. Oh shit and balls. Oh Clyde.

Clyde.

I trust Clyde. Oh Jesus, what sort of fool am I?

Beware the painted man's false promises until he shows his second face. The very first thing I was told. The very first thing. And I can still see, when I close my eyes, one of the Sheilas saying, *maybe it means you, Clyde.* Him saying they weren't really tattoos.

It was all there. All of it. He cast the spell. He brought the Dreamers here. He made the disk that knocked us all out. Jesus.

How long? That's the only question. How long has he been against us? It can't have been since the beginning. I can't believe that. I won't believe that. If I do…

Shit and balls and fuck, fuck, fuck.

I watch Shaw and Tabitha go through the same thing when I tell them. Tabitha has her head between her knees. And I can tell she's crying and trying not to show it because, well, because she's Tabitha, and she's not the sort of person who can cry in front of us all. But this has broken something, this betrayal. Something feels cracked in all of us. Shaw walks back and forth muttering to herself and shaking her head angrily, occasionally barking things into a walkie-talkie and ignoring the responses.

And in the background Ephie keeps on sobbing. And eventually I manage to pull myself together enough to go over to her, and stroke her head, and tell her it'll be OK, we'll find Ophelia, we'll find Clyde, we'll fix this, we'll make it right. And slowly, slowly she subsides until the squid and octopuses come and wrap her in sinuous limbs, carry her back into the pool, spread-eagled on her back, hair spread out like a peacock's tail, somewhere between sleep and catatonia.

Tabitha's next. She's sitting curled into herself. She won't show me her face.

"Talk to me," I say. "Give me something here. Please."

It takes a while, a little coaxing, but eventually she says, "No." It's not just a denial of my request, but of everything, of the whole world.

"I know," I say. "I don't know." I look about. "I don't know how to process this."

Finally she looks up, her heavy mascara in thick trails down her cheeks. Funny—I'm not sure if that's by accident or design. Not that funny really.

"He was the best of us," she says. "Best of us and not one of us. Fuck. Fucked up." She shakes her head, more and more violently. Her hair thrashes about her head. I touch her shoulder and she stops and looks up at me. Pain and distress. Hate too. Not of me. Of herself. "I fucking kissed him." She looks at her hands, her feet. "He's got a fucking girlfriend. They've dated since university. And I kissed him. Who does that? What bitch? He was the best of us." She shakes her head again, a final vicious spasm. "Fuck."

"He was the only person I was sure it couldn't be," I say.

"Me too."

"We'll find him," I say. I try to find something that sounds like confidence. "We'll fix this. Fix him. We'll get it out of him."

She looks at me like I've gone mad. "What? We can't. He's gone. Don't you understand that? Clyde's dead. He's dead. He just hasn't stopped moving yet. We're just waiting for Kayla to put her sword in him."

"His machine—" I start.

"Was a lie!" She's shouting now. Shaw looks over, but I hold up a hand to keep her back. This needs to happen. It's time to get everything out.

"Don't you get any of this?" Tabitha demands. "The machine to kick out the Progeny—it can't be made. Some Progeny fuck lied to us. Just made something to knock us all out. So he could take Ophelia. It was a lie. He was a lie."

"You did the research," I say. "You read what was in the book. You thought this was possible. He didn't make the machine he said he did, but that doesn't mean the machine we want isn't possible. You can make it. You can help us fix this. Help us make it right."

"I'm a research assistant." She enunciates the words. "Understand that. I shouldn't be in the field. I shouldn't be making shit. I do research. Just learn stuff. Don't apply it. I go out in the field—Clyde gets infected. Build stuff—he steals Ophelia."

"No," I say. I shake my head. "No, that's not right. You're wrong." I get down on my knees. I'm close to her and Tabitha's aura of "bugger off" is so highly developed that it feels like a violation of private space, but I think she needs some human contact right now. "You are not responsible for this. You didn't do this. Clyde didn't do this. The Progeny did this. Evil mind worms from outer space. Not you. Not me. Not Clyde. We're going to get him back. We're going to fix this. Me. Shaw. Kayla. You."

There is a glimmer of hope, something maybe. And then she drowns it. But she's not talking to me anymore. I see the shutters go down. I've done my best, what I can. I beckon Shaw over. She shoves the walkie-talkie back into her pocket.

"Please can you talk to Tabitha," I say. "I think she needs to talk this out. Shutting down will be bad." Tabitha reminds me of parents, of lovers, of husbands and wives I had to visit when I worked with the murder squad, when I delivered bad news. Some of them took it quietly, some took it loudly. All of them needed to talk. Not usually to me, but to someone. They needed to reconnect with humanity, to confirm, "It wasn't me." Tabitha needs that now.

"What are you doing?" Shaw asks me.

"I'm not sure… Something with Kayla. I mean, someone has to stop her."

"Stop her?"

"I think Kayla is going to kill Clyde," I say. "We have to—"

"Arthur." Shaw reaches out and grabs my arm. She has a sad smile on her face. "You really don't know Kayla at all."

"What? What do you—"

"The girls' prediction," she says. "That Kayla can't save Ophelia. Kayla believes that body and soul. With complete conviction. And with good reason. The girls tell the truth.

Kayla won't chase Clyde because she doesn't believe she can do anything. She wouldn't have stayed here as long as she did if she could have done something about it."

God. I just accused her of planning to kill her daughters. And then the one guy I trust took her daughter off to kill her. And she's sitting alone somewhere feeling powerless.

"Where is she?" I ask. "I need to talk to her." I need to try and make some of this right. Anything right.

"Try Halal House, near the bus stop."

"Where?" There was something about that sentence that I missed, I'm sure.

"She likes falafel, Arthur." Shaw speaks slowly, patiently. Her hand, I notice, is still on my arm. "Halal House. Near the bus stop. She likes the food there. She finds it comforting. Whenever she's upset she usually goes to eat there. Try there."

I nod and turn to leave.

"Arthur," she says. She still hasn't let go of me.

"Yes?" I turn.

"This is good work. It's good to see you taking charge of this situation." She gives my arm a squeeze and finally lets go.

I nod numbly. Taking charge. This is what I needed to finally take the lead? This? I'd rather I wasn't leading at all.

43

One of Oxford's curiosities—something that goes unadvertised to tourists—is that late at nights its streets are ploughed by a strange fleet of grease-stained vans. The sun drops below the horizon and they roll out from unnamed, and presumably equally greasy garages. They track the city's streets in search of their prey. Finally they will encounter a pack of drunken students and will proceed to ply these uninhibited, unsuspecting youths with spicy meat of dubious quality and origin. It's the stuff horror movies are made of.

Halal House is the sedentary version of Oxford's infamous kebab vans—an establishment where the owners have the pluck to attempt to sell the same wares to sober people. Only the hardcore falafel fanatics can be found there during daylight hours.

Kayla is among them, at the back of the place, wedged into the furthest corner of a booth, legs tucked up in the almost impossibly narrow space between table and seat. A plastic container lies untouched before her. Her face is hidden behind her long bangs and all I can really see of her are her fine hands turning an ornate pocket watch over and over.

Slowly, feeling like an animal trainer approaching a circus tiger without his chair and whip, I slip into the booth opposite her. She says nothing. Silence. Not one of those comfortable ones I've heard about. I open my mouth a couple of times. But how do I start? Any sort of apology seems paltry in the face of everything that's happened.

Eventually I just decide to talk.

"K—" is about as far as I get.

"Feck off."

I blow the rest of the word out in a long tremulous breath. Close my eyes. But I have to do this. I have to get this conversation working. She needs to talk. People always needs to talk. My palms sweat. A spot between two of my ribs begins to ache.

"Kay—" I say.

"I said feck off." Still she doesn't look at me, just works the pocket watch over and over. I'm not even sure if she's paying attention to me. It's as if the curse is just an automatic reflex, some vocal tic that I keep triggering.

"Kayla—"

A knife smashes down into the tabletop. A simple, stainless steel table knife. Not even an edge on it. Buried up to the handle in the peeling linoleum. Quivering slightly. I don't even see her hand move.

I am so very, very scared. I have accused Kayla of the worst imaginable bloody things. Of course she wants to kill me. I'm the worst possible person to be starting this conversation with her. I sit and stare at the linoleum's fresh scar.

Kayla starts up with the pocket watch again. We sit in silence.

"It was my da's," she says, letting the watch briefly pause upon her knuckles. She begins talking so abruptly and so quietly that I almost miss it, almost ask her to repeat herself before common sense kicks in and shuts my mouth for me.

"I took it off him after I killed him." She looks up from behind the shield of her bangs, not at me, but at some spot over my shoulder, not at the now, but at the past.

"They were in me, you know," she says. "The Progeny. They were feckin' in here." She taps the side of her head. "I was twelve years old. But they couldn't get a grip, couldn't keep hold. They kept trying to fix me. Kept trying to stitch me up in some new way so they could keep me, hold me, have me as a puppet. They feckin'… feckin' changed me. Made me different. They feckin' raped the inside of my skull. They're always getting in there. Every time I take one of those bastards down. I can feckin' feel them, worming in. Trying to stay there. I don't even know what's left of who I was. I don't know who I am. If there's anything of the original, or if it's just all… all stuff they feckin' made."

"I'm…" I start, but what is there to say? I don't know. I stay there, mouth slightly open, like some slack-jawed idiot. Which is maybe all I am. "I'm sorry," I say. It feels insignificant.

She lets out a grunt or a snort. I can't tell if it's derision or acceptance. She twirls the pocket watch once more, spinning it across her fingertips.

"Epilepsy," she says. "Seizures. Bad ones too. Something when I was born. Not right." She taps the side of her head. "So they went and did some surgery. Went in there and cut some things out. Scar tissue. Still get headaches sometimes." She shakes her head. The movement of the watch doesn't falter.

"Wasn't my Da they took first. Was my ma. Then him. Then me. Then Izzie. Except, like I say, it didn't stick. What the doctors had done. Couldn't stick."

I catch a gleam in her eyes at that, a slight, grim smile. "I'm their feckin' mistake. And I make them pay for it." Then the smile is gone.

"They'd been in the sheep. We had a farm, see. Up in the highlands. And the Progeny, they'd been at the sheep. Trying them on for size, I suppose. Breeding up maybe. Izzie told me. I called her a fool and told Ma on her. Then Izzie wasn't a little girl anymore. Nobody was who they'd been before. Not even me. Changed. A little more than human. A little feckin' less."

She stares ahead, jaw working, working, working.

"They were already dead. You know that, right? You understand that. That's feckin' important to realize. It's very, very, very feckin' important." One of her fingers is tapping the table, harder and harder. I can hear a creaking sound every time it strikes. Fresh cracks spread in the linoleum. "Dead. Just hadn't stopped moving. Progeny don't come out. Once they're in. Only me." She hangs her head.

"Slaughtering sick sheep we were. Up on the farm. Da, and Ma, and me, and Izzie. And the knife went in one and the eggs came out. Went into us. And the Progeny don't come out. Only out of me."

Her hand stops its tapping, hanging suspended above the table. "Didn't even know what I was doing at first, what they'd made me capable of doing. Not until Da was dead. Only hit him twice. Once in the stomach. Once in the neck. Then down and he was done. Didn't even understand it. Ma was attacking me then. The thing that had been my ma. They knew it hadn't worked. They didn't know why, I don't think, but they'd seen what they'd done.

"We were in the kitchen. Ma came at me. Izzie grabbed my hands. Feck she were but nine years old. She was strong as feckin' iron right then, though. Might have been the thing in her. Might've been the fear in me."

Tears are slipping down Kayla's face now, rolling one after the other in an ever-increasing stream. She speaks in a deadpan.

"Kicked Ma. Sent her halfway across the room. She still came at me, but I was free of Izzie. Grabbed the rolling pin off the counter. Swung it round. Cracked Ma's head. Down she went. Turned. And there's Izzie. Hands held out to me. And there was something in her head. In her brain. One of them. The Progeny. It was in her. Grubbing in her brains. And I brought the pin down. And I caved in her skull. Whole thing collapsed in upon itself.

"Don't know why she had her hands out. Sometimes I think maybe she'd had it beat, was just asking me for one more second, two more. Just so she could get it out. Just asking to be like me. Sometimes I think she was about to throttle me."

She buries her tear-stained face in her hands. "Feck," she says. Repeats it over and over. "Feck, feck, feck."

I sit in silence. The lump's in my throat too. I can't imagine something like it. I can't even picture it. A child. She was just a child. The age of Ephie and Ophelia. And, Jesus, what she must be going through right now.

I want to reach out and touch her, to show some kind of compassion, but Kayla's not that kind of girl, and I can still see the knife buried in the table. So all I have is words.

"We'll fix it," I say. "We'll fix this."

"I found them in a bath," Kayla says.

I shut my mouth immediately. Just let her talk.

"I was eighteen. Had been killing the Progeny fuckers for six years by then." She stares at her hands. "I was living on the streets. First I'd been down to Edinburgh. Sponge off the tourists. My head was still fecked with it all. Then I found them there. Two Progeny. Was easy. Maybe I knew a little about how they thought. After they'd been in here." She taps her head again. "Taken over a couple in their fifties. It was easy to kill them. So I started working my way south. Going to the big cities, finding the Progeny. Taking them out. Because if it was me they couldn't breed. Couldn't infect. They worked at me still, but I didn't get weaker, didn't get stronger, didn't stop what I was doing, just found them and killed them. Up and down the country. Feckin' scourge on the bastards.

"And then the girls. Tracked a bunch of Progeny to a warehouse in Sheffield. Five, I think. All women. And I went there, and I killed them all, and then, as I was leaving, I saw the bath. And I went over. Almost like something called me over. No reason to go over. I was done there. But the two of them were lying right in it. My girls. Weren't even eighteen months old. Could tell even then though they were twins. Ephemera in the arms of a squid; Ophelia cushioned by an octopus. Water swimming with eggs. The girls screamed when I lifted them out of the water. Went into convulsions." A smile peers through the veil of Kayla's melancholy. "I was so feckin' scared. Carried the whole bath back to where I could boost a flatbed truck.

"Slowed me down they did. Cramped my style. Got sloppy. Got found. Shaw found me. Thought she was one at first. Progeny. Almost killed her. But she lost a sister to them, same as me." She looks away. "Not quite the same."

Shaw lost a sister? To the Progeny? How did I not know that? I am such a bad team leader.

I picture again the scene Kayla described. Her twelve-year-old self crushing the skull of her little sister. And there is something in that image that rings a bell. And I realize my vision of that scene is so vivid because I have seen some of it played out. The head of the student on Cowley Road. The original painted man as he was transformed. His head changing from male to female, then abruptly collapsing in on itself. As if struck. Crushed by a blow from the past. And then Kayla froze. It was then that she froze. After seeing that.

The Progeny know. They have her Achilles heel.

That's not good. Not good at all.

Still, now doesn't seem like the moment to maybe remind her how out of luck she is. In fact she seems to know quite well herself, because she leans across the table and grabs my arms. She stares at me with enough intensity that it's like she's stabbing me all over again.

"I can't save her, Wallace," she says. "I can't do it. I don't know why, but it can't play out like that. And so all I've got is you. Do you understand me? You, and Tabitha, and Shaw. That's it."

"I understand," I say. And I do. God help me, I do. I feel crushed by it. "I'll fix it. I'm going to fix it. We're all going to fix it."

"You better, Wallace. You better fix it or I'll feckin' kill you."

44

THE NEXT MORNING

Tabitha sits in the lab and pokes things. Bits of metal. A soldering iron. The book. Occasionally she turns the pages of the book, handling it as if it's going to burn her.

"You can do this," I say. I've lost count of the number of times I've said it.

"What if I build it wrong?" I've lost count of the number of times that's been Tabitha's reply.

I want to point out it's not like she can do a worse job than Clyde did, but I'm not sure that would really motivate at this point. I feel frustrated and useless. There aren't leads to chase. Ephie hasn't made any prophetic statements. The Progeny haven't thrown down the gauntlet. I'd be worse than useless at building magical devices to disrupt aliens. All I can do is try and motivate Tabitha, and she is very reluctant about the whole thing.

"Look," I say. "This is our chance to save Clyde. To rescue him. To bring him back."

She turns and looks at me with complete hatred. Well… not complete, I think she's mixed in a little bit of contempt too. A 90/10 mix, let's say.

"You think I don't know that? Overly fucking aware. Thank you." She gives me the finger, which rather undermines the sentiment.

"Sorry. Sorry." I shake my head. "It's just... We have to get him back. Don't we? And I can't help. Shaw can't. Kayla can't. That's not what we do. But you—"

"Pressure," Tabitha says. "Totally helps. Cheers." Another outing for her middle finger.

I sit and stare at the back of Tabitha's head. She turns a page of the book. She even seems to read it. But as the anger runs out of her, her shoulders slump. She goes back to poking things.

Her anger, I think, is the key. That is, as Clyde told me, her way. If I can trust him. If he was who I think he was back then. But... Shit, I have to trust my memory. My hope. I have to. It's all any of us have.

So—anger. Tabitha runs on it. And she's lost it. And I can get a bit of it back. Just by talking, apparently. But that's misdirected anger. I need her to be angry at the book. At herself maybe. At Clyde even. I need her to be so pissed at this she fixes it.

Oh God, I can't believe I'm thinking this again. This is always such a bad idea... But, God help me, I need to do what Kurt Russell would do.

"This is so fucked up," I say. And it even sounds like cheesy movie dialog. Except even the guys playing second fiddle to Kurt Russell usually deliver their lines with the vague semblance of conviction.

"Know that."

"Clyde, wow," I say. I wish I had a scriptwriter. "The chap who actually got stuff done around here." I'm glad her back is to me, because I'm wincing as I say that.

"What?" Tabitha's voice is low, her shoulders are back up.

"I mean," I say, attempting nonchalance, "the one who could blast magic, could do the book work, could build stuff, and he's the one we lose. It's just..." I can't finish the sentence; the temperature of the room is dropping too fast. Even though I can't see Tabitha's face I can still feel the death stare. I'm worried I've gone too far.

Tabitha stands up.

"Don't walk out on this, Tabitha." I totally overstepped the mark. "You can—"

Tabitha crosses the room and punches me right in the balls.

I stop, drop, and squeal.

"Fuck you," she says. "Fuck you and your reverse psychology bullshit. Plenty bloody good at what I do. This is not what I do. Why I'm no damn good at it, you prick."

All of which is pretty much deserved I think. But, she doesn't storm out of the room. She goes back to the lab table and starts turning pages. She actually seems to examine stuff.

I try to tell my testicles it was worth it.

Goddamn you, Kurt Russell. You and your terrible bloody life lessons.

Shaw finds me still on the floor when she comes in five minutes later. Tabitha is writing something down on a notepad and ignores us both in a studied way. Shaw arches an eyebrow as she offers a hand to help me up. I shake my head, as I crouch there, knock-kneed.

"Can see you in the bloody glass," Tabitha says. She's pointing at a large fish tank that is currently home to two white rats.

"Shouldn't you be concentrating?" Shaw's voice holds only minimal disapproval but there's still a muttered curse word and Tabitha lowers her head.

"How are we doing?" Shaw asks me.

"Kayla's trawling the city for any Progeny she can find," I say. "A long shot, but worth doing anyway. Tabitha here is building our secret weapon." Without looking up,

Tabitha flips me off over her shoulder.

"And you?"

"Thinking."

"About?"

"The Dreamers."

There's a pause. She looks at me. "Do you want me to beg for something of actual substance, Arthur?" But she's smiling. Something has loosened inside her, I think.

"I saw them again," I say. "After Peru. Before Ophelia disappeared." I tell her about the skull-faced man, about his demand to keep the Twins safe.

"It's related," I say. "It has to be. All of this. The Peru thing. The summoning. It can't all be random. The Progeny had Olsted plant that book in the Bodleian. They led us to Olsted. They led us to his book. And it was his book that led us to Peru. So they led us to Peru. And it was Clyde who pushed for us to perform the summoning. And Clyde has to have been infected when he did that. He was infected in the fight perhaps. That's the last point at which it could have happened. That's probably when it was." I want to believe it was then, so that's what I stake my hopes on.

"You think the Progeny had us summon the Dreamers?"

"Yes." I nod. "I don't know why they had us do it, but they did."

"But the Progeny can't touch the Dreamers," Shaw says. "If they do they're bounced from reality. It's the end of their game."

And that begs the question of why the Dreamers haven't bounced them already. If the Feeders get here then the Dreamers go too.

"I think the Dreamers are scared," I say. I remember how they stared while the skull-faced man looked at me. I remember how silent and still they were. "It's something to do with the Twins, with Ophelia. They want her safe. Why? Why do they care?"

"A prophetic twelve-year-old somehow gives the Progeny leverage on them?"

"It's all I can think of," I say.

"You need to talk to the Dreamers," Shaw says.

I should really think about the natural endpoint of conversations before I start having them.

"Are you going to knock me out again?" I ask Shaw.

"I think Ephie's pool is probably more humane," she says.

It makes me sad that she's right.

45

My finger touches the pool. Ephie cowers. The squid and octopus convulse. The water darkens. Everything goes black—

THEN AND WHEN AND IN-BETWEEN

The alleyway is empty this time. No princess, no swirling dresses, no distracting curves. I go to the door she opened. There's no handle, but I do have a credit card and there's enough of a gap between the door and the floor to get some leverage once I've jimmied the lock.

The corridor is hard to negotiate without the candles. I put one hand against a wall and proceed to trip over an enormous amount of junk before I find the second door. It swings open as soon as I get the lock open. Still, looks like quick trips to the ATM are going to be absent from my future until I work out how to explain the damaged card to my bank manager.

As the door swings wide I see the Dreamers milling about in their two superimposed rooms, pulling wine glasses out of one reality and into another.

They all stop, turn, look at me.

I smile—a tightening of the lips that never makes it to my eyes. "Hello, everybody," I say. "Hope you don't mind the imposition."

They pull back to the walls of the room. It's not quite cowering, but it's far from confident. What has them so spooked? I watch them as they walk, mark out the princess and the skull-faced fellow. The two who seem willing to talk to me.

"Look," I say as quietly as I'm able. I try to sound reasonable. "I understand—you want something from me. I'm more than happy to provide it. I think our goals are in alignment. Neither of us wants the Feeders here. But, and I'm sorry I got a bit noisy about this last time… But a little more help, a few more specifics, would be dreadfully nice to have."

Skull-face turns to the princess. He shakes his head.

"Please?" I say.

But no one says a word.

"Look," I say. "I'm trying to help you all. Just let me know what actually helps. Talk to me. Tell me about Ephie, about Ophelia. Tell me something so I can help them."

The princess takes a slow step forward. Skull-face takes a quick one, then another. He waves her back as he stalks toward me. "Not your business," he says, his voice dry and cracked. "Our business. Never should have been asked. Failed anyway."

I look down at my feet. I need to be calm and collected. I need to not think about Ophelia in the hands of the Progeny. I need to not think about how that Progeny used to be my friend. I need to be calm.

"Maybe," I say, still not meeting his eye, "I wouldn't have failed, if I'd had a little more information." My voice is still low, but my tone might be a little less than civil.

Nothing from skull-face.

"I mean," I say, which is probably a mistake, probably I should calm down and appeal to the princess, but fear and frustration have control of my tongue for a moment, "you must have known that I couldn't really protect anyone without knowing anything. You must have known how helpless I was. And you must—" I don't know if this is true, but it suddenly feels true "—you must have known about Clyde. I mean, why would you not tell me that? If I'd known that then surely, I mean…" I blink at the enormity that change would have brought. Surely they knew. They hold reality together. How could they not?

But skull-face just turns his back on me.

And I forget myself, and grab his shoulder, saying, "Please."

Bad move, Arthur. Very bad move.

Skull-face turns, sneers at me.

There is a crippling pain in my shoulders, my arms twist unnaturally, my bones become putty, the limbs twisting in looping curves. Then my bones harden again. I stare at my looping, useless arms. Like an uncoiled slinky. I can feel the muscles, triceps, biceps, whatever the hell else is in there, twisted to the limit of breaking, beyond the limit. I drop to one knee, bellowing.

"Hush." Skull-face places a finger against my lips.

And then I do lose my temper. Finally. Utterly. Then I tap into whatever dark seam of energy fuels Tabitha. And fuck this guy. Fuck him to hell.

"You know," I manage, "I am getting sick of people telling me that."

And I nut him hard in the crotch.

He goes down hard, doubling over with a whoosh of pain. My arms spring back and for a moment all I can do is reel with him, the whiplash of reality returning. But I'm the one who recovers first and my fist catches him square in the sternum even as he tries to stand up, hands still buried between his legs.

He sits down hard. I grab him by the throat.

"Now," I say. "Enough bullshit and avoidance. Ophelia, Ephemera. The kids. Tell me something that's actually bloody useful."

Someone catches my arm and I flinch away. I look up and see the princess.

"Hush," she says.

"Don't you bloody start." But already the anger is leaking out of me. I look down at skull-face, still with his hands between his thighs, and I feel like an arse. That's not how to get results.

"Calm," the princess says. "I meant calm." She speaks hesitantly, the slight hint of an accent that I can't place.

She catches my arm again, pulls me away as skull-face slowly drags himself to his feet, a look on his face that acid might have etched.

"I'm calm," I say. I try on a smile. But it's a little early for that. A grimace comes out instead. I can still feel skull-face's eyes moving over my back, charting exciting places to damage me.

"It is hard for him," she says.

"For all of you, surely," I say. I try to accept the olive branch she's offering.

"For him, especially."

"Why?"

"I have told you," she says. "She is not what you think she is."

Round and round we go.

"Who?" I don't even bother hiding the exasperation.

"Ophelia."

She says it as if it's obvious, as if only someone with severe head trauma couldn't see it.

Ophelia.

Ophelia.

Ophelia isn't what I think.

What do I think she is? Some poor messed up little girl caught in the middle of some ungodly mess. But she's not.

"She's Progeny?" I ask, bewildered. Because how could Ephie have not known? Unless Ephie is Progeny too? But then... how does it work with Clyde? Is he still—

"No." The princess cuts off the stream of questions in my head. There's even something like a smile on her face. But sadness too. You'd think having control of all reality would cheer you up a bit.

"Her mother," she says. "Her mother was Progeny."

Another mental contortion as I try to wrap my head around that one.

"Infected," I say. "Someone infected by a Progeny." I so totally do not want to imagine alien mind worm love.

"Yes," she says.

"It's inheritable?" Do the Progeny get into the DNA somehow? Mix their eggs with ours?

"No," says the princess. "Nothing from her mother's side. Just human on her mother's side."

Which leaves...

"Who's her father?" I ask.

She doesn't answer at first, but I follow her eyes. And the words echo in my head. *"It is hard for him."*

"Skull-face?" I ask incredulously. It only occurs to me after I've said it that that's probably not what she calls him. Then, as my brain does more work, "Ophelia is a Dreamer?"

"She will be." The princess nods slightly, looking pained. "When her time comes. When the blood comes on her."

Blood. Blood in the water.

Menstruation. Puberty.

I don't know how to tell them. How to tell them it's too late. I'm not even sure if I can admit it to myself.

She's not who I think she is… A prophetic girl spending her whole life in a swimming pool full of octopuses and squid, and I thought she was human. What sort of fool am I?

"How?" I ask, because it's the easiest question to ask. It's the question I don't need answering.

The princess's hand comes out again. She doesn't touch my arm this time, but my cheek.

The room vanishes. A feeling like vertigo. I'm suddenly nauseous. And then my body is not my own. There's something in my head that is not my own. A terrible need, a terrible desire. A feeling like power and hatred.

And there's a woman too. Oh my God is there a woman. All curves and softness exactly where you would want it. My head is lost in her blond hair. She's naked. I'm naked. Our bodies together. Thrusting. And there is pleasure, such pleasure, in the tight embrace of flesh, but it is a pleasure in taking something, the kleptomaniac's joy in theft. This is something forbidden, something terrible.

The woman arches her back, throws her head back. Bright red lips. Large green eyes, pupils throbbing and wide, the slight upward curve of a petite nose. The exhalation of her breath. And in that cresting moment I recognize her. The part of me that is still me in this strange emaciated body recognizes her. I've seen her before.

Then something that is not quite here—something that is touching *my* body, not this new one—is removed. A hand abruptly removed from my cheek. And then—

46

THE EDGE OF A SWIMMING POOL FILLED WITH SQUID

I come to lying on my back. Shaw is bent over me, a look of concern on her face. Her hand is reached out toward my face, as if to replace the one the Dreamer removed.

"Back?" she asks.

My tongue doesn't feel like working. I cough and try to bring my systems back online.

Shaw turns away. "He's OK, Ephie," she says.

Sorry Ephie, I want to say. The last thing she needs is more scaring. Instead I just splutter at her.

"Robert," I croak when I finally get things going.

"Who?"

"The budget man," I say. "Didn't want to pay for Peru."

Shaw looks confused. "What about him?"

"There's a woman," I say. "She... works with him? For him? His boss? Pretty. Very pretty." A frown creases Shaw's brow. "In a magazine sort of way." I don't know why I feel compelled to say that.

"Yes," Shaw says, perhaps a little too fast. "I know her. His assistant." She purses her lips with something approaching disdain.

"Progeny," I say.

Shaw's eyes go wide. "What?"

"Progeny," I say, "and—" Then I see Ephie staring at

us. Ephie. Ophelia's sister. Twin sister. And that should have been obvious. I shake my head. "Not here," I say.

"What?" Ephie says immediately.

"Nothing."

"What aren't you telling me?" Ephie's voice is shrill, almost a scream. I half expect Kayla to swoop down out of somewhere and threaten to stab me for upsetting the girl. But Kayla isn't here. She's out hunting monsters. Trying to protect her other charge.

I pull myself up off the ground. "Not here," I say to Shaw again, backing away fast.

"Tell me!" Ephie is furious now, splashing the water. The squid and octopuses swirl around her, thick tendrils of ink stretching out through the water. I press the elevator button. Shaw stands between the two of us looking torn. The elevator door pings open. Shaw follows me. Behind us, Ephie shrieks.

"What's going on?" Shaw asks. "What happened? And are you serious that the airhead with more inches on her chest than IQ points is infected?"

"They showed me," I say. "The Dreamers. She's Progeny and she's the Twins' mother."

The expression of confusion, of horror, on Shaw's face gives me a good idea of how I must have looked pretty much since I joined MI37. I pat her arm. It's awkward.

"No wonder Robert is so happy to back our closure if it makes his little whore happy." The depth of Shaw's bitterness catches me by surprise.

"There's more," I say.

"Of course there bloody is." Shaw shakes her head.

"A Dreamer is their father. And that, unlike infection, is apparently inheritable."

"You're saying—" she starts then stops. I don't think she really wants to know what I'm saying.

"Ophelia became a Dreamer when she hit puberty."

Shaw's eyes are as wide as saucers. Then she closes them. "Blood," she says. "Kayla was screaming about blood in the water."

"The Progeny have themselves a Dreamer," I say. And there it is out in the open, a statement to sum up how completely screwed we all are.

"The Dreamers knew," Shaw says slowly. "They've always known."

And it makes sense. It's all starting to make horrible sense. "They wanted me to keep her safe," I say. "To stop her from falling into the Progeny's hands. To stop her from being… being…" I can't say it.

"Infected." Shaw fills in the blank. "God, no wonder they got away from you fast as they could when Clyde brought them onto our version of reality. They knew he was infected."

"Shit," I say. "Oh shit and balls."

"She can…" I try to think through the possibilities. "Can she bring the Feeder through?"

Shaw thinks about it, one palm pressed to her brow.

"No," she says. "I don't think so. The other Dreamers would fight the addition of a new reality. The Progeny will have infected her, but I don't know if one Dreamer could overcome the will of all the others."

Which is good for us. But… But… "What if the Progeny have another way to bring one in? A spell or something? Can she stop them from evicting a Feeder from reality?"

Shaw chews a lip. "Maybe. Maybe yes. Hold them at a standstill."

"You think the Progeny have a spell to bring the Feeders through?"

Shaw doesn't answer. Doesn't look at me. The elevator pings. The doors slide open. A corridor stretches out before us, seemingly without end. Just door, after door, after door. None of them offer an exit. Just empty dead-end rooms. Shaw stares off into space. I stand there next to her frozen just as still. The doors slide closed. Slide open again.

Shaw jerks to life. "Call Kayla," she says. "Get her back here. Then find that Progeny bitch and find out where they have Ophelia by any means you see fit to use."

I nod. "Sounds reasonable."

Shaw takes a step toward the exit of the elevator, then pauses. "Oh, and Arthur?" she says.

"Yes?" I try to read her expression.

"I think it's about time you were issued a gun."

In my mind's eye I can see Kurt Russell standing behind Shaw. I can see him nodding and smiling that lopsided grin.

"Yes," I say. "Yes, maybe it is."

47

Despite the unaccustomed new weight of the gun sitting beneath my jacket, tracking down the Progeny feels reassuringly familiar. It's nice to be doing something where I feel I have some actual experience. I've tracked down a fair number of lawbreakers across Oxford, and while today's lawbreaker may be a disgusting space worm hiding in someone's head, the principles seem to be the same. Known address first, then place of work, then regular hangouts that you've found out from co-workers, family members, friends. There's a process. Process is comforting.

I raise my hand to knock on the mailbox-red door of 11 Chapel Street, registered address of Madeline Ellman, assistant to budget director Robert Felkin. Before I can bring the fist down, Kayla kicks the door off its hinges.

It flies back across the small hallway and cracks in two as it hits the wall.

She sees my look and shrugs.

"Not complaining," I say. Though it's definitely a breach in standard police procedure.

"Better feckin' not be."

And it's not a joke the way she says it, but it's not quite as definite a threat either. We're not friends, but I think neither of us is as convinced we're enemies.

There's a door off the hallway and a staircase leading

up. Kayla kicks the next door off its hinges too.

"I'll take upstairs," I say.

"Whatever."

I hear her methodically crashing through each room downstairs as I make my way up. I've got the gun out, and I'm holding it in both hands, feeling the surprising weight of the thing.

And whatever felt comfortably police-like a moment ago is gone now. The gun, freed from its shoulder holster, changes that. This is not police work. And it's only been two weeks... a week, but I'm not a good British bobby anymore. I'm Agent Wallace. Kurt Russell wannabe. Inaction hero.

I have to admit, I was kind of hoping for a revolver really. A big old Clint Eastwood job, all barrel and cylinders. And a hip holster. Instead it's a sleek black semi-automatic that sits in the shoulder holster. Still, beggars can't exactly be choosers. And with Kayla downstairs, it's nice to have firepower all of my own. All I have to do now is to work out how to hit something smaller than the side of a barn.

The upstairs consists of a short corridor with four doors leading off it. I push them open with the gun barrel one by one. I would kick them, but I'm not sure I have Kayla's leg strength.

The first one opens up onto an empty bathroom, the next an empty bedroom, something made up like a guest room. The third door reveals an office neat enough to suggest OCD as a side effect of alien possession.

The fourth door. I brace myself, then pause and check the safety on the automatic. Rather embarrassingly, I discover it's on. Which undoes all the security I felt about having a gun in the first place really.

I push the door open. Another bedroom. Minimal furniture. A bedside table, a dresser, a lamp. No pictures.

Just plain white walls. Not a room that a person really lives in, just one someone… something inhabits. A holding place of a room.

And her. The Progeny. She's here too.

I swing the gun at her. Suddenly my hands are shaking, my aim all over the place. My mind's eye superimposes Olsted's daughter over the scene. But that was the heat of a moment. That was different. Jesus.

"Hands—" I manage to get out. But her hands are already rising. Though not above her head, just to her shoulder, her neck. And something, a clasp maybe, undoes, and suddenly a blood red dress is sheering away. And there is nothing beneath. Just flesh, and skin, and curves, and desire. The gun droops even as I stand to attention, all focus descending to live well below my waist. A lust so powerful, so all-consuming it obliterates everything else. I am as naked as she is, all my thoughts exposed to her. All my thoughts a need. For her. For flesh. To immolate myself to her. A moth to such a pretty, pretty flame.

I moan slightly.

There is movement to my side, someone pushing roughly past me, fast and hard. "Kayla," says part of my brain. A piece of it lying deep under the heavy layers of desire. She is moving toward… Her, moving toward what I want.

Kayla wants it too. Kayla wants Her for herself. She is trying to take Her from me. And I won't have it. Not at all.

I find the gun in my hands again, bring it to bear. Because Kayla won't take Her. She is mine. All mine. I want Her. Mine.

I try to focus, to get the sights lined up. But Kayla is too fast for my sluggish mind. And the hilt of the sword comes down like a lightning bolt, and then the Progeny goes down, disappears behind the bulk of her bed, and a little while later rational thought comes wandering back into my head.

"Feckin' men," Kayla says into my bewilderment. But it seems a general indictment rather than a specific criticism.

"What…?" I manage. "Did she…? Did I…?"

"A little bit of each." Kayla shrugs. "She took advantage of someone easy to take advantage of."

"How?"

"Bit of a glamour." Kayla fiddles with the downed woman's palm and pulls out a battery. "Bit of the old tit and arse."

I go closer, see her lying there. She's not been scalped. There's no blood. Kayla must have used the hilt.

"Cover her up would you?" I say. There's still a terrible beauty to her, even robbed of whatever power the battery was giving her.

I turn away and, to make myself feel better, think about how stupid she is to have listed her real home address.

Kayla lifts her by her hair. Throws a bedsheet over her. Throws the bundle over her shoulder.

Downstairs she ties the Progeny to a kitchen chair. Rough tight knots using twine she found in a drawer. The Progeny lies there, slumped forward, mouth slightly open.

"So," I say, still hanging back in the doorway of the kitchen. "How do we do this?"

Kayla twists her head, working a crick out. "It's hard to torture Progeny," she says. "The host's body isn't really theirs. So what do they care if you slice it up? Just shut down some of the infected brain's pain functions. They don't care." She taps the handle of her sword against the woman's bruised temple. "Don't feckin' care. It's their eggs they care about. Their young. Their ability to infect. To spread. They're like some sort of feckin' virus. So to torture a Progeny you've got to threaten that."

"Isn't…" I wonder if I want to pursue the thought. "Don't the Progeny nest near the brainstem?"

"Sure do," says Kayla, and promptly stabs the woman in the back of the neck.

The woman's body contorts, lurching forward out of unconsciousness. The mouth opens wide, wider than it should. There's an ugly crack as the jaw dislocates. It hangs, lolling open, and I swear I see a few rogue tendrils from the Progeny flicking back and forth in the back of her throat.

"Where's my girl, you feckin' whore?" Kayla's voice is flat deadpan.

The sword flickers again. Another guttural scream issues from the unhinged mouth.

I turn away, my gorge rising. Blood is trickling down the woman's neck. Another scream. Something spoken, but not English—something guttural and hard. A clacking of the voice box. An inhuman sound.

Jesus.

"Where, bitch?" Kayla's voice—still flat, emotionless, like this bores her.

I can't watch this. I can't hear this. I pull the kitchen door closed behind me. It doesn't do any good. I can still hear it all. And the pictures in my head are as vivid as if I saw it myself.

Jesus.

I go outside. Sit on the low wall that marks out the front yard. A small area of cracked concrete and weeds. Only the occasional scream reaches me now. I palm my eyes trying to erase the scene.

Madeline Ellman is not human. Not anymore. She's Progeny. I need to remember that.

I pull out my gun, turn it over in my hands. I make sure the safety's on. Part of me wishes Shaw never gave it to me. Not a shot fired. And would it have been better if one was? If I'd just killed the Progeny? Does anything deserve what Kayla's putting... *it*... through?

But then, what about Ophelia? She'd be gone. Dead and lost. The whole world lost. The Progeny have a Dreamer. I repeat that over and over.

Jesus.

Eventually the sounds stop coming from the house. Eventually I stand up, go back inside. Kayla is standing in the kitchen doorway. She is blood-spattered and satisfied. Behind her I can see the cloud of eggs slowly settling, can see the bisected body of the alien twitching in the exposed cavity of the skull.

I gag again, taste bile in the back of my throat, feel the acid burn as I swallow it back down.

Kayla smiles. Her teeth are stained red. "Got it," she says.

48

My nerves are still shot as we sit around the conference room. I can feel the weight of the gun pressed into my armpit. The great equalizer. Prized from Charlton Heston's cold dead hand. And I don't feel equal. I feel like the thing acts to expose my weaknesses, to show me exactly how right Shaw was. We need Kayla. I don't think any of us could do what Kayla did. Because it was horrible, and awful, and necessary.

I look over at Kayla. She looks totally calm. There's still dried blood on her cheek.

Tabitha is sitting next to her. She fidgets constantly. In her hands she fingers a new version of Clyde's device. One that should do what Clyde promised his would. Something to evict Progeny. She can't hold it still, playing with it, working it from one hand to the other. It shares its looks with Clyde's original—a small black disk with a red button like a mushroom. And though I know it's different, the sight of it makes me nervous. I really don't want to get kicked in the frontal cortex again.

But we need it. If it works. If it'll kick the Progeny out of heads. Tabitha doesn't think it will. But I know Shaw does.

And that's something else I couldn't do. I couldn't build anything close to what Tabitha has done. I couldn't decipher a single document, a single word.

We're a team. Everyone has a place and a role. And sitting here, I realize that's me too. I have a place and a role. And it's not glamorous. It's not throwing magic spells, or carving aliens apart with a sword. It certainly isn't gunplay. It's getting everyone working together. It is, as I overheard Shaw say, herding cats. Not in here, in the office, but out in the field. That's my job. Let everyone else do theirs.

We need each other. If we're to achieve anything. We have to be a team.

There again, given what we're up against, I'm not sure even that will be much help.

"Run through it one more time," I say. Because I'm sure I'll find a hope if I look hard enough. I have to find it.

"Didcot," Kayla says. "The power station."

I've seen the place when I've headed down toward London. Hulking over green fields and belching steam.

"Electricity," Tabitha says. And of course, that makes sense. The universal lubricant. Clyde told me that himself. Was that before or after he was turned? Was that some subtle Progeny joke? A clue he knew I'd never get?

"That's what they've been doing here," I say. "In Oxford. That's how we picked up on the trail. How the police did. Back when we thought Kayla was…" I don't finish that sentence. "Back when I didn't understand what it is she does."

Shaw gives me a smile for that one. It doesn't really cut through the tension, but I appreciate it.

"They were fiddling with the electricity in new construction," I say. "Something to do with the power there. I mean, God knows what they were doing but has to have been related. Something to amplify the power. To store it, I don't know."

"Need a lot of power," Tabitha says. She doesn't finish the thought.

"To bring a Feeder through." Shaw does.

"Yes," I say, because it's almost easier to concede the point now than it is to deny it.

"And they've got Ophelia there," I say.

There's a pause in which no one adds, "And Clyde."

"She's insurance," Shaw says, breaking the silence.

Kayla's face twists. Tabitha reaches out, hesitates, then pats her on the arm. The last person I saw her do that to was Clyde.

"But Ophelia's not insurance against us," I say. "It's against the Dreamers."

"They'll try to stop the Feeders," Tabitha says.

"But the Progeny will infect—" I stop myself. There is silence.

"They'll infect her," Kayla says. It sounds like a piece of her is breaking.

"The Dreamers need a consensus to kick out the Feeders?" I ask. "Without Ophelia they won't be able to do it?"

"We don't know," Shaw says. It's the answer I expected, but not the one I hoped for.

"Skull-face will back her," I say. I don't have proof of that but I know it all the same. "He's her father," I say. If Kayla hadn't already broken the arms of her chair from squeezing them so hard, she'd probably do it now.

"The Progeny are banking on that being enough," Shaw says. "They have to be. And they may well know more than us."

"So we get the Progeny out of her," I say.

We all turn to look at the disk Tabitha is playing with. She doesn't quite meet the collective gaze.

"This is such bollocks," she says.

And it is too much to ask of her. And it is too much to pin our hopes on. And there is a niggling voice in the back of my head that says, "Well, as Clyde's machine didn't work we don't really know that no one here isn't infected, isn't still a sleeper agent working against us," but I have to ignore it. I have to just trust. Because I can't do this if I don't trust these people. I can't do this by myself.

"Ephie," Shaw says. The word hangs there.

"The same parents as Ophelia," I say, trying to pretend those words don't affect Kayla. Her trying to pretend the same thing. "A potential Dreamer. Our potential Dreamer."

"She's coming with us," Kayla says.

I don't understand her position. It's the most divisive issue. Tabitha and I stand together on it. As she put it, "You don't bring a knife to a gunfight and you sure as shit don't bring a twelve-year-old girl."

"She's our one ace in the hole," Tabitha says. "If it all goes to shit. When it all goes… Why put her in harm's way?"

"She's only in harm's way if she's out of my sight," Kayla says.

"Kayla's her mother," Shaw says. "Her word is good enough for me."

And we can't argue Kayla out of it, and I don't want to harp on divisions at this moment. I want unity. So I change the topic and say, "There will be their… whatever they are," I say. "Their pet bloody monsters."

"Yes." Shaw nods.

"Not a feckin' problem." Kayla's voice hisses between clenched teeth.

"There will be the Progeny." Shaw picks up on the list.

"Still not a problem," Kayla says.

"And if one of them decides to look like your sister?" I ask.

She snaps me a look. Tabitha stares at both of us, perplexed. Apparently Kayla doesn't share that tidbit of personal history with everyone.

For some reason in the middle of this shit storm, that actually makes me feel a little bit good.

"That worked once," Kayla says. "They won't get me again. Not before I get them."

I'm not convinced but I don't actually have a plan, so I just say, "OK," and move on.

We all stare at the map of the site.

"And there will be Clyde," Shaw says quietly. Because somebody had to eventually.

"We get it out of him," I say. No hesitation. Not even my own doubts in the statement.

Again we look at Tabitha, at the little black disk.

"Such bollocks." She turns away before I can tell if she's tearing up or not.

Silence falls again.

"It's about thirty minutes away," Shaw says. "I'll be driving," she adds.

It's all hands on deck for this one. And with the way Shaw hits that can't be a bad thing.

"Shotgun," I say.

"Yes," Shaw nods, "you're right. We'll need one of those."

49

It's dark when we get to Didcot. The tourists they let go around half the plant have all headed home. Still, their presence here during daylight hours means the other half, plant B, is our best bet.

And still—what about the workers at plant B? They wouldn't let the Progeny just hang out there. So, the little brain-scampi have to be hiding somewhere out of the way.

Shaw bypasses the empty visitor parking lot and pulls up in the shadow of a massive cooling tower. Steam slowly leaks up into the dark sky, a pale smudge, like a thumbprint on reality.

In the trunk, an over-sized fish tank containing Ephie and several of the more adventurous squid sloshes loudly.

"You OK?" Kayla asks. There is something unusually tender in her voice.

"I will be," Ephie says. Whether it's prophecy or just a child's hope, I can't tell.

I stare at the car's door handle. I think about using it. I can't quite build up the nerve. This is different from the other times I've gone up against the Progeny. This time there isn't anger or the sudden blare of adrenaline. This time I'm scared.

Shaw touches my wrist.

"Aim low," she says. "Toward the gut. You'll end up

shooting higher. Don't go for head shots. Don't worry about getting the Progeny. Just slow them down. Their hosts need hearts and lungs just like the rest of us."

"OK," I say. And there is something reassuring in that, though I can't put my finger on exactly what.

"Let's go," Shaw says to the car in general.

We go.

Shaw takes point, gripping a pump-action shotgun that looks even more incongruous against her pants suit than the sneakers she's changed into. Tabitha and I stand behind her to form a rough triangle. We've been trusted with pistols. Tabitha's grip is shakier than mine, but not much.

Kayla moves—a brief flash of motion and then gone. Ephie stays in the car. She's got a walkie-talkie and I worry, but I think I'd feel like an arse if I asked her to make sure she doesn't drop it in the tank and electrocute herself.

Gravel crunches beneath our feet. I can see my breath in the air. I wish I'd worn a thicker coat. Which is a minor wish compared to most of the things passing through my head, but even that doesn't come true.

"Where is everybody?" Tabitha asks. "Should be lights. Guards. People."

She's right. Apart from our footsteps the place is eerily quiet. And I don't know the answer, and I don't want to know the answer. Apparently neither does Shaw, because she keeps leading us forward without a word.

There is a crunch of gravel to our right and we all spin. Shaw pumps her gun with a loud "ker-chunk."

It's Kayla.

"Voices," she says. "Movement." She points to another of the cooling towers.

"There?" I say.

"Inside." She goes three steps forward and then pauses, waits for us to catch up to her. And then I realize Kayla is scared too. Because as furious and as bloodthirsty as she is right now, she's not charging in alone.

Because she knows she can't save Ophelia. Someone else has to.

Me.

No pressure.

A flight of industrial-looking steel stairs leads up the side of the cooling tower to a small gray door set into the mass of sloping concrete. We climb as silently as we can, wincing each time a footstep rings out on the metal steps. Kayla waits silently at the top.

I can feel my heart beating slow and hard in my chest. My breath and footsteps coming at the same steady intervals. My body is drumming a steady funeral march.

I check the safety on my gun at the top of the stairs. It's off this time.

We're not high up, only thirty feet or so off the ground but I can see the countryside stretching off away from here, I can see the village of Didcot, low houses, fields and hedges, a small copse of trees. I can see the glow of Oxford as a yellow haze on the horizon. I can see the car we drove here in, the silhouette of Ephie in the boot. I remember why we're doing this, what we're fighting for.

Clyde's in there. My friend's in there. A little girl is in there, and she needs to be saved. We're going to fix this.

Kayla's hand is on the door handle. Shaw checks each of our faces one by one.

"Let's do this," I say.

So we do.

50

Kayla turns the door handle slowly, silently. Her hand doesn't even quiver. The mechanism doesn't squeak. Smooth. Silent. My heart crashes in my chest. The handle completes its descent. We all stand there. Waiting. One. Two—

Kayla slams her shoulder into the door. The lock gives with a short, sharp crack. Steam billows out as the door flies open. We push forward into its enveloping clouds.

For a moment I can see nothing, can feel nothing, can just taste the steam, a thick foul flavor coating my nose and mouth, sticking my hair to my scalp. We blink and cough.

Then light—sudden and abrupt. Spotlights coming on from all directions, casting the base of the tower in a sudden white glow. I shield my eyes, trying to see.

At first it's just shadows, shapes, holes in the blinding field of light. But not for long. Not for long enough. Because then I see what we're up against.

In the center of the room stand Olsted and the runner. Olsted with an oddly youthful energy in his old body. The runner—tall and languid, thin limbs swaying slightly. Clouds of steam come up through the grill-like floor, partially obscuring the Progeny, making them almost ethereal. In-between the pair stands Ophelia. She is not bound, is not held by either of them. She stands calmly. There is a little color in her cheeks. Her dress and hair have dried somewhat. Apparently she's OK out of water now. If that's part of her evolution as a dreamer or because of the humid atmosphere, or because of some other fact that would cause my brain to perform gymnastics it never trained for, I'm not sure. She is taller than I imagined her being from seeing her in the pool.

Between us and them—a hundred or more of their magic-twisted creatures. And I think I know where the staff of this place have gone. Overalls are stretched and splayed over pulsing slabs of muscle, are wrapped in ragged strands around mutated limbs, around arms become thick and branching, arms that end in flapping tentacles, in snapping claws, in groups of hands, around legs that end in hooves, in thin wiry tendrils, in vast splaying roots of flesh, in circular pods with a hundred toes waving in some unknowable pattern, around necks topped with overgrown baby heads, with ape-heads, with Neanderthal heads, heads with lizard skin, with eight arachnid eyes, with fractal insect eyes, necks topped by skulls crushed and whole. An impossible number of people with impossible forms.

Surrounding them, surrounding us, the arching walls of the cooling tower have been plastered with paper. Every inch of the concrete has been covered. The Progeny even taped them to the railing of walkway we're standing on. They're scattered on the floor grills, blown about by the wafting steam, caught around the legs of the field of monsters before us. Pink paper. The same image printed on it, over, and over, and over.

It's a black-and-white picture of a young girl's head. Half her head. Half is whole, anyway. One whole eye staring out from the field of pink. The other half is crushed almost beyond recognition. A mess of bone fragments and blood. It's a head I've seen before. But when I saw it last it was propped between the shoulders of a monstrously transformed student. And Kayla saw it even before that, saw it on top of her sister's shoulders when she lifted the rolling pin back up.

It's everywhere. It's an overwhelming experience even for me.

"Shiiiiiiiiii—" The word hisses out of Tabitha, never quite managing to reach the "t."

I look to Kayla. She stands perfectly still, unflinching.

"Kayla," I say. Then again, louder. "Kayla!"

"Hello, Arthur." Olsted's voice booms across the room. "Tabitha. Director Shaw."

The monsters stir, a rumble of breath, half-muttered roars of pain or rage.

"Kayla!" I shake her by the shoulder. It's like pushing on a tree stump. Her jaw is working slightly. I can't make out the words.

"Welcome to our little show." Olsted smiles, gives a little bow, the perfect circus ringmaster. "It's going to be one hell of a night."

A little too much emphasis on "hell" for my liking. I put my hands over Kayla's eyes and bellow her name into her ear. A soft moan seems to well up from deep inside her.

"What do you think we've been doing inside that skull there, Arthur, my lad?" booms Olsted, his voice bouncing off the circular wall, coming at me from all directions. "Why do we keep throwing ourselves at Kayla? We do hold on in her head for a second or two, you know. Our children do have a moment with her before they go on. Enough to strengthen a couple of neurological links, weaken others. Strengthen a response to an image, for example." He grins, showing each one of his little yellow teeth. "No matter her will, she cannot take seeing her sister's face. She's quite lost to you."

"We need to get out of here." Shaw's voice, low and urgent.

"No shit." Tabitha.

"We can't leave Kayla." Me. I almost surprise myself. But we need her. We really do. This won't go our way without her.

"But," Olsted carries on, "I'm not here to wag my chin all night. There are celebrations to be had. Games to play. Little mice to chase." He throws his head back to stare at the sky. "A panoply of delights."

The monsters are restless now. They shift on their feet, leaving eddies in the steam that drifts above their heads.

"Now, Arthur," Tabitha hisses.

"We can't leave her," I say again. But they're right too. We can't stay here. We're screwed if we stay here. This is a trap.

"Let the dance begin," howls Olsted.

The monsters move. A great surging of limbs. They bay, and howl, and scream, and shout.

"Go!" Shaw yells.

I grab Kayla around the waist, hoist her bodily into the air. She's stiff as a board, still muttering, "Already dead. She was already dead. Not me. She was—"

I stagger around. I can already hear feet smashing down the walkway.

Behind us a monstrous hand is heaving a monstrous body up over the railing.

I totter backward. Shaw is yelling something. Tabitha's feet beat a fast tattoo down the stairs. I smack Kayla into the doorframe and we spin around. Out in the cold night air, I smash into another railing. I can see a vast clawed hand emerging from the steam. Kayla's body pitches forward over the railing and it's a thirty-foot drop to earth. The air seems to vibrate with inhuman growls.

A body follows the fist emerging from the steam. I grab desperately at Kayla, but my hands are shaking. Shaw yells. Tabitha yells. I snag Kayla's collar, lose my footing. Then something massive brushes my back. A fingertip, a knuckle, something—and my feet go, and Kayla falls, still stiff as a store mannequin, and I fall, pivoting around her body until we crash to the ground far too far below.

51

I bite gravel as Tabitha and Shaw hit the last step of the stairs. My lip bursts open and I taste dirt and blood. The stiff weight of Kayla's body slams into my back driving my head down even as I try to raise it. Then someone has my hand, is pulling me up. Shaw. I struggle to help her, to find my feet. Tabitha is next to me, shoving Kayla's rigid form into shadows.

"No time!" Shaw yells, still pulling me away. I rip my hand out of hers, drop to my knees, grab the pistol, and then all three of us are tearing pell-mell away from the tower as monstrosity after monstrosity bursts out after us.

For a moment it's just my feet, and my heartbeat, and my fear—all thundering in my ears. The gravel shifts beneath my feet, and it's almost like I'm flying. Footsteps barely finding traction, but I'm going so fast I can't even fall. And behind me, I know, the monsters are gaining.

"Not to the car," Shaw says. "Don't lead them to Ephie."

Part of me hates her for that. For pulling the hope out from under my feet. But part of me admires her. Because she's right. Because it's the right thing to do. Hell, it's the heroic thing to do. It's what Kurt bloody Russell would do. Because right now, Ephie is about the only hope we have. An ace it could take years to pull out of the hole. But if she buys it, well then the world has really bought it.

We break left, and I skid, turn half on my feet, half on my hands, like a motorcyclist taking a corner at speed, and then somehow I'm back upright and moving again. There is a baying behind me. Like wolves. Like hounds. Like something gone horribly bloody wrong. Like tonight.

Of course the cooling tower was a trap. They've planned all of this for years. And they knew we would come. So they planned for us. And they pulled us into that place—a powder keg primed to blow Kayla's mind. And while we've escaped, now our biggest gun is down, and we're about thirty seconds from becoming canapés.

Wait. Scratch that. Four seconds.

More monsters from the left. Blindsiding us. I rediscover the pistol in my hand. Raise it. Fire point blank into something wide and snapping and terrible. The muzzle flare supplements the moonlight. Strobe-flash glimpses of the thing that's trying to kill me today reeling away. And I wish I hadn't seen it after all. I can feel its blood trickling down my face. But there's no time.

Shaw uses the shotgun to blow open a door, and I follow her. Behind us, something smashes a hole larger than the doorway, like something from a cartoon, except when a cartoon character does it I don't have the urge to soil my pants.

Focus. It's easy for my mind to wander away right now, to pretend this isn't happening. To just react. But I need to focus. Because I need to go—

—right! Right! Duck! Under a swinging fist that comes out of nowhere. And then Shaw is pulling me left, through another door. And I glimpse more things pouring down a corridor toward us. I fire my pistol with my eyes shut. I don't want a closer look. I hear screams, and caws, and howls. Another entrance, this building has too many entrances.

"Another building," I say.

"I know," Shaw breathes.

"They knew we were coming," I say.

"I know," she says.

"Clyde wasn't with them," Tabitha says, her speech punctuated by great inhalations.

"Too much talking," Shaw says.

"Ophelia was there," I say. And there's something in that. They weren't afraid to show us Ophelia. She was part of the trap. Part of the bait.

But they didn't show us Clyde.

Why would they hide Clyde?

"They're not summoning the Feeders in from the cooling tower," I say.

Shaw's shotgun booms and we kick through another door.

"What?" Tabitha's voice.

"Clyde," I say. "They're using Clyde. We need to find Clyde."

"We need to not die," says Shaw. She looses more shells into the night. I catch flashes of things falling away. I see blood from a long gash on her cheek. I've no idea where it came from.

"There!" Tabitha points to the vast bulk of the power station's main body. "Lose them in there."

Boom. Shaw blows another lock away. My foot hits the door. Kicking it in.

The door doesn't move. I bellow. My foot throbs with pain. I see the hinges. The door doesn't open the way I'm trying to kick it.

Then the door blows outward, torn from those offending hinges. Something massive and shadowy advances out into the night. Something that's been waiting for us and for this moment.

52

It's Tabitha who kills it. Her pistol barks and a bullet catches it in the eye. A chunk of its skull ricochets off the doorframe. Then we're over the tumbling corpse and looking onto a staircase leading down. Colossal machinery pulses to our right. We hug the wall to the left. Roars bounce up. Strange echoes that make it impossible to place things.

"Electricity," I pant. "Clyde will be where there's electricity."

"In a bloody power station," Tabitha points out.

"The generator." Shaw nods. "We need a map of this maze."

Down we go.

And then stop.

Because the monsters are coming up. We all open fire. A cacophony of gunshots and howls. Glimpses of beaks, and teeth, and claws. We back up the stairs. Until Tabitha screams.

It's a sound that sluices through my head despite all the other noise. Shaw and I both spin. We see the hand on her shoulder. The hand as thick as her waist. Massive, craggy nails, biting into Tabitha's flesh. Blood welling up. Her face twisted and horrified. Tattoos fading against her abruptly pale skin.

And then she's not there. She's just a scream fading into the distance. The creature just flings her away. Like a rag doll.

It's huge. Fucking gargantuan. Its head is the same size as my chest. Its chest is as big as my car.

"Oh crap." You would think I'd have come up with some better last words by now.

The creature pulls back its fist.

Shaw's arm is abruptly about my waist, and for a moment I think how odd a moment this is to hug me, and I think that there are worse ways to go, and then she pulls me over the edge of the stairs and I'm falling again, and I think that maybe there aren't worse ways after all.

53

The fall doesn't knock me unconscious, but I wish it did. We sit there groaning as seconds and chances tick by us. I make it to my feet first. Help Shaw to hers. I can't see Tabitha.

There's another door. I try the handle. It opens. We've lost Shaw's shotgun in the fall. Supporting each other, like contestants in the world's most horrific three-legged race, we stumble back out into a space we don't want to be in. We stumble back out into the open.

"Balls," I try to say, but mostly just spray blood from my busted lips.

Beside me, Shaw nods.

The space before us is oddly open and quiet. Cooling towers to the left of us. Buildings stretch away in front and to the right. Behind us I can hear monsters roaring at each other. The call and response of bellow and bark.

"Tabitha," I manage to say.

"Clyde," Shaw's voice is a whisper. "Focus on Clyde. He's the priority."

And it's a cold truth, but I don't think Shaw shies from those. There's something admirable in the focus. We're here to get this thing done.

Suddenly the night air shudders. The ground shudders. The whole of reality pulses. Shaw and I pause in our shuffling run. Everything is still. Not a sound behind or before us. And it's almost as if we imagined everything. As if it was all a dream. As if we are Dreamers, waking up from long somnambulism.

Then part of the power station explodes.

Concrete and bricks rain down from the building before us. They spatter down on the gravel. Too far away to hit us. Close enough for us to simply stand and stare as lightning arcs its way in reverse up into the heavens.

Bright and white and unfading. First one bolt then another joins it, twisting around the first. Then a third strand. Then a fourth. They dance around each other, out through a hole punched in the roof of the power station. More strands of lightning lance upwards. The illuminated clouds twist around them—a distant whirlwind. The strands of lightning are knotting together, forming one massive beam that sputters and crackles. The air smells of ozone. All the hairs on my body stand on end.

"Found him," I say.

Then, from deep inside the heart of the power station, whatever is left of Clyde brings a Feeder through.

54

It comes. Down out of the sky it comes. And then it *is* the sky. It is everything. Horizon to horizon is eclipsed, the night sky obliterated by its presence, by the simple weight of its shadow.

"Oh," I start, but I never make it to the expletive. The sound drags out of me, a long hollow thing. "Ohhhhhh…"

It's like a landscape. It's like another world hanging above my head. And that would be easier, if that was just it, if the Feeder were just some chunk of rock, no matter how alien, if it were dead and dry. Even if it was coming down, coming to crush us all—I think that would be better.

But it's alive. It's a thing. A he, she, or it. It has eyes. It has a million bloody eyes. I can see them rolling in sockets the size of lakes, of shopping malls. Yellow irises, purple irises, orange, and gold. Pupils like black holes. I can see scales, and crags, and cliffs of skin. I can see veins like rivers. I can see organs the size of cathedrals pulsing beneath translucent pieces of exoskeleton, or chitin, or some other alien shit. It's got bloody tentacles. It goes on forever. And it doesn't end.

The air around me ripples, shifts. The smell of ozone is stronger now. It's a sour taste at the back of my throat. Every hair on my head is standing up straight. Every hair on Shaw's head next to me. It should be comical. This should be a great laugh, a real knee-slapper.

And something in me wants to laugh. Wants to laugh and not stop. And weep, and scream, and dance, and dance, and dance, and sing songs of praise. Part of me wants to strip naked and rejoice. Part of me wants to dig, to dig and never stop, to bury myself in the earth's core. Part of me wants to start scratching the flesh from my bones, to get the gaze of it out of me. Part of me wants to claw out my eyes. Part of me wants to claw out Shaw's, to take them for myself. Part of me... Part of me... Part of me...

I can feel madness hammering in the door, begging to be let in. Madness can take the pain away, the abomination of the thing away, it can take away the impossibility made possible. If I'm crazy I don't have to be here anymore. Leave an answering machine on for reality. I'll get back to you when I can...

My throat is completely dry, my attempt to swallow just a dry clicking sound. It all seems so futile now. So bloody pointless. Everything we've done so small and stupid.

Tendrils descend, like those from a Progeny's mouth, but so... so... so much more, so much bigger. Jesus. They're, just, just...

And still I can feel my mind slipping, like a car missing the gears, an ugly crunching sound. And perhaps madness has made it in after all, has said "screw it" to the door, loaded up Shaw's shotgun and come on in, all guns blazing.

But madness doesn't come. It remains a dream, wishful thinking. Because it's not me losing a grip on reality, it's reality itself losing grip. The world is changing right in front of me, permitting this monstrosity, this untruth.

Beside me, Shaw puts what I cannot into words.

"Oh fuck," she says.

55

We start running. There's nowhere to run. The Feeder is everything. It is the sky, and the sky is falling. But we run, because that's all that evolution has left us with. This is our option.

We run. Run toward the beam of lightning, toward Clyde; run toward the hope that we can undo this, toward the impossibility that it is not too late. And above our heads is proof of the impossible—surely it's time we had a little for ourselves. Surely. If there's a God…

And there's a God all right. It's just he's floating above my head munching on parts of Essex.

There's an incredible pressure from above as we stagger forward. As if the atmosphere itself has grown denser, the air we're pushing through a greater barrier. Gravity seems weaker. My feet scrape over the ground, barely making enough contact to propel me forward. Smaller chunks of rubble are rising into the air. Tiny electric shocks race up my legs each time my feet make contact with the ground.

There is a sound like an earthquake. Part of one cooling tower suddenly rips free, hurtles skywards, disintegrating as it goes, vanishing behind a cloud to immolate itself against the vast mass of the Feeder. I manage to stop myself from tracking the rubble all the way up. I'm whispering a new mantra to myself: don't look up, don't look up.

I can see a car in the sky. I pray it's not the one with Ephie in it. I pray Kayla is still earthbound. In the distance trees are uprooting themselves.

As Shaw and I approach a door, the wood is torn free of its hinges and races upwards. Shaw and I are holding hands. I'm not sure when it happened. As if we are both victims of the mad belief that this way we're heavier, that this way we can survive.

And the insanity clamoring at the back of my head is using that belief as a crowbar, trying to force itself in. Give up Shaw, it's telling me. Give up Kayla. Sacrifice. Feed it. Feed it her. Feed him. Feed it anything. Just not me. Just not me.

And then Shaw half pulls, half shoves me through the maw of the doorway and into the darkness of a corridor and abruptly there is a ceiling over my head. No more sky. No more Feeder. No more vacuum. No more madness.

We stand gasping in our pitiable shelter. I can hear the walls creaking, can see cracks appearing.

"What do we...? What do we...?" I can't make it to the end of the sentence. Part of my brain is still trying to process what it saw, yammering at the overload, flooding the rest of my processing abilities with the horror of it all.

"Clyde," Shaw says, and the word is almost foreign. "Come on. Clyde. Down."

It gets easier the longer we're under cover. We stay away from rooms with windows. We stay in stairwells, in dark places. It's easier to enter denial that way.

It's not too hard to find our way now. We don't need a map. We just follow the electric charge in the air. We go through rooms full of blown monitors, our feet crunching on the glass. We pass dozens of small fires casting flickering shadows around the remains of shattered strip lighting. Shaw uses a flashlight. I could use mine, but I'm still holding my pistol in my free hand so I'd have to let go of her to use it, and neither of us seems willing to give up the human contact just yet. We're grounded by our palms— some circuit of flesh to counterbalance the circuits of wire that hiss and spit in the walls around us.

We hit the bottom floor of the place and the spaces start opening up. Shaw's flashlight doesn't penetrate the shadows too well anymore. But then we don't need the flashlight. The hulking pieces of machinery, the gangplanks and walkways, the bundles of wire— everything illuminated in a pale white light that grows stronger and stronger as we walk on.

"Almost there," Shaw says. And she makes it sound almost hopeful, as if there can still be hope. I'm not sure I believe that, but I cling to her words like a drowning man.

"I should reload," I say.

"Good idea."

We stand there, awkwardly facing each other as I fumble the mostly spent magazine out of the gun.

"What do you think happened to Tabitha?" I try to make the question light. I don't try hard enough.

"Nothing good." Shaw doesn't either. She swallows several times.

"I'm scared," I say. Because it's absurd to deny it any longer.

"Me too," she says.

"I don't feel like someone who can fix this problem," I say.

"Neither do I."

We stand there. The fresh magazine is still not fully loaded. I stare at it.

"Bet no one else does right now, either," I say.

"Probably not."

I push the magazine home.

"Bollocks to it," I say.

"Bollocks to it," she says.

And then she kisses me.

It's nothing really passionate. Nothing to write home about. Neither of us is swept off our feet. She just leans in, and pecks me quick and hard on the lips.

I stare at her.

"What?" she asks. "I'm relatively sure we're about to die."

I lick my lips. I can faintly taste strawberry Chap Stick. "I don't mean to complain," I say, "but you should probably work a little bit on your pep talks."

56

I have to shield my eyes as we go through the doorway. The lightning is a scorching white stripe, like part of the screen of reality has burned out.

And there, at the heart of the madness, is Clyde.

What's left of Clyde.

No. That's wrong. It's not what's left of Clyde. It's what Clyde has become. If it was what was left of Clyde, there would be less of him. Instead there is so much more.

His head is there, his torso. His eyes are wide open and bright white. His mouth is open and full of light too. Like the electricity is in him. Like he's brimming over with the stuff. He's pouring it into that beam of lightning, but I don't think he can get it all out in time. It's going elsewhere. Going deeper into him.

Clyde is growing. His arms and legs have become liquid, flesh flowing over the bundles of wires that lead to his twitching form. He lies in a spreading pool of himself, something half human, half generator. A pseudopod of pink, doughy flesh rises up and wraps around a pipe, squeezing tight, bending the thing. It climbs like a creeper, wrapping up and around, anchoring Clyde to the place. And that's not all of it, of him. A lapping wave of skin grasps at rivets in the floor, clamping down on them so that they poke whitely through the stretched tissue; his arm is bifurcating over and over, splitting into thick tendrils that wrap around every available piece of machinery; even his hair betrays him, becoming roots that push into cracks in the concrete floor.

He already covers an area as large as my living room and he's growing.

"Oh no," I say. "Oh Clyde." Because how can we fix this? How can we make this right? He's not even human anymore. And if we can't even fix Clyde...

"We have to stop him from casting," Shaw says. She speaks haltingly, one hand to her mouth, as if holding back the bile.

I can feel tears leaking down my cheek. This man was my friend.

"We can't just interrupt the power source. This place generates enough juice for fifty percent of Britain. If we interrupt it..."

I flash back to Kayla burying the sword into the car battery, to the explosion that ripped the student in two.

"We do more damage than the Feeder," I say.

"No." Shaw shakes her head. "We just do it quicker, is all."

I look at Clyde again. His eyes are sightless. He is oblivious. "How do we interrupt him?" I say. "How do we get the attention of... of *that*." It's not a "him" anymore. Things have gone way beyond that.

Shaw looks at me. The cracks in her mask of professionalism are spreading. Her lip is trembling. And I remember Kayla torturing the Progeny's insider, Robert's assistant. They live in the head and they don't come out on their own.

Except if Tabitha's little black disk works. But Tabitha is... I don't want to know what happened to Tabitha. Like Shaw said: nothing good.

"We have to kill him, don't we?" God, that hurts to say. Shaw nods. That hurts too.

I look down at the gun. Bloody thing. Nothing but bloody trouble, these things.

Oh shit. I raise the gun, try to sight it. My hand is trembling so hard I can't focus. My vision keeps blurring. I keep thinking about Swann. I don't want to lose another friend.

He's not my friend. He's not my friend. It's like Kayla said, my friend is dead. He just hasn't stopped moving yet.

In the distance I can hear parts of the building tearing away. I can hear explosions and animal bellowing.

I blink my eyes. I try to steady my hands.

"I don't know if I can do this," I say.

"You can't."

It's not Shaw who speaks. A thin whisper of a voice that seems to come from everywhere and nowhere. Shaw's eyes go wide.

Something detaches itself from the shadows. I spin, but I still can't get my hands steady, can't line up a shot. I don't even get to pull the trigger before the runner closes the distance and buries a fist in my guts.

57

I hit the floor, cracking my tailbone, rocking back in pain. The runner is already on me. His narrow fists pummel me at speed, fast as the lightning that crackles through the room. The gun spins from my hand. My head snaps sideways and I see Shaw leaping for it. But the runner is off me and across the floor, beating her with ease. One of his feet connects with the gun and it spins away. The second foot comes through and catches Shaw in the ribs. The air leaves her so fast she doesn't even cry out.

I'm trying to get up. I manage to roll onto my stomach, but my arms are useless at my sides. Not enough strength to lever myself up. The runner grabs Shaw by the collar, hoists her up and then brings her over his head, like he's windmilling a sack of so much flesh and bone. Shaw crashes to the ground next to me. Her head makes a dull thwack against the concrete. She moans in pain, balling up like a babe.

The runner finally moves slowly. He knows there's no hurry. I push against the floor again but I can barely even lift my nose off. My breath bubbles through blood.

He stands over us.

"We were to use the one you call Olsted for this," he says. His voice is the same thin whisper, rough and hoarse, but not weak. "He was to be the one to sacrifice himself. But once we had your creature we decided to use him. To try to tell you. To try to get you to understand that you cannot win. There is only one end to this. But you don't seem to understand. When will you realize how futile this is?"

Another foot enters my field of vision. A shoe. And it's not white. Not slender. Not elegant. A big, heavy-soled Doc Marten thing. It takes steps toward the runner. I let gravity take my head. It rolls sideways. And I recognize the figure.

"This was always inevitable," says the runner.

"Really?" says Tabitha from behind him. "Bet you didn't see this fucking coming."

58

Tabitha is a mess. One side of her face is caked in blood, her hair matted to the ruined flesh of her forehead. Her arm on that side is crooked, and cradled to her chest. Her knees are bloody wounds, scrapes and scratches cross-hatching their way up her thighs and down her shins. She's breathing heavily and everything seems slow and ponderous as she holds up the black disk with the red button so that the runner can see it.

And he moves. Quick as the lightning spewing out of Clyde behind us, so fast his whole body is a blur. And still he isn't fast enough to catch Tabitha.

She slams the disk down onto her chest, so her sternum crashes into the button. Something whines high-pitched and violent. Tabitha winces, still not convinced, despite her brave face, that this is really going to work.

The runner stops. Like he hits a wall. Like a stick has been thrust between the spokes of his wheels. He just jams, frozen in his lunge, twisted awkwardly. The disk's whine builds. It crackles with static, spitting white sparks out into the air.

The runner starts to shake, a tremor that seems to build in his legs then slowly climb until his whole body is vibrating, faster and faster as the noise builds. I can hear his teeth rattling. And this is what you get, you bastard.

This is what you bloody get. This is payback. You took Swann and now we're going to take your body from you. See how you like it, asshole.

The disk is shaking now. I can see Tabitha's hand vibrating almost as fast as the runner. Electricity plays over her skin. A moan escapes her lips, rising to match the whine of the thing. My eardrums are beginning to feel the pressure. I make it to my knees just so I can press my hands to my ears. It doesn't do any good.

Tabitha curses, releases the disk. Pulls her hand back like it's been burned. It probably has. The disk hangs there. Quivering in space. The runner quivers, jibbers, and shakes.

And then, when it feels like my eardrums are going to give, the Progeny does instead.

The disk suddenly rips apart. A tiny flare of flame, a crack of electricity. It explodes into plastic fragments and torn circuitry. The runner's head snaps back. The Progeny is flung out forward, straight through the throat. The tendrils of its mouthparts snap and fly. I can see ethereal strands protruding from the runner's neck, flapping uselessly. The maggot-caterpillar twists, arcs as if trying to free itself, the tiny beak of its mouth gnashing wildly. It twists back on itself, gnawing at its own flesh. And still it's shaking, faster and faster, until chunks of it are flying off. It spatters, twitching, leaking white fluid onto the floor. And then it's just white bloodless chunks that fade, and fade, and then they're gone.

The body of the runner falls. Just a body. The eyes roll back. Whoever was in there before the Progeny took up residence is gone. Completely, utterly gone.

Tabitha's crying. I make it to my feet—I don't really understand how—stagger into her, give her some sort of hug. I don't know who's really supporting who. She just leans against me.

"It's OK," I say. "He's down. He's gone." I don't know if it's what I should say, what she needs me to say, but what else is there to do?

Tabitha pulls violently away from me. "It's not!" She half screams it. "How the fuck is it OK? It's fucking broken." She points to the shattered plastic on the ground. "It's broken," she says it again, a fractured whisper this time. She looks up at me. "How the fuck are we going to save Clyde now?"

Oh no. Oh shit, and oh balls, she's right.

I look over at Clyde. I was too beaten up to even realize the hope we held for a moment. I'd written that plan off. But Tabitha had been holding that hope with her the whole time. She'd gotten here on her own, holding the disk. And a few feet from her goal she'd wasted our one remaining weapon on the runner. She'd wasted it to save Shaw and me. She didn't know it but she picked us over the man she… loves? Loved? I don't know anymore.

Tabitha turns away from me, turns toward the sprawling mess that is Clyde. He's bigger now. The skein of flesh covering the floor is thickening. Ropey veins are threading their way through it, blisters of fat and muscles pushing up through the surface. His face is lost in it all, eyes and mouth full of white fire. And maybe that's why it takes me a moment to realize that Clyde isn't totally given over to his power anymore. Maybe that's why it takes me a moment to realize that, while we're looking at Clyde, he's looking right back.

59

"Too late."

Clyde's voice, like his mind, is no longer his own. There's a bit of the old plumminess, the well-bred geniality left there, but it's buried deep and sinking fast. His voice hisses, an electrical crackle at the back of his consonants. He spits sparks every time his lips meet. There's something like distortion at the edge of his speech, a screaming echo to every word.

"I've done it," he says. "I've brought them through. And the Dreamers are too weak and too exposed and too fucking small to turn it all around. We've won. You're too late."

I pick up my gun.

"Don't," Tabitha says. I don't know if she's talking to me or to Clyde. "Don't. Just don't."

Shaw is still on the ground, but she's managed to uncurl herself, managed to get on all fours. Her head is still tucked down toward her chest.

"You know what you have to do," she says.

"Don't!" Tabitha screams it. She steps in front of me. But she's not looking at me.

"Come on, Clyde," she says. "I know there's a part of you left in there. You're bigger than this. You're better than this. You can fight this. You—"

But the Progeny is already laughing. And as Tabitha plunges on, a vast strand of flesh explodes out of Clyde's spreading form and smashes into her gut. A blunt, jointless arm of flesh and muscle that powers into her, lifts her off the ground, drives her backwards. She crashes into the back wall of the room, head bouncing off pipes and machinery.

"Too late!" The Progeny that was Clyde screams it, still laughing.

"Do it," Shaw says, and then the tentacle of flesh whips down, just to the left of me, drives into her, knocks her back down to the floor with a crunch, and a crack, and a spray of blood.

I've got the pistol bunched tight in my hands. I'm staring down the barrel. I can see Clyde's face. Clyde lost in what he's become. I see the face of the friend who is not my friend anymore.

"Too late, Arthur," Clyde whispers. "Too late, old boy." Clyde starts to cackle again.

And there's only one thing to do. What Kurt Russell, with a single tear running down his cheek, would do.

I pull the trigger.

60

I don't see the bullet. You never see the bullet. Not outside of Hollywood anyway. They travel faster than sound. I can wave my hand fast enough that my eyes can barely keep up—I can't believe they're going to manage the trick with a supersonic chunk of lead.

But the mind plays tricks. And magic is so thick in the air, I can taste it at the back of my throat. And for a moment time really does seem to slow. And I do wonder if maybe I see something in the air flying toward the face of someone who used to be my friend. Someone who just hasn't stopped moving yet.

He's still laughing when the bullet ricochets off thin air and falls away.

I stare. I fire again. Sparks fly in midair. The bullets whine away. Clyde remains—cackling and whole.

The tentacle of flesh teeters above me, then crashes down.

I barely make it. I hear the floor crack, feel splinters of concrete scoring my legs. I trip over Shaw and roll. I'm up and I'm trying to fire but he's coming at me again. I dive back, over the whipping arm of flesh, like this is some ballsed-up game of jump rope. I land better this time. Well enough, in fact, to stop myself from tumbling face first into the bolt of lightning that cracks across the room.

Flesh tentacles and lightning bolts? That is not even close to being fair.

I start running. Just running. I don't have a destination. I just run round and round. And Clyde keeps trying to kill me. So I keep firing. It's easy now. Easy to feel no remorse. Easy enough to point and shoot. It's just impossible to hit him.

Lightning crackles behind me. The flesh tentacle wheels around in an arc toward me. Less than a second to think. Adrenaline takes over. I jam my legs out, slide over the floor as flesh whips over me, the breeze ruffling my hair. And if Clyde hadn't needed to stop shooting lightning bolts at me to avoid frying himself I'd be cooked medium-rare right here and now.

I can't win this. I'm just delaying the inevitable. And, to make matters worse, my running in circles has managed to get Clyde's ever-spreading derrière between me and the door. So apparently, I'm not even delaying the inevitable quite as much as I'd hoped.

I throw myself behind cover—cower behind a chunk of humming machinery. Have to be careful not to touch it in case he shocks the whole thing. At least it isn't bloody raining. Then I'd be gone as soon as I trod in a puddle.

Electricity. It all comes down to electricity. And I can't disrupt the power source before he drops the spell unless I want to turn us all into so much meat mist. But I can't shoot him until the spell has no power source.

I can't disrupt the power source.

I can't...

I can't...

Grow a pair.

What would Kurt Russell do?

Oh sod it.

I shoot the metal casing in front of me. It's hardly like

I have an over-flowing platter of choices anyway. I hear the bullet smashing around inside. The thrum of machinery chokes and then with a crackle of smoke and a burst of flame it dies. Something whirs around and smashes into the casing, denting it.

There is an ungodly popping sound from the vicinity of Clyde. The light, the lightning—for a moment it flickers.

"Fuck!" Clyde's voice.

I reload the gun, sight on some more machinery, fire off two bullets. Another snap, crackle, and scream.

"What the fuck are you doing?" There's a narrow edge of panic in Clyde's electric voice.

I have to back away from the machinery I was crouched behind. The flame leaking from the bullet hole is jetting out more insistently now. I catch sight of something else critical-looking and shoot at that as well.

There is a grunt of pain and I can smell burning meat.

"It's too late!" The Progeny sounds furious, like Sly Stallone's Tango preaching the rules to Kurt Russell's Cash.

"Too late for me," I say. "I'm gone either way. It's just whether you come with me or not." And I've got to think that Clyde, that my friend, would rather die than go on like this.

I open fire again. And something really goes this time. Something detonates inside the machine. The casing deforms massively, metal ballooning out, looking like some art nouveau sculpture. Wires flicker out of jagged holes spitting sparks. The lightning storm flickers again. The Progeny screams again.

"Fuck!"

"You were always going to die," I tell him. I tell it. "It's the end of the world."

Drop the spell. Drop it. Please drop the spell.

I can't see anything else to shoot, so I stand up.

Clyde is getting crispy around the edges. One of the electrical wires has burned a hole through his spreading skin.

There are several important-looking chunks of metal beyond his bulk. I sight them down the barrel of the trigger.

"Think you can hit me before I pull the trigger?"

His white eyes regard me. They seem hollow, utterly hollow.

Drop the spell. Please, just drop the spell.

But he doesn't, so I fire.

Clyde screams. And the lightning storm dies. Just vanishes. The tear in the world healed as machinery explodes.

I turn, blind in the sudden darkness, and I've got to do this faster than he can think. I've got to move faster than thought. And I know I can't really do it, but it's my only chance. Firing into the after-image of his blazing eyes.

And maybe there is something left of Clyde in there. Maybe he still does have a scrap of control. Maybe that's why he didn't kill us all when we were lying there unconscious in the office before he stole Ophelia away.

Maybe not.

But the bullet goes through, and in the light of the muzzle flare I see it take my friend in the jaw and drive whatever is left of his brain out through the back of his skull.

61

I help Shaw to her feet in the blue glow of dying Progeny eggs. Tabitha sits against the back wall of the room and sobs.

"The Feeders are still here," Shaw says. "No more are coming through, but they're still here."

And I know it. I can feel it. That sense of pressure from above, that counter-intuitive sense of being pulled up while I'm being crushed—it's growing. The shrieks of the building's mortar and rivets are growing.

"Ophelia's stopping the Dreamers from sending them away." I'm stating the obvious, but it still feels far too much like offering a death sentence on a twelve-year-old girl.

Shaw can't quite meet my eye.

"So what now?" I ask. Dodging responsibility.

"Tabitha," Shaw says. Dodging it just as nimbly.

We both help her off the floor. When she's on her feet she punches me in the jaw. There's not much strength in it but it still makes the room spin. I don't have anything left to take the punch with. I'm a watch in need of winding.

"He's dead," she says. "You killed him."

"I know," I say. I don't deny it. It's not really deniable.

"The Progeny killed him," Shaw says. "Arthur just did what needed to be done."

"There was another way!" Tabitha sprays blood when

349

she shouts. "We needed more time. We needed to try harder. We needed to—"

"There was no time." Shaw catches Tabitha by the shoulders. "He was trying to kill us. To kill you."

It's true, but Tabitha's not really in a state to deal with the truth. She's like me on the rooftop after Alison... after that. But instead of finding rage she just sags in on herself. The tears come harder now.

Shaw takes her in her arms, holds her while she lets it out.

I turn away, uncomfortable and unsure of myself, unsure of how I feel. Part of me wants to join Tabitha, to mourn. Part of me wants to scream at Clyde's remains, to demand he tell me how he could be so stupid as to get himself infected. Ask him why he made me do this.

Shit.

Shit.

I just killed my friend.

The Progeny killed my friend.

I killed my friend.

I don't know. I just want it to stop. I just want the Feeder to take us all. I just want it all to stop.

I stare at Clyde. I could have told him about feeling this way. And now he's gone. I could have told Alison about it. She's gone too.

Maybe I could tell Shaw. Maybe. But she's comforting Tabitha. And that's comfort that needs to be given.

"You silly bastard," I say to Clyde's corpse. "You stupid, silly bastard."

God, he's even still got that mask from back in Peru around what's left of his shoulder.

I'm going to miss him.

I bite back tears, turn away.

The mask!

I turn back. Holy pants, and holy shit, and oh my God... No. No, it's too long a shot. It's way too long. But, imagine. Just imagine.

It's hope.

I run toward the mask, run over his body. My feet slip on the expansive wasteland of his spilling offal. I stumble and then I'm crawling on all fours across him. Thick veins squirm away beneath my palms. I feel like gagging.

"Arthur?" Shaw's voice calls out from behind me. "Arthur, what the hell are you—"

"Get off him!" Tabitha's shriek cuts through. "Get off him, you murderous bastard!"

"The mask," I say. "He overwrote the monk. He put his own personality on the mask. He's in the mask. An extra copy. That's what he said."

I'm holding it now, a concave wooden oval. Leather straps tangled in tendrils of flesh. I pull, and at first the flesh resists, but then some of it tears and some of it just gives, and with a rip and slight spray of blood and fat, it comes free.

"No..." The word slides out of Shaw. But she's not sure. Nothing from Tabitha. She just watches me in utter silence. Her whole body is rigid. But the tears have stopped.

I make my way back across Clyde's dead body. In the distance something explodes. A pipe suddenly lifts off the floor and flies up through the hole Clyde's lightning storm blew through the roof.

I kneel down next to the comatose body of the runner. Tabitha is still watching me, still silent. I can't tell if she's on the verge of hugging me or castrating me. Maybe she can't tell either.

I turn the runner onto his back, the narrow, effete face staring blankly up. His chest rises and falls, quick shallow breaths.

"Wait," Shaw says.

Tabitha's head snaps to stare at her boss. She's wound so tight she's at her breaking point.

"In Peru this happened, right?" Shaw says. "In the temple."

"Yes," I say.

"So he could have been infected then. Whatever's in there could be a Progeny too."

I drum my fingers on the plain wood of the mask, try to mull that over, try to be rational. When was he infected? Was it before I came on the scene? Was it in Olsted's apartment? Was it outside the Peruvian temple?

Outside the temple, surely.

Surely.

That was the moment, wasn't it? When he talked me into summoning the Dreamers. It couldn't have been before Olsted's—otherwise why would the Progeny have been chasing him? Unless… misdirection? There's been so much of it.

I don't know. I can't know.

But I have to decide. I have to make a decision I'm going to stick with.

I put the mask on the runner.

We hold our collective breath.

Nothing happens.

We wait.

And still nothing happens.

"Come on," Tabitha says. "Come on, you idiot. Come out of there."

Nothing.

And then… something. I can't tell what it is at first. Something subtle. And then, I realize it's the breathing. It's gone deeper, more regular. Then the head shifts, just slightly to the side. Then—

"Aaaaaaah!" The runner's body suddenly convulses. His arms fly out wildly, his legs kick. His hands come slamming down on his chest with a great wracking cough. The hands keep working up and down the torso, almost a patting motion, as if trying to work out the shape of the body.

"What in God's name…?" It's not Clyde's voice. Not exactly. There's a breathy quality to it, and it's a little higher. But the intonation, the pattern of the words—that's right.

"What in the blazes of blue is happening?" the voice behind the mask says. "What's going on with my body? Why isn't this my body?"

There's rising panic in the voice.

"What's wrong with my body?"

"Clyde?" I say. "Clyde?"

His head snaps to look at me. Just wood. Just a mask. And there's nothing there to recognize because there can't be anything to recognize.

And then he's obscured from me as Tabitha jumps on him. She's soothing him, and kissing him, kissing the wood of the mask, kissing the hands that aren't really Clyde's, that he moves as if he's some out-of-practice puppeteer. But the questions, the confusion, the joy he's clearly feeling as Tabitha's lips press against him…

"It's him," I say to Shaw. "It's Clyde." She comes and stands next to me. We're awkwardly close. But… well, shit, we just brought our friend back from the dead. We just bloody resurrected someone here. I put my arm around her.

Hell yeah.

62

"What's going on?" Clyde asks when Tabitha finally climbs off him. "I really... I don't understand anything." He sits up. Then he sees the ruins of his own body sitting across the room from him, and that sets him off again, sets Tabitha to soothing him again.

Above our heads, part of the ceiling tears away.

"We don't have time for this," Shaw says.

And she's right.

"Clyde," I say. "Clyde, please listen to me." I try to get between him and Tabitha with the minimum of success. I don't push too hard. I'd be less than charitable toward the guy who got between me and my resurrected sweetheart too.

"What is it?" he says.

"The Progeny took you," I say. "In Peru. You're the mask. The mask you made. You're the copy."

Clyde's hands come up. They trace the wood of the mask. He moans, keeps on moaning, the pitch of it sliding up toward a place called hysteria.

"Please, Clyde. I need you to hold it together. We all need it." Tabitha whispers and soothes some more. But I need him to get this. We really don't have much time.

"The Feeders are here," I say to him. "They infected you and made you summon them here. The Dreamers should have bounced the Feeders from reality but they didn't. You... you... when you were infected... you pulled the Dreamers onto our plane of reality... And..." I pause, try to think of a way to soften the blows, but there is none, and there's still no time, so I just plunge on. "Ophelia is a Dreamer too," I say. "The Progeny-you kidnapped her. She's here. She's been infected. And she's stopping the Dreamers from getting rid of the Feeders."

I pause, look up at the sky. And there's smoke everywhere, but I can still feel the Feeder up there, still feel the jibber-jabber of madness that it inspires in the back of my head. Clyde's eyeless face looks up, following the direction of my gaze.

"It's destroying this place," I say. "Everything. It's destroying everything."

Clyde takes a moment. And who knows what he can make out of that. It's a lot to drop on a guy—that he's just a copy of himself, just a mask on a man. That'd probably crack me in two right there.

Clyde lowers his head, looks at me, then Shaw, then Tabitha. He looks at Tabitha the longest.

"You're kissing me," he says to her.

"I'm not going to stop," says Tabitha.

"It was during the whole Progeny thing," I say. It's a longer story than that, but I don't really know it.

Clyde shrugs. A familiar movement on the unfamiliar body that makes me smile more than seems appropriate at the end of the world.

"Seems worth living for," he says. Then he heaves himself up. He's a head taller than me now. I have to tilt my head to look up at him.

"We should probably go stop all this then, shouldn't we?" he says. He pauses. "I'll need batteries."

I cross over the corpse once more. Clyde looks away,

and I can't really blame him. I have a hard enough time watching myself on video. Watching someone looting my corpse could definitely be defined as being a bit too much.

His tweed jacket is ripped and half-embroiled in reams of skin but I manage to wrestle a fistful of AAs and Ds out of the exposed pockets.

"Where's Kayla?" Clyde asks, as I work. Probably a good moment to change the subject.

"She's our next stop," says Shaw.

63

We find stairs up to the first floor, but we don't find the first floor. It's gone. The walls are stumps of brick, and concrete, and steel. Everything's gone. The entire village of Didcot is gone. I can see half of it suspended in the air above our heads, slowly rising.

"Oh my…" Clyde says. He looms, gaunt and elfin above me. Blond hair billows upwards around the wooden mask. "That's not good."

I'm only just listening. I'm trying to stop my eyes from traveling up, up, up. It's like the force of the thing is drawing them skywards. I can see… I can see… I don't know what I can see. A skyscape of skin. I reach up a hand to it. It could be miles away, it could be inches. Can I touch it? Can I go to it? My feet feel light.

"Arthur!" Shaw's voice snaps through the delirium. I feel hot and cold at the same time, like there's some fever working its way through me.

"Keep it together," she speaks softly.

On the horizon I see a hill tear itself in two. The whole top of the hill just gives up and goes up. Trees, houses, fields. All going up. And I've got to keep it together while the whole world is falling apart.

"There," Clyde points.

Standing like a lone finger giving the world an irreverent

salute is a single cooling tower.

"Go," Shaw barks. We follow. The familiar thrum of feet, and heart, and breath. Except everything is more ragged now. Our pace is slower than before. All except Clyde. His new limbs seem to naturally flow faster and faster, a torrent of movement that carries him further and further ahead of us.

"Brakes," I hear him yell. "Where are the bloody brakes on this body?"

I almost smile. Which is about when the ground splits in two.

A great fissure runs across the asphalt in front of me. Gravel pours down into the abrupt abyss. I leap—a mad hurdle—and I make it, because, well, even I can hurdle a split that's only six inches wide, but I glance back and already the gap's a foot across. And there are others. All over the expanse of ground, great cracks are running in every direction, as if the world has suddenly developed a scaly hide.

I keep running. Keep my head down. And then the ground beneath me lurches, cracks. I'm thrown to my knees. We're all on our knees. The ground lurches again. I'm on all fours. Tabitha is sprawled on her back. The ground is tilting madly. I can't see Clyde over the lip of the tilting ground.

Another lurch and then I see him. Below us.

A chunk of blacktop has torn itself free from the ground, dribbling gravel downwards. We are floating up toward the Feeder. Other chunks of earth are rising next to us. The air is filled with them. The whole parking lot becomes unstable, rising into the air. Some pieces slower, some faster. Clyde's chunk is slower than ours. He's pinwheeling his arms at us.

"Jump!" I can hear him yelling over the cacophony of tearing earth and tar.

I scramble to my feet. I grab Shaw by the arm and heave her up. Tabitha is already gone. Jumping toward Clyde. I bunch my legs. Our chunk of the world tilts and I stagger, backwards. Teeter toward an edge. Then the tarmac rights itself. The gap between us and Clyde is growing larger. I run. Head down, hand in Shaw's. We jump.

For a moment I fear we're not going to fall, that we're going to just go up, up into whatever maw the Feeder above us has. I fear we'll be slammed into its impossibly vast hide, liquidated by the impact, absorbed.

Then my feet hit the ground, then my knees, and then not-falling is just a delightful dream. I bellow and sprawl forward. Shaw and Tabitha pull me up.

"No time," says Shaw, which I have to say, I'd realized already, but it's understandable that such repartee isn't up to par with her usual standard of intelligent debate. Anyway, by the time I've thought all that we're running again. Always with the running. I really would have preferred an apocalypse that could have been handled at a more leisurely pace.

Up and down. Leap and grab. Pulling myself onto chunks of floating rock only to drop down into craters of clay. All the time the vacuum above my head growing greater and greater, sucking harder and harder.

And then it stops, and I really fall. I smack to the ground; my chin stops just short of a metal step. The cooling tower looms above us. It sits in a tiny bubble of normal air, of normal reality.

Kayla's lying there, bloody, bruised, nearly catatonic, jaw working as she mutters unintelligibly to herself—just the way we left her. The Progeny's monsters, wherever they are—probably a mile above our heads and climbing—haven't found her. They haven't killed her.

I look up at the cooling tower.

Now you get yours, you bastards.

And maybe it won't change anything. Maybe it won't fix this, or stop this. Maybe we're still all screwed. But, before the end, you bastards get yours.

I check the safety on my gun, just to be sure.

"Oh no." Shaw speaks quietly but we all hear her. "No." She says it again.

"What?" Tabitha, still wired tight, barks out the question. "What is it?"

"The car," Shaw says. "The car's gone."

Oh no. Oh shit and balls no.

"I know I'm late to this," Clyde says, "but transport home doesn't seem like our biggest concern right—"

"Ephie," I say, cutting him off. "Ephie was in the car."

64

We all look at each other. And despite the Feeder in the sky, it's this that feels like failure to me. This is why they brought me on board—to save these girls. And now both of them... Both of them gone.

I want to look up, to see if I can still see it up there, to see if the car is still within sight. But looking up means seeing the Feeder, means acknowledging it at more than just the periphery of my mind.

I stare down, stare at my feet. I don't want to look at Kayla either.

"We still have to fix things." Shaw is speaking quietly. I can only just pick out her words over the boom and crash of the world tearing itself apart. "Whatever is left to fix," she says, "we have to try for that."

No one says anything. We stand there. And I realize we're all on the verge of running.

Fight or flight. Pick one.

And, like Swann told me, it's time to grow a pair.

"Shaw's right," I say. I try to put some conviction in my voice, and if not that some volume. "Are we going to let this end here? At their doorstep? Them taking Ephie is just another reason to hit them. To hit them as hard as we can. This is another reason for payback." I walk back and forth in front of the small huddle of them. I feel like I'm

361

doing some terrible impression of Mel Gibson at the end of *Braveheart*. Just without the kilt or the make-up.

Tabitha shakes her head. "We're going to die in there," she says.

"Sod it," I say. "We're going to die out here too."

Tabitha looks at me for a long time, then back at Clyde. "Fair enough," she says.

"OK," I say. "I haven't got much of a plan, but this is what I have."

65

Clyde blows the door off its hinges. It slams back and embeds itself in the meaty body of one of the Progeny's monsters. Up to the bloody door handle. The creature keels over. Which only leaves about forty-nine more between us and Ophelia and Olsted.

I come into the tower behind him. Kayla's over my shoulder and for such a petite girl she does seem to weigh close to a ton. Her hands are where I put them, pressed over her eyes. She's muttering to herself over and over.

"I didn't do it. Already dead. Not me. They did it. I didn't do it. Already dead. Not—"

And I'm muttering right back, talking into her ear. "We're going to take it away, Kayla. You're right. It was them. You're going to make them pay." And I've no idea what sort of pep talk would really get through to her in this state, but I'm going with what I've got—promises of vengeance and violence.

Tabitha and Shaw bring up the rear, pointing guns. Shaw has my pistol. I couldn't really fire while holding Kayla anyway.

"Burn them," I say to Clyde. "Now."

He closes his eyes, starts whispering to himself. Shaw and Tabitha open fire. They don't really aim. Just buying us time. I feel a waft of heat from the walls.

When the flame comes, it's only for an instant. Steam whips across the walls, the air damp and heavy, but an instant is all we need. Every picture of Kayla's sister gone to ash.

"Now," I say into Kayla's ear. "Now. She's gone. It's just the bastards that did it. Open your eyes. Please, I'm begging you, open your eyes."

Shaw reloads. Tabitha reloads. Quick and fast. But still too slow. Because here the monsters come.

Clyde spits out a battery. It hits one in the chest. And Clyde doesn't spit far.

"Come on," I say to Kayla. "Please. For your kids. For the Twins. Open your eyes."

Kayla's eyelids flutter.

Clyde blows back one monster. Points at another and it starts vomiting blue, doubling over, heaving out bloody chunks that look like organs.

The third monster gets through. A fist flies forward. Clyde dances backwards but the blow still glances off him, and he barrels over the railing, onto the metal grid below. His new body was meant to run, not fly. He lands awkwardly, a mess of spindly limbs. The monsters that haven't clambered up onto the walkway with us circle him greedily.

"Come on," Olsted is shouting. "Come and play my children, my darlings! Come and dance, and sing!"

"Come on," I say to Kayla. "Get Ophelia out of this."

And Kayla opens her eyes. She blinks once, twice.

Shaw blows a neat hole between the eyes of one monster. Another one hits her with a fist the size of her chest and she flies back into a concrete wall.

Kayla moves her hands, sluggish at first, groping. She slides off my shoulder, her knees shake but hold. She looks around. A monster looms over Tabitha.

"Please," I whisper. "Not for my sake. Not for yours. For Ophelia. Please."

Kayla looks back to me. Her eyes don't quite catch mine at first; they slip off, her gaze sliding down my face.

And then her eyes snap up, lock with mine. "Feck this," she says. And she grins.

The monster before Tabitha brings down its arms in a two-fisted blow. Tabitha cowers. Understandably. She's about to lose her head.

Except when the thing's arms reach the apex of their curve the fists aren't attached to them anymore.

The creature swings and misses. It stares at its bloody stumps. And then Kayla's blood-soaked sword catches it in its throat and the thing drops to its knees and she dances over its tumbling form and throws herself full force, like a whirlwind of knives, into the fray.

Down on the floor of the tower, Clyde stands up. Steam is boiling off him. One creature bursts into flames. So does another. Another. Heat is spreading across the floor.

"Come on!" Olsted screams at us. "Do what you can."

I stand there, flanked by Shaw and Tabitha as they shred the room with bullets. I stand there as Clyde roasts his attackers alive, as he turns their bodies to water, to slime, as he shrinks them to the size of chickens and punts them across the room. I stand there as Kayla dances a ballet of death, of hacked limbs and ribboned flesh. I stand there and watch Olsted's defense fall.

Then, for a moment, Kayla and Clyde stand face to face. Kayla's sword rises, and I realize she doesn't know. I didn't have a chance to explain about Clyde. Then Kayla hesitates, a quizzical expression on her face.

"Changed my look," I hear him say as both Tabitha and Shaw reload. "Felt I should after the whole Progeny in the brain sort of thing that I had—"

Then Kayla has passed him, has brought her sword down in another throat, has cut another limb from another torso.

There are fifteen of Olsted's creatures left. Then ten. And against one wall of the cooling tower I see the shadow of more shapes. Of a small crowd of people. As if something is suddenly coming into focus. I catch glimpses of top hats, of ball gowns, of three-piece suits, the reflection on a monocle, on a pocket watch.

There are five monsters left. Four. The Dreamers stand arrayed behind Olsted. Three. Two. One.

Skull-face stands apart from the main bulk of the group. He has a hand out toward them. "You don't touch her," he hisses. "She's mine. My own. There are other worlds than this. You do not touch her."

Ophelia, he's talking about Ophelia.

Ophelia is still standing there. And this confirms it—she's definitely stopping the Dreamers from taking out the Feeder.

And skull-face is stopping the Dreamers from taking out Ophelia. No… He's threatening to take them out if they make a move against her. He's not as strong as Ophelia—he can't fend them all off at once. But that makes sense. The mind worms seem to have a way of enhancing people—Kayla, the body Clyde's in. They make people more than they could be on their own. Why should that be different for Ophelia?

So skull-face can't take them all out. Just the one who makes a move. And none of the Dreamers are willing to stick their necks out.

Sorry excuses for deities, if you ask me.

But why can't Ophelia just protect herself?

It must be because of the Feeder. She's protecting the Feeder. She's left herself open.

The logical move is to take out skull-face. Without him all this whole Mexican stand-off falls apart. And if he tries to take me out of reality... well then he'll be focused on me. He won't be focused on Ophelia. Her defenses will be down. The Dreamers will be open to take Ophelia out.

I realize I'm definitely planning on killing her. The girl I'm supposed to protect.

She's already dead. She just hasn't stopped moving yet. She's already dead.

Skull-face just needs to join her.

"Your gun," I say to Shaw. "I need the gun."

She doesn't ask why, just throws it to me.

It's not a hard shot. His back is to me. I can see the princess looking at me as I line up the shot, but she doesn't say a word, doesn't do anything.

I fire.

There's a crack. There's the whine of a ricochet. The smack of the bullet as it hits the concrete.

Skull-face is still standing.

Between him and me: Kayla's sword. It's bent slightly, dented from where the bullet struck, from where she deflected the shot.

"No," she says. "No you don't."

And Olsted starts to laugh.

66

"No." I shake my head. It doesn't make sense. "Not you too."

Olsted just keeps on laughing. I snap the gun around to him.

"Go ahead," he still chuckles. "You think you can get the shot from here? Think you can take me out here?"

"She's my daughter," Kayla speaks as if Olsted hasn't. "Of course they're not in my feckin' head. I've told you that every goddamn day since you feckin' started. But you don't get to kill my daughter."

"She's not yours," I say. "She's theirs. She was your daughter. Was. Not anymore."

"I will feckin' carve you apart if you don't shut your hole."

There is silence in the room. Skull-face still hasn't turned to look at me. He's still staring at the other Dreamers. He's still got his palms up. Ophelia is still staring up at the open mouth of a cooling tower, up where my eyes want to go, but I can't let them. Only the princess is still staring me right in the eye.

I move the gun again. I point it right at Ophelia.

"Don't you feckin—"

"Tabitha, your gun." It's Shaw's voice. Tabitha spins, looking startled. "Now."

Tabitha tosses the gun.

Kayla watches them, takes a step toward me. And if she

decides to go, I'm toast, I'm done. Shaw slowly, deliberately checks the magazine, checks the safety. She hoists the gun.

"Stop him, Felicity," Kayla says to Shaw. "Don't let him hurt my girl."

Sweat's coming down me now, threatening to blur my vision.

"He's right, Kayla," Shaw says.

My whole body seems to quiver with relief. I try to keep the gun barrel straight as the air whips out of me.

"You have to trust him too, Kayla," Shaw says. "Ophelia's not your girl anymore." And Shaw points her gun at Ophelia.

"I will take you all down!" Kayla's screaming it now. "Not again. I'm not losing someone to these people again."

"It's too late Kayla. It's too late." It's Clyde speaking. He spits out a battery from underneath his mask, pulls another from his coat, rolls it in his hands. He shrugs. "I'm so sorry. But it's too late."

"All of you," Kayla hisses the words.

"Give it up," Tabitha says. "Let it go."

Kayla stares at us each in turn, arrayed before her. We all know what has to be done. She looks to Ophelia, to the shell of her adopted daughter. She looks back at me. Her lip curls.

And she moves.

And God, Jesus, Mary, and any Holy Ghosts that happen to be in the vicinity... I have seen her move before, I have seen her move like she defies time and space before, but this is something else, this is something different, this is beyond the limits of the human body, surely. I can see cracks opening in her skin for the split second she's in the space between us, in the split second before she's on me. I don't even get to register the sword. I don't even get to pull the trigger before—

Before nothing.

Nothing happens.

Kayla is hovering in midair before me, utterly still, her sword frozen above her head. Above mine. A bead of blood hangs in the air before us.

For a moment I just stand there too. Watching, staring at the imminence of death, at my own mortality poised in front of me. And then my head and my body and my instincts catch up and finally I flinch away.

Except I don't. Not an inch. Not a muscle. I'm stuck there. I can't even twitch my eyes.

Someone walks past me. I see her in the periphery of my vision. And then, as if relenting, the freeze lessens, and my eyes slide in their sockets. That, at least, she grants me. That, at least, Ephie lets me have.

She walks between us all, ignoring us. Her hair is still wet, a dark twisted braid down her still-dripping dress. The water steams here, making the palest of mists around her, lending her an ethereal quality.

"O," she says, addressing her sister. "Is there any of you left in there?"

I can see Kayla desperately trying to twist in midair, desperately trying to say something.

But only skull-face's voice sounds in the space. Even Olsted is silent now.

"Come here, child," says old skully. "Come to your father. She is your sister always. We will all be together when this is over. A family. New blood. New life. New worlds."

"O?" says Ephie, ignoring him. "O, can you hear me?"

"Come here," and skull-face's voice has lost some of its cooing softness now. "Come. Do as your father tells you to do."

"You can't save her, Mum," Ephie says.

At first I don't know who she's talking to, but then I

catch the look in Kayla's eyes, the hollowness there, the tears welling.

"You never could. Arthur never could." She pauses. "I can't."

There's a lump in my throat, a weight in my chest. This is not a child's decision to make. But she's not a child anymore, I realize. That's the price for the Dreamer package. Leaving childhood behind. And so Ephie holds us all still and steady, and she makes her decision.

Ophelia disappears from reality. Ephie grunts, drops to one knee. There is a tear in reality where her sister was. A ragged gap, and again the bright darkness of the void beyond.

As Ephie drops, so does Kayla. I can move again. Olsted is howling. Skull-face screams, a roar of horror and fury. He thrusts out a hand toward Ephie.

But Ophelia, the source of the Dreamers' fear, is gone. And one of them finally grows a pair.

The princess's hands go out, something still graceful in the movement, something almost passionate. And she has skull-face beat. And reality bucks and tears, and more than one Dreamer seems to shriek, but skull-face is gone. Then Olsted. Just a dark gash of light. The Dreamers do what they do. They tear out the bits of reality nobody wants anymore.

"Now!" the princess bellows at the other Dreamers, and the whole place shakes. "Do it now before it's too late."

As if on cue, the top of the tower tears away. And I can see everything. I can see the world torn apart, the world rising in ragged chunks, the world going to smash itself apart against the great implacable face of a god that truly does not care.

And this is it. This is the end of everything, and I can feel the madness stretching up, up, up, black fingers closing over my thoughts, I can feel the unreality of reality tearing my thoughts apart. And then comes a great sigh. A great exhalation. Something like grief and something like sorrow. And something like joy too.

And then the Feeder is gone.

The Dreamers drop as one to their knees. Grunts of pain. Tears and bellows. Shouts of joy.

Above my head—just a night sky, just the night stars.

And then, finally, it's over.

67

The world still hangs in the sky. Everything is still there, everything still a mess. But the terrible pressure is over. The crushing, sucking power of the thing is done.

It takes me a long time to look down. To look at us. Tabitha is slowly clambering down the steps of the walkway. She leans heavily on the banisters with her left arm. She still cradles the right to her chest. The masked man that is Clyde takes graceful steps toward her. He offers a slender arm for support. She takes it and wraps it around herself. He lifts her gently off the steps and she buries herself in his chest. When he sets her down, even in her platform Doc Martens she still doesn't quite come up to his armpits. They stay there, holding each other like teenagers slow dancing at the prom.

Shaw is still slumped against one wall, looking bloodstained and dazed. I rummage in the back of my mind and eventually find the manual for taking a few steps toward her. My body feels distant and sore, like a problem I'm going to have to deal with in the morning.

I offer a hand to Shaw to pull her up. Kurt Russell waiting for the credits to roll. The man of action come to get his woman.

Well… I mean… Not exactly…

Shaw grabs my hand, and as I try to pull her up, she

pulls me down. I don't have the strength to resist.

"Sit," she says.

I nod, take a seat next to her. We both sit there, side by side. After a moment she rests her head on my shoulder. It feels as close to peace as anything I've come across in a long time.

I can see Kayla, still out on the floor of the cooling tower, on her knees. Her sword lies before her on the floor, and she stares down at it, shoulders shaking.

Ephie is there too. The princess as well. The princess's hand is on Ephie's shoulder, but Ephie shrugs it off and crosses to her mother. She lays a small hand on Kayla's forehead. She pushes Kayla's head up, pushes the bangs back.

"You should grow your hair out," Ephie says. "Your fringe hides your eyes."

A sound comes from Kayla that lies somewhere between a sob and a laugh. She grabs Ephie and pulls her into a savage hug. I'm surprised I don't hear the poor girl's ribs snapping. But, of course, Kayla would never hurt her daughter. I know that now. I shouldn't ever have doubted it.

I look at the space Ophelia occupied. No sign that she'd ever been there. Not a smudge or a mark. All gone.

Shit. Shit and balls.

"I'm so sorry, Mum." Ephie's words are muffled in Kayla's hair but no one else is talking. Everyone is staring. Even the Dreamers, still standing there, staring along with us.

"No." Kayla pulls away slightly, still holding Ephie. She shakes her head violently, sure Ephie can see her. "No," she says again. "Never that. I'm sorry. Not you. I'm the one. You should never... I never wanted you to have to do that. I never wanted history to..." She bites her lip, chokes something back down. "I should have been stronger,

Ephie. And I wasn't. And I'm sorry you had to be the strong one for us."

Something complicated and unspoken plays out on Ephie's face. Not the emotions of a young girl. Something very adult. Eventually she says, "There was never anything you could have done."

"It doesn't mean I shouldn't have tried."

Ephie holds her mother's gaze, then nods. "Thank you," she says. Then she steps away. The princess takes a step forward, puts her hand back on Ephie's shoulder.

"I have to go now, Mum," Ephie says.

"No." I can tell Kayla doesn't want to say it, but I can tell she can't help it either.

"I'm not a little girl anymore, Mum."

"I love you, Ephie. Ephemera."

"I know, Mum. I love you too."

Kayla's biting her lip so hard I'm scared her teeth are going to go through it. "I'll see you again, won't I?" she says. There's an edge of begging to her voice.

"All the time, Mum."

Kayla smiles, a little glimpse of something brighter in the clouds of her fear. She swallows hard. "You're going to make the world a better place," she says. "I know it."

Ephie smiles, big and pure. She runs forward from the princess's hand, throws her arms around Kayla. They embrace one last time.

"We shall put it back," the princess says to no one and everyone, sweeping her hand round, "as best we can. We will find what is left in the less probable realities. Bring it forward. Rewrite what is real." She looks kindly at Ephie. "Of course some things will always be lost. Some things can never be regained. But we shall do what we can."

Ephie pulls away from Kayla, goes back and takes the princess's hand.

"See you soon, Mum."

"See you soon, Ephie."

They both turn back to the main body of the Dreamers, but before they take a step, the princess pauses, turns back, looks me in the eye and smiles.

And then she's gone, and Ephie's gone, and they're all gone, and all around us, reality starts to pull itself back together.

68

TEN HOURS AND SUBSTANTIALLY MORE THAN ONE DRINK LATER
Light comes in sluggishly through my curtains and puddles on the floor. Morning has broken.

I should feel awful, I know. I should, at the very least, be hungover to hell. And failing that I should be bone-sore. Every muscle in my body should be screaming at me, asking me what in God's name I was thinking, what I thought I was playing at. And, all told, I should probably be regretting that I ever set my eyes on Felicity Shaw.

Except Felicity Shaw is looking at me right now, is smiling at me right now, and, quite frankly, I'm still a little bit drunk, but she looks pretty great.

I smile back at her. Her expression changes to something like suspicion.

"If you make any jokes," she says, "about working under a woman, I swear I will castrate you."

With a grunt, she rolls off me. I shiver as a breeze blows over my naked, sweat-slick chest. But I don't go to pull the sheets back from her. There is something wonderful and grounded about being here, now.

Outside I can hear traffic trying to make headway, can hear townies shouting insults at students, can hear the students ringing the bells on their bicycles as they plunge madly between buses and infuriated drivers. All the mundane minutia of everyday life.

"I like this," I say. "I really genuinely like this."

"Peace?" Shaw asks me, wrapping the sheets around her, a great rumpled bundle of white.

"Yes."

"It won't last."

"I know," I say. "I don't think I'd want it to."

Shaw leans over and shuts me up with a kiss. When it's over she rests her head on my chest.

Quite the night, all told. Quite the night.

"Do you think Kayla will be all right?" I ask. Now, with some distance, some peace, I can start to think about things, to process events. I see again the fractured smile Kayla gave as Ephie left with the Dreamers.

The Dreamers.

They put our car back. Put the road back. Most of the infrastructure of things seems to be back. There were signs of damage of course. Roofs gone. Trees lying on the ground. Patches of turf torn up. Cars trashed. There was a story on the news about terrible storms. Meteorologists were being fired. Not so bad really. Unless you were a meteorologist.

We'd dropped Kayla off outside a house in Southtown I'd never seen before. A surprisingly flowery-looking place with boxes of roses and a purple door. Not too far from the Sheilas actually.

"After everything we've been through," Shaw asks, "do you still really doubt Kayla's strength?"

"No," I shake my head. No hesitation.

"We'll go over later," she says. "Make sure she's got some company."

"Yes," I say. "Disturb the peace." Shaw laughs. And it'll be good to see Kayla, to check up on her.

Things I never thought I'd think...

And maybe Clyde and Tabitha could be there too. Pick them up from Tabitha's along the way. We dropped them both off there after Kayla said goodnight. It didn't seem like a good idea to take Clyde back to his place. I'm not sure how Devon would take the news that her boyfriend is leaving her for an angry goth, let alone that his entire physical form is now a wooden mask. She'll have to hear it at some point, but that's not today's problem.

I smile. Tabitha and Clyde. They're an odd couple, but I can actually imagine it working.

And this... Whatever this is. Shaw and I. Can I imagine this working? I feel like this has been sneaking up on me for a while, and I never got the chance to even think about it. I'm worried that if I do think about it, I'll just mess it up.

One day at a time. If this job has taught me anything: one day at a bloody time.

A cellphone rings, interrupts my thoughts. Shaw groans and rolls over, picks it up.

"Yes?" she says. Then she sighs. "What?" A pause. "Where? When?" Another pause. "Now?" She sighs. She nods. "OK. As soon as possible." She hangs up.

"What is it?" I ask.

"Apparently there's a thaumaturge re-enervating fossils—"

"Wait." I hold up a hand. Find out what people are actually talking about—another lesson I've learned. "Can you translate for me? Please."

She smiles. "Rogue wizard. Natural History Museum. Zombie dinosaur."

My eyebrows climb a good inch up my forehead. "Zombie dinosaur?"

"Apparently so."

I think about that. "You're talking bollocks," I say.

"No rest for the wicked."

"But I'm good," I say. This really doesn't seem fair given that I saved the entire bloody world last night.

Shaw smiles again. "You're not bad, Arthur. Not bad at all." She rests a hand on my thigh. "Now get out of bed."

I lie there, hesitating. I don't want to get out of bed. I have to get out of bed.

Shaw looks down at me. She raises an eyebrow. Just the one. It's a good look on her. "What?" she says. "You're afraid of a zombie T-Rex? After the Feeder? I'd have thought you'd have grown a pair by now."

And hearing that here, now, makes me a little sad. But it makes me smile too. Some things can never be regained. But we do what we can.

And anyway, with a zombie T-Rex on the loose, what would Kurt Russell do?

ABOUT THE AUTHOR

Jonathan Wood is an Englishman in New York. There's a story in there involving falling in love and flunking out of med school, but in the end it all worked out all right, and, quite frankly, the medical community is far better off without him, so we won't go into it here. His debut novel, *No Hero* was described by *Publishers Weekly* as "a funny, dark, rip-roaring adventure with a lot of heart, highly recommended for urban fantasy and light science fiction readers alike." Barnesandnoble.com listed it has one of the twenty best paranormal fantasies of the past decade, and Charlaine Harris, author of the Sookie Stackhouse novels described it as "so funny I laughed out loud." His short fiction has appeared in *Weird Tales*, *Chizine*, and *Beneath Ceaseless Skies*, as well as anthologies such as *The Book of Cthulhu 2* and *The Best of Beneath Ceaseless Skies, Year One*. He can be found online at www.jonathanwoodauthor.com.

YESTERDAY'S HERO

BY JONATHAN WOOD

Another day. Another zombie T-Rex to put down. All part of the routine for Arthur Wallace and MI37—the government department devoted to defending Britain from threats magical, supernatural, extraterrestrial, and generally odd.

Except a zombie T-Rex is only the first of the problems about to trample, slavering and roaring, through Arthur's life. Before he can say, "But didn't I save the world yesterday?" a new co-director at MI37 is threatening his job, middle-aged Russian cyborg wizards are threatening his life, and his coworkers are threatening his sanity.

As Arthur struggles to unravel a plot to re-enact the Chernobyl disaster in England's capital, he must not only battle foreign occult science but also struggle to keep the trust of his team. Events spiral out of control, friendships fray, and loyalties are tested to their breaking point.